Stacy Thowe was born and raised in Kansas City, Kansas, graduating from Washburn University with a degree in English, emphasis in writing. She started writing at an early age in the safe confines of her diary. She has published many short stories and a young adult series in the hope of reaching out and helping others with her unforgettable characters. If asked, Ms. Thowe will often say the stories were given to her. She once read a Ray Bradbury quote which said that all of his writing was God-given. The first time she read that, she knew where all her beautiful words came from.

This story is dedicated first and foremost to my husband, Glen, who I would be lost without. And my children who lived this story alongside me and without whom I couldn't imagine my life. Also my mother, Carmen, who struggled to make me who I am today.

Stacy Thowe

GOD BLESS MY BROKEN ROAD

AUSTIN MACAULEY PUBLISHERS™
LONDON · CAMBRIDGE · NEW YORK · SHARJAH

Copyright © Stacy Thowe (2021)

All rights reserved. No part of this publication may be reproduced, distributed, or transmitted in any form or by any means, including photocopying, recording, or other electronic or mechanical methods, without the prior written permission of the publisher, except in the case of brief quotations embodied in critical reviews and certain other noncommercial uses permitted by copyright law. For permission requests, write to the publisher.

Any person who commits any unauthorized act in relation to this publication may be liable to criminal prosecution and civil claims for damages.

This is a work of fiction. Names, characters, businesses, places, events, locales, and incidents are either the products of the author's imagination or used in a fictitious manner. Any resemblance to actual persons, living or dead, or actual events is purely coincidental.

Ordering Information
Quantity sales: Special discounts are available on quantity purchases by corporations, associations, and others. For details, contact the publisher at the address below.

Publisher's Cataloging-in-Publication data
Thowe, Stacy
God Bless My Broken Road

ISBN 9781645753568 (Paperback)
ISBN 9781645753551 (Hardback)
ISBN 9781645753575 (ePub e-book)

Library of Congress Control Number: 2021900053

www.austinmacauley.com/us

First Published (2021)
Austin Macauley Publishers LLC
40 Wall Street, 33rd Floor, Suite 3302
New York, NY 10005
USA

mail-usa@austinmacauley.com
+1 (646) 5125767

A special thank you to my professors at Washburn University who refined my skill without clipping my wings.

And to all of you out there traveling your own broken roads, I dedicate this novel!

Preface

We sometimes step back and question those moments that change our life forever. I can remember the instant, the moment my life's course changed. I step back outside myself and relive that moment again and again in my mind, and I cry out to that young girl of nineteen. I give her words of wisdom, from the life experience I have now, somehow hoping to rewrite the past.

Yet, this story is not a story of regret or what ifs. It is a tale of hope and of faith; a story of living and loving against all odds. A story of not subsiding to what life presents to you, but standing strong and fighting back. It is a story of dropping to your lowest low and somehow climbing out. It is a retelling of one's journey to find love again, and the angels that guide us along our way.

Chapter One
My Chosen Road

I walked into my closet and looked around at his things; the things he had acquired during our twenty years together. The things he had come for. He had not come for forgiveness or out of fatherly duty, but for those things that lined our closet shelves. The shelves that he built with his own two hands when he still loved me.

My knees buckled, and I fell to the floor, as I looked up at his things. I heard my daughter and my mother in the background. Their voices rose surrounding him like a whirlwind of clatter, of items being tousled. I heard his tone of disapproval screaming up at me from downstairs, demanding me to put a stop to their interference of his plan. He barked out his orders as though he still had the right, as if I still belonged to him.

My body felt weighted beneath me, as he made his way up the stairs, my daughter, Saline, screaming behind him. "You were the only one not happy, Dad! Why, why are you doing this to us? Where are you going? Are you just going to leave us?"

"No, I told you, nothing is going to change. Your mother and I just can't do this anymore!" Jack answered, trying to get past her.

"Mom didn't want this! Why are you leaving us, huh? It's not about us. It's about you!"

"I'm not going to do this with you right now, Saline. I just came to get my things. Now please, sweetheart, just let me get them, and I will get the hell out of here."

"But we weren't unhappy, Dad, it was just you." Jack pushed past her and my mother, making his way up to me.

"Sarah… Sarah, can you please get them under control? You told me this wouldn't happen. You promised me."

And he was right. I had promised. I promised anything to get him back in our home. I thought somehow if I could get him here, that seeing the children and myself and how broken we all were, he would be that man again. He would be that father and that husband again, and it would be as if he had never left. So, yes, I promised him anything.

"Yes, Jack, and what about your promise to them?" my mother screamed up behind him. "What about your broken promise to your family?"

I listened unable to speak or move surrounded by his things. His suits he bought just for show hung neatly on the top wire rack. His golf clubs lay perched against the wall, amongst his many shoes.

His baseball bag full of gear from the church league lay underneath his many baseball caps and the black cowboy hat I had just bought him for Father's Day.

He entered our master bath looking for me. He turned toward the closet where he found me kneeling on the floor. His cold pitiless eyes looked down toward me.

"Sarah… Sarah, are you listening to me? You said it wasn't going to be like this. I just need to get my stuff and get the hell out of here!" He looked down at me with his hands on his hips, bringing his right hand up in disbelief as he spoke at me. Like a silent movie, his words were invisible. I saw his mouth moving, but upon exit his words evaporated into thin air. He paced back and forth, glaring at me, longing for the cigarette that awaited him in his truck.

Then all of a sudden, his voice roared out, "Are you going to let me get my stuff or not?"

But I did not move; I did not speak. I sat there looking up at him, blank, a mute, frozen in time. I was waiting…

I was waiting for him to fall in love with me again, but he didn't.

Somehow, someway, he just stopped loving me, and I could see it in his eyes. At the time, I didn't know why. But a voice inside of me told me that I had failed.

I sat there looking up at his things, and his words became blurred. He stood there yelling and flinging his arms back and forth, and my rage started to flare like a dormant volcano, building up over centuries. The web of lies, all those years, and my rage grew. I looked around at his things, the things he had come for, and I began to grab them, one by one.

"You want your precious stuff, your shoes, your golf clubs?" I shouted, as I abandoned myself and drifted down deep inside of my brokenness. I gathered his shoes and golf clubs at first as if in slow motion and then as if I were a patient in an asylum, making my escape.

I slung them at him with all my might, leaving my conscious self and all the insanity that surrounded me, and I gave him what he wanted.

"You want your stuff that means so much to you. Here, take it!" I grabbed his dress shoes and launched them toward him. I grabbed the glimmering clubs, sending them sailing, like spears, through the air as he ducked to miss the flying metal projectile, aiming right for him.

"Never mind – just keep it! I'm getting the hell outta here," he yelled in disgust while batting away the flying objects. "I will get all new stuff!" he shouted as he left the room.

The objects continued to fly out of my hands, even after he had left, clamoring against the wall, causing scars upon scars.

I laid my hands over my face, collapsing onto the floor, melting into the carpet, slowly hoping to disappear.

"It didn't have to be like this, Sarah. I just wanted to get my stuff!" he shouted as he headed down our long hallway and down the stairs where Saline was waiting for him.

I then heard my oldest daughter weeping, and I forced myself up. My feet carried me to her, past my other three children. Unaware of their location until that moment, I memorized how they huddled together in the bottom of my son's bunk bed. They hugged each other as if life would somehow end should one let go, as their father flew past them, without a word, without a smile, and without a goodbye.

Saline, my oldest at the age of 17, stood there crying, more angry than weak. She fell into my arms as we heard the garage door slam behind him.

We gripped on to each other as the world rose up all around us and the clouds spiraled in the sky. The lights dimmed to a haze and we had made it through one more day, one more occurrence. My other children joined us, forming a circle of tears and interwoven arms losing ourselves, briskly swirling up, up above it all, then slowly returning to each other, holding on, afraid to let go, while my mother looked on in a tear-filled silence.

· · · ·

Twenty year earlier... I watched that girl of nineteen over and over again, standing in front of an oval mirror, dressed entirely in white. I want to scream out to her, but then I realize – it is just a memory...

"I'm going to take care of you, Sarah," Jack said as we sat in a burger joint, just blocks from the justice of the peace who had just performed our ceremony. "I promise you. I'm going to make you happy."

"I'm sorry, I just... I don't know, this is not how I pictured it."

"I know. I know you wanted the white dress and the big ceremony. I'm going to make it up to you though, if it's the last thing I do. I promise. I'm so lucky to have you," Jack said, as he lifted a strand of my hair from my eyes.

I smiled and turned my eyes toward the window as Jack wrapped his arm around me. We were seated on the same side of the vinyl-covered booth that faced the window looking onto the main street of the small downtown area, which included a hardware store, a used clothing store, and a small bank. The waitress strolled toward us, bringing us a miniature-sized wedding cake that they kept in the freezer for times just like these, for couples just like us, for weddings that are held in the little white house down the street and end up here in the burger joint.

I secretly thought about my mother who said I was throwing my life away. She was against me marrying at such a young age. My mother had doubts about Jack from the beginning. So, we eloped, on a whim.

I tried to smile as my mind drifted off to the makeshift ceremony. The preacher's wife, who answered the door, smiled and led us in, asking for identification and the results of our blood tests.

"Do you have a change of clothes, dear?" she asked me, as I had on a t-shirt and jeans. Jack and I had stopped at a local department store and picked up a plain white sundress, clear plastic sandals, and a white shawl that would become my wedding veil. Looking at the pictures later with my mother, we would both hold back tears at how far off this was from what we pictured this day to be.

"Yes, I have it in my bag."

"Good, good. We have a room especially for the bride. If you'll follow me, dear, I'll show you the way." She carried on small talk as I contemplated jumping out the nearest window and making a mad dash to I-don't-know-where, anywhere but here.

After changing, I stared at myself in the large oval antique mirror that was placed in the bride's room, my image blurred by the soft lighting of the room. I was entirely in white as I had always dreamed and yet not like any of my dreams at all.

I stood there for what seemed like hours, unable to move, as the image reflected off the mirror became engulfed in my memory.

My groom wore a polo shirt, jeans, and cowboy boots. I came out from the bride's room, and Jack smiled at me and took my hand and said, "You look beautiful." I forced a grin as the preacher motioned us before him. His wife played the organ as we walked down the aisle. And it was done.

I immediately thought of my mother who would never get to see me in my white dress. I thought to myself, I would never get this day back. It was gone, within seconds, that moment of my life was now a memory.

"It'll be all right. I promise. If your mom doesn't kill me when we get back, we should be okay." Jack grinned. I laughed as he drew me into his side. I still hadn't come to terms with being Mrs. Jack Harris.

When we returned, Jack dropped out of college and took a sales position at the local newspaper. And as if it were fate, Jack discovered his true calling in life. He quickly came to the realization of what a good salesman he was. He started to climb the sales ladder and developed a love of his newfound career.

Lying, stretching the truth, seemed to come all too natural to Jack. Something he learned from his years of living without a father. From knowing that his father was married to another woman and had two other sons that he claimed as his family. From having to lie to his mother about where he was all day, after getting up at four o'clock in the morning to throw newspapers from his skateboard and then sneaking back home while she was at work so he could sleep instead of going to school.

Yes, lying became second nature to Jack. He entered into a world where everything was perfect and lying became so entangled with the truth that he could no longer distinguish between the two, and the alternate world, the world of the lie, was much more alluring. Why should he live in the truth when the lie always got him what he wanted? It worked with me, it worked with his clients, and eventually it would take over his life to a point where the lie became a better place to live. The lie became the reality.

We rented a small, one-bedroom home on the outskirts of Lee's Summit, Missouri, and settled into what I thought was the start of a lifetime together. I had Saline two years later, and she brought a sense of normalcy to our chaos. She was a bright-eyed brunette with these enormous brown eyes, sitting on top of cherry-blossomed cheeks that ballooned every time she smiled. She had a lot of her father's features, but her eyes were mine. Saline stole her father's heart from the beginning, and she became his world – and Jack became the image of a devoted father.

Jack, a stocky, broad-shouldered man, stood at five feet nine and looked somewhat like a body builder, especially when he worked outside, which he did on occasion, having a love for the outdoors. He built his arms and legs up until all you could see was muscle. Unfortunately, his physique would not last long. Jack dove into convenience store delicacies as a means to fulfill his zest for food and for life.

He was a salesman, heart and soul. He walked into a room and immediately knew everyone on a first name basis and was considered everyone's favorite neighbor, t-ball coach, and go-to guy.

Like Jack, I grew up without a father. My mother left my father after ten years of marriage. Years filled with physical and mental abuse, but when my father started abusing us, my brother, my sister and me, she decided to leave. I would only see my father about eight or nine more times in my lifetime, and each time, as if it were on key, it started out like a fairytale. My father arrived as if in slow motion, bending down his long thin silhouette and taking us all into his strong arms as if there were nothing in life more precious than his children. Then the fairytale slowly melted into a nightmare.

One of the earliest occurrences I can remember was when I was seven years old and I witnessed my mother being chased outside our home by my father.

"What should we do, T.C.?" I asked my brother.

"Stay down, don't let them see you," he said, sending us all ducking down below the window frame, as if we were all doing reconnaissance for the military.

"We need to call the police," I said.

"On Dad?" asked T.C.

"Yeah, on Dad; he's going to hurt Mom," I pleaded.

"What's he doing now?"

I remember inching my way up to the window frame, so as to not be identified.

"I don't know, I can't see them. It's too dark." The images slowly started to form underneath the street lights. "Dad's got his belt in his hand."

T.C. curiously lifted his head over the window frame trying to see what was going on. "What's he doing with it?"

"Chasing Mom! T.C., call the police!" I begged.

"You call the police."

"I'll call the police!" our fearless younger sister Tia said, as she marched toward the telephone.

"Get back here!" T.C. said and grabbed her by her shirt, dragging her back to the window.

"Let go of me, T.C.!" Tia screamed at him. "I'm calling the police."

And the nightmare had begun. We three sat and debated what to do next.

"T.C., he's going to hurt her," I said again.

"Get down. They're heading this way," T.C. shouted.

"Aye you!" a voice screamed out in the darkness. We lifted our heads over the window frame. "What are you doin'?" our neighbor Sonya screamed.

My mother yelled back, "Sonya!"

"You betta get outta here! I've called the police. They're on their way. Claire, are you okay?" Sonya said, now grabbing for my mother.

"I'm okay," my mother replied, in tears.

"I said get outta here!" Sonya yelled.

"I'll be back, Claire!" We heard our father yell back. He then rushed to his car, jumped inside, and sped off with the tires squealing. We could see the back of his station wagon lights as he skidded onto the main intersection, fishtailing.

We all headed downstairs, sitting on the bottom steps. The screen door slapped the door frame and bounced behind my mother as she entered the living room.

"You guys go back to bed. I'm all right. I'll be right up."

We sat there looking up at her.

"I mean it, right now," she said, as if we had been the ones chasing her.

Another collision with my father had come to an end. We knew it would be months or years before we experienced another, but the thought of it always lingered in the air.

Growing up, my mother had us in church every Sunday. I remember vivid images of the Catholic Church, with its large multicolored stained-glass windows that stood beside the parishioners, portraits which as a child would catch our attention as we gazed up at their magnificence.

We sat among the silent pews where talking was forbidden, even to one's neighbor.

I had always felt a sense of closeness with God despite the craziness of my world, and I would come to see – through the actions of my mother – what faith really looked like.

My mother gave every week a tithing that we couldn't afford, and the image of her head bowed down in silence over the pew, as the weight of the world seemed to be slowly, silently lifted, stays with me even today…

Twenty years after I married Jack, I would be faced with a life-altering experience that would challenge my faith, rip my family from our home, and I and my children would never be the same…

Chapter Two
The Crash

"Dang it, girl, get in the chute!" Ben shouted at the lazy, black-spotted cow that was strolling inside the small milk barn, which barely gave the two brothers room to breathe, let alone milk six cows at a time, while leaving six others waiting in the small enclosed room. The smell of feces and sweat lured in buzzing flies that swarmed around the two men.

"What's the matter, Ben?" his brother Mike teased him.

"Oh, Betsy here's got an attitude, and I'm not in the freakin' mood this mornin'."

"Wouldn't have anythin' to do with that late night you had last night, would it?"

"I'm here, ain't I. Heck, I'm always here."

"I know, little brother. I'm just givin' you a hard time. I used to be able to party like that and show up for work. Age has a way of catchin' up with you." Mike settled the milker onto the udder of another cow while shooing the milked cow out of the stall. The milk hose ran along the wall of peeling paint like a vine, leading out into a middle room where a large glass canister slowly filled with the snowy white milk.

"I'm fine, I told you."

"Okay, okay, I'm just sayin'. I don't know who smells worse, the cows or your breath."

"You're just jealous, brother, 'cause Debbie doesn't let you go out anymore. That's why I'm still single."

"Well, I'm sure that's one of the reasons." Mike grinned, and shooed the black and white cow that stood before him out onto the gated field. "Dad wants us to start workin' the dirt on the fork today. Do you want to run the tractor?"

"Yeah, I'll do it." Ben finished up with the cow before him.

"I'm heading over to Alta Vista to check on some fence. One of the bulls keeps getting out," Mike said.

Ben continued to lead one cow after the other through the chute as the small room's aroma became stronger, now a mix of urine and feces, unnoticeable anymore by the two brothers, who had milked these cows since they could make their own way to the barn.

Dirt scattered along the old country road lined by barbed wire, oil cans, and cattle troughs. This road was traveled by Ben's family for generations, for the love of the land, and for the pride of owning the unownable. Ben entered the long, dusty, gravel road that he had traveled down most of his life, his body bouncing on the seat of the old tractor. As a child, he would run down the road to the school bus after breakfast, after chores, in the scorching heat or frigid cold. Ben, the youngest of four, would battle to stay up front as his brothers and sister pushed him behind telling him to stay out of their way.

He was a timid and shy boy who started to wear glasses by the age of nine and would never know life without them. He was the youngest, the most naïve, and the one who loved to travel beside his father in the pickup truck as they headed out to the fields to capture the cob as it swayed with the wind. They would count the rows of kernels along the cob's surface, trying to defeat that old sourpuss Mother Nature who continually threatened their crops, leaving them on the verge of homelessness. As a family, he witnessed them daily thank the Lord above every year for his grace, especially when the crops came in abundant and they made it through another year, but he also saw that they thanked Him when they didn't.

At the ripe old age of thirty-three, Ben witnessed his two brothers and his sister with their spouses and children and felt he may have already missed his chance for a family of his own.

He grew up watching how his parents stood by one another year after year, and he wondered if he would ever share that type of love with someone.

One summer's day in August, the climate of the small town filled again with the excitement of the local county fair held at the Alma Fair Grounds just west of town. Pens were lined with prize-winning sheep, pigs, and calves as the 4-H Club came to its summer's end. Children of all ages gathered in pens, brushing, feeding and navigating their hard-earned projects.

Ben did not intend to go that day but was talked into it by some of his buddies and showed up at the last minute as the fair started to dwindle down. After he talked with a few friends, Ben decided to grab a bite to eat before the kitchen closed.

As he entered into the dining area, Ben's eye caught the image of a young blonde woman dressed in a blue dress that landed just above her knees. The blue was covered by a long beige apron that was spotted with barbeque sauce, and she wore a pair of brown, well-worn cowboy boots with fancy stitching that met halfway up her calf. Ben watched as she immediately brushed back a strand of blonde hair that dangled in front of her face.

"Am I too late?" Ben asked, shyly.

"No, no, come on through. There's plenty left, just starting to get things packed up," she said, wiping her brow with a plastic glove and pushing back a blonde lock that had made its way over her red bandana. The woman struggled to uncover some food items that she had just wrapped up. "What can I getcha?"

"Oh, the brisket's fine."

"Great, comin' right up."

Ben walked over to pick up his drink and utensils while discreetly looking back toward the woman as she prepared his order.

After being handed his food, Ben just stood there with his plate in hand.

"Is there anything else I can get you?" the young woman asked.

"No, sorry, this is fine." Ben made his way over to a table as she came out to clear the tables around him. The blonde woman went right to work, seemingly tired from the long day. She politely smiled at Ben as she worked, unfazed by the six-foot-tall farmer.

"Looks like you had a good crowd this year," Ben stumbled for words.

"Yeah, well, we sure did better than last year," she responded, without a second glance, still wiping down the tables.

Ben sat pretending to eat, trying to think of something to say. "Yeah, I heard the turnout last year was pretty slim."

"It really depended on what day you worked. I didn't work every day, but it seemed when I did, it was slow. This year it was like they were coming out of the woodwork, but hey, it keeps me out of trouble."

"Well, with someone like you working here, I would think they would be beatin' down the door," Ben said, in between bites.

The woman suddenly stopped and looked into Ben's deep blue eyes that were hidden behind large brown framed glasses, obvious relics from the seventies. She glanced at the lower part of his face, which accentuated his manly virtues of a rugged, unshaven chin and pronounced Adam's apple under his strong cheek and jaw bones.

The woman found a way to slow down around his table, striking up a conversation. "So, you from around here?"

"Yeah, we farm just east of town here. My parents have a farm, and well, I grew up there, and me and my brother still work there every day."

"Do ya now."

"Yeah. So, you live around here?" Ben asked while trying to quickly choke down some of the food on his plate.

"Kinda. I travel a lot. I try to make it here for the fair though."

"Forgive my manners, ma'am." Ben stood, holding out his hand, "My name is Ben Thompson, and you are?"

"Christine, Christine Jensen," Christine answered, shaking Ben's hand.

"Nice to meet you, Miss Jensen. So, what do you do when you're not here working at the fair?"

"Oh, call me Christine. I'm a beautician by trade, but I like to travel so when I've saved enough money to go somewhere, well, I just go," she said, continuing to clean up a few tables around Ben.

"Really?"

"Yep, just got back from Florida. I have a cousin out there in Jacksonville. I love the ocean, but for some reason after a while I find myself missing the Midwest."

"Can I help you clean up here?" Ben offered.

"Ah... yeah. If you don't mind, I could use some help picking up some of these tables."

"Not a problem. I don't often get a chance to help a pretty lady." Ben stood amazed at his own forwardness that evening.

"You sure aren't shy with the compliments, are you?"

"No, ma'am, not when the occasion calls for it."

"Uh-huh. Why don't we start over here? I mean if you're finished with your supper and all."

"Yes, ma'am. I mean, Christine. I'm done."

After the last table had been moved, Ben offered to walk Christine to her car. They talked as they walked down the dark country road that was lit up by the stars that twinkled brighter against a clear country sky. The wind had picked up and a cool breeze replaced the heat from the summer's day.

"So, you always pickin' up girls at the fair?" Christine said, swinging her purse behind her.

"No, unfortunately, I'm not usually such a smooth talker."

"Really, 'cause you are doing pretty well tonight," Christine said while rummaging through her purse for her cigarettes, taking out the open pack. "Do you mind if I smoke? I know it's a nasty habit, but I usually smoke after a long shift."

"No, I... don't mind," he lied.

"Thanks. Do you smoke?" Christine asked, offering Ben the pack.

"No, I don't smoke myself. I think I was always too cheap to pick up the habit."

"I wish I had thought about that. These things are so damn expensive. I've tried to stop, but then I get stressed about somethin' and out comes the pack." As they walked, the sound of crickets serenaded them. The night was ignited by swirling lightening bugs that encircled the small yards like low hanging twinkling stars. "So where can someone get a beer around here? Or, do you drink?"

"Well, Henderson's Liquor is up on Main Street, but he closes every year for the fair, his kids being entered and all, and yes, I have been known to indulge in a beer or two."

"Good to know," Christine said, playfully bumping Ben with her hip. "My family farms too, but we also manage horses. I have my own horse, so I ride a lot. He's part of the reason I come back home. So… do you ride?"

Ben flashed back to a time when he was about six years old. His dad had acquired a horse to board from a neighbor. Ben being around cattle all of his life did not hesitate to approach the horse, unfortunately from the rear, the next thing he remembered he was waking up with his father hovering over him, asking him if he was okay. Ever since then. Ben had not had much use for horses. "No, I don't ride," Ben answered, honestly.

"That's sad, 'cause they're awfully beautiful animals. You should come ridin' with me sometime."

"Well, I don't know…" Ben felt the conversation taking a nose dive, as Christine looked away, tossing her hair back and taking a long drag from her cigarette. "Oh, I know they're beautiful animals. I just don't, you know… ride."

"So, are you going to call me sometime, farmer?" Christine asked while blowing out a cloud of smoke from her cigarette.

"Sure."

Ben observed Christine look around, and she smiled an ornery smile. She abruptly threw her cigarette to the ground, stomped it, and moved in closer to Ben. She grabbed his collar and pulled herself to him. Christine kissed him deeply, as if she had seen in his eyes that he had not been kissed in a long time. Ben breathed her in, surrounding her in his arms. He drew her small frame into his and got lost in the moment as suddenly Christine pulled away.

"That was unexpectedly nice." Christine smiled.

"Yes, yes, it was. Can we do it again?" Ben laughed.

"Later, Cowboy. Call me." She then handed Ben a piece of paper with her phone number on it.

"Oh, I will, and it's Farmer," Ben replied.

"Okay, Farmer, I hope to talk to you soon." Ben watched her enter her beat-up Pontiac hatchback and start the roaring engine. She rolled down her window and waved as she drove off, leaving a trail of smoke behind.

Ben stood there unable to physically move, still embracing the memory of her lips touching his. Sensing that he somehow already missed her, he slowly turned and made his way back up to the fairground.

Ben and Christine started dating and eventually moved in together. The life they shared included hosting some late-night parties that left them sometimes waking up in different parts of their two-story home.

Christine walked in to their home one weekend after a celebratory night, her arms full with grocery bags.

Ben, still groggy from the late-night party, awoke on the couch. He took a moment to gather his bearings. "Where are you coming in from?"

"I couldn't sleep so I decided to make us a nice brunch."

"You know I don't eat breakfast," Ben said while blocking the sunlight coming in from the large picture window in the living room from hitting his eyes.

"It's almost eleven, honey. I don't think we can call it breakfast anymore."

"What? I was supposed to meet Mike. He's going to be pissed."

"Oh, he'll get over it." Christine placed the bags down on the counter and moved over toward Ben. "How about you don't go to the farm today?"

"Don't go? You know we're plantin' this week."

"Yeah, but we haven't had a Saturday together in a long time. Can't you call in sick or somethin'?" Christine sauntered closer to Ben, grabbing him around his waist while unbuttoning his shirt. "I'll make it worth your while."

"Honey, I'd like to stay, but I was supposed to already be out there. Can't we do this later?"

"Whatever, just go," Christine said as she turned back toward the kitchen.

Ben tried to unsuccessfully grab her arm as she walked away. "Why don't you come out with me? You can ride in the planter."

"It's too cramped. You guys need to get a newer one with a larger cab." Christine stopped to light up a cigarette.

"I thought we talked about you cutting back on those."

"I am cutting back." Christine pulled groceries out of the bags and shoved them in the closest cabinet, slamming the doors as she went along.

Ben moved toward her and wrapped his arms around her waist. Christine attempted to pull away.

"Hey, how about we go into town for supper tonight and maybe catch a movie?"

Christine looked at him, now less disgusted with the outcome. "Okay, I guess I'll have brunch alone," she said, wiggling her way out of his arms, she headed back toward the counter, her cigarette hanging from her lips.

"I really got to go; I'm sorry, honey. I'll see you tonight. Look up what movie you want to see." Ben started to undress as he headed for the shower.

Christine's phone lit up, making a buzzing sound. She walked over, picked up the phone, and stared at the screen. After a few seconds, she opened a cabinet door and took out a half empty bottle of whiskey. Christine stuffed the bottle into her purse. She then headed over to the bathroom door, leaning into the door crack. "Babe, I'm going to go visit Momma and maybe do some riding if that's okay with you," she shouted through the door.

"Yeah, go. I'll be busy most of the day. Just be back later," Ben yelled over the sound of the rushing water.

Christine grabbed her purse and headed for the front door. Swinging the door open with a jolt, she looked back for a moment and then slammed the door shut behind her. The beige shades covering the window swung to a halt, sending dust up into the beams of the sunlight, just as Ben exited the bathroom.

He stopped for a moment, rubbing his face dry with a towel, feeling a sense of uneasiness as he watched the blinds settle to a stop.

Ben pulled up to the farm and felt a stare coming from his father, who was working on a truck in the driveway. Ben quickly exited his truck hoping to avoid a lecture.

"Mornin', running a little late, aren't cha, son?" Larry asked.

"Yeah, Dad, I'm running late. Where's Mike?"

"He went out to the pasture to check on the cattle. You still plannin' on plantin' today?" Larry said, as he pulled away from the open hood of the truck.

"Yeah, Dad, I said I would. Christine and I were just up a little late last night, that's all."

"Yeah, well, it happens. Ah… speakin' of Christine…" Larry hesitated, as he began to wipe his forehead with the handkerchief he kept in his back pocket.

"Yeah."

"Well, your mom and I were talkin', and she wanted me to kinda bring up something that's been weighing on our minds. You have a minute?"

"I guess, Dad. What is it?"

"Well, Ben, you know we like Christine, and son, well, this isn't easy to say. We think you might need to start thinking about settling down. Christine seems to be a nice girl and we just want you to do right by her," Larry said, shoving his hands into his front pockets.

"Dad, we're fine."

"I know, I know you youngsters do it differently these days, but son, you don't want to make her wait too long."

"I know, Dad. I wouldn't hurt Christine. I mean, we plan on getting' married. We just haven't set a date, that's all."

"Like I said, son, we just want the best for you."

"Okay, can I start plantin' now?"

"Yeah, you could have started four hours ago," his dad said and gave a slight grin.

"I was just givin' the day a little time to warm up, that's all, no use in rushing things." Ben grinned back at his father.

Ben was married four short months later in the backyard of his brother's home. The first six months eased most doubts Ben had been struggling with. They were happy. They fought every now and then but nothing serious. But after six months, Christine started to drink more and more, especially when she had to work long days at the beauty shop that Ben helped her to open. Ben would sometimes beat her home after a hard day's work and find himself phoning around town to locate her.

One evening after leaving the farm, Ben walked toward the sliding glass door leading into the dining area of their kitchen. Christine's dog, Oscar, barked playfully in the hopes that Ben would let him in. Ben petted the dog and headed in through the sliding door. He sat down at the round oak table and started to remove his muddy boots, unlacing them one by one. Ben heard the sound of Christine breathing in the silence. Smoke slowly rose above the couch. He turned noticing the bottles that lined the kitchen counter and then glanced back at the sink loaded with dirty dishes. Ben looked toward Christine. She sat numb, staring at the television, moving her lit cigarette to her pressed lips, and then out toward the beam of light streaming from the television, blowing smoke into an already smoke-filled room.

"Did you make any supper? Or is that your supper?" Ben asked, standing there looking at the beer bottles that hid their large maple coffee table, its imperfections hidden with the forgiving nature of the alcohol.

"Nope. What, didn't your mother feed you? She usually does. You eat there more than you eat here anyway, how am I supposed to know whether you're goin' to make it home for supper or not," Christine said, slurring her words.

"I'm going to bed." Ben turned in disgust, trying to avoid another fight. He headed toward the bedroom to remove his layers of dusty clothing, when suddenly he ducked just in time to avoid a bottle that slammed against the wall, just missing his head. Glass shards now embedded in the carpet, as the larger pieces reflected the light from a nearby lamp.

"Here's your supper," Christine yelled out from behind him. "Did you hear me?"

"Yes!" he yelled back. "I heard you! Now just sleep it off."

"Sleep what off, you coward."

"Christine, I'm not in the mood. I don't want to do this tonight. I swear to you if you don't stop, I'm going to leave."

"Go ahead, leave me! Do you think I care! Everyone leaves me. What do you think I need you around here for? Get out of my sight."

Ben entered the bathroom and shut the door behind him. He walked over to the sink and looked at himself in the bathroom mirror, gripping the bathroom counter, shaking it as he let out a silent grunt.

He heard the echo of objects being kicked around and the sound of bottles clanging. He closed his eyes, clenching his fists as he turned on the faucet trying to cover the sounds coming from the other side of the door. He entered the shower, washing off the dirt and animal smell from his body.

Upon sliding open the shower door, Ben heard a piercing silence coming from the other room. He dried himself off with a towel and headed back to the sink with a gasp of relief. Ben quietly started to brush his teeth, as the bathroom door slowly opened.

Capturing a glance of Christine through the smoke-filled room, Ben sighed in disgust. Christine slowly walked toward Ben opening her arms, hugging Ben from behind, forming her body to his, as she apologized for the things that she said. Ben then slowly turned around already knowing the outcome.

"It's all right, let's just go to bed. I'm tired and I know you're tired."

Christine pushed him away and shouted, "So now I'm not good enough for you, is that it!"

"Christine, calm down. I didn't say that."

"I'm here throwing myself at you, and you stand there rejecting me. You're always too tired."

"And you're always too drunk."

"Damn you, Ben!" she shouted as she walked away. "You know why I drink."

"Christine, I'm tired. Do whatever you want. I'm going to bed." Ben then followed her out of the bathroom, heading toward the other side of their bed.

"I'm being punished. That's what it is. That's why I can't have a baby. I'm being punished for all the bad things I did. I'm being punished because I was an awful daughter and my mother, my mother never wanted me…" she said sobbing, as she climbed up into the bed, laying her head down on to the pillow. "Ben, I want a baby."

"I know, I know you do," Ben said while removing his glasses and placing them on the nightstand. He stood there watching her curl into an infant position, hugging herself.

"Ben," she said, as she started to drift off into the numbness of the alcohol. "Why can't I have a baby?"

"I don't know, honey," Ben answered. "Go to sleep."

"But… I would be a good mother. I promise…"

Ben lifted her up and placed the blankets around her as she passed out on the pillow. He moved toward the open window shade and stared out onto the full moon. He turned, grabbing his glasses, and headed out the door, careful not to step on the shards of broken glass.

He headed toward the kitchen; his muddy boots, still waiting for him, sat next to the chair. Ben caught a glimpse of an open bottle of whiskey sitting next to the sink. He picked up the bottle, glaring at it through the moonlight. He opened the back door and walked out toward the rock walkway that led out to the road behind his house.

Oscar lay silent behind the large oak tree, hidden in its dark shadows.

Ben looked down at the bottle and with one hand lifted it high into the air and suddenly brought his arm down with tremendous force, sending the clear bottle flying toward the multicolored rock that lined their patio. The bottle exploded upon contact, shattering into millions of tiny pieces. Ben stood there feeling the pain from the tiny pieces of glass being instantly embedded into his skin.

"Ahh…!" Ben screamed out, staring out at the road. "What do you want from me?"

Chapter Three
In the Beginning

Four years had passed since Saline was born. Jack had taken a job with his uncle's landscaping business in Nebraska, after being refused a manager's position at the newspaper. He moved up there without us to see if he could make a go of it, but in the process, he somehow forgot he had a family back home.

I hadn't heard from him in weeks. After unsuccessfully trying to reach him again and again, I decided to stop calling. I put our home up for sale and had just moved in with my mother when my mother's telephone rang.

"Where have you been?" I yelled into the line.

"Where have I been? I've been working."

"Why haven't you called us? Why haven't you checked on us?" I said, not understanding Jack's nonchalant tone.

"I did try to call," he lied.

"You never tried to call me! How do you think we've been making it all this time?"

Jack spoke as if the last couple of months never happened. He was trying to pull me into his fantasy world, the world of the lie, where everything he had done was for the benefit of us all.

"I'm sorry…" was all Jack said, "I just wasn't getting paid what my uncle promised me and I couldn't face you. I couldn't send the checks I promised, and I knew you would be upset!"

"More upset than this! Do you even care about us at all? How could you do this to us?" I blurted out.

"Sarah, I have the money now to pay the bills!" he exclaimed, hesitating to let the words sink in. "I made a lot of money this week. I sold a lot of work. I have the money to move you and Saline up here now. I know I can do this." I started to calm down at the mention of him being able to pay the bills. He knew I would. He was aware of the state of desperation he left me in, and he used it to get what he wanted. "I'm on my way to see you guys right now."

"Right now? What do you mean you're on the way right now?" I said, not sure how to tell him I had moved out of our home.

"I'm almost there."

"Well, we're not home."

"What do you mean?"

"I had everything moved out of the house, and it's in my mother's garage. I'm selling the house," I said, now noticing my mother behind me.

"Well, that's great. I wanted to sell the house anyway to get you two up here," Jack said, using this new information to his favor.

"What do you mean move up there with you? I'm not moving up there now." My mother moved closer to me, placing her hand on my shoulder as I shrugged it off. Jack and I continued to argue. Jack played his part. He said his lines and danced his dance and the world of the lie was spun. He drew me in, and out of the desperation of my situation, I allowed myself to be consumed. I became an accomplice in the lie.

"I'm about an hour out," Jack said.

"Well… I guess you should know…"

"Know what?" Jack hesitated. "What happened?"

"I'm pregnant."

"Pregnant?" Jack paused for the first time.

My mother gasped a relieving sigh, and sat down on the couch next to me rubbing my back.

"Yes, Jack. Pregnant. I'm about three months."

"Sarah… I'm so sorry. I'll be there in about an hour. I promise, I'm not going anywhere without you again. And Sarah…"

"Yeah…"

"I do love you."

We arrived in Nebraska in the spring and settled into a small three-bedroom rental.

During the pregnancy, I slowly felt myself becoming physically weaker. I would often have to lie down in the middle of the day to regain my strength.

I was about thirty-three weeks along when I woke Jack up one late August night, unable to bear the pain any longer.

"Something's wrong, Jack."

"What's the matter?" Jack said, drowsily rolling over.

"I don't know. I feel a kind of pressure on the upper part of my stomach." I pointed to my enlarged belly, rubbing the top of it.

Jack laid there trying to write my symptoms off, making excuses for my pain, but I knew something was wrong.

"Okay, I'll take you to the doctor in the morning," he said, and he rolled over as if I were exaggerating my situation. "Babe, just try and get some rest."

I woke up a few hours later, the pain now throbbing in my abdomen, my blood pressure soaring.

"Jack, Jack," I said, as I nudged his shoulder.

"Yeah," he said, yawning. "What's the matter?"

"I have to go to the hospital, something's wrong." Suddenly, I gripped the headboard of our bed as a stabbing pain started to shoot through me. I arched my back and held on to the bedpost behind me as the pain that dug itself into my intestines twisted like a blade inside my abdomen. The pain forced me to throw my head back. My eyes creased shut. I gritted my teeth as the pain exploded inside of me. I heard a loud, agonizing scream being released from my lungs as the pain made its way through my body and out my vocal cords.

After hearing me scream, Jack jumped up and gathered Saline. The pain submerged, and I struggled to dress into whatever was close by. I fumbled in the dark, stroking my belly, trying to defer another attack.

Jack shook Saline awake and had her put on her sandals with her pajamas.

"Is the baby coming?" she asked, putting out her arms in a deep yawn.

"We don't know. Mommy is just sick, so we need to hurry."

Saline rushed to me in the hallway as I grabbed on to the nearby wall. The piercing pain started to rush in again, and I braced myself against the wall. I dropped to my knees, the pain rushing in with increased force.

Jack came up behind me, lifting me to a stand.

We made our way out and began to back out of the driveway, when a rush of pain forced me to grab on to the dashboard. I gripped it tightly, clenching my teeth and arching my back from the seat, letting out a long excruciating scream and I felt myself becoming light headed.

Jack flew through the darkened streets, running stop lights and stop signs as they became blurred red images flashing by me. The surge of pain kept coming in every few minutes with increased intensity.

Jack pulled up to the emergency room. We exited our vehicle, leaving the car outside the emergency room doors.

"Can someone help us?" Jack shouted, as we entered the hospital. "Something's wrong with my wife and she's pregnant!"

"Jack, I have to get to the restroom. I think I'm going to be sick," I mumbled, as I grabbed on to the nearest wall.

A nurse helped me to the restroom as I started to dry heave. They brought over a wheelchair, gently placing me in it. The nurse then rushed me to the elevator, exiting on the maternity floor.

That was when I met Dr. Johnson.

He was dressed in the customary white coat and was followed by several other white coats. I would come to find out that they were students doing their residency and were there to observe my condition. The residents followed Dr. Johnson around, turning and swerving with his every move, like a flock of geese.

I was taken to my room and placed in a bed. Immediately, I was surrounded by the bright white of their coats.

"Hello, Mrs. Harris. I'm Dr. Johnson. Can you tell me where the pain is?" he said as he gently took my hand in his, and then felt around my abdominal area.

"It is coming from the upper portion of my stomach, it is a kind of pressure," I moaned, as another surge of pain rushed in. I lifted my back and gripped the side rails of my hospital bed, dropping my neck and head back and letting out another piercing cry. I felt Dr. Johnson grip my hand tighter.

"We are going to get you something for the pain right away." He turned, barking out orders to the residents, as the white coats began to scramble in different directions.

The pain came in short segments, rushing in as if it were a tidal wave heading into shore and then receding in the same swift manner. After about an hour, the pain finally started to subside, and I could see the world more clearly.

Dr. Johnson came back in and took my hand as he explained the prognosis.

"You have pre-eclampsia. It is usually a disease that affects new mothers so that is why it probably went undetected up to this point. We are going to have to deliver the baby tonight in order to save both yours and the baby's life. Now, the baby's heartbeat is strong and she will probably be fine, but we will have to deliver immediately. Once the baby is delivered, your body should be able to heal itself. I want to prepare you though. She may not scream right away. Her lungs may not be developed enough. She will probably have to be rushed to the neonatal unit as soon as she is delivered. Do you understand what I'm telling you?"

I nodded my head yes as his words lingered in the air.

Minutes later, my bed and I were wheeled into a delivery room. Jack took my hand and sat beside me through the whole procedure.

"How are you doing?" he asked, trying to calm my nerves.

"Fine," I mumbled as the strains of the day began to catch up to me and all I wanted to do was sleep. I felt myself drift off and return to that little girl in the pews next to my mother, and the silence of prayer surrounded me.

"Whaaaaa!" Lily suddenly screamed, almost on cue as all the doctors and nurses stood amazed at the strength of this tiny child, who weighed a mere three pounds and eleven ounces, and could fit in the palm of their hands. The nurse, speechless, brought her around to me as Lily again let out a large bellow.

"Whaaaaa!" she screamed.

"I can't believe how strong her lungs are," the nurse said, in amazement.

I looked at our doll baby and our eyes met for a moment. I then started to feel very weak as they rushed her out of the operating room.

Jack, unable to contain himself, looked over at me anxious to leave the room. Jack whispered in my ear, and squeezed my hand, as one does before they are about to let go, and I waved him on.

The overhanging steel lights looked surreal, dimming in and out as I closed my eyes. I could hear the faint whispers of the surgeons falling off into the distance, as I slowly lost consciousness.

When I awoke in the recovery room, a nurse was standing over me taking my vitals.

"You'll just be here a little longer, honey. We are going to be moving you to your room in just a little while. Is there anything you need?" she asked, her voice sounding as if she were just an image, speaking to me from a distance. I nodded as I felt myself growing tired again. I peered around the room and discovered I was alone.

When I woke up again, I was in my room. Jack came in and announced that Lily was doing well, but had so many tubes coming out of her she looked like an octopus.

During the next few days, my mother and my grandmother were at my side every day. I could only see Lily from the incubator in the Neonatal Intensive Care Unit, and only after washing and masking. I became witness to all the wires and tubes coming in and out of her tiny limbs and miniature veins.

The clear glass surrounding the incubator reflected the glare of the overhead lights. It had two hand-size circles on each side. It reminded me of a submarine with covers lining the exterior and when the covers were removed we could reach in and caress Lily's wrinkled skin. Her skin seemed to be too large for her tiny body. She looked like an old woman with wrinkles that tucked into the crevasses of her arms and legs.

I looked around. Each incubator contained someone's child. Parents clung to the sides of the incubators, trying to stay afloat, drowning in the grim prognosis from the doctors, as all they had to hold on to was hope. There was one baby that had ballooned up so badly that his skin turned almost blue. It was painful just to watch him fight for each life-giving breath. His parents surrounded him daily, hand in hand, as they touched his bubbled body.

The nurse came over to us. "It's all right, she's doing beautifully."

"Can I hold her?" I asked, determined to do it regardless of her answer.

"No, I'm sorry, but you can hold her hand. She can feel you touch her. She knows you are here. She can hear you," she said in a soft voice as if talking to a child.

"Hello, Lily," I said taking her tiny hand.

Lily lay silent, her small stomach contracting and expanding with every labored breath. I whispered a song to her. It was crazy, but the only song I could think of was a song that Saline and I sang all the time before I put her to bed. And I sang…

Hey, baby girl,
with your eyes so bright. With your eyes so bright.

And I saw Lily's eyes twitch.

Mommas gonna love you Mommas gonna love you
with all her might. With all her might.

I caressed her wrinkled, bruised skin with my gloved finger.

I'll comb your hair, I'll comb your hair,
and turn out the light. And turn out the light.

She opened her eyes.

Shhh… baby girl, Shhh… baby girl,
sleep tight… Sleep tight…

And Lily looked at me with weary black eyes. She seemed to be trying to make sense of her surroundings, and then softly, almost as if the exhaustion of everything was too much for her, drifted back to sleep.

Jack was the most attentive father in the ward. He escaped from his sales job every chance he got to spend hours in the hospital caressing Lily and talking to her. The nurses commented on how lucky I was to have such a devoted father.

Lily came home after three and a half weeks, and she flourished. It was now fall, and the beautiful vibrant colors that spread across the Midwest had started to blanket Nebraska. The trees soon became bare as the leaves began to fall, and the ground took on a quilt like look of reds, oranges, and golds.

A short time after Lily was born, we made the decision to start our own landscaping business since I was at home with the children anyway. We ran the office right out of the kitchen and became partners in business.

It was a struggle but we struggled together, hiring and replacing equipment that broke down, surviving bad deals and employees who quit without notice. Jack's decision to leave his uncle's business created bad feelings between Jack's uncle and himself.

We hired a babysitter that year. Abby was the daughter of one of Jack's friends. She soon met my brother-in-law, who was ten years my husband's junior. Tad was working and living with us at the time. They met and seemed to be attracted to each other almost immediately. I would come to find out Abby was friends with a lot of guys.

At the time, I thought it odd the closeness my husband and Abby seemed to have developed. But she came over to babysit whenever we needed her, and my husband would take me out for a dinner and a movie, and then either he or I would drive her home. He never took any longer than I did getting her home, but it was just those secret conversations my husband and Abby would have. I would unexpectedly walk up on them and the conversation would abruptly end, but I thought to myself, he would never betray his brother. He would never betray me.

I received phone calls about that time from my husband's aunt and uncle that I assumed were due to their anger that he left their company and became a competitor. The calls were all pretty much word for word, "Did you know Jack is sleeping with Abby?" Then they would hang up. I knew who it was, and I thought they were just saying it out of spite to get back at Jack for leaving. My brother-in-law came to me one day and asked me a question, that to this day remains a mystery.

"Ah, Sarah, could I speak to you for a moment?" Tad was a hair shorter than Jack, but he was thin and strong. Because of his work, he had the arms of a bodybuilder.

"Yeah, what's wrong?" I asked, feeling the uneasiness in his voice.

Tad, unlike his brother, was honest. Honest to a fault. If he thought something, he usually said it and without thinking about it first. I respected his honesty and wished my husband had acquired that gene.

"Well, have you heard the rumors about Jack and... well, you know, Abby?"

"Yeah, I've heard them."

"So, do you think they're true?" Tad asked. I had been around to see Tad grow into a man. From a young age, Tad grew up admiring his big brother. He was just trying to get to the truth.

And I responded honestly, at least honestly for me at that moment. "Jack would never do that to you," I said.

"Yeah, that's what I thought. You know people were starting to talk, and well, I didn't know what to think. I was just wondering what you thought. I mean with all the gossip and things," he said, fumbling for words.

"I just don't think he would do that to either of us."

"Yeah, you're right," he said. "I just wanted to get your opinion."

Satisfied, Tad headed downstairs to his room in the basement, and we never spoke of it again.

Chapter Four
The Small-Town Life

Ben pulled the large grain truck up to the elevator which was located just east of town. Ron Conner, who worked in the warehouse, had reached the edge of the loading dock just as Ben pulled in.

"Hey, Ben, how ya doin'?"

Ron was a heavyset man who always wore faded overalls that were lined with patches. Patches that sometimes failed to entirely cover all the worn-out sections. So much so, that if you weren't careful, you would catch a glimpse of something you weren't intending to.

He and Ben's older brother, Mike, had graduated in the same class. If something was happening in town, Ron knew about it before the participating parties did. Yet, he always held tight to his principles and said that he was not one to meddle in other people's business. No not him, he just knew the facts and stated them as he saw fit. He was not one to spread gossip. Although, he had been known to drop a few clues every now and then, not obvious ones of course, and Ben had a little too much on his mind that day for a subtle hint.

"Great, Ron, how are things with you?"

"Ah, you know, can't complain, it being harvest and all. It's our busy season," Ron muttered while bringing over a dolly loaded with cattle feed. "I hear Christine opened up a beauty parlor in town."

"Yeah, she's got her license, and we decided to redo the old attorney's office there on Main Street and see if we can make a go of it. There's not much business yet though, but she seems to like it."

"So, no young ones on the way yet?"

"No, not yet. So, how's Cheryl doing?" Ben asked while loading some feed into the back of his truck.

"She's pretty busy. She got the job at the elementary school."

"Really, I didn't know they had an openin'." Ben stood, his eyebrows narrowed, dusting the sweat off of his forehead with the sleeve of his button-down cotton shirt.

"Yeah, old Clair Foster finally retired after all those years."

"Really, she had been there forever. She was there when I was there."

"I know, me too, but she was never exactly what one would call nurturing," smirked Ron, standing there with his hands gripping the top of his overalls, pulling them out from his chest while rocking back and forth.

"No, and I have a feeling that won't be changing any time soon."

"Probably not, but anyway, Cheryl was glad to get the job. So, how do you like being an old married man?" Ron inquired, discreetly looking sideways at Ben, fishing around for details as he helped Ben load his truck.

"You know, it has its ups and downs, but so does everything in this life." Ben, being an extremely private man, didn't like to let on about personal matters. He figured people had enough to gossip about. He didn't need to go adding to it.

"Ain't that the truth."

"So, nothin' new around town?" Ben asked, trying to prolong the small talk while taking a break from loading the bags of seed.

"Uh." Ron looked down and around the room, trying to avoid eye contact with Ben while discreetly changing the subject. "None that I've heard of. Uh… Ben, did you say you were needin' a copy of your monthly statement?"

"No, I think Mike picked one up last week. Why, is something wrong?"

"No, I just was wondering. I thought Bob mentioned something about you needin' one," Ron lied.

"Nope, not me," Ben answered, loading some more bags into the back of his truck.

"Well, as long as you got it," Ron finally said, now feeling more uncomfortable. "So… you got everything you need?"

"I think so," Ben sputtered, sensing Ron's uneasiness and unusual eagerness to get back to work.

"Good, well I got to get back to the office before Bob fires me. You know he's been achin' to do that. Ha, you take care there now, Ben," Ron uttered while he patted Ben on the shoulder, "I'll be seein' ya."

"Yeah… be seein' ya, Ron."

Ron looked back at Ben as the grain truck exited the lot. After looking around the lot for other vehicles, Ron headed back into the main office where Bob Stantlin was going over the day's receipts.

"Was that Ben Thompson pickin' up?" asked Bob.

"Yeah, that was him," Ron replied, closing the door behind him.

Bob, shuffling some paperwork on his desk, only glanced up at Ron. Ron took a seat in front of him.

"Hear Christine started a new beauty shop in town," Bob said over the noise of the electric calculator, still not looking up from the paperwork.

"Yeah, I was discussing that with Ben as he was waitin'."

"I hear she does a pretty good job," Bob continued, still not looking at Ron.

"I hear she does an extra special job for the mayor."

At that Bob stopped what he was doing. He sensed Ron's eagerness to fill him in on the local gossip. "What are you talking about, Ron?"

"The mayor, you know 'im."

"You mean Ed Harper?" Bob asked inquisitively, still shuffling some papers around.

"The very one," Ron smirked with a grin on his face, unable to keep the secret any longer. Ron then leaned back in the vinyl office chair as it let out a loud squeak.

"His hair doesn't look all that great to me. What he's got left of it." laughed Bob, still missing the point Ron was trying to make.

"Well, it wasn't his hair I was talking about."

"What are you babbling about, Ron? Just spit it out."

Ron looked around the room as if he were an FBI agent getting ready to unleash world secrets onto an unsuspecting public. He moved closer to Bob's desk as he began to whisper. "Well, word is… Ed is showing up about closing time and ain't leaving right away."

"What's that supposed to mean? That doesn't mean anything." Bob, now caught up in the story, looked up from his desk.

"I'm just saying I don't know too many fellers that have to get their haircut two to three times a week."

"Who told you this? I don't believe it. I've talked to several people who said Christine is a sweet girl."

"Sweet or not, there's somethin' weird going on over there." Ron shook his head slowly up and down as he leaned back in the chair.

"And Ed is married and has children."

"So was President Clinton," Ron smirked.

"You need to stop spreadin' this nonsense before someone gets hurt."

"I'm just telling ya what I heard."

"Ed Harper, huh. Nah…" Bob said, now shaking his head, trying to get back to work.

"Well let's just say, Ed isn't the most faithful husband in the world."

"Does Ben know?"

Ron leaned back in to whisper to Bob, "Not really sure. I just know it won't be good when he finds out."

"Well, I'm not going to sit here and listen to idle gossip. Ben is too nice a guy."

"Suit yourself. I'm just saying somethin's fishy."

"Somethin's always fishy with you, Ron; why don't you go check the docks? Someone might be waitin'."

Ron headed out of the office door as the conversation came to an abrupt stop. After shaking his head in disgust, Bob continued going over the day's receipts.

Ben circled the grain elevator lot, throwing gravel toward the railroad tracks and headed down Main Street. There were a few locals making their way through town that day. The hardware store, which was family-owned, sat next to one of the two banks in town. The fronts of the stores had been updated to modernize them, but they were set in the original old brick buildings that had been there ever since Ben could remember.

Ben passed the Co-op which was operating out of an old filling station, and the county museum, which was across the street from it. There were two antique stores in town and an art store some woman opened up to try and sell some of her sweat and tears. Ben thought while passing by the shop that he hadn't seen much for customers there.

The ice cream shop had a few customers sitting outside on their black cast-iron table and chairs, trying to beat the heat that was threatening their dripping ice cream cones. The ice cream shop ran out of the other old gas station lot. Ben thought someone was crazy to open an ice cream shop just down the street from the grocery store, but it seemed to be doing its fair share of business. Residential homes formed behind the business area as children rode their bikes to and from the public pool that sat behind the hardware store.

Ben headed to the end of Main Street and parked in front of a small, one-room, white building with a large picture window in front. The large picture window had written in large white letters: *Christine's Beauty Parlor*. Ben had paid his niece twenty-five dollars to paint that on the window and he thought she had done a mighty fine job. There were a few people walking up and down the main fairway as Ben climbed down from the large red grain truck. His brown boots were lined with dust that sprayed into the air and fell slowly to the asphalt as he stepped from the cab. Ben waved to a neighbor as he skipped ahead of them heading into the parlor.

Entering the front door there was a jingle, and then a clang from above his head as the large gold chime hanging over the door bounced against the metal rail. Ben stopped and smiled at Christine, who didn't notice him at first. Mrs. Willard was sitting in the only salon chair as Ben approached Christine, leaning toward her for a soft kiss hello.

"Hi babe, what are you doing here?" Christine asked, after giving him a peck on the lips. Ben absentmindedly rubbed the dirt from his shirt, and sent it sailing to the floor. "Ben, I just swept in here, could you dust off outside?"

"Oh, I'm sorry. Hey, Mrs. Willard, how ya doin'?"

Mrs. Willard looked up from her magazine. "Well, just fine, Ben, how's your momma doin'?"

"She's good; been cannin' for a week now getting ready for winter," Ben rambled as he grabbed one of the empty vinyl chairs and turned it around, sitting on it backward.

"Well, haven't we all. If it wasn't for your wife's fine establishment here, I would never get my hair done." Mrs. Willard now smiled and glanced at Christine.

"Yeah, she's a fine one," Ben agreed.

"Glad you see that. You need to take this young woman out on the town sometime. You farmers never make time for your women."

"Ain't that the truth. I was just stoppin' in here to see if this pretty lady was available for lunch," Ben smirked, now leaning into the rear of the chair. Just then Christine's cellphone vibrated in her pocket. She leaned down removing the phone from its confines and quickly shut it off.

"Something important?" Ben asked.

"Nah, some out-of-town number. I been getting crank calls all day. But anyhow, babe, I'm sorry, but I still have a ways to go makin' Ruth here irresistible for Howard. She says he can't keep his hands off her every time I get done with her. Isn't that right, Ruth?" Christine then winked at Ben.

"Oh, you are makin' me blush, Christine. I haven't gotten Mr. Willard that worked up since our youngest son was conceived. You are so bad, Christine. You just concentrate on my hair and keep my personal life out of it."

Christine smiled at Ben and spun Mrs. Willard back around to take out her last roller.

"I'm sorry, babe, but I will be busy here for a while."

"No, it's fine, I just thought I would stop by. You know, you keep sayin' we're not spendin' enough time together so here I am." He laughed.

"Well, thank you, but maybe we can have lunch tomorrow."

"Tomorrow it is. Well, Mrs. Willard, I will get out of you all's hair so she can finish making you irresistible for Howard." Ben now stood back up and replaced the chair to its original position.

"Oh you... you scat and don't be makin' any wisecracks about this in town," Mrs. Willard said sternly.

"Who... me... never," Ben said, winking at Christine. "Well, I'll see you ladies later," Ben said as he leaned down to kiss Christine goodbye.

"See ya later, hun," Christine uttered, giving Ben her cheek to kiss as she worked around Mrs. Willard's hair.

Christine smiled as Ben made his way back out the door. Without looking back Ben bounced back down the stairs and climbed back into the grain truck.

Christine watched as Ben pulled out. Mrs. Willard then got lost back in her magazine. "That is a fine man you have there, Christine."

"I know. I'm lucky."

"I wish I had your youth. I remember when Howard and I were just gettin' started. Course we were a mite younger than the two of you, but there's nothing wrong with waitin' for the right one."

"Yep, nothin' wrong with that. Now, where were we? Let's get you lookin' hot."

"I'll settle for warm," Mrs. Willard laughed, closing her magazine.

Christine snickered, turning Mrs. Willard toward the mirror in front of her. "Okay, well maybe we'll get Howard hot."

"I don't know, honey. At our age, that could be dangerous."

"Ha…" Christine grinned.

"But heck, let's live dangerously, shall we?"

"Now you're talkin'." Christine laughed, as she slowly returned to work glancing back at the large grain truck, which had pulled back onto Main Street and was headed back toward the farm.

Chapter Five
Web of Lies

The business and our family grew. I had two more children, the boy that Jack had always wanted and another girl. We moved the office outside our home, and the business continued to flourish. The children were always with me, even at the office.

Jack and I developed a business relationship. Sometimes when I got to work, there would be a brand-new work truck parked in the parking lot, already lettered with our logo and Jack would just hand me the payment schedule he had acquired through the bank without my knowledge. My job was to figure out a way to pay for it.

From time to time work became slower, and because of our debt, Jack had to travel around to other cities to find work, mostly in the winter time. So, I held down the fort every time he said he had to leave, every time a storm would hit nearby.

That year Jack had been away most of the winter working in Wichita, Kansas. From the start, this work trip seemed different than most. He didn't send money home right away. He said it was because work was slow. I insisted that if the work was slow, he should return home and try to sell work in our area. But he argued that he would do better if he could just have a couple of more days, so he stayed.

After returning home, Jack would return to Wichita several times. He said it was to collect checks and our small world began to collapse.

In the weeks following, Jack changed. Even the kids noticed it as they would come to me asking what was the matter with Dad. He seemed uninterested in the kids, in our home, and in our family. That winter was the first Christmas he was not on the floor taking pictures of the kids. He always took pictures of the kids. We had bins and boxes full of photographs I couldn't keep up with because he enjoyed it so much.

But that Christmas as the kids opened their gifts, he sat in the kitchen watching television, like an unwelcomed uncle. I thought it was just because work was slow, the winter was hard, and we were struggling to keep the men working. What I did not know was… Jack was actually preparing himself to leave.

You have life-changing moments during your lifetime, moments that the wind changes directions, moments when you fall apart, and moments when you pick up the pieces. One unforgettable night, my life, and my family's life, was changed forever.

We had been married twenty years when he confronted me, one extremely cold and frigid February day.

"I'm leaving. I want a divorce," Jack said as if he had been contemplating the words in his head for days, maybe weeks, waiting for this very moment. As if he had rehearsed it in front of the mirror so that it would come out all at once, because he knew once it was out, there would be no turning back.

In the echo of his words, I heard a whisper of a promise, a commitment he had made to someone other than me, someone who now meant more to him than I did, who meant more to him than his family. Someone who would make him walk away from his wife and his children and all that we had built together and never look back.

"What do you mean, you want a divorce?"

"It's just like I said. I want a divorce. I'm not happy. You're not happy. I'm not going to leave you and the kids on the street, if that's what you are thinking. I will still take care of you. I just can't do this anymore."

"Do what anymore? Our marriage?" I asked. He had called me out to the garage so that the kids would not hear our conversation. Unfortunately, the walls were much thinner than we both realized. Standing on the other side of the wall were fragile, little ears.

He walked back and forth in front of my closed garage door as if he were drowning, as if we were smothering him and he could no longer breathe.

"Go then," I said, not really wanting to believe that this was really happening, thinking he was just throwing a tantrum. "If you want to go, then get out!"

"I'm leaving, but I want you to understand I'm not abandoning you and the kids. I'm not that guy."

"What do you call leaving your family and wanting a divorce? Who are you?" And at that moment, before I had a chance to analyze my words, they were released into the air. "Is there someone else, Jack? Are you seeing someone?"

"I'm not seeing anyone. I just want out. I can't do this anymore," he announced, as if there was some sort of rationality to what he was doing, as though this were a common-day occurrence, like taking out the trash. "I'm not happy, and you're not happy. I promise you, this is what's best for everyone."

"For everyone? What about the kids? Is this what's best for them? Or what's best for you?" I was trying to grab words out of thin air that would somehow bring him to his senses, but my words seemed to evaporate long before they reached him.

"I'll tell them later, right now I just need to get out of here. I'll call you tomorrow after I find a place to stay."

"Who is she, Jack? Tell me! Tell me the truth for once in your life!"

"I'm not seeing anyone. This is the best thing for both of us. You'll see." Jack opened his garage door and began to climb into the cab of his brand-new extended-cab pickup he had unexpectedly purchased a couple of months ago.

I rushed over, trying to grab the keys out of his hands. He turned and jerked my arm away so aggressively, it was as if he was no longer afraid of hurting me. I no longer mattered. He had about as much feeling for me as he did the fly on the wall, and I was being swatted down. I stood there and watched him drive off down the road.

As I entered the kitchen, the children looked to me for answers, but I had none.

I passed the kitchen table picking up the dishes as I always did and instructed the kids to get ready for bed. They had heard everything. Lily looked at me and asked, "Where did Dad go?"

"Nowhere," I said to her, "just get ready for bed."

"But Mom."

"Please, just go upstairs and get ready for bed. Saline, could you please help Jackson and Hope get ready?"

"I guess," she said. She was angry and looking for answers. I think that was the first time I felt guilty for what was about to happen to them. What was about to happen to us.

I covered up so much for their father that I'm not sure they really knew who he was. I lied to our friends and neighbors about the late nights he worked and how they were a necessity for the business. Yes, I did my share of covering up, but I thought that was what wives were supposed to do. Divorce was not an option for me. In the end, the lies would all become a part of the deterioration of my husband's character, to a point I didn't even know him anymore.

That night, I made a plan. I would get up early in the morning and go to meet the work trucks before they pulled out to head to the first job. I had it all figured out. I would block the trucks from getting out with my car, creating such a big scene in front of his employees that they would all know what he was attempting to do, and I would force him to stay. This was my plan as I headed to our bedroom and the sleepless night that awaited me.

When I arrived at the lot the next morning, the crew was already there and had the large bucket trucks we used to trim trees already pulling out. He knew. He knew I would come. He expected me. After spotting me, Jack sauntered smugly over to my car leaning into my window.

He leaned in to my car as he had always done, as if we were still a couple, and he was leaning in for a kiss. He leaned in smiling as he had done so many times before as if we were discussing the work day, or talking about employees, or paychecks or bills, as if we were discussing the children.

"Sarah, what are you doing here?" he asked.

"I want the keys to your new truck. That truck is just as much mine as it is yours. You're not taking it," I said as I tried to grasp any small amount of dignity I could while making him painfully aware of just how much he couldn't live without me.

He then smirked, smiling to himself, as if I were somehow being humorous.

"Sarah, I'm not leaving you and the kids without anything. I plan to support you," he said this with such confidence, as we both entered the world of the lie. "You can stay in the house and keep the car. I just can't do this anymore. You are going to have to realize that this is happening."

He said it so matter-of-factly, I thought he was talking to one of the kids or one of his workers as he stood there and explained to me just how my life was going to be now.

"Are you going to tell the kids? Because you are going to have to do it yourself. I'm not going to do it."

"If that's what it is going to take, I will tell the kids," he said coldly.

"No, right now. They're home. I kept them home from school. You're going to have to face them and tell them what you are planning to do."

"All right, I will." He walked away as he had done so many times before, and I saw him smile and laugh with our foreman as if it were just any other day, as if our world wasn't falling apart.

He followed me back to the house, and the kids were waiting in the family room, wondering why I had not sent them to school.

"Your mother and I are getting a divorce." I didn't think he would actually do it. His words seemed to freeze in mid-air. The room was suddenly stricken with a disease and my children's faces went blank. They looked at their father for answers as they had done so naturally in the past. They looked at him searching for what they had done wrong.

He explained, "Your mother and I just can't do this anymore."

"What do you mean your mother and I," I interrupted. "You want this, Jack. I don't!" I immediately corrected him, not believing he had included me in his plan.

He then turned to them once again, and in the most calm, monotone voice, reiterated, "I mean, I want this. I am leaving." And I watched as my children grew more withdrawn with each syllable. It was almost as though he was comforting them after they had skinned their knee, telling them that it was all going to be better. He even had the nerve to tell them that nothing was going to change. He would just be living somewhere else.

And the words rang in my ears. I couldn't believe what I was hearing. *Nothing was going to change?* Everything was going to change.

I was too numb to move. My children huddled closer together. They didn't know what to say. Whimpers and sniffles filled my younger two as my older girls fought back anger, trying not to cry.

Their father then ordered them to go upstairs so he could talk to me. They moved, slowly rising off the couch, looking around as if lost in a strange place, looking at me, as I stood there with tears in my eyes showing as much confusion and sadness as they did.

We were all lost as Jack seemed again relieved. Another promise, a whisper, had been fulfilled.

The four of them headed upstairs, like zombies. Softly I heard Jackson lean into Lily asking, "Does this mean Dad doesn't love us anymore?" As Lily hugged him with one arm, I immediately felt guilty for making Jack confront them.

I felt something tugging at Jack as he raced for the door. He turned and took one last, long look at me and with a cold hard stare he announced to me, "Get used to it. This is happening. I'm not walking away from you. I'm running."

The next call I made was to my mother.

Chapter Six
For Better or for Worse

Christine greeted Ben as he walked out of bedroom heading toward the kitchen. She juggled her lit cigarette between her lips while scrambling eggs over the stove. Her hair, twisted to one side, fell loosely out of a long braid.

Ben came up behind Christine and gave her a small pat on her backside, as he reached around her, hugging her from the rear.

"You want some eggs or somethin'?" Christine asked.

"No, I'll pass. I got to get goin'."

"I know. I just thought maybe I could make something extra special for you this mornin'." Christine smiled.

"I think you did something special for me last night."

"Oh, you…" Christine said, as she set her cigarette down in an ashtray and swatted Ben with a dishtowel.

"I've got to get out there early today. Mike called and said we have some cattle out on the north ridge."

"Okay, well, I have two appointments today, nothing overwhelming, just two-color treatments."

"Told you. Word's getting out that you are the hottest thing in Alma," Ben bragged and headed over to give Christine a hug.

Christine stood, slowly being rocked by Ben. "I wish. I sure could use the business."

"Now don't you go to worrin'. It'll all work out. You'll see." Ben turned to gather his lunch and placed it in his metal lunchbox.

"I hope so. See ya later, hun." Christine watched, making sure Ben went through the sliding glass doors before she headed to the laundry room, just off the kitchen. She stopped, looked around and opened the supply closet, pushing past plastic bottles and cardboard boxes, exposing a bronze-colored bottle of whiskey. She grabbed the bottle and brought it over to the kitchen counter, watching the liquid slosh around inside. She took a glass out of the cupboard and set it on the counter.

A few minutes later, Ben pulled up next to Mike's truck, which was parked about a mile north of their parents' home.

"Mornin', I haven't spotted 'em yet. Ted said he saw 'em around the North Fork." Mike leaned into the steering wheel of his truck, taking off his ball cap and scratching the top of his balding head.

"Alright, I'm going to grab the four-wheeler and see if I can weave in and out of the timber." Ben waved, heading toward the shed.

Mike yelled out while putting the truck into gear. "Okay, I'll stay on the main road. I'll call you if I spot 'em."

Ben headed up the dusty drive toward the white farmhouse with peeling paint. Cathy, his mother, looked out the window just as Ben's father Larry exited the kitchen door heading toward his pickup.

"Mike's going up to the North Fork and I'm goin' to grab the four-wheeler," Ben said while he swiftly moved past his father.

"Good. I've got to run into town right quick, but I'll be back to help in a little while if you haven't already rounded 'em up." Larry entered his red pickup and slammed the door shut, quickly backing out of shed.

"Ben! Ben!" Cathy shouted from the door.

Ben turned and answered, somewhat irritated at the continued interruptions, "Yeah!"

"Your father had another spell last night so keep an eye on him."

"Is he going to the doctor?" Ben yelled.

"Are you kiddin'? He won't go till he's bleedin'; you know that." Cathy stood with her floral apron on and her hands embedded into her sides.

Ben laughed. "Yeah, I thought it was weird that he would be goin' voluntarily."

"You know how your father is. He's just goin' into town for some pain medicine, so keep an eye on him for me will ya."

"Yeah, Mom, I will."

"Okay, see you at lunch." His mother turned, heading toward the screen door.

"But who's going to be keeping an eye on me. Nobody cares about me," Ben yelled back with a smirk on his face.

"Oh you, stop that nonsense. Everyone always said I spoiled you too much." Cathy turned and let the screen door slam behind her.

Ben entered the milk barn and grabbed the red four-wheeler he had scrimped and saved for. He climbed aboard and sent the engine roaring.

The noise sent several different-colored cats racing in all directions. They ran swiftly through the hidden crevasses of the barn, like blurred shadows.

He sped out of the doors heading back down the lane with his large protective prescription sunglasses on, sparing his eyes from the dust and rocks heading his way.

Ben spotted Mike's brown two-tone pickup parked on the side of the road. Mike pointed toward the neighbor's field where the runaway cattle had gathered to graze on the corn stalk remnants.

Ben circled his four-wheeler around and headed toward the back of the field. Mike started honking his horn, awakening the grazing cattle who were engrossed in their current breakfast. The cattle raised their heads, chomping on the sweet stalks. Mike tried to coax them out of the gate, luring them with aged square bales of alfalfa.

Ben came up behind the stubborn cattle, swinging his arms. He swayed back and forth on the four-wheeler, trying to keep the cattle moving toward the feed truck, which displayed the stacks of rich alfalfa.

The cattle startled to a slow gallop. They then began a strong stride toward Mike, as the roar of the four-wheeler surrounded them. The cattle headed out onto the road as Ben followed behind, weaving back and forth, screaming out various commands.

A few minutes later, the cattle were safely inside the gate. Ben roared up and stopped beside Mike's pickup.

"Didn't look like they were missing us all that bad," Mike uttered.

Ben replied, "Yeah, Ted's corn stalks were lookin' pretty good to 'em,"

"Hey, where's Dad?"

"He went into town. Oh, that reminds me. Mom said Dad had another spell last night and she wants us to keep an eye on him."

"Was he going to see Doc Walters?" Mike asked.

"Nah, he just went in for some pain medicine. Mom said he wasn't bleedin' yet." Ben reached back for a bottle of water he set in the basket behind him and took a long swig.

"Makes sense. Well, what say we finish up hauling the corn into town?"

"Sounds great to me, big brother." Ben smiled. "Hey, where do you want me to start?"

"Probably head up to the east-ridge and work your way back. You can meet me there after I dump the first load." Mike placed the truck in gear, slowly starting to pull the truck forward.

Ben started the roaring engine of the four-wheeler and yelled back at Mike over the engine. "See ya in a bit."

He headed up to the steel barn, unlatching the giant doors and sliding them out of his way and climbed up the ladder of the combine.

Starting up the engine, he heard the roar of the machine come to life. Scattered leaves were sent soaring from beneath it. Squirrels scampered left and right, racing through the branches, trying to avoid the large green monster.

Ben took the machine down the road a ways, turning the machine into the field. He turned on the cab's radio just in time to hear Garth Brooks blare out that he *Ain't Going Down 'Til the Sun Comes Up.*

He adjusted his baseball cap and began to shake to the music in the cab as he lined up for his first row of corn. The withered stalks easily bowed down to the combine's gleaming edges. The corn was forced down underneath the machine shooting the small kernels into the large grain bin. After what seemed like an hour, Mike returned and Ben brought the combine up next to the dump truck, stretching out the long arm, and released the golden kernels into the bed of Mike's truck.

The two brothers continued this process until the day came to a close.

"You want to grab a beer?" Mike asked as he closed the door to the grain truck.

"Nah, Christine's making dinner, and I promised not to be late," Ben said, as he hurriedly put some tools away.

"How's things goin', anyhow?"

"Good, good, just settling into married life. I'm not an old pro like you yet." Ben grinned.

"Are any of us ever pros?"

"Guess not, brother, but what can you do? See ya tomorrow." Ben waved and headed down the lane toward his truck.

He entered the sliding glass door of his kitchen. Oscar stood barking in the center of the yard, hoping to be let inside for the evening. Ben, ignoring the dog, opened the door, quickly noticing that some of the pots were boiling over. Rushing to turn off the burners, and burning himself in the process, he looked around for Christine.

"Christine?"

"Yeah," Christine's faint voice came from what sounded like the bedroom.

"Honey, the pots are boiling over," Ben said, shaking his hand in the air to try and stop the throbbing pain.

Christine responded in a slurred whisper. Ben hesitated for a moment not wanting to see what was waiting for him around the corner. He headed for the bedroom and caught a glimpse of Christine trying to lift her head from the pillow.

"Oh, sorry. I'll get it." Christine tried to raise herself off the mattress.

"Christine! Where did you get it? You told me you were through with this!" Ben entered their bedroom as Christine tried to rise from the bed. The empty whiskey bottle stood silent on the nightstand.

"What dooo you care? Where have youuu been!" Christine said, slurring her words.

"I've been working, Christine. Did you even go to work today? Did you make your appointments?" Ben stood at the end of the bed with his hands on his sides, disgusted at the sight before him.

"No, I told them I was sick, sick and tired," Christine said, trying to raise her head.

"Why are you doing this to us, again?"

"I told yooouuu. I'm nooo… good. Your nooo… good. Youuu don't love me anymore." Christine tried to stand but stumbled. Ben caught her before she hit the floor.

"Ben, do you want kids?"

"Just sleep it off. I'm going to eat."

"I'm sorry, Ben. I'm so sorry." Christine sat back down and curled up against her pillow, slowly starting to drift back to sleep.

Ben went into the kitchen and stood looking at the pots. He picked up one and hurled it into the metal sink next to him, hearing the tin clatter against the steel sink as the steam slowly rose.

Ben raised his arms and looked up and screamed into the silence, "Ahhhhh! I've had enough! Damn it, I've had enough!"

The next morning Ben awoke on the sofa. He was covered with the throw that was usually laid across the edge of the sofa. Christine sat in the chair next to the sofa smoking a cigarette. Her hair was uncombed and dark circles from her mascara had formed underneath her eyes. Ben caught a glimpse of her and tried to awaken slowly, avoiding her stare.

"What do you want, Christine?" Ben said, rubbing his eyes.

"I just wanted to say I'm sorry."

"You said that last night."

"It won't happen again. I realize…"

"You realize what. You have been hiding booze again. Do you know how long it took you to get over your last binge?" Ben sighed, trying to slowly rise off the couch, wiping his eyes.

"I know. I just, you know, have been having a bad week. The shop has been slow. You've been working so much…"

"I have to work, Christine. The crops are going to be short as it is. Dividing the farm three ways is not going to leave us extra income."

"I know, I just…"

"You just what?"

"I just can't seem to help myself."

"Then let's get you some help."

"I don't need any help! I'm not an alcoholic. I just need a pick-me-up every now and then," Christine argued, as she shook off the ashes of her cigarette.

"Now and then? You are starting to drink almost every night."

Christine moved toward Ben and tried to hug him. "I just need you."

"You have me. That doesn't seem to be enough." Ben held Christine away as he tried to rise to a stand from the couch.

"You're a jackass," Christine blared out.

"Oh, that's just great, just what I wanted to hear from my lovely wife. I'm going to work."

"Yeah, you do that. That damn farm. You love that damn farm more than you love me. You eat with your parents more that you eat with me. Say it!" Christine yelled, looking toward Ben's back.

"Say what, Christine?" Ben said disgustedly without turning around.

"You never wanted to marry me."

"I never said that," Ben shouted, turning around.

"You just felt sorry for the poor woman that can't have children, the poor woman that can't give you children."

"Christine, I've never said that."

"Oh, but you've thought it." Christine picked up an ashtray, throwing it across the room. "That's right. Just run off, you coward!" Christine yelled.

Ben headed to the back of the kitchen and quickly grabbed his jacket off the back of the chair. He leaned down and picked up his work boots and headed out the sliding glass door as Christine followed close behind him. Oscar leaped up off the ground, trying to get Ben's attention as Ben walked right past him.

"Ben! You coward. I hate you. Did you hear me?"

"I heard you! The whole neighborhood heard you," Ben yelled back, flinging his jacket and boots into the air as he walked.

Christine continued to yell as they both moved through the yard.

Ben climbed into his truck and backed out of the yard as his tires hit the dirt.

Christine managed to run up behind Ben's pickup, picking up small twigs and branches and throwing them uncontrollably toward the truck. She slowed down, yelling obscenities behind the roar of Ben's truck, as the sound of the engine diminished into the distance.

Ben pulled up to the farm just as Mike exited their parents' home still munching on some breakfast.

"Mornin', Ben. You got the grain truck, today?"

"Yeah, I got it," Ben said, not wanting to look at Mike.

"Okay, it's full if you want…"

"I said I got it," Ben said irritatedly. Mike stepped back, realizing that something was wrong.

Ben climbed into the bed of the old grain truck as Mike turned and headed for the combine. Ben then took the truck into town for the morning dump. Ron Conner greeted Ben at the scale after Ben dumped his load.

"Mornin', Ben."

"Mornin', Ron," Ben said..

"How ya doin' today?" Ron said, pulling at the suspenders of his overalls.

"I'm in a little bit of a hurry, Ron. I need to get the truck back to Mike," Ben said shortly.

"Gotcha. Let me just get you a receipt here. Glad to see Christine's place is so busy," Ron said.

"What do ya mean?"

"Well, I saw her headin' into the shop early this mornin'. I thought it was a mite early for a haircut but…"

Ben stopped to think if Christine had told him she was working today. "She was, huh?"

"Yeah, at least I think that was her," Ron continued while finishing up Ben's paperwork.

"Oh, I didn't know she had any appointments today." Ben stopped when he realized he had said the words out loud.

"Well, I could've been mistaken. My eyes ain't what they used to be."

"Yeah, well, thanks, Ron," Ben said, now in a hurry to get back in the truck.

"You betcha. Have a good day there, Ben."

"I'll give it my best, but it ain't lookin' good."

"Yeah, I've had those days myself," Ron said and turned to walk back into the office.

Ben hit the gas and turned the grain truck around in the gravel lot. The truck sprayed rock out in all directions. Ben headed into town slowing down as he neared Christine's Beauty Shop parking about a block away. Ben spotted Christine's car parked in the back, but all the lights were out in the shop and the closed sign was up in the window.

Ben pulled out his key from his pocket and made his way to the front door. Juggling the key in front of the door, he spotted what looked like a naked man racing across the front of the picture window. Ben's key got caught in the door and the door jammed and wouldn't open. He began to hit door with his whole body. He finally broke the door open on his third try, sending it crashing against the wall, shattering the door's glass window in the process. The gold chime above the door rang out and came crashing to the floor. He walked in as the sound of crushed glass filled the silent room. Ben spotted what looked like Ed Harper trying to put his pants on in the darkened corner. Ed turned around, his shirt still unbuttoned. Ben came up behind him.

"What the hell are you doing?" Christine yelled from behind him.

"What the hell am I doing? What the hell is this!" Ben turned and screamed back.

"Now, Ben, this isn't what it looks like," Ed stated nervously as he backed away from Ben with one hand in front of him. Ben started to walk toward him. He stopped, glancing over at Christine in the beauty chair half clothed, her legs curled up in the seat, with a ruffled shirt covering her upper half. She was made up with dark red lipstick and rouge across her cheeks, no longer having the mascara smeared underneath her eyes.

"She was just giving me a massage," Ed said.

"Oh, is that right, Mayor? And why would she have to be half naked to do that!" Ben began to grow more and more irritated as he walked toward Ed.

Ed backed into a tight corner and looked around for a place to escape.

"Now, Ben, I promise you this was the first time I have ever," Ed lied.

"Oh, save it, Ed. Everyone knows what a cheating whore you are. I'm pretty sure even your wife knows. You are pathetic!" Ben moved closer to Ed.

"Ben, stop it!" Christine yelled, rising from the chair.

"You want me to stop it! Why? Why, Christine? Why behind my back? Is it more fun for you that way? Why not just leave me and be with this pathetic excuse for a man! I wouldn't have stopped you!"

"That's why I did it. Because you wouldn't have stopped me. You don't give a damn about me."

Ben turned back toward Ed Harper as Ed tried to squeeze by him, heading toward the front door.

"Don't you dare move! I swear to you. You had better not move. I'm not done with you yet," Ben said, clenching his fists.

Ed froze, realizing the seriousness of Ben's tone. Ed knew Ben. They had gone to school together, and hunted every now and then. They weren't good friends, but they knew a lot of the same people. Ben never cared for Ed and Ed knew it. Ed stood silent, feeling that his life might truly be in danger.

"You're saying this is all my fault! It's my fault that you, my wife, is sleeping with another guy, a married guy! You are just as pathetic as him. You are a liar and a cheat, and I'm sick of all the crap you have been dishing out on me. I'm sorry you don't feel woman enough on your own, but you're going to stop blaming me for all your pathetic self-destruction. I'm done."

Ed took this chance to try and crawl past Ben and make a break for the door. Ben saw him and quickly turned around, grabbing Ed by his waistband. He brought Ed back up to a stand as Ed, a small man, tried to squirm away.

"This is for your wife, you sorry excuse for a man!" Ben stood Ed up and brought his right arm back, planting his right fist across Ed's jaw, sending him sailing back into the wall. Ed tried to rise as Ben maneuvered him around, struggling to bring him to a stand by the collar of his shirt. A drip of blood made its way down Ed's chin from a broken lip. Ben brought his left arm back and hit Ed in his right eye, tossing him back in the opposite direction.

"And that one was for me, you son of a bitch. She's all yours, Mayor." Ben then dropped Ed to the floor and headed toward the front door, glancing at Christine who was still sitting in the chair with that same look on her face, the look he had come to recognize, the look of helplessness that had captured his lonely heart.

Without looking back, Ben left Christine and the beauty salon for the last time, as the passers-by stopped and looked inquisitively inside the small mangled shop.

Chapter Seven
Calling All Angels

My mother arrived on a Thursday; the same day Jack had come to retrieve his things, the things that lined our closet shelves. The things that now meant more to him than his family. She could hardly recognize me. It had been almost three weeks since he had moved out, and I was still answering the phone for the business and trying to hold on to any aspect of dignity Jack would allow. I was determined to make him see just how much he truly needed me. Then he took that away from me too.

I dropped almost fifteen pounds in three weeks and didn't even realize it. My neck was smoother, and I didn't have that bulge of fatty tissue under my chin. My friends kept commenting on my weight loss and how great I looked, but it didn't really connect with me. When I looked in the mirror, all I saw was failure. I didn't feel attractive. I felt ugly. I was like a zombie. I would respond and cope, and had enough energy to get through the day, but when the children were at school, I collapsed and would leave reality and break down in my car somewhere, in some parking lot, some place where no one knew me, where people didn't knock on my door.

My next-door neighbors came over daily to check on me. I was never given the opportunity to sink all the way down and drown in my rejection. Yet, I was at my best when my mother was there, and she was there often.

My mother gave nurturing its capital 'N.' She was one of my angels. When my mother came, I would lie in bed, and she would take the kids here and there. She would make dinner and do the laundry and take us all out to eat. She would listen and rub my hands and tell me it's all going to be all right. She was my lifeline. But she wasn't alone. I had people, some I hardly knew, coming out of the woodwork to help me as if it were all planned, as though it were destiny. Angels were gathering and waiting in the wings. Every time I needed them, they were sent, sometimes unbeknownst to them, and they guided and helped me throughout each day.

One day, during a period when my mother was gone, I heard a knock on my door. Upon opening it, I saw a small brunette woman standing there. Her name was Sandy. Sandy and I had been acquaintances because our boys were in the same grade.

As I opened the door, all I heard was, "Hey."

I said, "Hey."

"So, how are ya doin'?"

I said, "Fine."

"Oh, I just heard you were maybe going through some stuff with your husband."

And without thinking why is this woman asking me this, or what business is this of hers, I just blurted out, "He left me."

Sandy stood and studied me for a moment. She had her dog on a leash and was working him around her waist.

"He left you?"

I said, "Yeah, he just walked out." I just exploded with this information as if I were talking to my therapist or something.

"That jackass," Sandy blurted out. She lived around the corner from me and was a beautiful, dark-haired brunette with green eyes. She and I always seemed to be moving in different directions. I mean, we were pleasant to each other, but not what I would call friends. Her oldest son was in school with my eldest daughter, Saline, and she had a younger son the exact age of my son, Jackson. Yet, here she was in my front yard calling my husband a 'Jackass.' Sandy then said, "So, do you think he is seeing someone?"

I was shocked. No one had asked me that before. They kept asking me – even my close friends – what I had done to make him leave or what was wrong with my marriage that drove him away. I had always thought he was seeing someone, but I did not admit it to others. Partly because somewhere in the back of my mind I thought he was coming back and if I said I thought he was seeing someone, then how would I explain letting him move back home.

I think part of me didn't want to admit that he was having an affair, because that would be admitting that he didn't want me anymore, that he wanted someone else. It meant that he rejected me because he loved another. The little self-esteem I had left would not allow this.

Like most women in my situation, I wallowed in the darkness. There I could still have hope. And there he didn't leave me because he found me unattractive. In the dark, I still had a chance of gaining back my family. In the darkness, I wasn't a failure and in its safety, no one could see me falling apart.

I responded to Sandy, "You know, I think he might be. I don't have any evidence, and he denies it, but something tells me he is."

Then Sandy said something unexpected, "Yeah, that's what my ex said."

"Your husband?" I said as I felt my mouth drop to the floor.

I suddenly remembered Sandy had gone through a divorce, and I knew it wasn't pretty, but I had never taken the time to find out why they divorced. I figured it was none of my business and here was this good woman, knocking on my door, asking me how I was doing.

"Yeah, my husband."

"I didn't know…"

"Yeah, he left me for someone else," Sandy said, as if we were discussing the weather. "So, do you think he is seeing someone?"

"I don't know, Sandy, he just left."

"So where is he staying?"

"I don't know. He won't tell us."

All the while Sandy was standing there maneuvering her dog around trying to keep him calm.

"Is he still supporting you?"

"Yeah, he's still paying the bills, but I don't know for how long," I said, now wanting to know more about her situation. "So, your husband left you for someone else?"

"Yeah, he sure did and he denied it at first too. It was his secretary."

"How did you find out?" I asked, making my way to the stairs on my porch and taking a seat.

"Oh, he left me claiming the same thing your husband is claiming, that he didn't want to be married anymore."

I sat down, and I felt this overwhelming sense of connection with this woman. She knew exactly how I was feeling. She had gone through the same thing, and yet she seemed… okay.

I had a thousand questions, a million, and I didn't know where to start. I wanted to know how she had made it through it all. She always seemed so confident to me. I remember after the divorce that she became very private, almost defensive as she seemed to be going through the process. But I didn't know what had happened, and I hadn't bothered to ask.

"Well, does he come around?" she asked.

"Every once and a while to grab something out of the house and then he leaves again."

"My husband did the very same thing," she confided. "I remember I used to dress up, you know, in some really nice dress and have my hair and makeup all done up to try and, you know, impress him and show him what he was missing. He would just grab his stuff and leave almost as if I wasn't even there."

I snickered out loud as if I were looking in a mirror, "I do the same thing."

"Do you really?"

"Yeah, he comes in and doesn't even knock. He just walks in like he still lives here."

"Yep, that was my ex."

"Yeah, and he doesn't even notice me." I smiled, almost laughing now; we both were. "I stand there with this dumb look on my face, all dressed up, and he doesn't even look my way, and I'm thinking after he leaves, I must look like crap."

"He's seeing someone. I know it. Settle down!" she ordered her dog. "Is he spending more money?"

"I don't know. He gives me enough to get by, and I don't know what he does with the rest."

She asked me if I had a lawyer. I told her I didn't, but Jack wanted me to get one. He wanted to be divorced as soon as possible.

"Oh, he is definitely seeing someone. My ex couldn't wait to be freakin' divorced. Oh man, this brings back such memories," Sandy said, shaking her head back and forth as if she had just had a flashback.

"Did you get a lawyer?" I asked.

"Yeah, I did, and we were divorced two months later. I never saw it coming. I was in a state of panic." Sandy then explained that she got two jobs because she was afraid she was going to lose her house. "So, have you decided what you are going to do about the house?"

"I don't know. I can't afford the house, and I'm not sure I can depend on him for income. I was thinking about selling the house and moving closer to family."

"Why? The kids are here. Their school is here."

"Yeah, but I need to start over," I said. "I have to make a new start. I don't think I can move forward here."

"Well, it's up to you, hun. You do what's best for you and don't let anyone tell you different. It will all work out, you'll see."

"I hope so."

"Do you have a pen? I can give you my number. This dog is getting restless."

"Yeah, I do. I'm sorry, come in." I opened the screen door for her, and she and her dog entered my entryway.

"You have a nice home," she commented as she walked in and looked around. The rooms were all painted by Jack who painted like a professional and took pride in the perfection of each room.

She watched me as I walked back to her. She was reliving something she thought she had left behind. For some reason, this woman wanted to help me through this. She had experienced what she hoped no one else would have to, and she looked in my eyes and saw the reflection of a woman she thought was long gone. She reached out her hand to me and I grabbed on with both hands, as every day I felt myself sinking.

"Here is my number. You call me if you need anything or you just need to talk. I'm not kidding. I've been there."

"I will," I said, and wondered if I really would.

"I have been there, and it is not a place you want to be alone."

"How did you get through it?" I had to know, because it was getting harder and harder for me to breathe, and looking at her I saw a strength. I saw my future.

"My son," she finally responded. "If it wasn't for him, I would have never made it. He got me up in the morning. He was the reason I got dressed. He forced me to move forward."

I understood this because if it weren't for my children, I probably wouldn't bother to climb out of bed.

"If it wasn't for him, I can honestly say, I'm not sure I would be here right now."

"What do you mean?" I suddenly stopped writing and looked up from the piece of notebook paper I had grabbed to scribble Sandy's number on.

"I mean the lows got really low. There were times that if he hadn't been there, I would have just kept the engine running and closed the garage door. I know… I know what you are going through. You call me, do you hear me? Oh, and here, give me your number. If I don't hear from you, I'll call you." Sandy grabbed the pen out of my hand as I relayed my telephone number to her.

She knew that I might not call. I wasn't sure if I would call. She knew I might not have the strength to call. I didn't know it at the time, but she had just thrown me a lifeline. Sandy didn't know it either. She was being used by God. She was one of my angels. They were getting ready to surround me as God summoned them one by one and they showed up at my door. I couldn't really see it at the time. It would take time to see these things for what they really were… miracles.

Chapter Eight
The Long Goodbye

Ben's family, meaning well, quietly tried to help without sticking their nose too far into Ben's business. They knew he would tell them what he felt they needed to know. He would be the man they had raised him to be, and he would put one foot in front of the other and move forward. But they also knew down deep that he had been hurt and they took steps to somehow help ease the pain.

"So how ya doin'?" Ben's mother asked as she entered his kitchen.

"Fine, Mom, I'm fine," Ben responded, annoyed to be in a situation that would make his mother ask this question of him.

"Well, I got you some things at the Clark's garage sale. They were asking some ridiculous prices, but I managed to bargain them down." Ben's mother, Cathy, moved toward the counter and placed a box full of used pots and pans onto the counter. Cathy went through the cabinets finding several empty shelves, debating where to store the cookware.

"Mom, you don't have to go doin' that."

"I know, it's just a couple of necessities. I saw you didn't have a microwave. Even though I was against 'em at first, I sure use mine an awful lot these days." After cleaning a spot on the counter for the microwave, Cathy moved around the kitchen wiping down the counter as she went along.

"Well, how much did you pay for 'em?"

"Now don't you go worrying about that. It's a gift from your dad and me."

"Well, I thank ya, but Mom you really don't have to. I'm really doin' okay," Ben tried to reassure his mother, but he knew once his mother had made up her mind, there was no stopping her. It was better to just let it happen and live with the consequences.

"Do you want to come and help me unload this stuff or not? I can't carry in the big items by myself," Cathy said, growing irritated with her youngest son's unappreciative attitude.

"What all'd you get?"

"Just some pots and pans and dishes, stuff you'll be needin'," Cathy said, already heading for the back door.

"Alright, I'll be right there. Let me put on my shoes." Ben then headed back toward his bedroom.

"Take your time – Lord knows I ain't in no hurry." Cathy took a moment to wipe the sweat that had built up on her forehead with a dish towel.

Ben walked back to his bedroom. It displayed a single bed he had brought down from the upstairs bedroom. He stopped and stared at the wallpaper in the bedroom that had been there when they first moved in. It aged the home. Its faded large floral design sang of former owners, maybe original owners, and would have to stay right where it was because Ben had no intention of changing it. It was always Christine who spoke of remodeling and spiffing up the place. But she never did. She never seemed to have a need to make this place a home, to make it theirs. Ben sat on the bed and put on his shoes and sighed as he headed out. "I'm comin', Mom."

Ben drove down the roads he had become a part of. The roads he grew up on. He wondered about the past, and what he could have done to make things better, to salvage his marriage.

"It is what it is," he said aloud, talking to himself.

He got up every day and arrived at the farm before dawn. He started at sunup and worked until dusk. Mike and his parents watched as Ben struggled through the process of starting over. Helpless, they let him deal with it in his own way.

"Well, I see you're up early again," exclaimed Mike, as he pulled up next to Ben who was working just off the south fork.

"Just trying to keep busy," Ben said while loading some square bales into the back of the flatbed truck.

"Well, if you ever run out of stuff here, me and Debbie have lots of stuff at the house that needs fixin'. I mean since you're hell-bent on working yourself to death," he said jokingly.

"Oh, I think the farm will keep us pretty busy. Don't you?" Ben said, now wiping the lower part of his chin with his glove.

"True, little brother. Hey, Debbie wanted me to ask if you wanted to come to supper Friday. Rachael has a baseball game, and she said she would love for you to come watch her play, you being her favorite uncle and all."

"I appreciate the invite, brother, but I got things to do," Ben strained to say as he continued to walk back and forth from the hay barn.

"Well, if you change your mind, the offer's always open," Mike said, putting his truck back into gear.

"I know, brother, thank you, and thank Debbie for me."

"Alright, well, I guess I better get busy if I am going to catch up with you."

"Oh, I haven't done all that much."

"Hey, I'm not complaining, gets me home earlier." Mike grinned at Ben.

Ben woke up the next morning to the nagging bark of Oscar. Although Ben knew that Oscar was an innocent bystander in this mess, the dog continued to be a constant reminder of Christine and their past together.

"Shut up, Oscar," Ben screamed out the window as the black and gray German shepherd continued to bark at a neighbor's mischievous cat. The dog yanked at the steel chain that restrained him from reaching his goal.

Christine had moved in with a friend who lived on the other side of town. She was supposed to pick up the dog once she got settled. Ben got up that morning and put on some jeans and a polo shirt. He then slipped on his boots and a baseball cap and headed out the back door. He immediately put the anxious dog on a leash and continued to speak to him.

"Come on, boy. Yeah, that's right, you mangy mutt. Nothing personal, but you're going back to your owner today."

Ben started to walk the dog down the sidewalk, stopping and tipping the brim of his cap at people he met along the way.

Now, in a small town, not much goes on that everyone doesn't already know about. And no matter how "Private" Ben tried to be, he knew there had been rumors about his breakup with Christine. Ben walked with Oscar prancing gracefully in front of him. He walked into the alleyway and approached the back of a large two-story brick home. He knocked on the back door hoping to get someone to answer. Suddenly, Ben heard a window open on the second floor.

Christine, still in her pajamas, stuck her head out and yelled down from a second-story window. "Ben, what do you want?"

"I came to give you your dog back," Ben said, trying to hold back the hyper dog.

"Ben, you know I can't keep him here," Christine said.

"Not my problem. Either you come down and get 'im or I will set 'im loose." Ben stood in the middle of the backyard, which was covered with dirt and car tracks. What little grass that was there sat to the east and west of the yard.

"Ben, can't you just keep him a couple more weeks?" Christine asked, almost as if Ben owed it to her.

"Nah, Christine, I can't. Now what will it be?"

"Oh, you stubborn ass."

"I'll take that as a no." Ben then leaned down and released the dog from the leash.

The large German shepherd headed straight for some trash cans placed by the alleyway. The dog commenced to tip over the large silver trash cans, bringing them down with a loud clang. The cans hit each other and began rolling as garbage slowly seeped out. With his tail a wagging, Oscar continued to playfully rip the bags apart.

"Ben, just let me get down there," Christine yelled out.

"Nah, Christine, not my problem anymore," Ben said. "Why don't you call the mayor and file a complaint?"

"I'll see you in court!" Christine shouted back out the window.

"I'll be there," Ben replied.

Ben started to walk off as Christine exited the back door in a robe trying to grab Oscar's collar and pull him off the pile of trash.

"You'll be sorry!" Christine announced to the neighborhood.

"Oh, I'm already sorry!" Ben replied as he walked back down the alleyway without looking back.

Ben entered the courtroom and took a seat toward the back. He didn't tell his family about the hearing. He hadn't told them much about what happened between him and Christine. He didn't feel they needed to know all the gory details. At that moment, failure surrounded him. Christine's affair had hit him like a coal train. He thought he would feel more relieved today, but all he felt was failure and loneliness. He was alone again. Down deep he felt that Christine was wrong for him from the start, but he was drawn to her neediness. He was captured by the necessity to reach across the bed and feel the warmth of a woman's body next to his. And in that way, he did miss her, though he would never have told Christine that. He would face her and give her most of what she wanted that afternoon and he would walk away.

As he left the courtroom later that day, he vowed never to marry again.

On the days that followed, Ben made plans for his future. He needed a change. He wanted to move on and put the past behind him. With this in mind, Ben began a journey that would take him out of his comfort zone and out of the confines of the small-town life.

"I'm thinkin' about getting a job in Topeka," Ben stated to Mike one foggy morning.

"What?" Mike answered.

"Well, you know as well as I do that we are barely hanging on here, and you with the kids, you're going to need a bigger portion of the farm income."

"This is our farm. All of us. You have worked on it just as hard as anyone," Mike argued, knowing his little brother was just trying to help.

"I know. I just know those nieces of mine are getting kind of expensive," Ben smirked.

"Ah, you noticed…huh? Ben, that's my business and it wouldn't be fair to you. I'm not going to let you do it," Mike said, now nudging his brother's shoulder. "I appreciate the concern, but we will find a way to make it work. We always do."

"Hey, it's okay. I'll still work, but I'll just take a smaller portion for a while."

"I don't know," Mike said, rubbing his head.

"Listen, I'll be making extra money and still have the farm. I hear they're hirin' farmers at a plant in Topeka."

"Who told you this?"

"Walt Anderson."

"Is he workin' there?"

"No, his cousin is. He said he works there and is still able to farm part-time. That's all I need, and I hear the pay is pretty good."

"Okay, well, we can give it a try if this is somethin' you really want to do. Hell, I might even try to find another job too," Mike said.

"Well, let's not get crazy," Ben said. "How about we see how this works out first."

"You got it, brother."

The next morning Ben drove to Topeka to apply at the Westchester plant. The massive white building stood out amongst the smaller businesses that surrounded it, sitting on about five acres. It must have stood about twenty floors high. Ben exited his car and looked up at the massive structure, unsure if he was dressed properly. Unsure if he should have brought a resume as his mother suggested. He had never worked off the farm before, and he felt like a deer entering alligator-infested waters. He hadn't felt this nervous since he got caught drinking by his dad after his last senior football game. Yet, he walked in, with all the honesty of a country-bred, farm-raised, Lutheran man who had never known what it was like to punch a clock.

Chapter Nine
And the Truth Will Set You Free

My next-door neighbors were Jamie and Daniel Grange. They were the type of people everyone aspires to be, but usually fall short. I almost believe that my husband felt less worthy because he wanted the image of being the best neighbor, the best husband, and the best father, but he couldn't compete with Daniel. Daniel was true and he was honest, and it wasn't just an act. Unlike Jack who had been living a lie for so long, he couldn't seem to distinguish between the lie and reality.

The Granges had moved next door to us six years ago. They had a boy and girl that were around the age of my two youngest children. Our children played together, had sleepovers, and became best friends. My husband and I would go out on couple dates with the Granges during the good times. They found out through my kids that Jack had left.

Part of me wanted to reach out for help, and the other part wanted no one else to find out because there was still a small part of me that hoped for reconciliation. Like a fool, I wanted to believe Jack when he said he wasn't seeing anyone. I thought if he really wasn't seeing anyone, this could still work. We could still be that family and everything would be okay.

Then I found the note...

Jack had come home to shower and get some clean clothes as he always did. I was cleaning up the kitchen when he arrived.

"I'm just going up to shower," he announced. Jack seemed to think since he was still paying the bills, he could show up unannounced whenever he wanted. At the time I was too weak to object.

Part of me still wanted him there. I kept hoping that maybe one day he wouldn't want to leave. One day he would just stay.

I didn't respond to him. I just turned away. He placed his briefcase on the table and went upstairs to shower. I guess he underestimated me, or just out of habit, left his briefcase right in front of me, as he had done a million times before.

I heard the shower start and like a child afraid of getting caught, I crept over to the closed briefcase and slowly opened it up. I knew if he was seeing someone, he would be writing to her. He would be drafting love letters to her as he once had done with me. I opened the briefcase and shuffled through his paperwork, and among his invoices, scratch paper, receipts, and pens, there it was… the note.

It wasn't on stationery or even notebook paper. It was on the back of an invoice and had been wadded up a couple of times and had other doodling on it. He was practicing his love letter to her. The note said: *Dear Kelly, I love you. I can't wait to be with you again. You are everything to me. Love always, Jack.* I heard her name and it resonated around the room, and for the first time, she became real.

I took the note and hid it in the cupboard, knowing that he wouldn't remember what he had done with it. It's strange. Somehow, I knew the note would be there. I knew what I would find before I opened the briefcase, as if it were waiting for me. Lying there amongst his many forms was… the truth.

He came down from his shower and grabbed his briefcase and headed out the door. He looked at me briefly, but said nothing as I glanced at him before he left.

I confronted him the next day.

"So, who is Kelly?" I asked while sitting at the kitchen table.

"I don't know a Kelly. Who's that? I don't know who you are talking about," Jack said with a kind of smirk, as if a secret had just been released. He looked as though he had seen a ghost, as if the name brought an image to his mind, an image that didn't belong next to me.

"Stop lying. Just stop it. Can you at least admit it?" I said, frustrated by his continual fabrications.

"Admit what? I don't know what you are talking about," he stuttered. "Where did you get that name from?"

"Don't worry about how I got it," I said.

"Well, I don't know who you're talking about. Sarah, I told you there is no one else. I just don't want to be married anymore."

"Who is she, Jack?" I asked, as I stood up trying to restrain myself from throwing the closest item directly at his head.

"I can't tell you what I don't know." Jack was good. It was almost as if he truly believed the lie himself. As if it were the truth. And that is how he got away with it. I truly believe it was real to him. I wanted to believe it. I wanted to believe it with all my heart, but I knew, I knew now that she existed.

Our son had a basketball game that evening, Jack was there. He tried to sit by me as if we were still a family, continuing the façade, so he could save face with our friends. Jamie and Daniel were there. Jamie, seeing that I was upset, came over and sat with me on the bench. She asked how I was doing. And I told her.

"Jack is having an affair."

"Are you sure?"

"Yes, her name is Kelly," I whispered to her.

Jamie did not know what to say. I think part of her wanted to go over and punch his lights out. And part of her, like me, couldn't believe what was happening.

It made sense. He was never around on the weekends. The kids hardly saw him anymore, and he was in such a hurry to get a divorce and didn't even want a lawyer.

He told me to get a lawyer and he would agree to whatever I needed. I believe the guilt over what he was doing started to overtake him and he just wanted everything to be over with. He wanted to start his new life with her. He consoled himself with the thought that he was doing everything he could to make sure we were taken care of. Another lie…

I finally started to let go after finding the note. I could no longer deny her existence. The note was the push I needed to start accepting what was happening.

The next couple of days were just a blur. I had to make decisions. I prayed about it. I was looking for a lawyer that could transfer our home into my name. Jack had agreed to give me our home if I gave him sole ownership of the business. I agreed.

I started to call several lawyers, and no one would help me. I had literally been calling around for hours when I reached Leonard, and he became my lawyer for the divorce as well. He was a kind man and handled the divorce for as cheap as he could after hearing my situation. And yet another angel had been sent to cross my path.

The kids struggled in their own way, but my eldest girls were the ones who worried me the most. I struggled day after day trying to decide whether or not to move them closer to my family or stay in Nebraska. My daughter, Saline, was just finishing up her junior year in a school district she had grown up in all her life. She had attended school with her classmates since kindergarten. She had no idea her life would be turned upside down with the one act of her father.

I decided to speak to Saline before I made my decision, since moving would affect her in a huge way.

"So how was school today?" I said coming up to her as she entered the kitchen.

"Fine, nothing special," Saline said while lowering her backpack to the floor.

"Did you get that article written for yearbook?" I said, trying to make small talk.

"Yeah, but it didn't fit, so I have to shorten it. How are you doing today?" Saline asked, looking up at me after sitting down at the table.

"Fine, just, you know, doing some cleaning."

"Did you hear from Dad?" she asked.

"Yeah, he's working. He said he was going to drop off a check tomorrow to cover the bills."

"Well, that's good," Saline said trying to sound upbeat for me.

"Yeah, well, sweetheart, I've been trying to decide what to do as far as moving. I know it's your senior year and all," I struggled getting the words out, because I wanted her to tell me how she honestly felt.

"Yeah, it is."

"Well, how do you feel about it? I mean about moving."

She spoke with the confidence of an adult. I almost felt our roles changing, parent and child, as she was the one consoling me. It was almost as if she had been waiting for me to ask this very question. She sat there contemplating her answer. And without hesitation, she looked me straight in the eye. "We'll do whatever you need us to, Mom. I'll be fine."

And tears filled my eyes as my daughter thought only of me, and we hugged as we would many times during the next few months.

"It'll be okay, Mom."

"Oh, I hope so, sweetie. You know I didn't want this for you."

"I know. We'll be okay. Whatever you need, we'll do," she reiterated.

"Okay, sweetie."

And she left, and the decision was mine.

Lily was just finishing up her seventh-grade year, and I wouldn't know until years later how many hours she had spent in the school counselor's office. Thank God for that counselor. Lily didn't tell any of her friends about what was going on. She was a lot like me. She had many friends, but no one knew, not even her best friend. She bottled everything inside and like me, hoped it would somehow go away, but it didn't.

Her counselor was another angel who was sent to be with her when I couldn't be. The counselor was her outlet. She was someone whom Lily could go to and cry with, and it would have no repercussions. I thank God for that counselor.

One Saturday, I was praying all day about moving my family. That particular evening, the kids and I were outside with the Granges when some neighbors from up the street came by. Jack had coached their two sons in baseball for a couple of years, and they also could not believe what was happening.

Like most people, they did not know what to say to me. They would just ask how I was doing, and I answered as I did with most. I was getting by.

"So, how are the kids doing?" they asked.

"Well, they seem to be hanging in there, but it's hard. He doesn't come by very much," I rambled, almost as if it were a recording.

"So, I hear you're thinking about moving," the husband said out of the blue.

"Yeah, I just can't decide. I would love to be close to my family, but it's just pulling the kids out of school and moving them to a new area. I really don't know what to do."

"So, you have family that lives there?" he said inquisitively.

"Yeah, my mother, my stepdad, and my grandmother," I said, surprised by his interest as he hesitated for a moment. Then he looked me straight in the eye as if he were placed there just to answer the question I had been praying about that entire day.

"You are doing the right thing," he said.

"What?" I said, almost not believing what he just said. He just said it with such conviction, as if he had not a doubt in his mind.

He repeated, "You're doing the right thing."

"What? How do you know?" I asked, as if I didn't believe he knew what he was talking about.

"Because I went through the same thing when I was a kid, my dad just left one day and my mother was left with me and my sister and my brother to raise. Well, anyway, we ended up moving. My mom found a home close to my grandparents, and they helped get us to school and picked us up after school, and when my mom had to work, we stayed with them and we were fine."

"Really," I said, still stunned by what he had just said. He didn't know why he had answered my question. To him, he was just stating a fact. He was stating his childhood experience and something in him said to share this with me.

It was as if he was sent there to answer my prayers.

It was the way he said it, *You're doing the right thing*, as if there was no doubt. I'm not even sure he planned to tell me anything that night, but yet there he was – another angel.

"Yeah, my father was never in the picture from then on, but we made it work," he said. "My grandparents were there and because of that we were able to move forward. If we weren't with my mom, we were with them."

He then looked at me square in the eye and said again, "You're doing the right thing."

And I just gasped as I said, "Thank you so much. I have been praying about this all day."

"No, it's fine. I know somewhat what you are going through. My mom went through the same thing. I'm telling you, if you have family around, you guys are going to be okay."

And I knew at that moment, I was doing the right thing. It was like there was this light that went on and all the fog lifted, and I knew what we must do. At that very moment, I decided we were going to move.

Unfortunately, there was still the process of saying goodbye, of letting go, and of feeling the heartbreak that would inevitably follow. But my prayers were being answered, and the angels were surrounding us, one by one.

Chapter Ten
City Life

Ben entered through the large glass door of the plant, walking into the tiled lobby area. He caught a glimpse of three other men sitting in plastic chairs that lined the large, gray, cement blocks that made up the wall. Ben, eyeing his surroundings, walked over to the receptionist's desk that was made of solid oak and encircled an attractive younger looking brunette woman like a half moon.

"I'm here about the plant position that was advertised in the paper. It said they were looking for farmers and well, I'm a farmer," Ben said confidently.

"Yes, sir, just a moment, and I'll get you an application." The young woman twisted her chair around, grabbing a clipboard and pen that was set behind her on a gray filing cabinet. Upon turning back around, she handed Ben the clipboard.

"Here is the application. You can sit right over there and fill it out if you'd like. If you have any questions, you just let me know," she rattled off politely, as if she already stated the script to one hundred other applicants before him.

"Thank you, ma'am, I'll do just that." Ben sat down and was so nervous he had to stop his hand from shaking in order to write legibly. Having no previous experience other than the farm, he sat there debating on the empty slots. He tried to think of organizations he had been involved in, listing ones that were farm-related. He took out a folded notebook paper that listed all his personal references. He came to the section of hobbies and interests and took the application back up to the receptionist's desk.

"Excuse me, miss, do we list any hobbies even if they are not work-related?"

"Yes, sir, any interests. They are just trying to get a sense of what you're interested in."

"All right, thank you."

"Not a problem. You let me know if you have any other questions." She smiled.

Ben then headed back to his chair and sat down, noticing the man sitting next to him. Ben thought he had seen this man somewhere before.

He finished filling out the application and handed the completed form back to the receptionist. Being curious, and trying to relieve some of his tension, Ben struck up a conversation with the man sitting next to him.

"Excuse me, but is your last name Johnson?" Ben asked.

"Well, yes it is, Kyle Johnson. How'd you know?"

"Well, I'm a Johnson on my mom's side; I think we may be distant cousins. Is your dad's name Bud?"

"Yeah, that's him."

"I'm Catherine's son, Ben."

"Oh, well, are you all still livin' out in Alma?"

"Yeah, we're still there," Ben said, now leaning back in his chair, stretching out his long legs before him.

"So, you still farming?" Kyle asked, now turning to talk to Ben face to face.

"Oh yeah, I'm just trying to get a more stable income comin' in. It's kind of hard with Dad, me, and Mike all splitting the profit."

"Yeah, I know exactly what you are talking about," Kyle answered.

"I saw the advertisement and thought maybe it was time for a change."

"Yeah, well, I live in Topeka now, and I have been lookin' for work for about three months," Kyle said.

"So, you know anything about the job?" Ben asked.

"Well, a friend of mine works here. He's also a farmer. He says they like to hire farmers because they are supposed to be dependable."

"They must not get around to some of the farmers I know." Ben smiled.

"Ain't that the truth. It usually depends on the person." Kyle laughed.

Just then, a professional looking man with black-rimmed glasses came out and called Kyle's name.

"Well, good luck to ya," Kyle advised.

"You too. Hope I'll be seeing ya," Ben said.

Ben sat and waited, picking up the local newspaper that was sitting on the glass table in front of the chairs. He opened it up, trying to calm his nerves as he read through the headlines. "Ben Thompson," a voice rang out as Ben slowly rose, shaking the hand of a well-dressed black woman as she came up to greet him. "Nice to meet you, Ben."

"My pleasure, ma'am."

"I'm Felicia Conners. If you'll just follow me, we'll get you to a conference room." Ben got up and walked with Felicia down a long hall. "So, are you from around here, Ben?"

"Yes, ma'am, I mean Felicia, I grew up in Alma."

"Oh, I've been there. They have some nice antique stores." Felicia walked steadily as she talked. Ben found it hard to talk and not hit something as he walked so he tried to concentrate more on what was coming before him.

"Oh, I wouldn't know about that. I haven't been in one, but I hear that they're real nice," Ben replied.

They reached a small conference room and entered. Ben took a seat next to Felicia.

"So, says here you're a farmer," Felicia stated looking at the paperwork placed before her.

"Yes, born and raised," Ben replied, noticing that he was rocking his chair. He stopped.

"Well, what do you farm?"

"Well, mostly corn and beans. We have some cattle. We also do dairy."

"Wow, you're pretty busy," Felicia said.

"Well, I share the farm work with my brother and my dad, but my dad is gettin' up in age, so he doesn't help out as much as he used to."

"I can understand that. So, have you ever worked in a plant before?"

"No, Felicia, I haven't. I've actually never worked outside the farm before," Ben spoke honestly.

"Hmm… you've never worked anywhere else?" Felicia verified.

"No, ma'am."

"Well, we have had good luck with farmers in the past, and that's why we ran the ad, so you're in good company." Felicia smiled, trying to make Ben feel more at home. "Anything you can tell me about yourself as far as your work ethics?"

"Well, Felicia, I'm a hard worker. You have to be to be on the farm. I do love outside work, but I need a steady income, and benefits wouldn't hurt none either."

"I can understand that." Felicia laughed. "So, what brought you to Westchester?"

"I have some friends that work here. I listed them on the application. They seem to like it, and they seem to be getting along okay, and well I just thought it was time to expand my horizons a little bit. I love farmin', but you know I need to pay the bills, too."

"Understandable."

"It's just hard, you know, making ends meet sharin' the farm three ways."

"Makes sense. Well, Ben, I have to be honest. I would have really liked to see more work experience here, but I'm going to look over your application and we should be giving you a call in about one to two weeks."

"Well, I appreciate your time, and I look forward to hearin' from you," Ben said, noticing that Felicia had started to rise. Ben then followed.

"It's been very nice meeting you, Ben," Felicia said, as she walked Ben back to the lobby.

"You also, Felicia. You take care now." Ben turned to shake Felicia's hand before he exited.

Ben got a call two weeks later. He had got the job.

One week later, Ben entered the metal plant with an apprehension he hadn't felt since starting high school. Ben was shown around the first couple of days and led to computers he would need to become familiar with, even though he didn't have the slightest knowledge of how to use them.

Ben – determined to do the best job he could – would always arrive early and leave late making sure he had completed everything that was asked of him. His supervisors, amazed at this country man's honesty and general commitment to hard work, advanced him to coordinator, in charge of three or four men after being at the plant only six months.

Due to his new employment, Ben had also begun to make friends outside the small borders of Alma. Ronnie Clasp was head maintenance worker on second shift. Ronnie was known as a lady's man.

Ben became acquainted with Ronnie and started to go out with him after work and associate with a crowd he would soon come to call his friends.

During this time, Ben never slacked off on his farm chores. Even if he had a late night of drinking and playing pool, he would arrive at the farm every morning to do his share of the work before his shift at the plant.

The loneliness of the night would come creeping up on him every now and then like an old lover. The women he met in the bars all seemed to be turned off by Ben's honesty and 70s-style looks of shoulder-length hair and large thick glasses. Determined to never let anyone do to him what Christine had done, Ben kept his distance. Besides, the women that he met at these places all seemed to remind him of Christine.

One night, Ben and Ronnie were out drinking with a woman that Ronnie had picked up at Jakes, the local pool hall. Jakes was your typical dive, lined with motorcycles and cars that were put together out of spare parts. Yet, there was always a pool table open, if you could find it through the smoke. The bar was always open, and the ladies were usually dressed in black, fringed leather jackets.

"You ready to go, Ben?" Ronnie asked, slightly slurring his words.

"Can you drive?" Ben responded, raising his head from his glass.

"Yeah, I can drive. What the hell are you talking about, I can't drive."

"Well, you know my life will be in your hands, and that pretty little lady on your arm is hopin' she gets home all right."

"Hell, I can drive with my eyes shut," Ronnie announced, grabbing both hips of the blonde woman standing next to him and turning her around as she kissed him, almost knocking him off the bar stool he was resting on, as a roar of laughter was heard around the room.

"Hey, get a room," Ben said, jealous of Ronnie's prospects.

"Who needs a room, not us, baby," Ronnie announced to the pool hall as he backed the woman up to the wall, pinning her to it with his body as she tried to squirm away.

"Calm down, Ronnie," she said. "Let go of me. Not in the pool hall. Come on, lover, let's get outta here."

"You'll have me anywhere I say you'll have me," Ronnie announced, swaying as he moved.

"Shut up!" the young blonde woman shouted. She was prettier than most in these places, wearing a black leather jacket and blue miniskirt that flared as she walked.

Ronnie, realizing he had pushed her a little too far, tried to amend his last statement. He grabbed the young woman, bringing her close to him, kissing her as she tried to break away from his grasp. Ben instinctively got up thinking he would have to referee another encounter, always amazed by Ronnie's nerve and stupidity. Ronnie then stumbled back toward her apologizing, "Courtney, baby, I'm sorry. You know I want you. I just get a little crazy sometimes."

Courtney, struggling to stand straight, started to stagger away from him. "Let's get the hell out of here. Ben, where the hell are you? Are you comin?"

"Yeah, I'm comin'. You're my ride home, remember?"

"Oh yeah," Ronnie said, as he made his way to the door. He and Courtney leaned on each other for balance. "Hey, Ben, we'll have to sit Courtney here in between us."

"Hey, I don't have a problem with that." Ben, who was almost just as drunk as Ronnie, stood up and started to follow the two out of the bar.

"All right then, let's get out of here, Courtney and I have business to attend to."

Once outside, the trio all climbed into Ronnie's red convertible that had a black cloth top. They squeezed Courtney in the center since the car was only a two-seater.

"This should be fun," Ben proclaimed. Courtney couldn't seem to sit steadily in the middle of the two seats. Her head was tilted sideways, trying not to make contact with the cloth roof.

Ronnie, after starting the engine, hit the gas, sending the convertible fishtailing out of the gravel lot and onto the asphalt road, almost sending Courtney into Ben's lap. They drove onto the black pavement, hitting it so hard it lifted the car's rear end a couple of feet off the ground. Ronnie lit a cigarette while he drove. Courtney sat unbuckled on the armrest. Ronnie had one arm on her thigh and one arm on the steering wheel while trying to hold on to his cigarette. Courtney played with Ben's hair as Ben brushed her arm away, annoyed.

"Hey, what is your name, anyway?" Courtney asked Ben.

"Ben."

"You're kind of cute, Ben."

"Stop trying to sleep with everyone you come in contact with, damn it," Ronnie screamed out at her, removing his hand from her thigh and taking the steering wheel.

"Ronnie, I didn't mean anything by it," Courtney apologized, trying to grab Ronnie's arm as he snatched it away from her.

"I should just take you home. I'm sick of you."

"Go ahead, loser. Like you don't sleep with anything that comes your way," Courtney screamed, as she started to hit Ronnie on the head uncontrollably.

Ben tried to grab Courtney's arms to calm her down, as she tried to squirm away.

"She didn't mean anything, Ronnie," Ben exclaimed.

"She did too. She sleeps with…"

Just then lights flashed over the occupant's eyes as the car drifted into oncoming traffic. A semitrailer, which was coming straight at them, released a loud foghorn sound. Ronnie grabbed the steering wheel, overcorrecting as Ben screamed, "Watch out!"

The car veered back to the right lane as the road curved, sending the convertible over the edge of the road and rolling down the slope on to a field. The top flew open and all three passengers were thrown out of the car and into the grassy field. The car finally landed on its side in the ditch.

Ben woke up in a daze as he heard Ronnie yelling at him from what seemed like a distance.

"Ben, Bennn… are youuu okayyy?" Ben saw only blurred images having lost his glasses.

"What? What happened?" Ben questioned, not knowing where he was. "Where are my glasses?" Ben instinctively got on all fours and started to search around the brush for his glasses. "I can't see without them. Where are they?"

He shook off Ronnie's hand in a state of panic as he frantically began to look through the weeds. He reached up to the right side of his face and realized blood was dripping down.

"Ben, I've got 'em. They're a little smashed," Ronnie said, making his way toward Ben, trying to calm him down.

Ben sat and tried to put them on, still unaware of where he was. He located a cut behind his ear as he began to mumble.

"I'm bleeding. Here behind my ear." Ben suddenly felt nauseous. The field began to spin as he felt himself falling backward.

Courtney sat on the side of the hill holding her stomach. Ronnie looked over at her and yelled, "I'm calling for help."

Next thing Ben knew, he was being awakened by Chuck's voice. Chuck was another maintenance guy from the plant who went out with them every now and then. He lived just down the road. Chuck and his girlfriend, Amanda, showed up just minutes after they received Ronnie's call. Amanda was driving her car in case they needed another vehicle to drive.

"I can get the car out of here tomorrow!" Ronnie shouted.

"Do you think Ben's okay?" questioned Chuck nervously.

"I don't know? Do you think he needs to go to the hospital?" Ronnie asked. "Ben, Ben, do you want to go to the hospital?" Ronnie, now sitting next to Ben, raised Ben's head gently into his arms..

"No... Chuck, just take me to your place," Ben muttered. Ben tried to stand with the two men's help and felt his legs giving way beneath him.

"Are you sure?" Chuck asked.

"What? Why?" Ben still seemed to be unaware of the last few hours. Ronnie and Chuck then spotted the small gash behind Ben's right ear. They placed a flannel shirt that Chuck got out of his car on the cut to help stop the bleeding. The red spot started to consume the shirt as they gently moved Ben into the backseat of Chuck's car.

"Alright, I'll take him to my place. I'd get this freakin' car out of here before the police show up," Chuck urged.

"Can't do that right now," wailed Ronnie nervously. "Do you think he's going to be okay? Ben, man, I'm sorry. Are you okay?" Ronnie asked, as he nervously leaned into Chuck's vehicle.

"I'm okay, I'm okay... just take me home. I need to get some rest..." Ben reassured them.

"Damn it, I shouldn't 'ave... Chuck..." Ronnie started to say as he moved away from the car brushing through his hair nervously.

"Just get the heck outta here. I'll call you later," Chuck said, now annoyed with Ronnie.

"Okay... okay. Courtney, you okay?" Ronnie asked, now realizing he had forgotten about Courtney who was still sitting on the ground.

"Yeah, but I want to go home," Courtney said as Ronnie helped her up.

"Okay, baby, let's go. Ben, man, I'm sorry!" Ronnie shouted behind him.

"Just go, Ronnie, damn it!" Chuck yelled. "We'll get a tow truck out in the morning."

Ronnie jumped into Amanda's car and took off down the road. Chuck and Amanda headed off with Ben in the backseat of their car. Ben kept coming in and out of consciousness.

"It's okay, Ben, we're taking you to our house," Chuck tried to reassure him.

"Okay, thanks, man," Ben moaned.

"No problem. Are you sure you're okay?" Chuck asked him again.

"Yeah, why do you keep asking me that?" Ben murmured, and he passed out in the back seat.

"Chuck, he doesn't look good," Amanda said, "Maybe we should take him to a hospital."

"They'll want to know what happened," Chuck answered.

"Yes, but what if he's seriously hurt?" she asked.

"We'll take him home, and if he doesn't get any better, we'll take him to the hospital, all right?"

"Hey, it's your friend," Amanda said sarcastically.

Ben woke up five hours later with a splitting headache. They placed a trash can next to the bed because he kept throwing up every few hours. Chuck came into check on him every hour. Ben, not feeling any better, asked to be taken to the hospital.

Chuck and Amanda took Ben to Midland Memorial. He was immediately admitted with a story that he had fallen down some stairs. A police officer was called into question Ben as to why he had not immediately come to the hospital after the injury. After the officer arrived, he explained to Ben that there had been a report of an accident off Highway 24.

"Have you been drinking tonight, Mr. Thompson?" the officer asked while taking out a report pad.

"Yeah, I was drinking."

"So, you fell down the stairs at your friend's home?"

"Yeah, we were playing poker in the basement and I fell down the stairs."

"And you are sure you want to stick to that story?" The police officer stopped writing long enough to look directly at Ben's face.

"Yeah, that's the story I'm sticking with because that's what happened," Ben proclaimed. Ben hated to lie. He just didn't want to get his friends into trouble. He felt he was just as much to blame. He had been just as drunk and had entered the car under his own free will.

"Alright, Mr. Thompson. Is this the number where you can be reached?" the officer said, pointing to the report.

"Yes, sir, it is."

"You're lucky. It could have been much worse," the officer said, with an insinuation that he knew Ben was lying.

"Yes, sir, I know that."

"Well, take it easy around those stairs because you just may have looked death in the face."

"I know that, sir," Ben replied, now looking away.

Ben was checked out of the hospital the next day with a concussion and five stitches behind his ear. He was told to get plenty of rest, but to stay with someone who could keep an eye on him. Ben went home alone… He never took another drink for the next two and a half years.

Chapter Eleven
Broken

The weeks that followed were a blur. They consisted of talking with my lawyer, getting ready for the move, and preparing my children for I-didn't-know-what. My lawyer set a court date for the end of May, just four short months after Jack had driven out of our garage.

I didn't know how to help my children. I didn't know how to help myself. I began painting the house, updating what I could. We had built the house on this lot seven years ago and it began to show small signs of deterioration; like our family, our home was slowly starting to fall apart.

I cleaned out what was left in our business account for moving expenses before Jack had a chance to take my name off the account. It was about forty-five hundred dollars. Jack never said anything to me about it. He just opened another account and continued to run the business on his own.

The children would go to school and come home as we tried imitating some kind of normal routine, but the hollowness was always there. When my mother was there, I was at my best. When she left, the depression would move in. It seemed to retreat at the first footsteps of my mother entering my kitchen and returned every time I watched her drive down the road heading home.

Sandy made herself available to me at a moment's notice, even giving me her work number where she said I was welcome to come and just hang out. I called her many times from various parking lots where I would just park and sit after dropping off the kids at school. I blended in there. No one could find me. There the tears were silent. There the rejection took over, and I melted into my seat, slowly disappearing.

I would slowly dial her number and she would ask where I was and I would tell her, not at home. She would tell me to come over. Wherever she was, she invited me in.

I didn't want to be at home. It was a constant reminder of my failure and the sadness that had engulfed us. I would have given it all up for my marriage. I even suggested it to Jack several times, thinking that it was just the pressure of all the things we had accumulated that led him to leave. I told him we could sell the house, sell the business, start over, and he would just smile at me and say, "No."

He seemed to change daily in a kind of bipolar routine. One day he would be caring and sensitive and the next he would be cussing at me and yelling so loud anyone around the proximity of my phone conversation could hear his insanity. Sandy had to restrain herself from taking the phone from me a couple of times as I just sat there letting him tear into me.

"Why do you let him speak to you like that?" she would ask.

"I don't know."

"He has no right to talk to you like that."

But at the time I didn't have the strength to fight back. I was broken. I couldn't have fought back if I wanted to. So, I took it.

I wasn't sure I was even in love with Jack anymore. At the time, I wasn't sure I had ever loved him. Yet, the good times we had as a family kept going through my mind. The bad times had left and would return later, after the divorce, after the move, and after Jack brought her into my children's lives.

My best friend Tiffany came to stay with me one week when my mother could not be there. She and her husband had been our best friends since before we had children. We were all trying to make sense out of something that didn't make any sense.

"Tiffany, why is he doing this?" I said as we sat on the sofa, Tiffany taking my hand into hers.

"I wish I knew," she said. The unfamiliarity of her friend, her strong, confident friend falling apart in front of her, left her speechless.

"I heard about this group that meets at local churches. It's called Divorce Care. Have you heard of it?" Tiffany asked.

"No," I said, not really caring to know more.

"It's a support group for people who are going through divorce. I don't know if it will help, but it might. I looked up a location that was close to you. I think you should go."

"I don't know," I said. The thought of getting together with other divorcees didn't excite me. I assumed they would be handling it differently than me. I felt weak. I felt like I was falling apart, and I didn't need to be around people who were holding it all together.

"No, really, you should go. They meet on Thursday nights. Is Saline available to babysit?"

"Yeah, I think so." I tried to think of excuses to get out of it, even though part of me knew I needed help.

"How about we call and get you signed up?"

We spent the rest of the week painting and getting my house ready to go on the market. Then she and I started to plan my future move.

I started grabbing for any straw that I could find that would get me through to the next day. Anything that would help make sense of this craziness in my life. I was sinking. My faith was still there, but the why questions had me running to Brentwood Bible Church as fast as my feet would carry me. I went in embarrassed and ashamed to announce to everyone my failure. I had failed my family, my kids and yes, Jack. I thought that everyone was looking at me as the poor little wife who couldn't keep her husband. I even had friends, or so-called friends, who asked me what I had done to make him leave. Your self-esteem is a funny thing. I had always been a confident person, and with one blow from Jack, it all changed. I was broken.

I walked into the meeting trying to hold back tears. As I entered the large room, I saw several tables facing one another in a 'U' shape. The director stood in the middle of the tables, handing out our workbooks and pens as everyone entered. He greeted us and said how glad he was to see each of us. The room was as silent as a morgue.

I sat in my seat flipping through the workbook trying to hold back tears. I hated that I had to be here at all. I hated that I was in this situation. And mostly I hated that I couldn't handle this on my own. I sat next to people who I could tell were just as broken as I was. Men and women, who had been hit by the same brick wall.

Every day I had this uncharacteristic urge to smash my husband's windshield with a baseball bat. I thought I was going crazy. I visualized going to the new truck that he had just bought before he left me, and smashing the entire thing with a crowbar or something. I felt the peace that this would bring. I would visualize the shards embedding themselves into the interior of his cab.

I sat there and tried to hide this from the others as the leader of the group started to speak.

"My wife just left one day," Kevin said. Kevin was a tall man with dark hair and a mustache, and had a demeanor that commanded attention. "I didn't know what had happened. What I had done. It was like being hit by a freight train."

And we all slowly looked up at him. He had made a connection.

"I begged her to come back. I didn't want this for our family. My children didn't want this, but her mind was made up. She left me. She left us for another man. Then I heard about Divorce Care. Divorce Care carried me through, and that's why I am here today. If it hadn't been for my support group, I don't know where I would be right now. My children and I gathered together in our brokenness and somehow made it through. That was two years ago, not that it still isn't difficult at times. Being both a mother and a father is difficult. It's unnatural, but through God's grace we have made it work. I know it's difficult for you to see this right now, but it will get better. I'm living proof, God has a plan for you."

He then said as if reading my mind, "At one point I wanted to smash every window in her vehicle, and possibly flatten a couple of her tires. I wanted her to feel the deep hurt I was feeling." We all looked around at each other and he continued, "But I didn't. I thought I was losing my mind."

"I smashed my husband's windshield in," blurted an older-looking blonde woman sitting across from me.

"What happened?" Kevin, our leader, asked.

"Well, I found out he was divorcing me to be with this other woman, and I just lost it. I went to his work and took out my crowbar and smashed it through the front of the car. I don't even really remember doing it. It was like I was dreaming or something. Well, anyway, the police showed up at my house that afternoon."

"He saw you?"

"No, but he knew it was me. I mean, I don't normally do things like that. I was just hurting so bad. At first it felt good. I mean, releasing that crowbar and watching the glass shatter." She suddenly laughed and we all smiled back at her. "Until the police showed up at my house, so no, I wouldn't recommend it." She laughed again.

At that moment, somehow, we were all able to laugh and cry with one another. The walls slowly started to crumble, and we held each other in our brokenness. I said to myself, *I'm not crazy. Everything I'm feeling is normal.*

I then began to climb again. I began to slowly believe again. I looked forward to every meeting because it got me through another week. We became a family of support. We laughed together, and we cried together. We got each other through with a hope of a new tomorrow and the thought that God really did have a plan for us.

I started attending the services there and taking my children. The contemporary Christian music rang out as if it were speaking directly to us, giving us restored hope. Praying became second nature, and I called on God throughout these times and he sent angels flying my way. Every time I turned around, another angel was waiting to help us, letting us know that it was going to be okay. And I began to plan the road that we would travel, guessing and praying along the way.

After the decision to move was set, I started having angels show up to help me pack. I don't remember packing anything. I remember seeing people pack and answering questions, but I don't remember actually packing.

I went to my children's elementary school on the last day of the school year to pick up Hope and Jackson. It was a sad occasion because everyone knew that they would not be returning the next year. Their dad and I had been very involved in the school. After he left, I really didn't tell many people what was happening to our family. The kids' teachers knew. I had to tell them so they would know what the kids were going through. They were both very sympathetic and said they would keep an eye on them for me. I was ashamed. I didn't want people to know. Failure wouldn't allow me to.

As I was walking in that day, Mr. Roberts, the principal, met me at the office door.

"Hi, Sarah, do you have a minute?" Mr. Roberts asked.

"Yeah, sure," I said.

I followed him into the office where he handed me an envelope.

"It's just a little something to help with your move," he said. "Your family has been such an incredible help to the school in the past that we wanted to do something for you."

The envelope had my name written across the front. I looked at him blankly.

"What is this?" I asked.

"All the teachers took up a collection to help you with your move."

I stood there numb, realizing that these people, who didn't make all that much in the first place, cared enough about me and my family to donate money to us.

He just stood there and said, "Good luck to you."

The money in the envelope totaled $180.00 and it was my special fund. I took it wherever I went. This became my emergency money when something unexpected happened and I needed cash immediately. The money lasted me about nine months, and each emergency was answered by the generosity of these people, angels in disguise.

Chapter Twelve
Time Doesn't Stand Still

"How's Mom and Dad feelin' today?" Mike questioned.

"Oh, about the same," Ben said. "I picked Dad up some ice cream on the way in. Mom says he sure has a sweet tooth these days."

Mike grabbed some tools from the back of his truck and slowly lifted them over the sides and took them into the barn, yelling back at Ben. "Yeah, I'm just not sure how good it is for him."

Ben, grabbing the rest of the equipment, followed behind. "Hey, if it makes him happy, I'm okay with it. After all, he doesn't really have all that much to look forward to these days. If a little ice cream raises his spirit, I'm all for it."

"True, didn't really look at it that way. I guess it doesn't hurt anything." Mike looked at Ben with a new realization. Their parents were getting older. "Hey, did you get those heifers pinned up?" Mike asked, as he slid the large barn doors together and padlocked them for safekeeping.

"Yeah, I did," Ben replied.

The two men then started to walk down the hill toward the two parked trucks sitting right in front of their parents' home.

"Oh, by the way, Debbie and I were wonderin' if you'd like to come over for dinner on Saturday. That's if you're free. We're celebrating the end of baseball season."

"Yeah, I think I can be there."

"Good. You know Rachael and her team took first place this year," Mike bragged.

"Yeah, I heard. That's great. Tell her I said not to get a big head though." Ben laughed.

Everyone knew Rachael was Ben's favorite niece. Rachael was a hard worker and would come over and clean Ben's place for him, for a small fee, of course. Ben sometimes found himself thinking that if he would have had a daughter, he would have wanted her to be just like Rachael.

Rachael was a strong-willed teenager who made straight A's and was involved in every sport in school. She was also the niece who showed up with Mike quite often helping out at the farm. Rachael loved the farm almost as much as Ben and Mike. She would ride out with Mike and often end up riding around the farm with her uncle to do odd jobs.

"So, you goin' to the dance at the fair this weekend?" Rachael questioned while she rode back to the farm with her uncle one lazy fall afternoon.

"Nope," Ben answered.

"Why not? There should be lots of pretty women there."

"Don't need any. Don't want any," Ben said, kidding with her.

"You're just afraid to show your moves," Rachael teased her uncle, bouncing around on the bench seat, mimicking his dancing inabilities.

"Yep, I don't want to show up all those younger guys."

"Well, I can't say that I blame you. Dancin' doesn't seem to run in our blood." Rachael frowned while adjusting the radio in Ben's truck.

"Why? Aren't you goin'?"

"No. Scott likes to dance, but I get out there and just make a fool of myself."

"I've seen you dance. You're not that bad," Ben said, looking over at his niece.

"Oh… not that bad, huh," Rachael smirked.

"Well, I mean, you're not quite as good as me but then again, who is?" Ben smiled as Rachael pushed his shoulder with her hand, knocking him gently into the door.

"I don't know. I just feel like a fool every time I get out there and all those people are starin' at me. I don't like it."

"What? You who hit seven home runs last year and was captain of the basketball team doesn't like a little attention?"

"That's different. I'm on a team. They can hide me."

"Oh, Rachael, you should go and enjoy yourself with Scott."

"No, because then I feel stupid because I can't keep up with him."

"I don't think he likes you for your dancin' abilities." Ben turned his face briefly toward his niece.

"Yeah, but he may leave me for my lack thereof."

"Well, that is a concern." Ben smiled, trying to lighten the moment.

"What?" Rachael laughed, pushing her uncle's shoulder again. "But seriously, you should go; there will be older women there too."

"How old? I don't like them too old," Ben joked.

"Old like you."

"Oh, that old, now I feel better." Ben grinned.

"You know what I mean," Rachael said.

"I know what you mean. Don't you worry about your old uncle here. I'll be just fine."

"Yeah, but you'd be better if you had someone to do stuff with."

Just then the two turned onto the gravel driveway leading up to the farmhouse. The cool fall air swayed the branches above them as the truck moved in and out of the shadows from the overhanging branches.

"Okay, okay, I'll try," Ben replied, sensing his niece's concern.

"Great, now don't forget, I want to borrow your car for homecoming. I don't want to show up in Scott's old clunker."

"I haven't forgotten. Oh, and thanks for cleanin' the house last week. I'll write you a check when I get back."

"No problem. But you have somethin' growing in your shower. I'm going to need to get somethin' special from Mom to take care of it. You need to get more cleaning supplies."

"I'll try to do better."

Rachel exited the truck as Ben's mother waved him down.

"I'm making meatloaf for supper. You want to stay and have some?"

"Nah, Mom, I'll just eat somethin' at home."

"I made more than enough. Your dad wants to watch the KU game tonight, and he would love to have the company."

"Well, then, okay, but only for Dad." Ben smiled.

"All right then, I'll see you inside."

Ben parked the truck down by the field and got out, noticing the sun going down in the west. The farmhouse stood on the top of a hill that overlooked the farm fields and hills to the west. Ben walked out just as the sun was making its way down. He stopped and looked for a second as beams of oranges and yellows slithered across the fields, bringing an end to another work day.

The sound of the bulls serenaded him from the east. He glanced over at the garden he planted every year for his parents. Most of the plants were already drying up as the ground prepared for the long hard winter heading their way. His mother's flower garden was blooming just beside the house, the colors ranging from whites, to reds, to purples.

The shades of fall were beginning to peek out, the leaves already showed signs of changing from the deep emerald green to the golden red, oranges, and yellows.

Ben walked over to the old apple tree which struggled each year for new life. His dad had planted that tree and several others in the orchard behind it. The orchard used to be rich with different types of fruit trees, pears, apples, and peaches, but they had long since died and all that was left was this one apple tree, a single remnant of a time long gone.

As their parents had gotten older, Ben and Mike took up most of the workload around the farm. Their mother had suffered a heart attack about two years ago and was told she only had one year to live. Well, it had already been two years, and she had slowed a bit, but she was still going strong. Stubborn, Ben figured his mother wasn't going to let some city doctor tell her when her life in this world was going to be over.

Unfortunately, Ben's father had taken a turn for the worse, as the arthritis that had plagued him most of his life started to take its toll and left their father home-bound and getting around with the help of a walker.

Mike checked on them in the evening when he came out to do his chores, after leaving his day job. Ben would be around most of the day, checking in on them throughout the day, in between chores, until he made his way to the plant in the evening. Ben's mother still made their lunch every afternoon as he and his parents settled in for the daily noon meal and watched the farm markets on television.

Ben had a weak spot for his parents, whom he saw suffer through the many years of droughts, floods and storms, making a life for him and his siblings. As the roles started to reverse, Ben saw his parents starting to fade right before his eyes, and his dreams of a family – like the plants in his garden – slowly withering away.

Chapter Thirteen
The Goodbyes

The day of my divorce was the day Jack finally admitted that 'she' was real.

Not long after, Jack picked up my youngest daughter, Hope, from what used to be our home, to take her out for her birthday surprise. The surprise was on all of us, as Hope came home innocently rambling on about the woman named Kelly, who was Daddy's girlfriend.

The poor little thing, I questioned her so uncontrollably about this woman, she had to stop and tell me, "I don't know, Mommy." This woman became even more real when he invited all the children to go to dinner with the two of them… and my children went.

I felt betrayed. I felt that I had lost my children. They seemed to accept what their father was doing, and I began to fall again and failure brought me down once more. He had left me for her, and everyone seemed okay with it. Everyone, but me.

Moving day was dreary with an overhanging reality that we were leaving our home, our friends, and the only life my children had ever known. Throughout the day, friends stopped by to say goodbye.

Lily anxiously waited for her best friend, Laura, who was supposed to come by that morning to say goodbye. We were all standing in the front yard loading boxes into the rental truck when Laura's father pulled up in his car, alone.

"Hi, Sarah… Lily," Mr. Rhoades said, awkwardly looking around as if he were trying to find the words. He reluctantly approached us holding something in his hands.

"Hi, Mr. Rhoades. Where's Laura?" Lily asked.

"Oh, well, she wanted to come, Lily," he said. "But she just couldn't bring herself to tell you goodbye. I'm so sorry. She really wanted to be here. She just couldn't face you, so I told her I would bring this to you."

"Oh," was all Lily could manage, and I saw her demeanor darken as if a cloud had formed right over us and the darkness pulled us down again. Her already swollen eyes tried to imitate a smile as Laura's father handed her a brown wooden frame. It held a picture of Lily and Laura hugging in front of Laura's house after a sleepover. The frame's heading read: *Best Friends Forever.*

"Tell Laura it's okay," Lily said. "Tell her I'll call her."

"I will, Lily. I'm so sorry." He then turned to walk back to his vehicle, turning back half way and waving. "You all have a safe trip. We're sure going to miss you." And he reentered his vehicle. Lily stood there looking at the picture as tears filled her eyes. I hugged her with one arm, bringing her close to me, knowing it would not be enough. She tried to smile at me, as she reentered the house and slowly made her way to her room that was halfway packed. She sat on her bed looking out the window to the back yard, unable to move, unable to cope, as tears ran their course.

I stood there and watched in silence. I didn't know what to do. I didn't know what to say as the weight of the day pounded down onto my already slumping shoulders.

The day had been filled with so much heartache. Saline sulked in her room, unable to leave its confines.

Jackson and Hope played with Mitch and April Grange the entire day. They played just as if they would be seeing each other tomorrow. They played as if they would still grow up together, their innocence of the unknown an eerie comfort.

We and the Granges, our next-door neighbors, were coming to the realization that the day had come when we would have to say goodbye. Our younger children, who were supposed to grow up together, were now being separated. The dreams of homecomings, proms, dating, and weddings were something they would now experience with someone else. Looking into each other's eyes, we faced our future.

After boxes were loaded and rearranged, and the house was empty – after everyone had left, and we had said our tear-filled goodbyes – my parents came to me and said it was time to go. I stood in the garage of my home and said, "I have to say goodbye to my home."

I walked back into my house and looked out the back windows onto the trees that lined the back yard. There stood the wooden jungle gym that Daniel and Jack had assembled, thinking it would be enjoyed for years by both families. I turned toward our family room, now silent, as thoughts of birthday parties with yellow balloons floating through the air filled my mind. I pictured the Christmas tree that sat in the corner each year, accentuated by red and gold bulbs and twinkling white lights.

I ventured upstairs passing each of the kids' rooms, remembering them as they once were, cluttered with life. I pictured the children stretched out over their beds or lying across the floor playing a board game or checkers. I walked into my bedroom and looked around. It felt as empty as me. Maybe it was just me, or maybe it was what we were all feeling that day, but this house that was our home seemed so sad.

At that point, I turned and walked back downstairs and out the kitchen door, hearing it slam behind me as I felt the house give out a deep sigh. I got into my car as my children all looked out the window at their home, one last time, and I pulled away.

When we arrived in Topeka, children in the area had just finished up the current school year. The kids and I moved in with my parents. We all seemed to adjust differently to our newfound living arrangement. I was totally fine living with my parents. There I could concentrate on finding a job. My mom literally took care of everything. So, I was fine, but my children were taking on a different view as their relationship with their grandparents began to suffer.

"When will we be going to check out our new school, Mom?" Lily asked, bouncing onto the bed Saline and I shared.

"Well, I'll check with Grandpa. I'm not sure where it's located."

"Will we be finding a house close to the school?" Lily asked.

"I hope so, but a lot of that depends on your dad."

"I don't want to talk about him," Lily sternly responded. Her whole demeanor changed at the mention of her father. I didn't blame her. Her world had been set upside down and she was coping with her dad no longer being an active part of her life.

"I'm sorry, honey, but it does."

"I just want a place of our own. I don't want to live here forever."

Just then Saline walked in the room. "Mom, we have to move," Saline said, throwing herself onto the bed next to Lily, face first. She then lifted her head enough to restate her need to relocate. "I love Grandma, but I just can't live here anymore."

"What happened?" I asked.

"I told Grandma that you let me talk on the phone until bedtime and she doesn't believe me. She said we need to start going to bed earlier and that I am staying up way too late."

"I'll talk to her," I said, rubbing Saline's shoulders. "She's just trying to help."

"I just can't stay here anymore," Saline reiterated. "Grandma thinks I'm not helping you with the kids and I'm trying to."

"I know you are."

My mother took care of us. She took care of things I felt unable to do at the moment. Unfortunately, my mother also decided to try and help with the kids' discipline, which wasn't going over well with any of them. I was in no hurry to move, but I was beginning to realize that my children, and my parents, needed a home of their own.

I started applying for jobs, but the limitations of my work history hindered my job search. After all, my cheating ex-husband was the only real reference I had at the time. At first, I hit the pavement with enthusiasm, knowing that the job that would save us all was waiting just around the corner. Well, days became weeks and still not even a call of potential employment. I started to drop back into my depression, wondering what exactly was God's plan for me.

I came home one day after a day of futile job searching and Saline came into our shared bedroom slamming the door behind her. "Mom, we need to move." I crawled up to my pillow, leaving the want ads lying beside me as I tried to close my eyes, drowning myself into the pillow.

"Mom, I mean it," her voice rose. "We need to move now. We need to get our own place."

I thought to myself, *Doesn't she see me trying? What does she expect me to do?*

"You need to find a job," she said, sounding more and more disgusted with our situation.

I sat up and looked at my strong daughter sitting there beside me, and I brought the job ads back before me and started to cross them off one by one, circling anything that looked even remotely promising. I tended to forget that I was not the only one affected by the divorce. I wanted to just curl up and dwell in my sorrow, but my children wouldn't let me. They kept pushing and wanting more. They still needed me. They gave me the strength to keep trying, the strength to not give up.

I eventually came to the decision we needed to move. Yes, without a job and without guaranteed child support. But who was going to rent to a newly divorced woman with four kids, who doesn't even have a job? Well, God works in miraculous ways.

I started searching for a duplex to rent because I hated the thought of apartment living. I also wanted the kids to feel as if it were some kind of home. They had already been through so much. I wanted something they could be proud of. Well, with four thousand dollars in the bank, I started looking for rentals. The cheapest I could find rented from $900.00 to $1,100.00 a month. With the optimism that Jack would come through with some child support, and the reality that two other landlords had already told me no, I pulled up to a duplex in the school district I wanted my kids to attend.

That is when I met Barb, an elderly woman with bright red hair, green eyes, and pale skin. Barb was fashionably dressed in a green shirt that brought out her eyes, and an orange scarf that was wrapped around her neck.

"Hello, you must be Sarah," she said.

"Yes."

"Nice to meet you. I'm Barbara, but you can call me Barb. Would you like to go in?"

"Yes, we would love to," I said while I looked around, thinking I didn't have a prayer in the world of getting this place.

The kids immediately loved the duplex. It was spacious and was something we could all call home. The rent was $900.00 a month, which was one of the cheaper rentals.

After we looked around, Barb brought out an application. "I would just need you to fill this out and get it back to me as soon as you can."

"Oh, I can fill it out right now," I said without hesitation, even though I had no idea how I would pay the rent.

Barb looked over the application, her eyes drawn to the employer section. "So, you're not working right now."

"No," I responded, "But I have some child support coming in, and I plan on finding a job as soon as possible."

Barb looked at me. She then looked at all of us.

"You know, I trust you for some reason. I don't usually do this, but I'm going to let you have it. I have a good feeling about you."

"I promise, you won't be sorry," I told Barb enthusiastically.

The kids immediately started jumping around as if we had just won the lottery. They didn't even try to hide their excitement, as my parents and Barb looked on, caught up in the kids' joy. And we had found our first home. As I said, God works in great and miraculous ways, and we moved in at the first of the month.

I soon found a job with a temporary service that paid next to nothing, but it was an income. It didn't take long for me to realize I wasn't going to be able to make ends meet. So, I took on another part-time job in the evening at a local department store.

I would leave my temporary job and rush home and either put fish sticks in the oven or pick up some fast food before I had to leave to my second job in the evening. Jack was still not paying regular child support, and my patience with him grew thinner, as my time with the kids grew shorter and shorter.

Coming home from my second job one evening, my phone rang. My caller ID told me that it was Jack. I threw my purse down on the counter, quickly picking up the receiver.

"Why haven't you paid the child support, Jack?"

"Sarah, I'm trying. Work is slow right now."

"How is that my problem, Jack?" I said, now throwing my keys across the counter. "How do you expect me to feed and clothe these kids?"

"I will send more, there just isn't a lot of work right now," Jack said, truly believing that he was doing everything he could. He had transformed into someone I didn't even know anymore. He was sinking down, drowning in all his lusts and selfishness, and unfortunately, he was bringing us down with him.

"I don't care. I need that money," I said.

"Kelly and I are having a hard time right now. We are trying to get things going…" And the words burned themselves into my chest. If he had been standing right in front of me, I truly think I would have slugged him right across the jaw.

"I don't want to hear about you and Kelly! I don't care what you two are doing, but I do care that you are not helping with the kids."

"Sarah, I'm trying."

I slammed my palm onto the counter and held the phone away from my mouth until I could gain my composure. "No Jack, you're not."

"Whatever, Sarah…"

I suddenly heard a click and was left looking at my receiver. I leaned onto the counter putting both of my hands over my eyes, wondering how long I could go on like this.

Chapter Fourteen
What Are Friends For?

Ben would arrive at the plant thirty minutes early every day so that he could tie in with the day crew and get an update on what still needed to be completed. The large steel machines let off heat and steam by the minute. In the winter, this heat was used to warm the plant, but in the summer the heat only added to the already rising temperatures inside the confined work area.

Ben, being used to the heat on the farm, was never bothered much by the high temperatures. He worked on the farm in the blistering heat of a summer's day and the rigid cold of the winters, never complaining, and it was no different at the plant.

Having more free time than most, Ben signed up for as much overtime as he was allowed, especially in between seasons, when work on the farm was slow. Ben would always manage to maintain a number five or six spot on the overtime list. He was now making more money than he ever had.

He enjoyed the ability to spoil his parents, buying them whatever they needed. *Heck*, he thought, why shouldn't he? They had taken care of him all those years. Ben just thought he could make whatever time they had left here on this earth a little bit nicer.

His mother would send him home with a hot meal every day. Ben was their company, so whenever he was free, he took the time to stop in and just talk with them, not about anything in particular, just sharing company. Ben would enter the screen door always finding the familiar sight of his parents, usually sitting at the kitchen table.

"So, you know anythin' interestin'?" Larry asked.

"No, nothin' much, Dad," Ben answered, taking a seat at the table.

"Hear the city is repairing the curbs in town. I hear they got 'em all tore up."

"Yeah, they're putting some type of brick down to make it look nicer, I guess. I think it's just a waste of money."

"Well, they got lots of it," Larry said, snickering.

"Don't they now. How you been feeling?"

"Oh fine, fine. Can't complain. Your mother's keepin' me fed."

"Well, you're looking kind of thin, Dad," Ben kidded. "Don't you like what she's cookin'?"

"Sure, just doesn't seem to stick. I don't have much for an appetite these days." Larry's once broad frame had begun to melt away. His tall physique was starting to deteriorate as he sat hunched over the table, unable to sit up straight.

"I wish I had that problem. I can't seem to keep the weight off," Ben said, slapping his gut.

"Oh, you look fine," Ben's dad replied.

"You stayin' for supper, son?" Cathy asked, as she headed over to the table with a couple of plates in her hand.

"No, Mom, I have some plans in Topeka, but I'll be out early in the mornin'."

"Could you maybe pick me up a couple of things at the grocery store?" she asked.

"I sure can. What do ya need?"

"Well, your dad was looking at the ads; looks like the grapefruit and bananas are on sale at Walmart," she said, then taking a second to recall any other items. "Oh, and some ice cream, your dad's been hankerin' for some. But you better get that in town, otherwise it'll melt."

"Yeah, I was figuring on that, Mom." Ben rose from the table, getting ready to leave. "Okay... well, if you two are okay, I'll see ya in the mornin'."

"We're fine," they said in unison.

Ben then exited the farm house, heading for his truck.

Ben, having time on his hands, had to find ways to entertain himself. His family often made an effort to include him in whatever they were doing. They also tried to be there for him whenever he needed someone to go to the movies with, or a football game. Ben still went out with his friends every now and then, but not to the extent that he once had. Change had once again begun to spin its web as Ben's friends started heading in different directions, marriage, kids, divorce, all fated by the hands of time.

Coming into the plant had become as normal as walking onto the farm to Ben. Although he still hated working inside and being confined, he enjoyed the perks and benefits of working for a large company. He often tried to make the best of circumstances and greeted most people with a friendly hello. He figured he was certainly more fortunate than most and didn't see any need in concentrating all his efforts on the negative. Ben had begun to live a life he figured he was meant to live, alone.

After arriving at the plant one day, Ben found that the dough batching machine seemed to be running fairly well on its own, so he stepped into the breakroom to take his lunch break. The aroma of the vegetables they made at the plant seemed to seep into Ben's clothing and skin, trailing closely behind him wherever he went. He hardly noticed it anymore until he got home and could smell the plant's scent follow him inside.

Entering the breakroom, he ran into Alex, a maintenance worker who was about ten years Ben's senior. Alex, like Ben, was a single man, and they had on occasion gone out together to get a bite to eat or driven to the local casino for a night of gambling. Ben found that he liked talking to Alex more and more because of the commonality they shared, both being divorced and single.

"Hey, Alex, how's it goin'?" Ben said, as he grabbed his lunch bag.

"Oh, all right. I guess I can't complain, but I probably will," Alex said routinely while spreading mayonnaise on this sandwich.

"What's the matter now, Alex?"

"Well, I took this woman out the other day, someone my daughter set me up with, and she gets mad at me on the first date."

"What'd you do to her?" Ben said sarcastically.

"I didn't do anything. We go out to this restaurant I had heard about, and she gets mad 'cause I pull out a coupon."

"A coupon?"

"Yeah."

"You used a coupon on the first date?"

"Yeah. I didn't see anything wrong with it."

"Well, I guess she did," Ben said, laughing.

Alex, being an older man, was almost completely bald and wore round eye glasses, giving him a distinct resemblance to Mr. Magoo. He was short and stout and had a tendency to run on and on about things that sometimes did not seem as important to the receiving party.

"What? I was trying to save some money."

"Hey, it makes perfect sense to me. I don't see why she would have a problem with it," Ben snickered, trying to hold in his laughter.

Just then the sound of clanging metal came raging in, as the door to the breakroom opened and Ronnie came walking in. "I thought I heard you laughing, Ben. What the heck's so funny?"

"Do you want to tell him, or should I?" Ben, unable to control himself anymore, sat down on a metal chair, roaring with laughter.

"Oh, go ahead. You seem to be busting at the seams," Alex said, annoyed as he stood over the sink washing off some vegetables.

"Well, our good friend here finally gets a date and takes this woman out to a restaurant."

"What, did he take her to McDonalds?" interjected Ronnie.

"No, but he pulls out a… a coupon," Ben said, finally allowing the laughter to overtake him, as he sat hunched over, holding on to his stomach.

"I don't see anything wrong with it," Alex said.

"You cheap, stubborn ass," said Ronnie. "No wonder you can't ever get a second date."

"Oh, you two are starting to annoy me," rambled Alex, heading over to the table to take a seat.

"Alex, I'm sorry, we didn't mean…" Ben said while he tried, a little late, to get control of himself.

"Not me. You are one of the cheapest… On the first date, huh?" Ronnie reiterated.

"Yes, on the first date," Alex answered proudly.

"I wouldn't call her back anytime soon," Ronnie said.

"No, she told me never to call her again." Alex looked over at Ben waiting for him to say something.

"What? I didn't say a word." Ben smiled. "I really don't know why she would have a problem with it."

"Oh, I don't know why I tell you two anything," Alex said, shaking his head, still trying to get his lunch ready.

"Well, I have to get back. Keep your chin up, Alex. There's sure to be someone out there someday who will appreciate your frugalness." The sound of the machines came busting through as Ronnie headed out of the breakroom. "I'll catch you two later."

"You're darn tootin'," Alex stressed. "I don't need any more women anyway. The last one almost broke me."

The breakroom was now empty except for the two of them. Ben brought his lunch across the commercial tile floor to a table where Alex had settled. Employee updates and safety posters were pinned to bulletin boards that lined the walls surrounding the two men.

Ben began to look around the room. "I don't know, Alex. Maybe I'm getting sentimental in my old age, but it sure would be nice to have someone to do stuff with once in a while."

"Yeah, I guess that's why I keep going out on these first dates my daughter is always setting me up on, even though they never seem to work out."

"Don't get me wrong, I don't ever plan on getting married again," Ben said.

"Oh, be careful what you say, my friend."

"No, I mean it. My first wife cheated on me. I mean, I'm sure I did things wrong, too. I could have been a better husband, but I would have never cheated on her. I just think I have lost the ability to trust any woman."

"Doesn't mean they're all like that," said Alex.

"I guess. I just don't know anymore. I think she took that part of me with her."

"I know how you feel, but sometimes, you know, the loneliness just really sucks," Alex said, frowning, throwing down his fork.

"I have been on my own for almost six years now, I mean. I'm better. I think I'm happy, but sometimes you just miss having someone to do stuff with."

"Yep," agreed Alex, taking a bite out of his sandwich. "Hey, that reminds me, Stan Hamilton was telling me the other day about a singles agency he joined not too long ago."

"A singles agency? What's that?"

"Well, he says for a fee this singles agency will get you in touch with single women who belong to the agency. That's how he met his girlfriend."

"Really?"

"Yeah, but they want some ridiculous amount to join. It cost him like five hundred dollars or something like that."

"That much, huh?" Ben asked, rubbing the bottom of his chin, contemplating the information he had just been given.

"Yeah, and you're not even guaranteed to meet anyone. I told him they wouldn't be getting any of my money," Alex said.

"What's the agency called? Do you remember?" Ben asked, trying not to seem too desperate.

"I don't remember, but you could check with Stan. He's working today."

"Hmm, maybe I will." Ben then scooted his chair back and got up to place some items he was finished with in the trash.

"Well, you go ahead. I think it's all a scam. They won't be getting a cent from me."

Ben then walked back from the trash can giving Alex a grin. "Hey, maybe they have a coupon you can use, Alex."

"Oh, shut up."

"Just a suggestion."

Alex's words started running through Ben's mind as the rest of Alex's conversation got lost in translation. Ben's mind started to wander. He was filled with the anticipation of dating again, of meeting someone he would enjoy spending time with. Ben thought he had finally resigned to the fact that he would spend the rest of his life alone. Yet, it seemed, unbeknownst to him, that part of him still held on to the hope that someone was still out there for him.

He sat and debated the pros and cons of a dating service as Alex rambled on. He didn't like the idea of paying someone to find him a date, but he felt leaving it to destiny might take a little too long.

That evening, Ben made it a point to get over to the packaging area where Stan Hamilton worked. Stan was also a farmer, and Ben had talked with him on a few occasions, so he felt comfortable approaching him about the agency. Somehow, the thought of meeting someone outside of the bar atmosphere appealed to Ben.

"Yeah, it's called Friendship Match," Stan shouted over the machines, eager to spread the wealth of his knowledge to someone. The sound of the machines hummed around them and Stan had to take out his earplugs to hear Ben more clearly.

"That's what Alex was telling me."

"Hold on." Stan reached down to slow his machine down. "Yeah, they have a location off of 29th and Cedar."

"How'd you hear about it?"

"Oh, my cousin met his wife there."

"Really?"

"Yeah, why?"

"Oh, I was talking to Alex and he was telling me you met your girlfriend there."

"Yeah, I did, but the newness has kind of worn off. We still spend a lot of time together, but we're dating other people, too."

"That's what I'd like to do. So, do you think it would be worth me checking out?"

"Yeah, I love it." Stan then reached into his wallet, pulling out a business card. "Here's their number. Give 'em a call."

Ben seemed renewed by this newfound information. Later, on his break, he took out the card that Stan had given him and started to dial it into his cellphone. As he waited, he heard the phone click and start to ring. Ben thumped his fingers against the phone, nervously fighting the urge to hang up.

Chapter Fifteen
Hollow

I entered my home after returning from my temporary office job and had only a few minutes to get dinner ready, check on homework, and assign cleanup duties before I was off to my department store job. I didn't have time to think. I seemed to be running from one thing to the other, trying to keep our heads above water.

Saline and Lily were always there to help out, but Saline was getting older and had started to have a life of her own. She had actually made a friend. Christa was our next-door neighbor and was a senior at the school Saline would be attending. Christa, not being shy, immediately took a liking to Saline and was determined to make her way into Saline's life. Saline, having been through so much with the divorce and her struggle with leaving behind her boyfriend in Nebraska, was not exactly up for socializing. But luckily, Christa would not take 'no' for an answer. Christa, a fiery red-headed teenager with freckles and a strong will who usually got her way, was also, unknowingly, one of Saline's guardian angels.

After finally getting Saline out of the house, Christa introduced Saline to numerous friends, and Saline spent the summer getting to know people she would actually be going to school with. So Saline, who did not know a soul in Topeka, would actually start her senior year knowing some of her classmates. As time went on, I would have never dreamed Saline would later be attending her senior prom with eight other couples she called her friends, and she was even escorted by her long-lost Nebraska boyfriend. And we were witnesses to yet another miracle sent our way.

We struggled when school started trying to build some sort of workable routine as we settled into our new environment. Saline was responsible for getting herself and Lily to school and then picking up Jackson and Hope after school. I took full advantage of having my parents living in close proximity and would drive Jackson and Hope to my parents' home to stay until school started. Then my parents would drive them to school. I swear, between us all, we circled the entire Topeka area every morning. But somehow, we made it work.

"Jackson, Hope, get down here, now," I yelled up the stairs.

"Coming," Jackson yelled down.

"That's not what I need to hear. I need to hear you two getting into the car, immediately."

Just then a rumbling of footsteps echoed down the stairs as the two scrambled for backpacks and jackets, pushing and poking each other into irritation. I grabbed my purse and headed out of the kitchen door, climbing into my vehicle followed by Hope and Jackson, who sat in the back seat.

"Mom, did you sign my field trip form?" Jackson asked, looking through his backpack.

"Yes, I did. I put it in your backpack," I said as I rummaged through my purse for keys.

"Oh, here it is. Huh, must have missed it."

Hope then took her thumb out of mouth and asked, "Mommy, does Grandma have waffles today?"

"I don't know. You'll have to wait to find out," I said while trying to rearrange my purse so it stayed on the seat, while backing out of the garage.

"I love the waffles," Jackson said.

"Me too," Hope added, rubbing her tummy. "They're delicious."

"Well, you be sure to tell Grandma thank you."

"We will," they announced in unison.

My mother would always be waiting for Jackson and Hope at the top of her cement porch that displayed black cast-iron railings, as she did every morning, still in her white robe and slippers. She smiled and waved as the kids headed through the gate and ran up the stairs. My mother looked young for her age. Her ebony hair carried the same soft wave that mine did. She waited for the kids as if they were the highlight of her day. And my neighbor back in Nebraska was right. When I wasn't there, my parents were, and we were better for it.

The loneliness that came with the end of the day, when the kids were tucked in and my older girls were in bed reminiscing about their day, was the hardest part of the day for me. There was an emptiness that came along with divorce. It was almost like a part of me had died. And in a way, it had. Divorce is like grieving the loss of a loved one, except the loved one is still alive. Even with all the craziness from our hectic schedule, the hollowness was always there. It never seemed to leave. I didn't feel whole. I had lost the ability to feel normal. Nothing felt normal.

One evening after I had put the kids to bed, after all the homework had been done, the dishes were washed, and laundry was put away, I made my way to my bedroom, finally alone. This was my time, the time when I did not have to be brave, or strong, or Mommy. The darkness of the room would conceal me, conceal the tears. I climbed into my bed that I had once shared with Jack. The black cast iron canopy surrounded me with sheer drapes falling to the floor on either side. Visions of the past and present regrets would haunt me, draining me to a point of exhaustion. This one night I phoned my friend, Tiffany.

"I just can't do this anymore. I feel so lonely," I whispered into the line as if trying to conceal my weakness from the world.

"I wish I could help, Sarah," Tiffany responded sincerely. "Have you prayed about it?"

"Yes…"

"No, I mean really got down on your knees."

"No…not really." The hollowness that surrounded me was swallowing me and at that point, I began to embrace it.

"Then this is what you need to do. I want you to hang up with me and give it over to the Lord. Stop trying to handle this on your own."

"I just… just want to feel normal again."

"Oh, honey, you will, but you are going to need God's strength. Lean on him. Tell him what you are feeling."

"I don't know," I said, trying to hide the tears.

"I promise it'll get better."

"I know," I said, not being truthful. I didn't believe it would all get better. I didn't think I would make it one more day. I felt the weight of the world around me pulling me down, and I didn't have the strength anymore to fight back.

After hanging up, I slowly sat up in bed and brought my legs over to the side of the bed. Without thinking, I suddenly fell to my knees on the carpet. I curled up in a ball, my head now lying over my bent knees scattering my hair across the floor, as my mind began to wander.

I prayed a prayer that night that was not an ordinary prayer. It was a prayer of desperation, a prayer of last resort. Prayers that I would assume most come to know, only in the deepest valleys of despair. When one is faced with losing one's self.

Chapter Sixteen
Sign Me Up

Friday morning rolled around, and Ben found himself questioning his decision to call the dating service. He wondered if he should just stay within the small confines of his defined little world, where it was safe. But being a stickler to his word, Ben headed out his back door.

He didn't tell anyone about what he was doing. He felt if this last attempt didn't work out, he was more than happy to spend the rest of his days on this earth alone. Maybe God just didn't see him as a father or a husband. Maybe he was put here on this earth to take care of his parents... to take care of the farm.

He reluctantly pulled into the parking lot of Friendship Match. He entered the glass door and strolled up to the secretary. The room looked barren. The furniture consisted of a sofa, two chairs, and a coffee table. The carpet was worn and displayed an ugly off-green color. There was a rectangular table, set against one of the paneled walls, that was covered with pamphlets and flyers.

The walls displayed framed pictures of presumably happy couples. The frames were randomly spaced. Most were hung crooked as if they were placed there in a rush and no one had time to straighten them. He looked at each photo, wondering if they were real people or just faces cut out of magazines. An attempt, Ben thought, to prey on people like him.

The secretary looked up at Ben. "She's ready to see you now, Mr. Thompson."

"Thank you, ma'am," Ben said as he slowly rose off the sofa and was shown to a small office displaying the same brown paneling.

"Hello, Ben, nice to meet you. I am Heather Taylor," the petite woman said, standing up to shake his hand. "I believe my husband spoke with you on the phone." Heather was a brunette with a very slim figure, who looked older than she probably was because of the amount of makeup she wore.

"Yes, he did. Ah... but before we get started, Heather, I wanted to let you know I am really just lookin' to get some information about your agency. I wasn't definitely sold on the idea yet."

"Well, before you make any rash decisions, hun, let me tell you a little bit about our agency." Heather leaned back, sitting half-way on her desk. "I started the company six years ago when I found myself unexpectedly single after ten years of marriage. I started going out like most, going to the local bars, trying to meet someone that I could relate to, and, well, you probably know what I'm talking about."

"Oh, yeah. It gets old really fast."

"Exactly. Anyway, I just thought there should be other options for singles out there. I had heard about singles agencies in other cities, but there was nothing close by that I could join so I thought what the heck, and that's when I started Friendship Match."

"Really?" Ben said, leaning back in his chair a little bit more comfortable.

"Yep, and it's worked out so far. I mean, I'm not getting rich off it, if that's what you're thinking, but it's a living and I really enjoy doing it."

"I heard you met your husband through your service."

"Yes, I did and he's wonderful. We now run the agency together. So, I'm living proof that this does work. I mean, if I hadn't started the agency and he wasn't looking to join one, we may have never met. I meet all of my clients personally and I try to get to know each one individually and get a sense of who they are and who would be the best match for them."

"Well, Heather, I have to tell you somethin'. I'm not exactly sure I want a serious relationship again. I had a really bad marriage, and I just don't think I want to relive that all over again."

Heather froze for a moment, giving Ben a blank stare.

"Well, I have to tell you, Ben, most of our female clients are looking for a long-term relationship." Heather eyed Ben, as if trying to determine if he would make a good addition to her clientele.

Ben, feeling her hesitation, tried to explain, afraid that she may have misunderstood him.

"I mean, I have no problem with a long-term relationship. I just don't know if I want to be married again. I mean, she'd have to be pretty dang wonderful to get me to do that again."

"Oh, honey, never say never. To be honest, I have to tell you that most of our female clients are looking to be married. If the profile that you fill out, and that most of our female clients will see, does not specifically state that you are hoping to be married one day, I can almost guarantee you much fewer responses."

Ben sat for a moment, drumming his fingers on the arm of the chair, considering his reply. "Really? All those women out there are ready to jump back into marriage?"

"Oh, I wouldn't say jump, Ben. For instance, how long have you been single?"

"Six years."

"Six years, and you still think you'd be just jumping back into a relationship?"

"Well, yes," Ben said, laughing. "You don't know my ex-wife."

"You're right, I don't. Are you sure you're ready for this agency? I don't take it lightly, and I don't want to sign up someone who's not ready because, I have to tell you, most of my clients are, and I don't want to waste anyone's time."

Ben sat a little stunned at Heather's directness. He thought about just walking out, but something inside him told him to stay. "Well, I mean, I can understand that. I just don't want to, you know, lie on an application."

"I can respect that. How about I tell you a little bit more about our agency, and then you can decide if it's right for you."

"All right..." Ben said, still reluctant.

Heather then proceeded to walk back around her desk and had a seat in her chair. "We are online, so you can view any potential matches without making a commitment to anyone."

"One problem, I don't have a computer."

"Oh, sweetie... that is a problem."

"Well, there's one at work, but I hate to use it."

"Well, you could always come here. We have an extra office I've made available to clients before, and there's always the public library. Otherwise, we do have face-to-face meetings weekly, from dinners, to parties, and 10-minute introductions, so there are many ways we can get you connected. I mean, I can mail you out the monthly schedule if that's what works best for you."

Ben, a little bit more optimistic, responded, "Yeah, that may work."

"Great. Well, the way it works is you fill out the profile, pay the fee, we then get you entered into the system and finally we run a background check. If you check out okay, we will then try to match you up with people who share your common interests."

Ben sat for a minute reflecting on the information Heather just gave him. "So, I can mark considering marriage?"

"Yes, I don't see why not."

"Hmmm. okay... I'll give it a try."

"Good, let's get started. I promise you, hun, you won't be sorry."

"I hope not."

"Oh, have a little faith, Ben."

One week later, Ben received his first call from Heather saying that he had been approved for membership. She invited him to a singles' dinner that was being held at a local restaurant in town. Ben reluctantly said he would attend, still not sure about the whole thing, but he had already paid the fee and felt he should get his money's worth. He and Heather talked about some changes she felt might be necessary for Ben's success within the agency.

"Do you own some khakis or dress pants, Ben?"

"No, I really only own jeans."

"Well, I think maybe you should get some."

"Why?"

"It just makes a good impression," Heather said, trying not to sound too bossy.

"Hey, I just want to be myself."

"You will be. It's just a nice restaurant, and I think khakis would be appropriate."

"What are they again?"

"Just go to any salesperson, and they will be able to help you. They're usually a beige-colored pant."

"All right, I will, but I won't like it," Ben said, smiling into the receiver.

"Okay... Ben," Heather sighed. "Trust me on this one."

The next day Ben headed into town trying to get to the mall early. He went through the glass doors, hearing the soft music playing all around him. Ben soon spotted a young woman working behind a register, and approached her, inquiring as to where he could find khaki pants.

Ben followed her to a section where there were many different colors of what looked like dress pants. "Here they are," the young clerk announced.

Ben looked around not knowing where to start. "Ahh, ma'am, what do you recommend?"

The young woman quickly looked through the various racks of clothing. "Well, the beige is quite popular. They go with practically everything."

"And what should I wear with them, if you don't mind me asking?"

The young clerk smiled, sensing Ben's apprehension, as she helped him pick out a couple of outfits.

Ben believed shopping to be more of a chore than farming, as he stood there dripping in sweat, trying to decide which outfit looked best. The young saleswoman checked on him quite often, helping him pick out a few items, relieving some of Ben's anxiety.

The night of the dinner, Ben arrived at the restaurant early and was seated in a side area on a cushioned bench. He was wearing the beige khaki's and a maroon shirt the saleswoman helped him pick out. He had bought some brown shoes and a couple of other shirts just in case he got asked to more outings.

The new attire gave Ben a look of sophistication that he wasn't used to as he sensed a couple of women passing by looking his way. The tall farmer, unused to this type of attention, almost turned around to see who they were staring at.

The rest of the group finally arrived, and consisted of three women and two men. Ben making the third man. There was one woman, with strawberry blonde hair, named Stephanie, who looked about Ben's age, and another man named Dan who wasn't too much older than Ben, but the other three in the group looked quite a bit older. So much so, Ben thought for a moment that he and Stephanie had been placed in the wrong group.

The evening went as planned; everyone ordering supper. Ben tried to join in on the conversation when he could and secretly hoped Stephanie did not see him as a complete idiot. Stephanie seemed to catch the attention of all three men as she smiled and laughed at their wit throughout the meal. The other two women, not seeming to mind the attention Stephanie was getting, were active in the conversation and seemed to be happy just to be out somewhere.

As the dinner came to a close, Ben wondered how he could contact Stephanie to see if she would be interested in going out sometime. The group walked out to the parking lot together and said their goodbyes. Ben thought about approaching Stephanie right then, but didn't know if that was allowed. Ultimately, Ben decided to wait and contact Heather about arranging a date.

Almost two days later, Heather called Ben with Stephanie's phone number, informing him that Stephanie had agreed to let him contact her.

According to her profile, Stephanie was the mother of two children, a boy and a girl, and had been divorced for about two years. She enjoyed going to the movies and reading. It also said she came from a small town, which appealed to Ben, thinking they would have something in common.

Stephanie lived in the south-central part of Topeka – older homes, traditionally found in the center of most towns, homes that had survived a multitude of families over the years. Stephanie's was a small blue house with a torn screen door.

"Hi, Ben," Stephanie said as she opened her front door.

"Hi, Stephanie. How are you?"

"I'm fine. I'm sorry, but the dang babysitter is running a little late. Do you mind if we wait in the living room?"

"No, no, that's fine."

Ben walked in, noticing a disarray of toys on the floor and leftover dirty dishes lining the counter. A trail of laundry led up the stairs. He could hear the patter and rustle of small feet running overhead.

"Would you like something to drink?"

"No, I'm fine." Ben sat rubbing his hands together. "Ah… did your babysitter need a ride?"

"Oh, no, she drives. She's a teenager though, so she had some type of sporting event which ended late, but she said she was on her way."

"Oh, okay, I just thought I could pick her up if you needed me to. I mean, I'm in no hurry or anything."

"Oh, thanks, that's sweet of you, but she should be here soon," Stephanie said as they both heard a loud thump come from upstairs. "Ah… could you excuse me for a moment," she said as she made her way up the stairs.

Ben could hear the conversation even though Stephanie tried to keep her voice to a whisper.

"I told you two to settle down. Lauren will be here soon."

"No, I don't want Lauren. She never plays with us. I want Grandma," a small voice blared out.

"Grandma couldn't watch you tonight," Stephanie responded, trying to keep her voice down.

"No! No Lauren!" the young voice shouted, banging something against the wall. "I want Grandma."

Just then another young voice joined in as the children started shouting in unison over and over again: "We want Grandma! We want Grandma!"

"You two, back in your room this minute!" Stephanie ordered, as the ruckus seemed to diminish.

"No!" Ben heard a young voice say. Ben suddenly had a flashback to a time when he told his mother no. He, 'til this day, still had a vivid image of the leather hitting his hind end.

Just then Ben heard a rustle and then silence as a door finally closed and Stephanie reappeared at the bottom of the stairs.

"I'm sorry, they have been this way ever since I told them I was going out," Stephanie, obviously frazzled, apologized. "I may need a drink. Do you want one?"

"No, I'm fine," Ben said, thinking about her last comment. He felt almost embarrassed for Stephanie and tried to think of something comforting to say. "I'm sorry, I have no children… but I'm sure it's normal."

Just then the doorbell rang, and a brunette around seventeen bopped in, apologizing to Stephanie for being late.

Feeling relieved, Ben stood ready to go. Stephanie then called her children down to say goodbye.

A blonde boy, wearing nothing but underwear and a Spider-Man t-shirt hopped down the stairs, followed by a red-headed girl who was a little plump for her age and had a nose covered with freckles.

"You two say hello to Ben," Stephanie said to them as they automatically turned their faces to the wall and shouted out a hello in unison.

"Hi," Ben said back, not knowing where to look exactly since they were facing the wall.

"Lauren, I'll be back fairly early."

"Don't worry about a thing," the teenager said politely as she tried to gather up the two young ones who had now taken off to the living room.

As they walked out the door and into the night, Ben tried to recover from the activity inside, thinking to himself, *How does she do it without losing her mind*?

Stephanie said, "I swear, I can't have a moment's peace with those two. I'm sorry they were crazy tonight. They obviously had too much sugar today."

"No, it was totally fine. I'm sure all kids would react the same. I mean, I'm sure it's hard being a single parent," he said, trying to sound convincing. "They seem like great kids."

"Well, thanks."

"You're welcome," he said. Ben then opened the passenger door to his truck to allow Stephanie in. "So, shall we go?"

"Yes. Where are we going?"

"There's a barbeque place off of 30th. Do you want to try there?"

"I've been there before. It's okay, if you like that kind of place."

"Is there somewhere else you'd rather go? I'm new to the area, so I don't know a lot of places round here."

"There's a nice steakhouse pretty close. You're a farmer, right?"

"Yep, born and raised."

"So, you must like steak."

"Very much, let's go."

Ben was finally enjoying himself as they drove to the restaurant. They waited about 20 minutes before being seated. Ben noticed there was a candlelight on each of the tables and there was soft music being played in the background. Every table had a white table cloth, and everyone seemed very dressed up. Ben was glad he had worn his new sweater.

After they were seated, the waiter came over with menus. Stephanie quickly ordered a glass of wine. She wore a dark blue top that was sheer at the arms and brought out the strawberry color in her hair. She had on a matching skirt that fit a little too snug. She was not really heavy. She just bulged out in certain areas that the skirt seemed to accentuate. She wore dangly earrings that showed through her hair when she turned to look the other way.

"So, you don't have any kids," Stephanie said.

"No, I don't."

"Were you married before?"

"Yes, I was married for about five years, but my wife couldn't have children," Ben said casually.

"Oh…" Stephanie responded, biting her lip. Stephanie looked around the room at the other couples as Ben decided he better hold up his end of the conversation.

"And you were married eight years?"

"Yes. Their father lives in town and gets them every other weekend. This just happens to be my weekend."

"Oh, I'm sorry. We could have made the date for another weekend."

"No, it's fine. I mean, I have them all week," Stephanie said.

"It must be hard caring for them and workin'."

"Yeah, it is. And my ex is worthless as far as helping out."

"Well, that's too bad. I don't really see my…"

Stephanie then interjected before Ben could finish, "Yeah, well, I couldn't depend on him then, so I don't know what made me think I could depend on him now."

"Soooo… have you eaten here before?" Ben said trying to lighten the conversation.

"Yeah, my ex would bring me here every now and then, but I haven't been here in a while."

"Oh…" was all Ben could manage, sorry that he had asked.

"I have a date with Dan next weekend," Stephanie said. She looked at Ben as if he should know who Dan is. Stephanie crossed her legs and set her napkin in her lap, leaning forward with her chin resting on the top of her fingers as she waited for Ben's response.

"Dan?"

"You know, Dan from the other night at the singles' dinner."

"Oh, yeah… Dan. I had forgotten his name."

"Yeah, he's bringing me here too. Did you make a date with someone else?"

"No, just you."

"Oh, you're sweet, Ben."

The conversation dragged as Ben and Stephanie continued to make small talk. Stephanie talked a lot about her kids and how they never listened to her and how worthless her ex-husband was.

Ben was glad when the meal finally came so they could slow the conversation down while eating. He didn't talk a lot about Christine. It seemed ages ago, and he hated rehashing the past, so he politely nodded at Stephanie as she continued to relieve herself of all the negativity that seemed to surround her.

As the night finally came to an end, Ben drove Stephanie back to her house in an awkward silence. After pulling into the driveway, he quickly got out of the truck and went around and opened Stephanie's door.

He walked her politely to the door and said good night. Ben sensed that Stephanie felt the same as he did about the evening as she murmured a cold goodbye and entered her house without looking back.

Ben entered his truck, took a deep breath, and slowly reversed out of the driveway, beginning the long drive back home.

Chapter Seventeen
Looking for Mr. Right

The kids and my friends encouraged me to get out and meet new people. But how does one start dating after being married for so long?

I looked around me and witnessed my friends, at the department store, and their relationships. There was Gina, who had been divorced for seven years and was living with a man whom she had known for over two years. She was very petite and looked like she was almost ten years younger than she actually was. I would have thought men her age would be lining up for a woman that looked like Gina. She always talked about what a great guy her boyfriend was and how lucky she was to have him. I believed her. I had no reason not to. I would later learn that he wasn't such a great guy. Not even mediocre.

Gina opened up to me about one night in particular. She and her boyfriend had a huge fight after his office Christmas party and were driving home a little after midnight when he pulled over his vehicle and told her to get out. Now beside it being midnight, Gina had on a black cocktail dress and black heels. She was only wearing a light jacket, even though there was snow on the ground and the temperature was about 12 degrees. So, her prince charming practically forced her out the door and left her there on the side of the road. Luckily, a police officer came by and gave her a ride home. But still she stayed with him.

And there was Kate. Kate was a dental hygienist that worked at the department store in her spare time. Kate, only thirty-three years old, had just finished her schooling when she met her prince charming. She took on the part-time job to help compensate for her boyfriend's drug habit. Kate was sweet and compassionate, but she had a need to fix this man who didn't want to be fixed. Kate was one of the kindest persons I had ever met, and she was stuck. She found herself dependent on this man as if he were her drug.

I didn't quite understand my friends who I thought were quite special and unique in their own ways, these women who had lost themselves, and settled for men who in my eyes didn't deserve them. I spoke to Gina once after she confided in me about how her boyfriend really treated her. I asked her if she thought this relationship was what God truly wanted for her. And she said, "No." But still, she stayed.

I wasn't sure what my future held, but I knew I didn't want to become one of the statistics of women who settled. I couldn't. I would not allow it for myself, and I would not allow it for my children.

Saline and Lily would watch my younger ones most of the time when I went out. I loved to dance and had recently discovered the two-step and country line dancing. Harrington's was the only country dance place in Topeka. Its exterior sign displayed a large wagon wheel on the 'O,' that lit up and turned during the evening hours. During the daytime, the building didn't look like much with its shingled wood walls and peeling paint, but at night as the sign lit up, it became the singles destination of Topeka.

My friends and I discovered that there were many older couples who would come there early, before the crowd, and before the youngsters took it over. We would intentionally arrive early and sit there and watch these older couples who shared a lifetime of history, couples who moved around the dance floor as one. The women wore square-dancing skirts that flared out and bounced with every move. Their sequined skirts caught the gleam of the overhead lights as their partners twirled them across the floor. Their male partners, with cowboy boots and hats to match, looked more like ranchers than dancers. Yet, they danced with ease. Their life-long partner anticipated every move, every turn, as they glided them across the dance floor.

We sat there envious – envious of the past these couples shared and the future that awaited them. Fantasies were always better than reality, and the thought that we expected to meet someone of character in a place like this seemed almost ludicrous to me now. I mean, we had a good time, but to put our hopes and futures in the hands of people we would be meeting in these places was unrealistic.

I came to this realization one night when I made what could have been a fatal mistake. I let my guard down for an instant.

Brenda, a friend of mine from the department store, and I were seated by the dance floor having a drink when a stout, muscular man, just a few inches taller than I was, approached me.

"Would you like to dance?" he asked.

I looked over at him and accepted his invitation. He stepped back, allowing me to walk in front of him.

We walked up the steps to the dance floor, and he took me in his arms and swayed me across the dance floor as George Strait belted out, "She let herself go," and we two stepped in rhythm to the tune. He seemed very confident as he held me in his arms – almost cocky as he led me across the dance floor. He held me out at a distance from him, and swayed and turned me within the small confines of the dance floor. He danced so swiftly that we didn't really have time to talk. Once the song was over, he walked me back to my seat and said, "Thank you for the dance," and then turned around and went back to a table, where some of his friends had gathered. Brenda looked over at me.

"He seems nice."

"Yeah, and he's a really good dancer. I see you were out there," I told her.

"Yeah, he's a pretty good dancer too."

We sat down on our stools, nursing our drinks as the next song started. Before I had time to put my glass down, there was my partner once again standing right behind me.

"Would you like to dance this one?" he asked very politely.

"Sure."

"I guess I should introduce myself. I'm Bradley Wilson, but you can call me Brad."

"Nice to meet you, Brad. I'm Sarah."

"Well, you're certainly a good dancer, Sarah," he said to me as we climbed the stairs to the dance floor.

"I was just about to tell you the same thing."

"Nah, I can keep up," he said, trying to downplay his talent.

"No really, I have a hard time keeping up with you."

We stepped onto the dance floor as the disco ball spun above our heads, casting shadows on the people sitting and standing around the dance floor.

I looked around the room as we danced and witnessed the sadness and laughter that was unique to a place like this. The lost gathered here in hopes of finding their soul mate, and I had become one of them.

It was still hard for me to face that I was single at my age. It seemed like yesterday that I was in my driveway, watching the kids run back and forth from my house to my neighbor's house, as I waited for Jack to return home.

The song was a steady, slow two-stepper, and it was a little easier to follow Brad on this one, so we were able to hold a conversation while we danced.

"So, you from around here?" Brad asked.

"Not originally, but I moved here about six months ago," I said.

"Oh, me neither. I'm originally from Tennessee, but I'm stationed here at Fort Riley."

"So, you're in the military?"

"Yes, ma'am."

"So, how do you like it?"

"Oh, I love it. I get to see the world. Places I never dreamed I'd see, and I'm not finished yet," he said, as he took me in his arms twirling me around the dance floor.

"I wanted to tell you that you look very nice tonight," Brad said.

"Well, thank you."

"Would you like to dance the next one?" he asked before the song was over.

"Why not?"

We danced the next couple of dances, stopping to talk off to the side. He seemed to want to keep me near to him so that no one else could ask me to dance. At the time, I thought it was flattering.

Brad seemed very polite, never trying to hold me too close. We talked as we danced, laughing and smiling as if we were old friends. He came from a small town. He grew up near Nashville and caught me up on all the local Elvis myths. He talked about his family. He had been divorced seven years ago and had a son and daughter that still lived in Tennessee. He said he used to make a trip down every other weekend to visit, but his kids were older now. One had just entered college and the other was a senior in high school.

I told him about my children. I always expected men to run in the other direction upon hearing that I had four children, but Brad didn't even seem to blink. He told me his mom had four children. He was the oldest. He grew up without a dad and said he understood what I was going through, his mother being a single mother and all, and I found myself wondering if he was as true as he seemed.

We danced most of the evening. I stopped every now and then to head to the restroom to call the kids, but every time I called that night, I got a busy signal. I tried several times and started to get worried. The kids were notorious for knocking the phone off the hook when I wasn't home and not noticing it. I hated to leave, but my concern got the best of me as I approached Brenda after I left the restroom.

"Brenda, I'm sorry. I can't seem to get my kids to answer. Would you mind if we left now?" I shouted over the loud music.

Brenda frowned at me because she also had been dancing every dance with someone and was sitting and talking with him at the time. But being a mom, she understood and immediately responded with, "Sure, let's go."

As she turned to tell her companion the bad news, Brad came up beside me asking what was wrong.

"I'm sorry," I said. "My kids won't answer the phone. I keep getting a busy signal so I'm going home to check on them."

"Well, I can drive you. My truck is just outside. I promise to bring you right back," he said sincerely.

Brenda sensing my nervousness said, "I can drive you. We can go," she said, since she had been the one to drive that night. Her companion looked over at me briefly.

I felt bad so I turned to Brad stating, "Are you sure?"

"Yeah, we can go right now."

"Well, I don't live far."

"Great. Then we can come right back after we make sure they're okay."

I hesitated for a moment. "Okay," I said, turning back to Brenda. "Brenda, I'll be right back."

Brenda looked at me with concern in her eyes, not feeling it was her place to stop me.

Brad and I then walked out and headed for his extended-cab truck. He opened the passenger side door for me and then went around and got in. On the way, I kept calling the house to see if the kids were okay, and I kept getting the same loud beeping in my ear.

"I can't believe they won't answer the damn phone," Brad suddenly blurted out after hearing my complaints about the busy signal I was getting.

"Well, it may be off the hook," I said as a look of horror crossed my face at the tone of his voice. He spoke as if these were his kids and he couldn't wait to get his hands on them.

"Still, they should know better than to leave the damn thing off the hook." He seemed to be growing more and more irritated by the minute.

"Well, it's probably nothing. They knock the phone off the hook all the time," I said, not understanding his irritation.

"What the hell? That's just irresponsible," he said angrily, hitting the steering wheel. The Doctor Jekyll, Mr. Hyde routine was scaring me as we finally pulled up to my driveway.

"I'll be right back," I explained to him and I headed inside.

I went in, and sure enough the phone was off the hook and the kids were there safe and sound, watching television and eating popcorn.

"I'm sorry, Mom. I didn't know," Lily apologized.

"I have to get back because Brenda is waiting on me. I just got a ride here."

"Who brought you, Mom?" Lily asked.

"Never mind, I'll be right back," I said, embarrassed that I had gotten a ride from a man I barely knew, something I would have killed my daughters for doing.

I had told Brenda that I would come right back, but I wasn't sure I wanted to ride with this guy again. I didn't want to leave Brenda at the place alone, so I returned to the truck after telling the kids goodbye.

"They knocked it off the hook!" he said angrily.

"Yes," I said, regretting I had entered the truck as he was backing out of my driveway.

"Well, that's just crazy. They should know better than that. What kind of crap is that? We had to drive over here for nothing!"

"They're just kids," I said, now defending them.

Brad looked at me, sensing my queer look, and realized that he had said too much.

"Well, they still should know better," he said, trying to somehow make his overreaction plausible.

We drove back in silence. Brad tried to start a conversation, but my answers were all very short. I tried to remain calm, hoping that he had intentions of driving me straight back. He looked over at me occasionally as if trying to read my mind. He finally pulled into the parking lot slowly. He headed to a back row on the east side of the dance hall where the lights didn't quite meet his truck. He turned to me as if to apologize, and as I started to open my door, he grabbed my wrist firmly and brought his other arm around to grip my shoulder.

"Do you want to stay out here for a while?" he asked.

"No," I blurted out. "I mean, I have to find Brenda. I told her I would be right back," I said.

"So, you're just going back inside?" he said angrily, as if he was agitated with me. As if he expected more.

Just then one of the security guards from the hall came around the corner. Brad saw him and released my wrist. I took this chance to climb out of the truck and headed straight toward the security guard, who asked, "Is everything all right?"

"Yes," I said and headed back into the hall.

I looked back at Brad, who was also making his way back in.

The crowd had gotten thicker, and Brenda was nowhere to be found. I started to panic as I decided to head back to the front where the security guards were and call a cab. As I exited the hall, Brenda pulled up in her vehicle.

"Sorry, my friend left, so I was waiting for you in my car," she shouted out at me.

I had just gotten into her car when Brad made his way out of the front, looking for me in the parking lot. I ducked down as Brenda drove by him and made her way out of the parking lot.

That was the last straw. I decided right then to take destiny into my own hands. Brenda told me about a singles agency she had heard about. It was called Friendship Match. Brenda said she had a friend who had met her husband there. The next week I called the singles agency. I made an appointment with a man who said I would be meeting with his wife.

I knew I didn't want to return to the bar scene. I wanted to meet men who were looking for a long-term relationship, not just a one-night-stand. His wife, Heather, ended up giving me a special rate to join, so I took her up on it.

Heather gave me immediate access to their website so I could start looking it over. After we had finished all the paperwork and I paid the fee, I immediately went home and checked my status and was consumed with the hope that there were others out there, like me, who wanted a true, honest relationship.

I began to look through the photos Heather sent to me, and I started a dialogue with a few of them. I didn't really meet anyone until I attended some of agency's small get-togethers, and then I was immediately dating. But, unfortunately, a few frogs made it past Heather's microscope.

Chapter Eighteen
Ghosts of the Past

Heather kept her word, sending out the monthly activity events to Ben. At first, Ben tried to attend regularly. He went on a couple of dates that didn't quite work out for one reason or another. Before long, Ben was not attending any events at all. Days turned into weeks, and weeks turned into months as the year of his membership started to dwindle to an end. Heather's calls became more and more infrequent, saying she would inform him of new members when they became available. Ben eventually just stopped checking the website.

"So, what you been doin' lately?" Larry asked his son one lazy Saturday afternoon, as Ben started to wrap things up to head home.

"Oh, not much, Dad. Why, did you need somethin'?"

"No, son, just wonderin' what you been up to lately."

"Nothin' interestin'. I've gone to the casino a couple of times but nothin' exciting."

"Didn't strike it rich, I see."

"No, Dad, I didn't. I guess I'll keep workin' at the plant."

"Well, it's only a matter of time."

"Yep, that's what I keep tellin' myself."

"So, you got plans for supper?"

"No, I'm just goin' a grab somethin' at home."

"Your mom's makin' round steak. You feel like stayin'?"

"Not today, Dad, unless you two need somethin'. I mean, I can run into town for you if that's what you need."

"No, we weren't needin' anything."

"I may meet up with Alex from work. He had talked about goin' to a coin collector's exhibit in Topeka."

"Really, I hadn't heard about it."

"Yeah, I've started collectin' some gold coins. Alex does it, and, well, he got me started, so I may head into town and join him. I'll probably just eat in town."

"All right by me."

Ben and his dad headed into the kitchen as Ben said goodbye to his mother and grabbed a shopping list she had made out of items they needed from Topeka. Ben took it and then headed home to shower. He caught a glimpse of his light blinking on his answering machine. It was a message from Heather. Ben, disgusted with the agency, didn't play the message. He instead headed out the front door on his way to Topeka.

It had been almost a year since he joined the agency, and the time between calls from Heather became longer and longer. Even the New Year's party was a bomb as Ben sat in a strange home, on the couch, by himself, amongst people he did not know. He ended up leaving the party early and headed up to the hospital about 10:00 p.m. to visit his father, who was having some tests run. He spent the rest of New Year's Eve playing cards with his dad until after midnight, and then drove home.

When he arrived in Topeka, there was a large crowd waiting to get in to the coin exhibit. Ben, unfamiliar with the whole process, let Alex do all the talking as he stood and listened. There were many women at the display cases, and Ben found himself wishing he could introduce himself to one of them, as his friend Alex edged him on.

The two eventually left the exhibit alone, with only a few coins.

Being it was still early, the two decided to head to the local casino. Ben was starting to become a regular there, some of the dealers began to recognize him by sight. He had a rule to never play too long, and always set a limit to what he could lose. The two men ate at the buffet, and then headed for the tables. After a couple of hours, and about a hundred dollars poorer, Ben left with the plan to stop at the local Walmart to pick up his parents' items before heading back to Alma.

Ben entered the store just as he had many times before. It was crowded for that time of night, Ben figuring he might avoid the rush by going later in the evening. He grabbed a steel cart and headed to the drugstore section. The wheel squeaked as he moved the gleaming cart through the aisle, checking off his mom's list as he went along.

He came around the corner of the pain medication and had an eerie feeling. He then caught a glimpse of her…

It was Christine.

Ben stood there numb as she seemed too interested in the man she was with to notice anyone else. Ben recognized the man she was with. It was Danny Shelton. He was one of Ben and Christine's former friends from Alma. They had hung out together when Christine and he were still married.

Ben took a few steps back and saw them quickly pass the aisle he was in. They were too engrossed in each other to notice Ben eyeing them. Danny, he had heard, had just gotten divorced, but he didn't know he had been seeing Christine. He didn't even know where Christine was living anymore. He didn't want to know.

Ben peered around the corner while still gripping his cart, hearing the wheels quietly squeak forward. He stood silently watching them walk down the large aisle in the front of the store, before they exited with their bags. Ben just stood there for a moment, unable to move. He continued to add items to his basket, now more slowly than before as images of the past crossed before him. He thought about how happy she looked. Ben pressed on, throwing items into his cart until he had everything on the list. He entered his car for the long drive home, wishing he hadn't ever stopped drinking.

Ben arrived at home. He entered the dusty living room. His niece had been too busy to get over to clean lately, and Ben never saw it as a priority. He hated clutter, but actual cleaning, he never seemed to get around to.

He opened his refrigerator and took out a cold bottle of Pepsi. He sat down on his couch looking out the large picture window that faced the street in front of his house. The light beams from passing cars gleamed at him out of the darkness. Bringing the bottle back down to the table, he sat there with his arms hanging across his knees, hands together and his head bowed and he began.

"Lord, if this is how I am supposed to live, I can do it. Just please take this lonely feelin' away. Tell me how you want me to live. I know I can do anything you need me to do and if this is how it is meant to be, then this is how it will be. Just please, remove this need from my heart." Ben hadn't prayed in a long time. He didn't want to bother God with his needs; he figured God had bigger things in this world to worry about than him. He didn't need to be adding to God's problems. But at that moment, in the silence of the night, Ben had nowhere else to turn.

He gave out a sigh as he looked around the dusty living room. The house felt empty and he wanted to leave, but he had no place to go. Ben then lifted his head, clicked on the television, and placed his feet on the coffee table. He quietly lifted his Pepsi to his lips and eventually fell asleep on the sofa.

The next morning, Ben woke up to the annoying blinking of his answering machine. He reluctantly played the message:

"Ben, it's me, Heather. Hey, I need a favor. I know your membership's almost up, but I will renew it for six more months if you can be at this dinner next Saturday. I know it's a singles' dinner, and you said you didn't want to go to any more of those, but I'm in a spot. This other guy just bailed on me, and I need you to cover. I have to know something by tomorrow. Call me on my cell please, hun. Thanks."

Ben glared at his cellphone on the table. He picked it up, scrolling through his numbers until he saw Heather's number. He slammed it closed and then reluctantly opened it back up. He paced back and forth a few times and then threw the phone back down to the table. He walked into the kitchen opening the refrigerator door, glancing back at his cellphone lying there.

"Ah, what the heck."

Ben walked back over to the coffee table, picking up his cellphone and dialed Heather's number.

"Ben, glad you called."

"Heather, it's been almost a year."

"I know, I know, but don't give up hope, sweetie. I think this might be the night for you."

"I thought you just needed a body there."

"Well, I do. I mean, these are not people I would regularly pick for you, but I'm in a spot. You'd really be helping me out."

"Yeah, well, I have nothin' else to do."

"Well, don't sound so enthused. You never know. This might be your night."

"You always say that."

"Well, I'm always thinking positively, and you should too."

"So, I get six more months free?"

"Yep, and it won't cost you a penny."

"All right, I'll be there, but I better meet someone," Ben said, trying to lighten the conversation.

"Well, honey, you never know. The stars may be aligned for you this time."

"Stars, I just want to meet someone normal," Ben declared.

"Well, your idea of normal and someone else's can be quite different. Hang in there, sweetie. We'll find you someone. Don't give up yet."

"I'm starting to think it may just not be in the cards for me. And I'm okay with that."

"That's your problem, Ben. You lose hope too soon. You have to be positive to make positive things happen for you."

"Okay, I'm positive I won't meet anyone," Ben said jokingly.

"Just be there, Ben. I will take care of the rest."

"I'll be there."

Chapter Nineteen
When It Rains, It Pours

I started dating through the singles agency but still hadn't met anyone that I connected with. One guy I went out with couldn't keep his hands to himself. One guy talked about his ex-wife the whole time and ended up eating my restaurant leftovers stating he didn't want it to go bad. And then there was the guy who just wanted to hang out at my house after the date. I eventually had to ask him to leave… these were the frogs.

Needing some extra money, I decided to have a garage sale. I needed to get rid of various pieces of office equipment that I had inherited from the business and some furniture that wouldn't fit in my small duplex. I also needed to get rid of some of the kid's clothes and useless photography equipment Jack had purchased just before he left.

Working two jobs was barely making ends meet. Jack would send money sporadically, but not the money I was supposed to be receiving. The state agency for child support was useless. Every time I called, I got the same response: Call back in a week, or a month. We can't do anything because he is self-employed. We can't do anything until we hear back from the state he lives in. Jack had moved to Louisiana, near the coast, with Kelly to start a new life, one that didn't seem to include the kids he already had. I soon gave up on the state agency and had to rely on Jack for the time being. I had to settle for anything he felt like sending my way.

The garage sale went really well. A man I had often seen – who worked across the street – stopped by. I noticed he got to work about the time I was leaving for work. He spotted me at the mailbox a couple of times. He seemed nice enough and would sometimes wave as he got out of his car. He stopped by my garage sale on his way back from lunch that day. His name was Dave.

I was showing a woman some bedroom furniture when Dave walked up behind us. "These dressers are brand new," I explained to the eager woman.

"I just don't know how I will get them to my house. I only have the car," she said, pointing to her small Toyota. I looked over, disappointed to lose the sale.

About that time, I heard a voice from behind me say, "I can take them for you."

We turned to see a man about my age, with a somewhat receding hairline, pointing to his pickup truck. The woman turned to me, looking for affirmation that he was a friend of mine, and I just kind of shrugged my shoulders, indicating I didn't know who he was. Suddenly I recognized him. It was the man whom I had only seen only from a distance until that moment. At the time, I thought it was odd that he wanted to help this woman that he didn't know, but I went along with it, hoping to get rid of the dressers.

The woman then said to Dave, "Are you sure? I mean, I really don't live far away, but I hate to have you drive this stuff over there."

"Oh, I'm sure. I don't have to be back at work just yet," he said, smiling at me. "It's really not a problem."

"Well, I would really appreciate it," the woman said gratefully.

Dave then started moving the furniture onto his truck by himself. He wasn't very tall, but seemed fit. I guess he would have to be, working at a health center. I looked at him, unsure of his motives, as the woman and I both helped to lift drawers into his truck.

"This is very nice of you," I said, still unsure why he was helping this woman he didn't even know.

"Oh, it's nothing. I was just stopping by to look over your garage sale. I'll be right back."

"I'll be here," I said. And he left.

So, I continued to wait on other potential customers when Dave, keeping to his word, returned.

"Well, we got it all unloaded," he said.

"Thank you. I'm sure she appreciated it."

"I'm Dave Sullivan by the way."

"Oh, I'm sorry, I'm Sarah Harris."

"Nice to meet you, Sarah."

"I see you work across the street."

"Yes, I manage this division. You should come check out our facility," he said and turned to look at the building.

Not knowing what to say, I stood there wondering what he was really after. Was he trying to sign me up for a membership?

"Ahhh… you have a lot of nice stuff here."

"Well, I used to be in business with my ex-husband, and I have all this office equipment I don't use anymore, so I'm trying to get rid of some of it."

Dave went through some of the items, picking up a few and asking some questions. He then suddenly looked at his watch.

"Oh, I have to get back, but do you mind if I come back later and look at it?"

"No, I don't mind. I'll be here." I thanked him again for his help.

I finally found out Dave's motive when he stopped by later and asked for my phone number.

He called me that night, and we talked for quite a long time. He had two children of his own and was recently divorced. We decided to go out that weekend.

Dave picked me up for our date in his pickup. He had decided, unbeknownst to me, to take me on a tour of Topeka. I thought this a little strange, but enjoyable. He drove me through the older residential areas and explained their significance to Topeka. He had grown up in this area and knew I was still unfamiliar with some of the city. He explained he had just moved back from St. Louis to be closer to his children.

We then entered the city park, and he stopped at the new swimming complex.

"Have you been to the new complex?"

"Yes, it's very nice. They really did a nice job with it."

"Thank you," was all he said.

"What do you mean?" I said confused.

"I used to work for the Parks and Recreation Department. I was put in charge of redesigning this complex."

"Really?" I said. "The kids and I have come here several times. We love it."

"That's good to hear. I'm very proud of it."

"Well, you should be," I said. "So how did you end up in St. Louis?"

"Well, I went there to take over as director of the Department of Parks and Recreation. It was my dream job, but my wife for some reason refused to move down with me."

"Why?"

"She's a nurse here and didn't really want to leave her family. I moved, thinking that she and the kids would move down later, and she never showed up."

I thought this odd since moving is something a family usually plans together. Why would Dave leave and just expect them to follow later?

"I just think she later decided not to move. Anyway, to make a long story short, I stayed down there for two years and missed my kids too much. So, I moved back and took this job to be close to them."

I really liked Dave, but parts of his story just didn't sit well with me. I was pretty cautious by then, and some of the statements he made just didn't seem to make sense. His wife didn't follow him? I just wasn't sure I was getting the whole truth, and truth, based on my experience with Jack, was very important to me. I mean everyone makes mistakes. I know that. I just had a feeling Dave wasn't giving me the full story, and that bothered me.

"Yeah, my daughter is pretty mad at me."

"Why would she be mad at you?"

"I don't know. I guess she felt I abandoned them?"

"Why do you think she feels that way?"

"I guess she thought I should have moved back a long time ago."

"I still don't understand why your ex-wife didn't move with you. I mean, had you planned the move and she later refused to join you?"

"Yes, we had planned it, and I just left assuming she and the kids would follow me, and they didn't."

I left the story at that. We finally reached the restaurant, Annie's Kitchen. It was a local family restaurant. I thought maybe I was overstepping my boundaries with the questions, but I needed to know if Dave was being truthful with me. After my experience with Jack, honesty was very important to me.

Dave told me he attended the nearby Lutheran church. He said he was head of one of the youth ministries there. We shared good conversation and said our goodbyes that night, with a handshake. We made plans to go out again. I kept thinking that night, here, I had spent all this money on the singles agency and I found this guy on my own.

Still hopeful, I looked forward to the singles' dinner Heather had invited me to that Friday. She said there would be a lawyer and a businessman there. I had a full schedule at the department store that week and was given only Tuesday and Friday off. Saline had agreed to babysit for me, but as in life, things change.

"Mom, I have to work on Friday," Saline said coming in from school on Thursday evening. "I'm sorry, I won't be able to take Jackson and Hope to soccer practice. I checked the schedule, and they just changed it."

"That's okay, sweetie, I may just have to just skip this one." I was openly disappointed, but I understood that the girls also had lives of their own.

"No, you should go. Call Grandma, maybe she can take them."

"Don't worry about it. I'll figure something out."

"Okay, but you should go," Saline said, heading out the door to work.

"Where are you going, Mommy?" asked Hope.

"Oh, Mommy was invited to a dinner."

"Are we going?" Hope asked.

"No, sweetie, this is just for adults."

"Mom has a da-ate, Mom has a da-ate!" Jackson said, making fun of me while wiggling his hips back and forth.

"I wish," I said. "Mommy has to pay for this date."

"Then who's going to take us to soccer?" Jackson asked, now realizing that this impacted him.

"Well, I'm going to try and get Grandma."

"Yay!" Jackson and Hope said in unison. They were excited because my parents always took them for ice cream or some type of snack after an event.

Just then Lily came down from her room.

"Mom, do you work tonight?" Lily asked.

"Yeah, sweetie I do," I said, trying to get some clean clothes out of the dryer and put another load in before I had to leave for work.

"What are we having for supper then?" Lily asked, stretching her slim body across the kitchen counter.

"Well, there is leftover spaghetti, or you can put in some frozen fish," I said while trying to get my load quickly folded.

"What do you guys want?" Lily asked Jackson and Hope.

"Spaghetti," shouted Jackson.

"Fish," said Hope.

"I'm not making both. Mom, tell them to pick one."

"Honey, it's just warming up spaghetti; you don't have to make it."

"I know, I'm just tired."

"I know, sweetie, but I have to work tonight. It shouldn't take long to get it ready."

"All right," Lily said disgustedly as she slouched off toward the refrigerator.

I felt bad for Lily. She sometimes got stuck with more than her share of chores around the house because Saline and I were usually running out the door somewhere. She rarely complained, but I knew it got to her sometimes. I knew the strain that Jackson and Hope could be. But during this time, there was no choice, and Lily knew this. So, she tried to make the best out of a situation none of us had any control over.

I woke up that Friday morning and headed to my temporary job at the distribution center. The day seemed to drag. I finally reached my mom to see if she could take the kids to soccer practice. She said she could, and I started to make plans to go to the singles' dinner that evening.

When I got home, Saline and Lily had picked up Jackson and Hope for me from school. I put a frozen pizza in the oven, and the kids settled in to watch television as I got dinner ready.

"I'm leaving for work, Mom," Saline announced in a hurry. "Have a good time at the dinner."

"I'll try."

"You never know, you might meet Mr. Right," Saline said, smiling as she grabbed her purse and headed out the door. I smiled back at her.

"Yeah, Mom, Mr. Right…ooww," teased Jackson.

"Who's Mr. Right, Mom?" asked Hope innocently.

"A figment of our imagination, honey," I said sarcastically. "You guys need to get your soccer stuff ready. Grandma will be here any minute," I said, now looking at the clock.

"But we're still eating."

Jackson and Hope just kind of looked at me as Lily got up from the table.

"I'll get it ready," Lily said.

"Thanks, sweetie."

My mom arrived 20 minutes before they had to be there and honked from the driveway. The kids ran out, excited that Grandma would be getting them ice cream on the way home. Lily went along to watch them on the field because my mom usually stayed in the car. I waved from the garage as the door slowly closed.

I had decided to wear my gray pants and my new pink shirt I had bought with the money my kids and my parents gave me for my birthday. I was so thin by this point, I almost had to buy a whole new wardrobe. I looked in the mirror, thinking a year ago I would have never guessed I would be wearing this size again. The pants were very form-fitting, but loose in the legs. The pink shirt showed off my arms and came down a little past the waistband of the trousers. My dark hair had been trimmed around my face into long layers and came down past my shoulders. I looked young for my age, mostly because of my weight loss. I don't know if it was the stress of working two jobs or just worrying about the kids and the rent, but I continued to lose weight.

The Pink Elephant was a restaurant on the east side of town and was known as one of the better restaurants in Topeka. I knew I would be paying for my own food, so I made sure I took enough cash to cover the bill. After I got into my car, I realized I didn't have my cellphone. I wanted to take it in case my mom needed to get hold of me. Checking my watch, I quickly re-entered the duplex and climbed the stairs, locating my cellphone lying on the bed. Now I was late.

I quickly drove across town as images of the past week flew through my head.

I pulled into the parking lot of the Pink Elephant Restaurant and quietly whispered, "Here I go."

I walked as fast as my three-inch heels allowed and headed north toward the restaurant's wooden stairs. I looked around, the sun was shining, and there wasn't a cloud in the sky. The parking lot was packed full of vehicles.

As I was walked, I caught a glimpse out of the corner of my eye of another person heading toward me from the east side of the parking lot. I was in too much of a hurry and the sun was much too bright for me to make out the image.

As I neared the stairs in front of the restaurant, I saw a shadow heading right toward me. The dark silhouette formed through the rays of the sun, and out of the corner of my eye, I could see the image forming as we reached the bottom of the stairs at exactly the same moment…

Chapter Twenty
The Makeover

"So how you doin'?" Rachael asked while taking out the cleaning supplies from the laundry room closet.

"Just fine. How are you?" Ben replied.

"Good. Dad said you were thinking about going to their bridge club dinner next Saturday."

"Yeah, I was thinkin' about it. Why?"

"Well, there's usually a lot of women there, but I don't know what Mom and Dad are thinking."

"What do ya mean?"

"The women there are pretty old."

"Really?"

"Well, you know what I mean."

Ben laughed at his niece. "Oh, old. Old like me or old like your mom and dad?"

"You know what I mean, Grandma old."

"Oh, Grandma old. Okay. That's way older than me. I better think about this some more."

"I guess you could meet someone there."

"Well, it beats sitting at home, I guess," Ben said.

"Yep. Well, if you're goin' to go," Rachael said, "I've been thinking."

"Oh, that usually means trouble for me." Ben smiled.

"No, really. I think maybe your look needs an update."

"My look? What's wrong with the way I look?"

"Well... you know, the glasses today are usually a bit smaller."

"Are they now?"

"And nothing personal, but you are getting a little old for the long hair."

"What kind of update are we talking about? Give it to me in dollars."

"Well, I was thinking maybe new glasses and a shorter haircut."

"New glasses? But these fit me fine. I've had these forever."

"Exactly. They're getting kind of dated, don't you think?"

"Dated? These are priceless antiques."

"Yep, that's what I'd call 'em."

"So, you think I need updating, huh."

Rachael smiled while dusting the living room. "Well, just a little."

"So... do you want to go with me to get this stuff done? I know I have good taste and all, but I'm not sure I could pick out the current styles as well as you can."

"I'd love to. When do you want to go?"

"How about today?"

"Great, because it may take a while to get the glasses; just let me finish up here and I can call Mom and let her know."

"No hurry. We'll probably want to get to Topeka before the stores close, though."

"True. Oh, let's go now. I can finish this when we get back."

"Sounds good to me. After you, madame," Ben said, opening the door for his niece.

"Can I use your cellphone to call Mom and Dad?"

"Yep, but it will cost you a quarter."

"Take it out of my wages."

"What? You think you're getting paid for goofing off with your uncle?"

"Oh, you're funny, Uncle Ben."

Ben and Rachael returned seven hours later with two pairs of smaller, metal-framed glasses and a new, shorter haircut for Ben.

Ben looked in the bathroom mirror, trying to smooth down the little hair he had left.

"Do you like it?" Rachael asked.

"I do. It's just going to take some getting used to."

"Well, I love it. You look so much younger."

"I do, huh."

"Yeah. Watch, you will be fighting the women off now," Rachael said.

"Well, we'll see about that."

"So, you going to the bridge club dinner?"

"Well, I guess so. I have plans this Friday night also."

"Oooo...a date?" Rachael asked excitedly.

"Not exactly. It's more like a small get-together."

"Where at?"

"In Topeka."

"Good. You can show off your new look."

"Yeah, my new look," Ben said, still looking at himself in the mirror.

Ben wished he hadn't accepted the invitation from Heather. He started to worry about what kind of people would be at there. He thought he might feel out of place. He believed it was mighty nervy of her to call and expect him to step in at the last minute, even though he was getting an extra six months for free.

Ben took that day off from the plant, so he would be at the dinner on time. He spent most of the day out at the farm checking on the cattle. He had lunch with his parents and caught up on the local news.

As the evening approached, Ben left the farm, thinking about what he should wear to the dinner. He debated on if he should just wear jeans. He decided he should probably play it safe and wear the khaki pants Heather had suggested.

Ben entered his truck preparing to leave for the Pink Elephant in Topeka when he suddenly realized he didn't have his truck keys. He went back in the house and discovered they weren't in his jeans. Ben took this as a sign that he should stay home as he rummaged through his bedroom, finally finding the keys on the floor. Ben was now running about 10 minutes late as he got into his truck and headed east on I-70.

"I should just make it," he said to himself as he drove down the road. "Ah, I don't know why I'm even going." He sighed.

Ben put the truck on cruise, thinking about his day. His mom seemed to be doing fine, but his dad got slower and slower every day. The arthritis had taken over his body to a point where he couldn't even stand straight anymore. Ben wondered what would happen to his mom if his dad became ill. She waited on his dad hand and foot. She brought his plate over to the table for him and made sure his coffee was always filled. What would she do without him, or him without her? Sharing 50 years together, any change was bound to take a toll on them.

Ben realized at that moment that he may not celebrate 50 years with someone. He wondered why that was. He figured it was all somehow God's plan. This realization didn't seem to comfort him as much as it should have as he continued down the interstate, heading to Topeka.

Ben pulled up in the parking lot, noticing the wooden steps that led to the front door. He made a hard left and parked in the east end of the parking lot. He quickly got out of his truck in an attempt to be on time.

Ben was walking so swiftly that he didn't notice the woman walking from the south end of the parking lot. He jogged across the lane, his dark silhouette hitting the sunset at just the right moment. He was moving so fast, he almost bumped into the woman in a pink shirt, passing right in front of him at the bottom of the restaurant stairs…

Chapter Twenty-One
The Meeting

And there they stood, face to face… the farmer and the single mom.

They met almost as if it had been predetermined, as if all the stars in heaven were aligned, and they were meant to meet at that exact moment, on this exact spot. All the turmoil and broken roads that had led them here to this one moment in time were now winding down, withering away as if a whisper.

"I'm sorry, excuse me," Ben managed to spit out, as he found himself almost running into the attractive brunette who stood before him.

Something seemed familiar about her. Ben couldn't explain it. It was almost as if they had met before. Ben brought his arm down to signal for Sarah to go ahead of him.

"Thank you," Sarah said, startled by his presence, now moving slowly past Ben. Sarah glanced at the tall farmer as she passed in front of him. She silently wondered if he was possibly part of her singles group. She caught a glimpse of his smile as he signaled for her to go forward. A gentleness radiated from this stranger, the type you usually feel from running into an old friend. Sarah felt a warm sensation evoke as she stepped in front of him, moving toward the stairs.

Ben followed her up the stairs. He noticed how her pink shirt accentuated the shine in her brown hair as it bounced with every move she made.

Walking only two steps behind her, he sensed her looking back at him. Ben tried not to stare, but he couldn't seem to take his eyes off of her.

As they neared the top of the stairs, Ben, as if it were a natural thing to do, reached forward to open the door for her. Sarah glanced at him, noticing his strong, gleaming smile.

"Thank you," Sarah said.

"You're welcome," Ben replied.

Sarah walked quickly through the door and approached the young hostess standing behind the counter. "I'm looking for the group from Friendship Match."

The hostess glanced up briefly and pointed to the left. "They're meeting right over there." She motioned in the direction of a small waiting area.

Ben also approached the desk. "I'm also with the group," Ben said loudly, so that Sarah could hear.

They both stood smiling at each other as Sarah turned to where the hostess had pointed.

"I guess we're over here," Sarah said.

"I guess so." Ben smiled, as they both made their way over to join the others who were already waiting.

Two women were seated on a bench, and there were two men dressed in slacks and button-down shirts standing beside them. They looked over at the late comers as they approached.

One by one, the group slowly introduced themselves to Ben and Sarah. A heavier set older man with a bald spot and a pot belly introduced himself as Don. Don extended his hand to each of them. Sarah noted his forceful handshake that left her hand throbbing.

The other man, named Albert, was younger but not by much. Albert's distinguishing feature was his dark slacks that did not seem to quite meet his shoes.

One of the women introduced herself as Katie. Katie, a full-figured woman, had permed hair that was orange in color. Her pale skin accentuated her green eyes that creased in the corners when she smiled.

The other woman, named Olivia, had gray hair that was pinned back on one side by a single diamond studded hairpin. Ben thought she reminded him of his sixth-grade school teacher.

After the introductions, Ben then turned to Sarah to introduce himself.

"I guess we haven't formally met, yet."

"No, we haven't," Sarah responded, still feeling a sense of familiarity toward Ben.

"I'm Ben Thompson," he said, extending his arm to shake her hand. Sarah held out her hand, as they both felt an immediate connection and naturalness to one another's touch, neither one wanting to pull away.

"Sarah…Sarah Harris."

Sarah stood speechless as Ben spoke, "It's very nice to meet you, Sarah."

"Well, shall we find our table?" Don suddenly blurted out, taking charge of the group.

"Yeah, but I think they have to seat us," Albert interjected, as Don flagged down the young hostess.

The hostess then gathered some menus and stated, "Follow me, please."

As the group started to move forward, Don immediately stretched out his arms as if he were a school crossing guard, holding back both Albert and Ben, letting the three women go before them. Ben – annoyed that he had lost his place next to Sarah – thought about trudging ahead and pushing through, but he didn't want to seem rude, so he waited politely next to Albert. They all then followed the young hostess single file to a large round table.

"Shall we sit boy girl?" suggested Don.

Don and Albert took a seat on either side of Sarah, and Ben, disappointed, slowly made his way to the chair in between Katie and Olivia.

The restaurant gleamed with large tin fermentation tanks that brewed the handcrafted beer the restaurant was famous for. The fermentation tanks sat behind large glass walls that went all the way to the lower level of the restaurant. Customers crowded at the edge of the glass, eyeing the magnificence of the tanks.

The voices of the crowd hummed all around the group with unknown conversation and laughter. From where they were seated, they could see the outside deck that looked over a small wooded area.

The conversation seemed to drag, as the awkwardness of the unfamiliar resonated in each individual attendant. The group quickly looked over the menu, trying not to make eye contact with one another. Ben and Sarah stole secret glances of one another, but usually when the other one was not looking. Everyone continued to smile pleasantly at each other, when Don finally broke the silence.

"Has anyone ever been here before?"

They all shook their heads no.

Being eager to talk with Sarah, Don turned to her, "So what do you do for a living, Sarah?" Everyone's eyes turned toward Sarah.

"I'm working for Sage Distribution right now. I'm in Human Resources," Sarah said, embarrassed that she didn't have a permanent job, intentionally leaving out the part about it being temporary.

"That's interesting. So, what is the work force there now anyway?"

Sarah – having no idea – searched for an intelligent response that would not divulge her limited work history. "You know, I'm really not sure. I haven't been there all that long. The facility is fairly new though. They only built it about five years ago," Sarah said, trying to grab at any tidbit of information she knew about the place.

"Really, I didn't know that," Don said, trying to sound interested.

Sarah, satisfied with her answer, asked Don what he did for a living, as the rest of the group sat and listened in.

Don turned toward the group as if he were addressing a board of directors. "I'm in banking," he said. "I travel all around the area auditing different banks. I've done it for years. I really enjoy it, and I'm at the level now that I have the freedom to do pretty much whatever I like outside of work." His comment now being directed toward Sarah.

Ben sat, hesitant to join the conversation. He envied Don's quick wit and ability to speak to people he just met. Ben was always uncomfortable meeting new people, and in these circumstances, he usually only spoke when he was being spoken to.

"So, Albert, what do you do?" Don asked.

"I'm a lawyer in Kansas City," Albert said shyly.

"Well, you had a long drive then," Don said, as everyone else at the table shook their head in affirmation.

"Yeah it is, but I enjoy the dinners and traveling to towns I haven't visited before," stated Albert.

"I work at Western Energy," Katie interjected, now grabbing everyone's attention. "I'm a supervisor in the customer service department there. I've been there about 17 years."

Sarah thought at that moment how she wished she could get a job there. Western Energy was one of the many places Sarah had applied and never got a response from.

"My husband passed away two years ago from cancer," Katie said. "I joined the agency so I could get out and meet new people."

"Me too," commented Olivia. "I mean, I lost my husband five years ago."

Don looked over at Ben as he sat with his hands on his knees, kind of leaning into the table, as if he were at a campfire. Ben dreaded this moment when everyone announced their careers. They all sounded so exciting. He worked in a plant and farmed. He wasn't sure what Sarah would think of his chosen occupations. It certainly wasn't anything glamorous and she didn't seem to be the country type. She looked sophisticated and worked in an office.

Ben knew his time was coming, and he would answer as honest and as direct as he knew how. After all that had happened, Ben's word still meant a great deal to him, and no matter what the group would think of him, the truth is what they would be getting.

Don sensed Ben's hesitance and immediately tried to bring Ben into the conversation. He turned and asked Ben what he did for a living.

Don, somewhat jealous of Ben's youthful rugged looks, felt a reluctance from Ben to participate in the conversation and decided to use this to further his advantage with Sarah.

"I work for Westchester."

"And what do you do there?" Don asked.

"I'm a coordinator for the line," Ben said. "I also farm with my brother in Alma."

"I've been out to Alma; it's a fine town," Don said. "You still live there?"

"Yes, I do. It just seems easier livin' near the farm, and I kinda like the small-town life."

"I've been to the antique stores out there," added Olivia.

"I hear they're quite nice," Ben said. "But I haven't actually been in one, so you probably know more about them than I do."

"So, you raise cattle?" questioned Don.

"Yes, we do. It's a small herd, comparably," Ben said, now feeling more comfortable as the conversation turned toward farming.

"How many head do you have?" Albert asked.

"Oh, maybe 150, 160 head, somewhere around there," Ben replied.

"Sounds like quite a bit to me," laughed Don.

"It surely can be." Ben grinned, now looking over at Sarah, who smiled back.

Sarah then took this opportunity to speak to Ben. "So, Ben, you grew up there?"

"Yes, ma'am, born and raised."

"I've never been to Alma."

"Well, it's a beautiful place, lots of open roads and pastures."

"Is it a lot smaller than Topeka?" Sarah asked.

Everyone in the group then started to giggle.

"What?" Sarah said, now embarrassed.

"Oh, don't mind us," Ben said smiling. "It's just that Alma is one of those towns where if you blink, you might miss it."

"Oh…" Sarah said, laughing as they both smiled at each other still feeling a sense of familiarity between them, "I thought Topeka was small."

"No, you haven't seen small till you visit one of our local farm communities," laughed Don.

"But I have a feeling you might like it," Ben quickly uttered.

"Maybe I would. I'll have to get out there some day," Sarah said.

"Well…" Ben started to say as Don interrupted him.

"So, Sarah, where are you from?" Don asked.

Sarah, annoyed that Don had cut Ben off, reluctantly answered, "Well, originally I'm from Kansas City. But I spent about twelve years in Nebraska," she said, as Ben looked over, also growing annoyed with Don.

"Oh, whereabouts?" Don inquired.

"I lived in Bellevue, right outside Omaha…"

The conversation continued throughout the dinner as each participant started to feel more comfortable with one another. Sarah never noticed Ben's secret glances, and not once did he make an effort to direct a question toward her. Ben spoke when spoken to and seemed to feel out of place as he squirmed in his chair.

As the evening slowly came to a close, Don continued to go out of his way to try and impress Sarah, dominating most of the conversation. While Ben just kind of sat back and watched from a distance, always answering any questions very politely, and with a twist of country accent that Sarah found very attractive.

As they said their goodbyes, Ben and Sarah found themselves stealing secret glances. Ben contemplated asking Sarah if he could walk her to her car, but Don stood again, as the group prepared to leave, holding back both Ben and Albert, allowing the women to walk out before them. Ben stood behind again, irritated that he couldn't walk Sarah out.

Sarah, unaware of Ben's true feelings, headed straight to her car. She looked over toward where she saw Ben park, hoping that he might try to approach her before she left. She slowed her pace down to a stroll, but then picked it up when she noticed Don looking her way. She entered her vehicle, thinking maybe Ben just wasn't interested. She looked down, stroking her hand, which still tingled from Ben's touch.

Thinking she was acting like a school girl with a first crush, she placed her keys in the ignition and started her car. Ben just seemed so honest to her. He wasn't trying to impress anyone, and he seemed to go out of his way to state the truth, even if it meant acknowledging that he wasn't as worldly as the others. This type of honesty from a man was new to Sarah.

Ben looked over in Sarah's direction as he fought the urge to run over there before she left. He wondered if she would like to have dinner sometime. He came to the conclusion that asking her now would seem too forward, and what if she said no.

Ben, giving in to his ambiguity, decided he would call Heather on Monday and ask for Sarah's number. He eased his mind with the fact that this was probably the best decision for them both. This way Sarah would have the chance to say yes or no and not feel obligated by him putting her on the spot.

With these thoughts flurrying through his head, Ben suddenly hit the steering wheel of his truck with the palm of hand, irritated with himself for not taking more initiative. He felt like he had once again let a moment pass him by and it was gone.

He forcefully put his truck into gear and backed out of his parking spot, starting the thirty-mile drive back home, alone.

Chapter Twenty-Two
The Odd Couple

"So, you met someone," Heather smirked into the phone.

"Yes, I met someone, but I didn't get to talk to her much," Ben said.

"Why?"

"I don't know? She was sitting a ways from me."

"Like a seat away or like a table away?"

"A ways, okay."

"Oh, honey." Heather laughed. "You are too much."

"I know. What can I say?"

"You have to initiate a conversation."

"I do. It's just hard when there's other people around. I do better one on one."

Ben heard some shuffling of paperwork over the phone before Heather answered, "All right. Well, let's see. Who was there that evening?"

An image of Sarah flashed before Ben's eyes. "Her name is Sarah."

"Oh, Sarah. Yeah, she is quite lovely, isn't she?"

"Yep, that she is."

"Well, I'll tell you what, Ben. I'll get a hold of Sarah and make sure it's okay with her that I give you her number."

"Okay, don't forget to tell her what a great guy I am," Ben smirked.

Heather grinned. "Ben, you don't want me to lie to the woman, do you?"

"Huh, you're funny."

"I'm just kidding. I'm sure she will be happy to hear from you. I'll get back to you as soon as I talk to her, deal?"

"Works for me."

Heather hung up with Ben and sat looking at her desk for a moment. "Wow, I would have never put those two together," she said to herself, as she picked up the phone, dialing in Sarah's phone number.

After several failed attempts, Heather finally reached Sarah late in the afternoon. Being a workday, Sarah was between jobs and dealing with kids while trying to get out the door when Heather called.

"Hi, Sarah. It's Heather from Friendship Match."

"Oh, hi," Sarah replied as she struggled to get her coat on and find her purse. Sarah sounded rattled, as she juggled the phone in her hand. "Ahh... could you hold on a minute, Heather?"

"Sure, honey, take your time."

Sarah then scrambled to put on her heels while kissing Jackson and Hope goodbye. Heather unavoidably heard the conversation between Sarah and the kids. Smiling into the receiver as the scenes unfolded, Heather reminded of her own crazy life at one time.

"Mom, Lily won't read us a story before bed," Jackson whined.

"Lily, could you please read them one book?"

"But, Mom, they always want two books. I have homework," Lily said, annoyed.

"Guys, I have to go. Lily, can you read one book?"

"Well, then I want it to be my book!" Jackson shouted out, as they all gathered around Sarah like a distraught mob.

"No, mine," Hope said.

"Look, you two will have to agree on one book or no book at all," Sarah said trying to settle the quarrel.

"What!" they said in unison.

"Okay, today, Hope, it's your turn, tomorrow it will be Jackson's, and I don't want to hear another word about it."

"Why does Hope go first?" Jackson said, disgusted.

"I'm sorry, guys, I have to go. Do your homework and have Saline do the dishes when she gets home, bye, love you."

"Love you," all the kids said, dragging themselves to the sofa.

Sarah finally got back to her phone call as she exited out the garage door and climbed into her large SUV. "I'm sorry, Heather. Go ahead."

"No, it's fine. You forget I have children too. Well, anyway, I have good news, two of the men from the dinner the other night want to get in touch with you."

"Two?" said Sarah surprised, now putting her car in to drive and entering the evening traffic.

"Don and Ben," said Heather. "Do you want me to give them your phone number?"

"No, ah... not Don. I just didn't feel a connection there. Ah, sorry. Could you hold on?" Sarah put the phone down, trying to grab her purse which had fallen to the floor. She then suddenly snapped her head back up to see the oncoming traffic while juggling the phone. "Sorry, no, not Don. I mean, he was nice, just…"

"Just no connection."

"Right," Sarah said, relieved.

"Gotcha, not a problem. No to Don. What about Ben?"

Sarah hesitated recalling their initial meeting before the wooden stairs of the restaurant. An image of Ben smiling at her as she passed him flashed before her eyes. "Ben."

"Yeah. I don't have to give out your number if you don't want me to."

"No, no, it's not that," Sarah hesitated. "Has he seen my profile?" she asked.

"Probably not. He doesn't have a computer."

"Oh… well, have him take a look my profile, and I'll look at his, and if he still wants to see me, give him my number."

"Okay, but it might take a while. I may have to mail him your profile."

"That's okay. Have him take a look at it first."

"All right, sweetie. I'll call you back either way."

Sarah hung up with Heather just as she got stopped at a stoplight. She touched her hand, remembering the tingling sensation she had when Ben touched her.

Sarah, for some reason, had a strange feeling that Ben did not have any children. She couldn't explain it, so on her break Sarah hurried to the computer in the breakroom. Luckily, it was free. She rushed to pull up Ben's profile, unable to wait till she got home to find out if she was right. His photo was exactly as she had pictured it. He had a gorgeous smile that accentuated his pronounced jaw and cheekbones, giving him a rugged, outdoor look. Ben sat there with one arm over the other, leaning on one knee, almost pulling himself into the camera.

Sarah read on, discovering that he had put down "considering marriage." She looked under children, and sure enough… he had no kids. She smirked as this newfound discovery settled and her suspicions were validated. *He has no children*, she thought to herself. *There's no way someone with no kids is going to date a woman with four.* Sarah sat laughing so hard she threw her head back, looking at the ceiling, as she announced out loud into the chorus of the department store music, "The man has no kids. Ah… now that's funny. And I have four… okay." A fellow employee walked by just as Sarah blurted this out, the employee giving Sarah a curious look.

The rest of Ben's profile read as she thought it would. He worked for a large manufacturing company and farmed. Sarah knew nothing about farming.

She could barely keep a house plant alive. She sat on her stool behind the counter and wondered what exactly, if anything, the two of them had in common.

Heather finally got hold of Ben the next day after calling several times. "Man, you're a hard guy to get a hold of."

"Oh sorry. I had my phone off."

Heather narrowed her eyebrows in question. "Why? May I ask?"

"Didn't need to call anyone."

"Okay… whatever, well anyway, I got hold of Sarah. She wants you to read her profile before I give you her number."

"What? Why?"

"I don't know. I guess she wants you to know everything about her before she agrees to go out with you."

"Why? Is there somethin' wrong with her? I mean, she looked pretty good to me." Ben laughed.

"Yes, she's very attractive, anyway Ben, can you bring up her profile at work?"

"Not right now. Our computers are down. Why don't you just read it to me."

"Okay… hold on a minute… let's see here. She's originally from Kansas City. She moved here from Nebraska. Oh, and she has four kids."

"What? That tiny woman has four kids?"

"That's what it says here."

"Gosh, I never would have guessed that," Ben said, as the information sunk in. "Anything else I should know?"

"Well, she's a Christian and wants a serious relationship, and hopes to be remarried one day."

"Oh, I mean, that's not awful. I mean, my mother had four kids."

"Oh, and she loves to dance."

"Huh, well, that's it. That's a deal breaker. I don't do dancing. Dancing is just not in my blood," Ben said jokingly.

Heather was silent for a moment, not finding Ben's sense of humor quite as humorous. "Okay. Seriously, what do you want to do? You want to take dancing lessons first and then give her a call?"

"No. I'm just kiddin'. I would like to call her. I thought she was great. I mean, everyone has kids. Well, everyone except me. This dancing thing though. I don't know." Ben sensed Heather's growing irritation with him as he continued to egg her on.

"And what did I tell you, Ben?" bragged Heather.

"What?"

"This may be the one."

Ben, currently working second shift, wanted to call Sarah as soon as possible, but he had to wait for an opportunity where he would have plenty of time for the call. He wanted to avoid feeling rushed while on the phone with her, so he placed the paper with Sarah's number on it in his pocket and waited for exactly the right moment.

Luckily, the machines continued to run smoothly that evening, needing little maintenance, which gave Ben ample time to make the call. He headed to one of the smaller offices, removing his hard hat and safety glasses, and turned his pager to vibrate. The small dusty office held one computer that sat on an old metal desk. The room, surrounded by grim brown paneling, had no windows and was very dark. Several of the employees used the office to order new parts and products for the line.

Ben sat down in the chair, which displayed a small rip in the green plastic cushion. He clicked on the desk lamp, fumbling around in his pocket for Sarah's phone number. Ben looked forward to hearing Sarah's voice again. Without hesitation, he punched the numbers into his cellphone and sat and listened to the buzzing sound in his ear.

"Hello," Sarah said.

"Hi, Sarah?" Ben asked, not sure if the voice belonged to her or one of her kids.

"Yes, this is Sarah."

"This is Ben, Ben Thompson, from the singles' dinner the other night. Heather gave me your number."

"Oh, hi, Ben. How are you?"

"I'm fine. I wanted to apologize for not talking to you more the other night."

"No, it's fine. Those get-togethers are always kind of awkward. I was just surprised to hear from you, I mean, since we hadn't talked much."

"I'm really sorry about that. I just feel a little uncomfortable sometimes in group settings."

"Yeah, it can be a little intimidating." They sat for a moment as there was an awkward silence. "So, you had a chance to look over my profile, right?"

"Yeah, I did. Was there a reason you wanted me to see it before we talked? I mean it was fine, I didn't mind doing it."

"I just like everything to be out there before connecting with someone. So, you know, everyone knows what they are walking into. That's all."

"So, you have four kids, is that right?" Ben said cordially.

"Yep, I have four."

"So how old are they?" Ben asked.

"Well, I have one that's seventeen, one that's thirteen, one eight, and the youngest is six."

"Wow! There's quite a difference in age."

"Yeah, well, I didn't plan it that way, but that's how it worked out," Sarah said, suddenly uncomfortable. "So, Ben, you have no kids?"

"No, I don't," Ben said.

"So, how is it you don't have any kids, if you don't mind me asking?"

Ben didn't mind. He wondered why people always thought he should have kids. He figured God had a reason. "No, I don't mind. I've been divorced for about seven years now, and my ex-wife couldn't have children. But I knew that when I married her."

"Oh," Sarah said, somewhat intrigued by his answer, wondering what kind of man would marry a woman he knew couldn't have kids. She thought at that moment, he must have really loved her. "So… a… you said you worked for Westchester?"

"Yeah. I've been here about six years now."

"And you farm?"

"Yep. Well, my brother and I farm together. My parents still live there, but they aren't able to get around like they used to, so we take care of the farm, and check in on them while we're out there."

"Well, you're a busy guy."

"Yes, I am. My dad built the house we grew up in, and they still live there. He farmed most of his life."

"So how many siblings do you have?" Sarah asked.

"I've got two brothers and an older sister."

"You're not the youngest, are you?" Sarah suddenly blurted out without thinking.

Ben, wondering why that would be a problem, answered nervously, "Ahh… yeah… why?"

"Oh, nothing. I just have a younger sister who was pretty spoiled."

Ben, taking this opportunity to show his sense of humor, answered without hesitation, "Oh, you don't have to worry about that. That's not the case here. My parents hardly fed me growing up."

"Oh, is that right?"

"Yep, I always got the leftovers in food and clothes. And every time somethin' went wrong, my older siblings were always blamin' me, because I was too little to defend myself. I think the youngest ones are the most unfortunate ones." Ben snickered.

"Oh, you do, do you?"

"Yes, I do."

"Well, that wasn't the case with my sister. She pretty much got whatever she wanted, and what a temper, boy."

"Well, that's because we younger ones have to fight for everythin' we get," Ben joked.

"Oh, is that the reason? I'll need to confirm that with your mother."

"Go right ahead. She'll confirm everythin' I've said," Ben said as they both began to laugh and the conversation took an almost too natural turn.

"She'll confirm everythin' you said?"

"Are you making fun of my accent?"

"No, not me. That's not somethin' I would do."

The phone call carried on longer than they both intended. Sarah, more so than Ben, sensed a kind of familiarity with one another, a naturalness. She didn't know why, but Sarah already felt as if she knew him in a way, and could trust him. It was like talking to an old friend she had had grown up with. And he never went out of his way to take her side, but voiced his own opinions, in a mannerly way of course.

She actually didn't know a man could be this honest. They talked about family, religion, and politics, and found they had a lot of common beliefs, but a lot of uncommon upbringing. She was raised in the city, and he was raised in the country.

His accent was quite different. She found herself holding back laughter at the way he said "dang near" at the end of most of his stories.

Sarah immediately had feelings for this man that she couldn't explain. His honesty and character had shone through, and for some reason she knew it wasn't just an act. Somehow, she knew that this could possibly lead to something more than just dating.

As they made plans to go out that Saturday, Sarah wondered if Ben could be the answer to her prayers.

Chapter Twenty-Three
Family

Ben got up early Saturday morning and headed to the farm. He hoped to make a short day of it because he wanted to get his hair trimmed up a little before his date with Sarah.

He didn't tell a soul about his plans for the evening. He figured it probably wouldn't work out anyway, so why get their hopes up. He thought he would probably eventually do something to screw this up, too, and the less people that knew about it, the better.

When he arrived at his parents' house, his dad was sitting at the kitchen table with his pipe and coffee, reading the morning paper. Ben, seemingly a little bit more chipper that morning, caught the attention of his parents who sensed his good humor.

"Good mornin', you two."

"Well, good mornin'," his mom answered. His father looked around his paper, not recognizing his son's usually somber voice.

"What's got you so chipper this mornin?" his dad asked.

"Oh, nothin'. The sun's shining and the good Lord has blessed us with another beautiful day. Isn't that enough?"

"Sure is," his father said, as he went back to reading the newspaper, pulling out his magnifying glass to help read the small print.

"You want some breakfast, son?" his mom asked.

"Nah, Mom. You know I don't eat breakfast."

"Oh yeah, that's right. Well, if you don't mind, I'm gonna have mine. Your father has already had his."

"No, Mom, you go right ahead."

"So, what you and Mike got planned for today?" his father asked.

"Well, I think he wanted to move the heifers back into the south field. Is he here yet?"

"Haven't seen 'im," his father responded.

"Well, I'm going to feed. I need to head back to town early today," Ben said, not realizing he left himself open to question.

"Why, you got a hot date?" His father laughed.

"You never know, Dad. You never know."

"Well, you two be careful," Ben's mom said.

"We will, Mom. Don't you worry. Are you two doing okay today?"

"Yep, we're fine," his mother answered.

"All right, see you all later."

Ben headed out of the screen door and heard it bounce behind him.

The fall air was cool that morning. Ben could smell the beginnings of winter in the air. The windshield of his feeding truck was already tinted with frost. He opened the truck door and then turned around looking at the field below the house. He loved this time of year when it started to cool off after the hot summer months.

He opened the door and leaned in to start the truck. He stood back up after hearing the roar of the engine.

Slamming the truck door, he walked toward the barn, noticing the trees that lined the rock road were now blanketed with an array of colors, forming a canvas of warmth around the roof of the barn. Ben had always thought this scene captured the unique strokes of God's hand as He laid yellows next to reds, and golds next to oranges, with just a splash of green.

Ben meditated for a moment, breathing in deeply the cool morning air. The dried leaves rushed around his feet as he strolled leisurely up the hill.

The leaves raced along, stopped only by the barn wall, succumbing to its vastness. With the rush of the next strong wind, they were off again. Now free, the leaves were suddenly picked up and lifted high in the air, reaching out toward the branches of the nearby sycamore, and then falling to the ground in a quick stride across the pasture toward the lazy, grazing cattle, who slowly lifted their heads to watch the race.

It still took his breath away, even today, as Ben wondered how anyone could live anywhere else.

Ben entered the feed truck and headed toward the barn to refill the grain bin. Mike and Rachael suddenly pulled up. Rachael exited her father's truck looking for her uncle.

"You headin' out to feed?" asked Rachael.

"Yep, I am," replied Ben.

"You mind if I ride along?"

"No, I'd enjoy the company."

"I just have to run in and say hi to Grandma and Grandpa. I'll be right back."

"No hurry," Ben replied.

"So, you feeding first?" Mike shouted from the window of his truck.

"I thought I would," replied Ben.

"Okay then, I'll get the trailer ready," Mike said, putting his truck in gear.

"All right. It shouldn't take me long."

"There's no rush."

Ben leaned into the steering wheel, looking up at the one side of the house that had yet to be painted. The other three sides of his parents' home had been done months ago, but due to lack of scaffolding on this side, which was the tallest side, the painting never seemed to get completed. Ben's father said it gave the house character. Ben's mother stressed that it was just an eyesore.

"So, what are you doing tonight?" Rachael asked, as she climbed into the truck.

"Oh, I'm just going to Topeka, nothing special."

"I was wondering if I could bring a friend over to watch your cable television?"

"Sure, you have your key, don't you?" Ben asked as he put the truck into gear.

"Yeah, I got it."

"Well, feel free to whatever is there. The snacks may be pretty slim though."

"I know. We'll bring our own."

"Well, I'll be gone for a while so you'll have free run of the place."

"So, where you goin'?"

"Ah, just out with a friend."

"Someone from work?"

"Not exactly, why?" Ben said, trying to end the inquisition.

"No reason, thought maybe you had a date."

"Oh…"

"Sure is a beautiful day," Rachael said.

"That it is. How's school going?" Ben asked, trying to change the subject.

"Okay, boring."

"Just seemed like yesterday you and your sister were running around making mud pies."

"I know right. I don't know what to do with myself when I graduate."

"Oh, you'll figure out somethin'."

"Scott's going off to college at the end of the year."

"Is he now?"

"Yeah, I'm going to miss him. Do you think he'll forget about me?"

"Now, who could forget about you? He's just spreadin' his wings a little. He won't be that far away."

"True, it just makes me nervous."

"Well, it shouldn't. From what I've seen, Scott thinks the world of you."

"I know. I just wish I was graduating with him."

"Oh, it'll come soon enough. You enjoy your senior year. It will end all too soon."

"What about you? Have you met anyone?"

"Don't worry about your old uncle. I'll be just fine. The women are sure to realize how great I am any day now. I'm sure of it." Ben smirked.

"Sure, they will." Ben's niece smiled.

The day went on as usual. Ben ducked questions about his plans for the evening as his family all seemed hell-bent on making plans for him that evening. He loved their intentions, but they were making it awfully hard on him to keep his secret.

He figured he might be able to get one or two dates with Sarah before she realized he wasn't right for her. He thought he would just enjoy her company while it lasted.

Ben dropped Rachael off with his parents and finished loading the cattle with Mike. After they were done, he rushed to town trying to get to the barber before the shop closed.

Ray the barber had been working in town since Ben was a small boy. Almost Ben's father's age, Ray still worked three days a week, cutting hair for the locals.

Ben pulled up to the barber shop and exited his truck. He entered the old wooden shop, hearing the familiar ringing of the bell overhead. The smell of tonic filled the room as if it were embedded in the wood. The 'one-chair' shop looked almost as aged as Ray.

"How you doing, Ben?"

"Great, Ray. Any new news around town?"

"Oh, there's always news. Not always good, but there's news."

"Ain't that the truth."

"How's your parents doing? I haven't seen your dad in for quite a while," Ray said while maneuvering the man in the chair around, using the razor to finish up around the edges. The man sat blanketed in a cutting cape that allowed the hair to fall to the vinyl-tiled floor.

"Well, Dad hasn't been doing too well. He's been having Rachael trim up his hair. He doesn't like to leave the house much these days."

Just then the barber chair became open as Ray finished up with his current client. Ben recognized the man sitting in the chair to be Sam Reynolds, a local farmer, who farmed just up the road from Ben's family's place. Sam looked at himself in the mirror, took out his wallet and handed payment over to Ray.

"Hey, Ben."

"Hey, Sam. Any news with you?"

"No, not today. Just preparing for winter."

"Us too," Ben said as Sam prepared to leave. "You take care now."

"You too, Ben, see ya," replied Sam.

"Sorry to hear about your dad. I always liked him coming in. Your dad is quite the character," Ray said, as Ben made his way to the chair.

"That he is."

"So, just trim it up?"

"Yep."

"You got a hot date?"

"No, just trying to look good for the prospects."

"Oh, I see. You havin' so many of 'em."

"Having to beat them off with a stick, Ray."

"Yeah, sure you do." They both laughed.

Ray finished up Ben's hair. Ben paid him and headed home to pick out something to wear. Being more nervous than usual, he rushed to get ready so that he would arrive about ten minutes early. He wondered if Sarah had dated much. She was so attractive, he figured she must have. Being newly divorced, he thought Sarah would want to date around a while. He hoped he would at least get a few dates in before she grew tired of him. Besides – he thought to himself – what would a woman like that want with a man like him?

Chapter Twenty-Four
Anticipation

Sarah stood in front of her closet, running her fingers over her limited wardrobe as she fought off the urge to make a run to the mall. With her current limited funds, she turned to the section of clothes her girls had gotten rid of and decided on a pair of cropped pants and a sweater.

The first part of the day was spent taking her three younger children to a family birthday party. Her parents volunteered to bring the kids home for her, so she could leave in time for her date with Ben.

Sarah headed back home with an anticipation she couldn't explain. It was as if she were about to meet her future. She had not been able to shake this feeling she had after her phone conversation with Ben. There was an immediate attraction, and it was like nothing she had ever experienced before.

She paced up and down the upstairs hallway in anticipation of his arrival. *I need to keep myself busy*, she thought to herself as she rechecked her makeup and hair for the fifth time. Sarah glowed with a bronze-colored skin she had acquired after several trips to the public pool over the summer. Her thick, naturally curly hair was straightened and lying over her shoulders, framing her face.

She had just picked up a basket of laundry to fold when she heard the doorbell ring. Her heart skipped a beat and began a crescendo of rapid beats as she made her way down the stairs and to the front door. Feeling as if she might choke on the lump that had formed in her throat, Sarah took a deep breath and slowly opened the door.

The natural light slowly spread across the white tile, lighting up the dim room. Ben stood there as the sun's rays made their way in and out of the crevasses of his silhouette. He stood against the door frame with one arm reaching above the frame, leaning into the opening. His bright smile stretched across the lower part of his face, accentuating his strong cheek and jaw bones that were colored by the sun. Sarah smiled back, thinking how handsome he looked in his blue button-down shirt.

"Hello, Ben," Sarah said.

"Hi, Sarah, how are you?"

"I'm good. Come on in."

"It's really quiet in here," Ben said as he stepped in, scanning the room.

"Oh, yeah." Sarah laughed, realizing Ben was probably expecting a lot of commotion from the kids. "My kids aren't home."

"Oh..." Ben said somewhat relieved, while wondering if she just didn't want him to meet them yet.

Ben looked around at the stylish furniture. He thought about the second-hand furniture at his own place. With four kids, Ben thought she would possibly have a lot of disarray around, but the house looked... spotless.

"I'm ready," Sarah announced.

Ben tried hard not to show how nervous he was. He had to stop and catch his breath as Sarah turned around in the light and he could see how truly beautiful she was.

He thought at the moment, *I don't have a chance.*

"So, you still want to go to the Pink Elephant?" Ben asked as they walked out the door and headed toward his truck. Ben rushed before her to open her door.

"Yeah, that's fine with me," Sarah replied.

"I wish I knew the area better," Ben apologized, "I would try to take you some place different, but I'm just not that familiar with the restaurants in this area."

"No, really, it's fine," Sarah assured him.

Ben closed the door behind her and went around the front of the truck, climbing into the driver's seat.

"So, you're new to Topeka?" Ben asked while backing out of the driveway.

"Yep," Sarah replied.

"Well, how do you like it so far?"

"I really like it. I didn't think that I would, coming from a larger city, but I love the people here."

"Yeah, smaller towns can be really inviting," Ben said, trying to be agreeable.

"I mean, everyone I've met here has been so welcoming. It was really weird walking in to stores and restaurants when I got here."

"Why?" Ben said, curious, now turning his head toward Sarah.

"Well, I'd be walking in Walmart or something and people around me would randomly say hello."

"And you didn't get that in Nebraska?"

"Not like here. The first time it happened, they were so friendly I had to turn around and check to see if they were talking to someone behind me. They talked to me as if they knew me. I love that about Topeka."

After an awkward silence, Ben started to tell Sarah a little bit about the small town he was from. He seemed to love it so. Sarah had always wondered what it would be like to grow up in a small town, and Ben made it sound so inviting.

"So, what is the population in Alma anyway?" Sarah asked.

"Oh, about eight, nine hundred on a good day."

"What was the size of your senior class in high school?"

"I graduated with about thirty-six."

"Thirty-six people?"

"And that was a large class."

"Oh, that's funny. I had about four hundred in mine."

"That's half the size of Alma."

"That's true," Sarah said, as they both began to laugh. "So, what do you farm?"

"Oh, mostly wheat, corn, and beans."

"I've never been on a farm before."

"Really?"

"Nope."

"Well, we'll have to fix that. I'll have to take you out to the farm sometime."

"I'd like that."

"So, you have family here?" Ben asked, having an urge to put his arm around Sarah and pull her close to him. He tried to remove that from his thoughts, telling himself over and over again that it was only their first date.

"Yes, my mom and dad, well, it's my stepdad, and my grandmother. That's another thing I love about being here. I get to see them so much more. I lost so much time with them when I lived in Nebraska, especially with my grandmother."

"How old is she?"

"Oh, she's about eighty-eight."

"Does she live with your parents?"

"No, she has an apartment of her own near my mom."

"Well, that's amazing, considering her age."

Just then Ben and Sarah pulled up to the restaurant. Ben got out first and came around to open Sarah's door. They walked close, but neither of them made any gestures toward the other. Sarah kind of strolled next to Ben with her hands behind her, her purse swinging with each step. Ben followed her pace, having to slow down his usual long stride.

When they reached the bottom of the wooden stairs, Sarah suddenly stopped and looked up at Ben.

"What?" Ben asked.

"Don't you remember?" Sarah asked. Ben looked back at her with his eyebrows narrowed, trying to recall what she was talking about. "This is where we first met."

"Oh… yes… you're right," Ben said, now grinning.

Ben then slowly bowed at the waist, gesturing for Sarah to move before him just as he had the night that they met. Sarah smiled as she moved toward the stairs feeling a sense of déjà vu. The hostess seated them in a private area due to it being just the two of them.

Ben pulled back Sarah's chair for her and then moved toward the seat across from her. Her olive skin complemented the white sweater she was wearing.

"Would you like some wine?" Ben suggested.

"Yes, that would be great."

"I'll have red wine," Ben stated to the waiter. Ben surprised himself. That was the first time in two and a half years he had ordered a drink. He just felt the occasion called for it, and it somehow felt right with Sarah. The waiter then brought over the two glasses of wine, setting them in front of the couple.

"Thank you," Sarah said.

"No, thank you," Ben answered sincerely. "It's not often I get to take a beautiful woman out to dinner."

Sarah smiled trying not to turn red with embarrassment, as she quite often did when unexpectedly complimented. It was just the way he said it. He was being truthful. He truly felt lucky to be with her. Sarah found this image of him the most attractive of all.

Ben could feel the men in the room turning to look at Sarah as she walked by. Yet, she seemed to be oblivious to it. This surprised him. He thought to himself, this woman has no idea how truly beautiful she is. Ben sat there looking across at her as he wondered what the heck a woman like this was doing here with a man like him.

"So, what are you still doin' single?" Ben blurted out.

"Well, I haven't been divorced all that long," Sarah answered. "And how is it that you have managed to dodge matrimony?"

"I don't know. I went through a pretty bad marriage, swore off marriage really."

"Really. Why?" Sarah questioned, now raising her wine and taking a sip.

"My wife had an affair, and ever since I just haven't been able to completely trust anyone. Honestly, I thought maybe I was just supposed to spend the rest of my days on this earth alone."

"Well, that seems awful lonely."

"It can be."

"I knew I would be getting married again the day I got divorced."

"Did you really?"

"Yep."

"How could you have known that?" Ben said, now intrigued.

"For that exact reason, I have no intention of spending the rest of my life alone."

"So, you really think you can trust again so soon? I mean, you're newer to single life than I am."

"Yes, I do. How is it you don't?"

Ben stopped and looked at Sarah for a moment. He wondered how she could be so ready to jump into a relationship so soon after getting divorced. It took Ben almost two years to even consider dating another woman.

"I just don't find it that easy," Ben said.

"It's not. I guess I just won't let him win."

"Who?"

"My ex."

"What do you mean?"

"I mean if I become bitter, not saying that you're bitter of course," Sarah added.

"Oh no, of course not." Ben laughed.

"And, well, decided I would never love again. He wins."

"I never thought of it like that."

"I've never thought of it any other way. I mean, I don't do it to get back at him. I just have no intentions of giving up my dreams just because he messed up."

"Dreams?"

"To grow old with someone."

"You have a strange view on life, Sarah Harris."

"Probably, but it's how I feel."

"No, I don't mean that in a bad way. I'm sorry. It's almost refreshing. It's honest. I had almost forgotten what that sounded like." Ben smiled.

"I have the same feeling about you," Sarah said, looking into Ben's eyes.

They dined and revealed things about themselves they had no intention of sharing, finding each other's company almost natural. Everything seemed natural.

They finished up their meal and headed out to the only movie theater in town.

The day had made its way into night as they pulled into the parking lot. With some time on their hands, Ben and Sarah decided to sit in Ben's truck and talk for a while.

They watched young and old couples alike make their way into the theater. They reminisced about their younger days and how fast time seemed to be flying by.

And with each word, each syllable of their pasts, these two lonely roads seemed to be winding down and intersecting. Here were two people who never should have met, who were suddenly thrown together as if it were destiny, as if the bend in the road was always there.

They finally entered the crowded theater, watching the schools of teenagers drift from one group to the other. The darkened theater corridor was lit only by the rows of framed posters. The two made their way into the theater and found their seats. As they sat, they immediately continued their conversation.

Ben sat and listened intently to Sarah as she explained how she hasn't been able to find a permanent job. He realized the extents this woman had to go through to keep her family together, while working two jobs, and for some unknown reason he felt the urge to help her.

"So how are you are making it, if you don't mind me asking?" Ben asked, concerned.

"The grace of God."

"Really?"

"It has to be, because I have no idea."

"Well, I'd sure hire you."

"You would, huh."

"Yeah, you're kind of nice to look at."

"Oh, so you wouldn't worry about my skills or work ethics?"

"No, not really. Like I said, you're pretty nice to look at."

"Oh, you," Sarah said, playfully pushing against his shoulder, making his body sway over toward the next seat.

The previews to the movie started to run when suddenly…

"Excuse me," a large man who was sitting behind them tapped Ben on the shoulder.

"Could you please be quiet? We aren't able to hear the movie."

Ben and Sarah looked at each other, each thinking how rude it was for the man to come up to them when the only thing playing was the previews.

The movie previews continued as Ben and Sarah absentmindedly again found themselves lost in conversation, when a man from the other side of the theater came over to them making the same request, to please be quiet because they were being too loud.

Ben, embarrassed, became silent, turning toward the screen. After settling into the movie, the two of them only whispered to each other a couple of times, making sure to keep their voices down to avoid another embarrassing episode from the crowd, whom they were sure all hated them now, and were making plans to throw them out should they provide any type of distraction at all.

When the movie finally ended, Ben got up to leave thinking he had ruined their first date. Sarah, sensing this, suddenly had an urge to grab Ben's hand to comfort him. She walked up behind him as they exited the theater, and Ben felt Sarah's hand slide into his as he gently gripped his large hand around hers. He looked down, surprised that Sarah had made this gesture, and then looked up and smiled, as they made their way out of the theater.

"I sure wish you hadn't been so loud in the movie," Ben teased Sarah.

"Me? I think they were talking to you," Sarah quickly rebuked.

"No, no it couldn't be me. I'm not that loud," Ben lied, knowing how his laugh usually resonated around a room.

"So, you're saying I am?" Sarah laughed.

"Well, both of those men did approach you. And I couldn't help but notice how loud you were bein'."

"How loud I was bein'?" Sarah said jokingly, as they walked hand in hand to Ben's truck. Ben opened Sarah's door, letting her climb in and then leaned into the cab just inches from Sarah's face. Sarah took a deep breath as if she was afraid he was going to kiss her.

Ben just smiled. "Are you making fun of my accent again?" Ben teased.

"Nooo…" Sarah said quietly as she caught her breath, "Thanks for the movie."

"You're very welcome," Ben answered, hesitating for a moment as if he thought about kissing her, but then slowly backed out, closing Sarah's door.

When they finally arrived at Sarah's duplex, Ben and Sarah sat in the truck talking. They got so caught up in the conversation that they lost track of time, neither one of them wanting the date to end. When Ben finally did check the time, it was almost 1:00 in the morning.

"You probably need to get home?" Sarah asked.

"I'm okay," Ben said.

"I know, but it's getting late and you have a long drive back."

"Oh, I'll be all right," Ben said, still languishing in the moment. "So maybe we can do this again sometime."

"I'd like that."

"Good, I'll call you toward the end of the week." Ben then climbed out of the truck and went to open Sarah's door, and walked her to the front door.

Sarah secretly hoped Ben would kiss her goodnight. She didn't show it, but walked intentionally slow beside him, her small palm resting in his hand. Ben waited for Sarah to open her door, and without any warning, Ben leaned down and tenderly kissed Sarah goodnight.

And he didn't ask. He just did it, as if he had been waiting to do it all night and couldn't wait one more moment. Sarah smiled and waved as Ben started to walk away, looking back once.

"Good night, Sarah Harris."

"Good night, Ben." And she slowly closed the door behind her.

Chapter Twenty-Five
The Wait

And he didn't call.

Sarah had to stop and think about what Ben had said. *I'll call you in a week.* Did he mean Thursday, Friday? *He sure wasn't one to rush things*, Sarah thought to herself.

Earlier in the week, Dave called Sarah about arranging another date. He had left a message on her machine and said he would call back, but Sarah wasn't sure she wanted to see him again. She felt almost drawn to Ben. She immediately had very strong feelings for him, and she wasn't sure why. Sarah thought Ben could possibly be the real thing. Maybe he was the one she had been praying for.

Sarah's temporary job was about to end. She only had a couple of weeks left. Her manager tried to keep her working past their hiring phase, but found it hard to drum up work to keep Sarah busy. Sarah started applying to the city and state as positions became available.

At least once a week, Sarah and the kids got invited over to her parents' house for dinner. Her parents, seeing how Sarah struggled to make ends meet, made sure to invite them over whenever they could. Sarah enjoyed not having to be responsible for another meal. Her parents pampered her whenever she and the kids joined them for dinner. They cooked for them and cleaned up, telling Sarah to sit and relax. They didn't have much, but they shared whatever they had. Angels seem to come in many shapes and sizes, and parents seem to sign up as soon as you are born, a selfless love innate to most parents' souls.

Sunday – after church – was usually the day Sarah and the kids made their way over to her parents' house and this Sunday was no different.

"So how was your date?" Sarah's mother, Claire, asked.

"It was great. He works for Westchester and he farms."

"A farmer, huh?"

"Yep."

"Oh, that's funny since you know nothing about farming."

"I know, but he's so nice, Mom. I have a weird feeling about him."

"What do you mean a weird feeling?"

"I don't know. It's hard to explain."

Claire looked over with her eyebrows lowered in disapproval. "I still think it's way too soon for you to be getting involved with anyone."

"Oh, it wasn't too soon for Jack. He's got someone."

"Yeah, but still, you shouldn't rush into anything."

"I'm not rushing, Mom. And I'm not going to get involved with someone I don't think would be good for me and the kids."

"Oh, and this man's different?" Claire said shortly.

"I don't know. He seems to be."

The heated conversation abruptly ended just as Lily and Jackson walked into the large dining room, where Sarah and her mother were located, right off the kitchen.

Her parents' home was dated with seventies' décor that was left over from Dan's first wife. Her mom and Dan had been married for almost nine years when Sarah found herself single again.

Her stepdad was a godsend. He was the only grandpa the kids ever knew. He took her kids in as if they were his own grandkids, and Sarah in as if she were his daughter. Dan had also been a cook in the army, explaining why he always made enough food to feed one.

"What are we having?" Lily asked.

"Spaghetti and meatballs," answered Grandma, as Grandpa cooked over the stove, stopping every few seconds to join in the conversation.

"Almost ready," Grandpa yelled.

Lily hurried to get everyone drinks as Sarah and her mother started setting the table. The odor of the Italian meatballs now filled the room with an aroma of garlic and Italian spices.

Sarah left the room to go and call Saline and Hope into the dining room. Saline, on the phone with one of her friends, waved her mom off, finishing up her conversation. Hope lay across her grandparents' bed, watching a movie on their private television. And they all felt at home.

Sarah's parents' home was a place they could all go and relax. No one had to worry about what to cook and even the clean-up was taken care of. Sarah would always offer to help, but her parents always refused, telling her to go sit and relax.

To Sarah, this was her sanctuary. This was the one place where she could kick up her feet and rest, drowning in the current movie on Lifetime. Sarah would usually fall asleep on the couch and be awakened by one of the kids asking to finally go home.

"So, Saline, how's school going?" Grandpa Dan asked when they all sat down to dinner.

"Good, Grandpa."

"So, how many dates have you had so far?"

"None, Grandpa."

Her Grandfather then smiled. "Oh, that's not what I heard."

"I don't have any boyfriends," Saline defended. "The boys at my school are all stupid."

"What about you, Lily?"

"She has one, Grandpa," Jackson interjected.

"Oh, she does?" Dan responded, raising an eyebrow.

"Yeah, his name is Darren," giggled Hope.

"Darren, huh."

Lily, now embarrassed, defended her current single status. "He's not my boyfriend. He's just a friend."

"Just a friend, huh?" teased her Grandfather.

"That's what she tells us," said Sarah, as she filled her plate with spaghetti noodles and meatballs.

"Dan, you leave the kids alone," said Claire.

"I'm just trying to get at the truth. You leave me alone, woman," Dan said and continued the inquisition. "And what about you, Jackson?"

"I don't like girls."

"No? What's wrong with 'em?"

"They're okay as friends, but they don't like to play dodgeball because they say we throw the ball too hard."

"Well, do you throw it too hard?" asked Grandpa.

"Yeah, because we want to win."

"Oh... okay," laughed Dan. "What about you, Hope?"

"What, Grandpa?"

"You got yourself a boyfriend, yet?"

"No," Hope managed to spit out after removing her thumb from her mouth. "I mean, I had a boyfriend in Nebraska."

"You did?"

"Yep."

"What was his name?"

"Zach."

"Zach, huh. Well, I'll have to check him out."

And without hesitation Hope continued, "It's okay Grandpa, because he's my 'ex' boyfriend."

"Oh, your ex-boyfriend, huh," Dave said, not able to hold in his laughter, as everyone at the table started to roar, leaving Hope sitting at the table, dumbfounded on what could be so funny.

"What?" said Hope innocently.

"Nothing, sweetheart. Eat your spaghetti." Sarah smiled.

Ben, still thinking about his date with Sarah, had to get up early the next morning to help Mike get some cattle moved at the farm. Tired from his date, Ben walked into his parents' kitchen a little less spirited than the previous morning.

"Mornin', you two," Ben said.

"Mornin', Ben."

"So how are you two doing this mornin'?" Ben asked as he headed to the kitchen table to sit down. His father had his pipe lit and hanging out the side of his mouth as he read the morning paper, holding his magnifying glass just inches away from the small print. His mother, standing next to the coffee maker, brought his dad over a cup of coffee.

"So, you going to the party tonight?"

"No, Dad. I had a late-night last night, so I might just hit the sack."

"Oh, well…" Ben's dad hesitated. "Mike said you might be going."

"I thought about it, but I think I'll just stay in."

His dad, hesitant to push too hard for information, reiterated, "Well, you're more than welcome to join us."

"I know. I just need to catch up on some sleep."

"So, what kept you up so late?"

"Oh, just hanging out with some friends."

His dad, nodding his head in approval, then stated, "Good… good, it's good to get out."

"Yes, it is. Well, you two need anything before I head out?"

"No, we're fine," Ben's mother answered.

"Okay then. I'm going put up some more fence. Tell Mike I'll be on the north fork if he needs to get a hold of me. My phone doesn't always work out there."

"Will do," his father answered, returning to his paper.

Ben headed out the door as the wind rushed into his face, slamming the screen door behind him. He walked over to the white feed truck and climbed in.

He couldn't seem to shake the urge to call Sarah right away. He had told her he would call her in a week because he didn't want to seem too pushy. After all, his friends at work told him never to call a woman too fast after the first date, because she would think he was pressuring her to go out again. Ben thought it was all nonsense, but thought since he had told her a week he should wait. He figured one more week in this life wouldn't mean all that much in the grand scheme of things. He had made it this far on his own, and a few more days wasn't going to kill him.

Ben started the engine, putting the truck into gear as he hoped the week would go quickly. He started down the lane, looking over the cattle as they gathered near the fence. They all moved in a herd, following the feed truck along the fence line, like a swarm of bees to honey.

Ben knew Sarah hadn't been divorced all that long and figured she would probably want to date around. No use getting his hopes up, Ben thought to himself. Sarah just seemed so different from other women he had met.

Ben sat and daydreamed, feeling the warm sun break through his windshield, squinting his eyes in the sunlight as he moved out of the lane and onto the main dirt road.

The week seemed to drag as Sarah waited in anticipation of Ben's call. Her fear was that she would be at work and miss his call. She thought she should have given him her cell number, but was reluctant to give it to anyone she had just started dating. The kids were infamous for not answering the phone and letting the machine pick up. Sarah feared Ben would feel awkward about leaving a message.

After getting off work on Thursday, Sarah rushed home from the department store to see if Ben had called. She entered the duplex, hearing the phone ringing as she opened the door, and the kids were just sitting there in front of the television letting it ring.

"Answer the phone!" Sarah screamed out as she entered the kitchen with her hands full. Saline and Lily just looked up at her with the phone ringing right beside them.

"Answer the phone!" Sarah said again, trying to get to the phone as Lily juggled the receiver, panicked at her mother's voice and finally greeted the caller.

"Oh yeah, hold on. She just got home," was all Lily said, as she rolled her eyes at Sarah, wondering why her mother was freaking out.

"Hello," said Sarah out of breath.

"Sarah?"

"Yes."

"Hi, it's Dave."

"Oh… hi, Dave…" Sarah said, forgetting that Dave was supposed to call also.

"How are you?"

"Oh, I'm fine, and you?" Sarah said, trying not to sound disappointed.

"I'm good. I left a message a couple of days ago. I wasn't sure if you got it."

"Oh, yeah, I'm sorry, I've been working and…"

"No, it's fine. Are you busy?"

"Well, I just got home from work."

"Oh, well, would you like me to call back another time? I know it's late."

"Yes, if you don't mind. It's just the kids are still up, and they have school tomorrow."

"Not a problem. Well, I won't keep you. I'll talk to you later."

Sarah got off the phone, disappointed Ben hadn't called. She wondered if he had called earlier when she wasn't home and the kids hadn't answered. Irritated, Sarah began to pick up the kitchen and told the kids to get ready for bed.

"Mom, I have a spelling test tomorrow," Jackson said.

"Did Saline or Lily go over the words with you?" Sarah asked.

"No, they didn't have time," Jackson said, as Sarah looked over annoyed at Saline and Lily.

"What?" was all Saline said.

"You guys didn't have time to go over his words?"

"No, Mom, we didn't," Saline said, now aggravated as she walked past Sarah stomping up the stairs. Sarah just dropped the subject, being too tired to get into an argument.

"All right, sweetie, go get 'em. Hurry up because you need to start getting ready for bed."

Lily, curious, asked, "Who was on the phone, Mom?"

"It was Dave. The guy I went out with a couple of weeks ago."

"You didn't like him?"

"No, I did. I was just hoping it was Ben."

"Dave, Ben, I wish I had that many guys calling me." Lily smiled.

"How come you two didn't give Jackson his spelling test?" Sarah questioned, tired and irritated that she now had to do it.

"I had a test to study for," Lily answered.

"So why are you two watching television?"

"We just started watching it. Gosh, we were going to give him a test," Lily said, now irritated by her mother's comments.

"All right, where's Hope?"

"She's putting her pajamas on. She just got out of the tub."

"Jackson!" Sarah yelled up.

"I can't find my backpack," Jackson yelled back.

Sarah began to look around the room. The kids' backpacks were lying next to the front door, next to their shoes.

"It's down here."

Jackson ran down the stairs, jumping from the second step to the floor and then rushing toward his Spider-Man backpack, tackling it as if he were a linebacker in the Super Bowl.

"Here it is," Jackson announced.

Sarah settled down on the couch and Lily headed upstairs. Hope then came trotting down the stairs in her nightgown, curling up to Sarah on the couch.

"Can you read to me, Mommy?"

"Oh, sweetie, why don't you have Lily or Saline read to you?"

"No, I want you."

"I have to give Jackson his spelling test," Sarah said, as she saw Hope's disappointed face. "I'm sorry, sweetie, but it's late."

"All right," was all Hope said as she moped back up the stairs.

"Saline, can you please read Hope a story?" Sarah yelled up the stairs.

"I will," Lily yelled down.

Sarah, feeling guilty that she didn't read to Hope, yelled up the stairs, "Thank you, Lily."

Jackson had his pencil and paper ready on the glass coffee table that sat in front of the sofa. "I'm ready, Mom."

Sarah went through the list one by one. Jackson only missed one word. Sarah had him write the word he missed ten times and gave it to him again before he headed upstairs. Just then the phone rang again. Sarah looked at her watch wondering who could be calling so late.

"Hello?" Sarah said.

"Hi, Sarah, sorry to call so late, but I wasn't sure what time you got home from work," Ben apologized.

"Oh, no, it's fine. I actually just got the kids off to bed," Sarah said, feeling rejuvenated by Ben's voice.

"Oh, have you been home for a while?"

"No, about forty-five minutes."

"I'm sorry. I would have called you earlier if I had known."

"No, it's fine," Sarah said, excited to hear from Ben.

"You sound a little tired. Would you like me to call back?"

"No, no," Sarah said swiftly, not wanting to hang up. "It's fine really. It's actually the only part of the day when I'm somewhat alone."

"Okay. So how was your day, pretty lady?"

Sarah smiled as she could hear Ben's country accent come through the phone. She was dumbfounded at Ben's ability to say just what she needed to hear, when she needed to hear it. When he talked to her, it was always all about her. He never complained about his day and was always so positive. He seemed so easy-going, taking life one day at a time.

Sarah caught herself complaining a few times about her life and Ben would always listen attentively and somehow put it all into perspective, telling her with uncommon certainty that it would all work out somehow. She loved that about him.

"You sure seemed to take your sweet time calling me, Mr. Cool," Sarah teased.

"What?"

"A week. You waited a whole week." Sarah walked back to the couch, curling her legs beneath her as she melted into the cushions.

"I told you I would."

"I know you did." Sarah laughed. "I guess I'm just not used to such honesty."

"I don't know how to be any way else."

"No, well, I love that about you."

"Well, good or bad, you'll be gettin' the truth from me."

"Was that a part of your country up-bringin'?"

"I guess so. My parents never stood for any lyin'. You didn't lie to my parents and live to tell about it."

"Really?"

"It's just the way they were."

And they got lost in conversation, making plans to see each other on Saturday. Saline and Lily looked on from the staircase, trying not to interrupt as they saw their mother smiling again for the first time in months. They walked downstairs, pretending to get a glass of water as Sarah smiled at them. After getting their water, they headed back up the stairs, giggling at their mother who was acting like a lovesick teenager, and somehow, they knew, even before she did…

They knew their mother was falling in love again…

Chapter Twenty-Six
Swing Your Partner Round and Round

Now love was not the first thing on Ben's mind when he signed on the dotted line at the single's agency. But then again… Ben never expected Sarah.

Ben was called in for overtime and arrived four hours early for work that Friday. The schedule was light with no new changeovers on the line. Later that day, Ben headed for the breakroom where he ran into Sam Garcia, one of the engineers at the plant. Sam had a gift for gab that often had the breakroom rolling and today was no different as several of the employees gathered into the small tiled area warming up their dinner in one of the two microwaves provided to them. Ben, having plans to get on the computer during his lunch hour, hurried toward the refrigerator housing his dinner.

"How's it going, Ben?" Sam asked. Ben noticed that Alex was sitting next to Sam, so he headed over to talk to his two friends for a minute.

"I'm good, Sam. How are things with you?"

"Fine. Hey, I'm having a poker game tomorrow evening and was wondering if you wanted to come. Alex here said you like to play."

"Oh, he did, did he? Why aren't you going?" Ben said, looking over toward Alex.

Alex shifted in his seat as he debated on his answer. "Hell, I don't have the kind of money to keep up with these guys."

"The heck you don't," responded Ben.

"I'm just not lucky at poker," Alex said. "You like the game."

"Well, regularly I would, Sam, and I appreciate you askin' me, but I have plans tomorrow night."

"What plans?" asked Alex.

"I got plans," said Ben, trying not to divulge any unnecessary information.

Sam nudged Alex's shoulder, determined to continue to interrogate Ben. "You got a date?"

"I might," responded Ben, immediately regretting his words, realizing he had already probably said too much.

"A date with who?" asked Alex.

"A woman," Ben said, opening the refrigerator door to find his food, hoping that this would stop the cross-examination of his personal life. But his friends were having way too much fun to let him drop the conversation at this point.

"What woman?" asked Sam. "Does she work here?"

"No, it's no one you two know," Ben said, slamming the microwave door and hitting start.

"How'd you meet her?" asked Sam. "We're just concerned. We don't want our baby boy going out with just any riffraff."

"Now, that's none of you all's business," Ben replied.

"None of our business," Alex joined in. "I've told you about every date I've had in the last year."

"Yeah, all two of them," announced Ben.

"That's more than you've had," teased Alex.

"Yeah, who is she?" Sam reiterated. "I mean, can we all see her or is this just some woman only you can see?"

"I'm not about to tell you two losers."

Ben then quickly grabbed his heated lunch and backed out of the breakroom doors, leaving them with a sly smile, as he heard both his friends calling out his name in unison. He headed past the noisy machines and into the office where the department's computer was kept.

Sarah had said she wanted go dancing. Ben – not being a dancer – figured this might be their last date due to his lack of rhythm. Flicking on the computer, Ben typed in the words *Country Music Dance Steps*. Ben shut the door, locking it. Faint fumbling noises began to seep under the door and make their way out toward the corridor, as Ben tried to follow the small image displayed on the computer screen, stumbling around the small confined area, hoping nobody could hear.

Saturday finally rolled around as Ben pulled up to Sarah's garage door almost fifteen minutes early for their date. Ben ran dance steps through his head as he moved his feet to the left and to the right, under the brake and gas pedal. Feeling like he couldn't stall any longer, he walked up to Sarah's front door, ringing the doorbell. Saline and Lily, Sarah's eldest two children, answered the door.

"I'm Saline," Sarah's oldest said, sticking out her hand to greet Ben. He immediately noticed what looked like Saline's younger sister, Lily, standing next to her.

"Nice to meet you, Saline, and you must be Lily."

Lily smiled, elated that Ben knew her name. "Yep, I'm Lily, nice to meet you, Ben."

At that moment, Jackson and Hope came running down the stairs. They stopped for a moment to eye their new visitor, and then crouched down in front of the television. The two of them giggled and stole glimpses of the strange man who had come to take their mother on a date.

"Are you my mom's date?" asked Jackson, now flipping his legs over his head in a stalled backward roll.

"Yep, that's me," said Ben. "Hey, doesn't that hurt?" Ben laughed, wondering if he had ever been that flexible.

Ben stood behind the couch not sure if he should sit down.

"Nope, I can flip all the way over," said Jackson as he finished the roll. "See…"

"Don't do that in the living room," Saline said sternly. Jackson immediately sat up, entranced again by the cartoon on the television.

"You must be Hope," Ben said, turning his attention toward Sarah's youngest daughter.

Ben smiled as Hope turned around with her thumb in her mouth, clutching a blanket, giving Ben a quick smile, still not relinquishing her thumb, and then turned back toward the cartoon. Ben took a seat on the sofa as Saline and Lily typed something into their computer.

Feeling she was being rude, Saline turned back toward Ben. "So, you work on a farm?"

"Yes, well, and I work at Westchester," Ben said, feeling more comfortable talking with the older kids, being that his nieces were about the same age.

"So, you're a senior this year?" Ben asked.

"Yep, I'm graduating this year."

"Your mom was telling me how you had to start a new school this year."

"Yeah, I did. But it wasn't so bad. I've made a lot of friends."

"Good… good."

"So, you're taking my mom dancing?"

"Yep, that's the rumor."

"Well, you should know, she's a really good dancer."

"Oh…" was all Ben could manage to get out, feeling the room getting warmer.

A few seconds later, Sarah made her way down the split stairway dressed in jeans, a black shirt, and black boots. Sarah had left her hair curly, leaving long waves forming around her face. Ben absentmindedly stood up, not realizing he was doing it. He looked at Sarah as if it were the first time he had ever seen her. It had felt like ages to him. He was almost breathless as she made her way toward him. He had this uncanny urge to look around to see if she was really heading over to talk to someone else, but there was no one else. *Surely this beautiful woman is not lighting up to see him*, he thought to himself.

"Hi there, stranger," Sarah said, tugging at Ben's shirt.

"Well, hello," Ben answered.

"Have you met everyone?"

"Yep, we all met. We're just getting to know one another."

"Mom, can we have popcorn?" Jackson asked.

"Yes, but just one bag."

"Yes!" responded Jackson, as he hopped up, making his way to the kitchen.

Ben, now looking at Sarah, was oblivious to anyone else in the room as Saline and Lily started to giggle.

"You ready to go?" Sarah said, reaching down to grab her purse and jacket from the bench in the entryway.

"I'm ready if you are," said Ben.

"We'll see you guys later."

"Bye, Mom," Hope and Jackson yelled out.

"I'll try to have her back early?" Ben joked, talking to Lily and Saline.

"Nah, we trust you," said Saline.

"Oh, you do?" said Sarah.

"Yeah, bring her back whenever you want." Lily laughed.

"Alrighty." laughed Ben, as he and Sarah exited the duplex.

Ben immediately slipped his hand over Sarah's as they walked toward his truck.

"So, how are you today, pretty lady?" Ben asked.

"I'm good… now."

"I was just about to say the same thing," Ben said, opening the passenger door for Sarah, hesitating to lean over her. "You know I wanted to kiss you as soon as I saw you."

"Why didn't you?"

"Well, the kids and stuff," Ben said and leaned down and kissed her without hesitation.

The two sat at an Italian restaurant conversing over candlelight. They looked into each other's eyes as if they had known each other for a lifetime. The conversation flowed so naturally, almost able to tell what the other was thinking before it was said. People around them stopped and stared at this couple who held one another's hand over the table, admiring the young couple who seemed to be so much in love.

"So, dancing, huh?" Ben finally said.

"Yep, I thought it would be fun. Don't you?"

"Ahhhh, sure."

Sensing Ben's sarcasm, Sarah realized she hadn't really asked if Ben liked to dance or not. "Do you not like to dance, Ben? I'm sorry, I should have asked you."

"No, it's fine. It's what you like to do."

"Yeah, but I think I just saw a look of terror in your eyes."

"No, not terror. I was just thinking this may be our last date once you have seen me on the dance floor. It's usually not very pretty."

"Oh, you can't be that bad," Sarah said.

"Oh no... but I can."

"Do you want to do something else?"

"No, it'll be fine. I'm sure you have nine other toes that will probably make it," Ben kidded.

Sarah, resting her chin in her right hand, asked, "Oh Ben, you do hate it, don't you?"

"I wouldn't say hate. I don't know how, never learned."

Sarah then sat up. "Can you dance to slow songs?"

"Yeah, I think I could manage those."

"Oh, you'll be fine then."

"Okay, but I can't be held responsible for any physical injury, yours or mine."

Sarah laughed out loud, squeezing Ben's hand, and leaned over and kissed him softly on the lips without even thinking about it. As if it was a natural reaction.

"What was that for?" Ben asked.

"Oh, just cause you're so cute."

They arrived outside the dance hall early. There were only a few of the regulars on the dance floor. Ben stopped and looked at them and was surprised by how graceful each couple was. The 'early bird' older couples danced, song after song, twirling their partner around the dance floor, trying to get in some time before the younger crowd began to arrive. Ben and Sarah found a table near the dance floor.

"They seem to be enjoying themselves," Ben commented.

"Yes, they do. See, it's not that scary."

"Oh, you don't expect me to do that," Ben said, now pointing to an older man with a black cowboy hat, twirling his partner like a spinning top around the floor with ease.

"Well, not on the first try," Sarah said, teasing Ben.

"Well, I wouldn't expect it on the fifth or six either." Ben laughed, now more nervous, taking a large gulp of his drink.

Just then a slow song came on as the lights dimmed and the rest of the elderly couples made their way out to the dance floor. They moved with such precision, such grace, Ben actually found himself gazing at them, almost envious of their natural rhythm.

"Well, shall we give it a try?" Ben said, as the younger crowd started to make their way into the dance hall.

"I'd love that," Sarah answered, taking his hand. Ben held her hand behind him as they made their way to the dance floor.

"She's Everything" by Brad Paisley rang out through the dance hall as Ben took Sarah in his arms, swaying her gently across the floor. Sarah leaned close to Ben, having to look up to meet his glance. He held her hand near his heart, engulfed in his palm and put his other hand around her waist. Ben felt Sarah's thin physique press against him, as the sway of their bodies fell into a natural rhythm.

"You aren't so bad," Sarah said, gazing up at Ben.

"Oh sure, I haven't stepped on your foot yet."

"No, really."

"Well, this is my favorite part."

"What?"

"Holding you in my arms."

The two of them danced as if no one else was in the room. The older couples turned and smiled, remembering what it felt like to be young and in love.

As the song ended, Ben and Sarah started to head toward their table. Suddenly, without warning, a familiar voice called out from behind Ben…

"Uncle Ben? Is that you?"

Ben turned around to see Tina, Rachael's older sister, making a beeline toward Ben and Sarah.

"Uncle Ben?" Tina yelled again. Ben turned slightly, glancing over his shoulder, but kept walking, pulling Sarah along with him. Sarah, now hearing Ben's name being called, turned and looked over toward the voice, as a young blonde woman made her way straight toward them.

"Uncle Ben! It's me, Tina!"

"Yes, I see you, Tina," Ben said, turning toward his niece, obviously annoyed she had spotted him.

"What are you doing here?" Tina said excitedly, looking over at Sarah. The two women now standing on each side of Ben waited to be introduced.

"I'm doing what you're doing, dancin'."

"Since when do you dance?"

"Since today, okay." Ben then noticed Sarah's stare and reluctantly introduced them. "I'm sorry… Tina, this is Sarah. Sarah, this is my nosy niece, Tina."

"Nice to meet you, Tina," Sarah said, not quite understanding Ben's reluctance to introduce her.

"Nice to meet you. Excuse me, I've got to call my mom." Tina then blurted out, racing toward the women's restroom, cellphone in hand.

"No, you don't," Ben yelled out behind her.

"I'll be right back," Tina answered, ignoring Ben's comment, as she flew through the crowd.

"So, that's your niece, huh?" Sarah asked.

"Yes, one of them. I'm sorry, it's just now my whole family will know I was out here. It's just, I don't normally, you know, dance."

"Oh… well… do you want to go?" Sarah said, thinking possibly Ben was embarrassed to be seen with her.

"No, it's fine. They would find out eventually anyway."

"Okay," Sarah said, taking her seat, not sure what Ben meant by what he said.

Ben, sensing Sarah's change in demeanor, tried to explain himself, "I mean, it has nothin' to do with you. I just didn't want anyone to know I was seein' someone yet."

"Why?"

"I don't know, the questions, I guess. It's fine. I'm over-reacting, I'm sure; I'm sorry. Do you want to dance this one?" Ben said, not knowing why he said that because it was a fast song and Ben had no idea what he would do once he got out there.

"No, I'm fine, Ben," Sarah said laughing, having not seen Ben so insecure before. He always seemed so confident. Sarah caught Tina heading back in their direction. "Here comes your niece, again. Be nice."

"I can't believe it. So, how did you two meet?" Tina blurted out, not waiting to be invited to sit down as she took the open seat. "Was it here?"

"None of your business," Ben said jokingly. Sarah turned toward him feeling like he was still over-reacting to his niece's obvious joy to see him out with someone.

"Okay, well…" Tina said, trying to calm her excitement, realizing that she may be overstaying her welcome. "You two should dance. And have fun… I have to get back to my date, but I'll be back."

"Great, we'll be waiting," said Ben sarcastically, as he and Sarah leaned against the table. "Sorry, my niece tends to get very excited about things."

"No, it's fine. She seemed very nice, and she really seems to care about you."

Just then, another slow song came on and Ben asked Sarah to dance again. They headed out to the dance floor just in time to see his niece and her date take the floor. His niece laughed and pointed at him, waving. Ben, still annoyed with his niece, took Sarah into his arms, and Sarah couldn't help but laugh, laying her head against Ben's chest. Ben started to move more naturally. He looked down at Sarah as if she were meant to be right where she was. He lifted her head and gazed into her eyes as his niece looked on. Sarah smiled at him as he held her chin up toward his face.

"What?" Sarah asked.

"You're so beautiful," Ben said, without even blinking. He pulled Sarah close to him and held her tight, finishing the song and moving into a second without stopping, oblivious to those around them.

After the song ended, Ben excused himself to go to the restroom and Sarah sat staring out at all the couples dancing. Just as the next fast song started, Sarah felt a tap on her shoulder. Startled, and almost spilling her drink, she turned around to see Brad standing right beside her.

"Hello, Sarah."

Sarah sat speechless. Her mouth dropped open as she quickly looked around the room for Ben and for Ben's niece. Images of the nightmarish evening with Brad flashed before her as she wondered what he could possibly want.

"Brad," Sarah managed to say.

"I won't take up too much of your time. I just wanted to apologize for the other night."

"No, it's fine," Sarah said, trying to end the conversation quickly while looking around nonchalantly for Ben's niece, who had been eyeing them all evening.

"I realize I screwed up, and I'm sorry. I just wanted you to know that I'm not usually like that," he said, moving around to look Sarah in the eye and blocking her view to Ben's niece.

Sarah tried to think of something to get rid of him before Ben got back. "Okay, ah… I'm here with someone."

"I know. I saw you dancing. I just wanted to apologize, that's all. I hope you will accept my apology. I am not usually like that."

"Well, I appreciate it, but I am not sure this is the time or place," Sarah said, not knowing what else to say as she felt her skin begin to crawl. Yet, for some reason, Brad seemed to hold his position right next to the table.

"Well, I can't leave you alone for a minute," Ben said loudly, returning to the table as Brad's cowboy hat turned toward Ben.

"No worries. I was just apologizing to the lady," Brad said confidently.

"Okay, and you are?" Ben asked, staring at Brad.

"Just an old friend," Brad said, now tipping his hat. "Again, I'm sorry, Sarah. You two have a nice evening." And Brad picked up his drink and walked back toward the bar.

Sarah just sat there stunned, not knowing what to say to Ben.

Ben sat down next to her, taking her hand.

"Are you okay? You look like you just saw a ghost."

"More like a nightmare. I'm fine. Just one more bad decision I made not so long ago."

Ben leaned against Sarah and whispered, "Do you want to get out of here?"

"Yes," Sarah said, relieved, as if he were reading her mind.

Once they got outside, Ben strolled next to Sarah, holding her hand.

"I swear, I leave you for one minute and every guy in the place is hittin' on you."

"What?"

"So, how do you know him? If you don't mind my askin'."

"Just from here. I was here one evening with a friend... and, well, it's a long story."

"Sorry, it's really none of my business."

"No, I... I just misjudged him. He came off as this nice guy, and in reality he's far from it. Can we just leave it at that?"

"Yeah, it just seemed like he kinda liked you maybe a little bit."

"Well, it's totally one sided. I don't want to have anything to do with him."

"Feel like some ice cream?"

"What?" Sarah laughed.

"Ice cream always makes everything better, don't you think?"

"I do. You must have read my mind. It's my go-to comfort food." Sarah then laid her head on Ben's shoulder as he placed his arm around her, and they made their way to his truck.

They visited the nearest ice cream shop and headed back to Sarah's duplex. Sarah and Ben found themselves once again talking in the driveway until 1:00 in the morning.

"I guess I better go in," Sarah said, not really wanting to leave.

"I guess you better," Ben said, just sitting, looking at her.

"What?" Sarah said.

Ben took Sarah's face into his hands and leaned over, kissing her. He then grabbed her, bringing her in close to him, kissing her longingly, as if he didn't want to let her go. He felt her soft lips press against his.

Sarah leaned back, gasping from the familiarity of his kiss.

"What?" Ben said.

"Why does everything seem so easy with you?"

"What do you mean?" Ben asked.

"It's just feels natural, like this is what I'm supposed to be doing."

"Well, maybe it is." Ben laughed. "Why fight it?"

And before Sarah had a chance to answer, Ben kissed her one last time.

Chapter Twenty-Seven
And Then There Was Love

"You're going to get me fired."

"What are you talking about?" Sarah laughed as she hugged her pillow, while watching the late-night show, the television flashing a light across her complexion as she muted the sound.

"I'm dragging here at work." And Ben was. Between the farm and the plant and talking with Sarah each evening, Ben felt like a walking zombie. But he was also the happiest he had been in a long, long time.

"Do you want to hang up now?" Sarah asked, concerned about Ben's comment.

"Well, no. It's a nice tired," Ben said, changing the conversation. "So, how's the interviews going?"

Sarah shifted on the bed, setting the pillow behind her. "Good, I had another one this week. I just have to go in for my polygraph, and if I pass it, I'll have the job. So… how's work going for you?"

"Oh, lonely without you."

"You're sure are a sweet talker for a country boy."

"That's because you're so sweet."

"There you go again. Are you sure you're from the country?"

"Yes, and dang proud of it."

Sarah couldn't seem to help it. She couldn't wait to talk to Ben. Their days were on such different work schedules that they really didn't get a chance to talk until late into the night. And Sarah, who was as exhausted as Ben, was starting to feel normal again. She was beginning to feel whole again. And a lot of this, she felt had to do with Ben.

"So where are you taking me Saturday?"

"Where do you want to go?"

"Oh, I just thought out to dinner and then maybe a coffee shop or someplace where we can talk."

"Sounds good to me."

"Have the kids heard from their dad?" Ben asked.

"No, they haven't."

"Has he started sending you any money for them?"

"No, not yet."

Ben hesitated for a moment, not knowing how to continue without making Sarah feel like he was intruding. "You know, Sarah, if you need anything, I'm here for you."

Sarah stopped for a moment, tears welling up in her eyes. She took a deep breath because she didn't want Ben to hear the trembling in her voice. Had he really offered to help her, this man who had no real responsibility to her or the kids? Those words – that came out so easily – made her fall all the more deeply in love.

"We're okay right now, but thank you, Ben."

"Well, just remember, I am here if you need anything. Please don't hesitate."

"I won't," Sarah said.

"Promise."

"I promise."

. . . .

Everyone at the plant noticed that Ben had been in an exceptionally good mood lately. He was always very friendly, but there were times a sort of sadness would make its way to the surface. But lately, Ben walked around as if he had won the lottery. Ben started to slowly open up to his friends about Sarah as things with her became more and more serious. Ben's friends were happy for him but couldn't resist giving him a hard time about his newfound, ready-made family.

"Four kids?" Sam said. Ben was sorry he had told him.

"Yes, Sam, she has four kids," Ben said, looking away toward the large raging machine next to him. Sam had come up to do some work on the belts that had been getting stuck recently. The two men had to shout at each other over the loud noise of the gleaming machines as they worked.

"And you have no kids. That's hilarious."

"What's so strange about that? My mom had four kids," defended Ben.

"So, what does she look like anyway?" Sam asked while adjusting some belts.

"What does that matter?"

"She's probably as big as a house, and you just don't want to admit it," Sam kidded.

"She's not either."

"Okay, hey, I'm happy for you, man," Sam hesitated. "Hey, so, have you taken the whole family out yet?"

"No. Why?"

"Nothing, I just thought, well, if you needed to take them out, I could lend you my station wagon. So you, you know, have room for everyone." Sam, unable to control himself, hunched over grabbing his sides as Ben stood there grinning with his hands on his hips. "You know, you needin' the extra room and all."

"You just wait till you see her. You're going to be eatin' your words."

"Okay, but I have the keys to the station wagon on me if you need 'em."

"Uh-huh."

"Hey, what are friends for?"

"Get back to work." But even Ben had to chuckle at that one. Ben turned away so that Sam couldn't see him smiling.

"Are you bringing her to the Christmas party?"

Ben turned back around. "You know, I never thought to ask."

"You should."

"I think I will, just so I can have the pleasure of watchin' your mouth drop open when she walks in the room."

Sam yanked one of the belts free. "Yeah, whatever, Ben."

"That's if she hasn't already dumped me by then."

Saturday finally rolled around, and Ben was in a hurry to get back to his house. His family wondered if he was still seeing the woman that Tina saw him with at Harrington's. No one in the family had said anything to him, knowing how private he was. They figured he would tell them when he was good and ready. Everyone except Rachael...

"Hear you got a girlfriend," Rachael said while dusting off his coffee table, looking over at her uncle.

"Were you supposed to come and clean today?"

"No, but I figured I would. I thought you might be wantin' to have someone over for a romantic dinner."

"Oh, really? And where did you get your information? No, let me guess. Your sister."

"Yep, Tina said she was real pretty."

"And what else did Tina say?"

"That you can actually dance."

"She did, huh."

"Yep."

"Well, I just started seeing her, Rach. No use to jumping to any conclusions just yet. She may dump me any day now."

Rachel continued to dust around the wood. "Nah, she won't," Rachael said, getting up to grab the broom.

"Oh, why won't she?" Ben said while tucking in his new button-down shirt.

"Because she'll discover how nice you are."

"True," Ben said, smiling.

Rachael entered the kitchen and started to sweep the floor while continuing to question her uncle, "Have you taken her any flowers yet?"

"No, not yet."

"Well, some women like that. I don't. But some do."

"And when did you become such a worldly woman?"

"I have dated Scott for two years now."

"Oh, yeah, I forgot. I guess you got me beat," Ben said, now wondering if his niece was right. It had been a long time since he had dated anyone this long, and he wondered if he could be doing more to show Sarah what she meant to him.

He had never felt this way about a woman before. He worried about her and found himself wondering how he could help her and the kids. This was new to a man who had spent most of his life alone.

. . . .

Sarah was getting ready for her date with Ben when Saline walked in, grabbing the bed rail of Sarah's bed and spinning herself around, sitting, watching Sarah get ready.

"So, you going out with Ben again?" Saline asked Sarah.

"Yes, sweetie. I am."

"Where is he taking you?"

"I think we're just going to get something to eat and maybe stop by the bookstore or a coffee shop."

"He seems really nice, Mom."

"I think so. So, how are things with you and Matt?"

"Oh, so-so…"

"What do you mean? I thought you two were talking again."

"We are. It's just hard. His parents don't want him dating anyone." Sarah looked over at her oldest daughter, feeling her sadness. Sarah walked over and sat down beside her, taking Saline's hand in her own.

"What about that baseball player you were talking to?"

"He's all right. He's kind of full of himself though." Saline flopped down onto Sarah's bed, hugging one of her pillows.

"I thought you two went out last weekend."

"We did, but we always end up getting into an argument."

"Well, that's not a good sign."

Saline hesitated for a moment, turning her head toward Sarah, "Mom?"

"Yeah."

"I just wanted to say I'm very proud of you."

"Oh, sweetie, I'm very proud of you, too."

"No, I mean it. You have two jobs and all of us to take care of, and I don't know how you do it."

"Well, Gods a big part of it. Did you ever imagine you would actually have friends your senior year?"

"No…" Sarah then started to twirl a piece of Saline's hair in her fingers, just like she had done when Saline was a little girl. "Yeah… I guess it could have been much worse."

"Yes, it could've, but somehow we made it through."

"I know… It's just hard sometimes. I don't know why these things are happening to me. First the move, then Matt, and now… I can't figure out why I keep having to start over and over again."

"Well, sometimes we don't know why, sometimes we just have to trust… I know it is hard… and you have been so brave."

Saline laid in Sarah's bed staring at the wall, as Sarah brushed Saline's hair away from her face.

"Well, I've got to go get ready. I'm going out with Allison," Saline said, suddenly hoping back up from the bed.

"I like her."

"I know, right. She's like me but a blonde."

"Well, you two be careful."

"We're just going to the movies to drown our sorrows."

Sarah looked at Saline with her eyebrows narrowed.

"She just broke up with her boyfriend too," Saline explained.

"Oh, tell her I'm sorry, sweetie."

"It'll be fine. Have fun with Ben."

Just then Lily came hopping in. Lily, excited to have a rented movie for a change, was looking forward to watching it with Jackson and Hope.

"Mom, is it all right if I put the movie in now?"

"I guess so. Did Jackson and Hope finish their dinner?"

"Yeah. You sure look pretty."

"Thank you, sweetie."

"What time is Ben picking you up?"

"Anytime now."

Just then the doorbell rang and Sarah felt her heart skip a beat as she hurried to finish getting ready.

"I'll get it," yelled Lily. She ran down the stairs, trying to beat Jackson to the door.

"Whooo… isss… it?" asked Jackson, who had his face pressed against the door.

"Itt'ss… Bennn," Ben replied, mimicking Jackson.

"Get away from the door," Lily told Jackson, physically pushing him out of the way.

"You get away," Jackson said, pushing back.

"Stop. He's going to think you're crazy," Lily said firmly. "Now go sit down."

Jackson moved back reluctantly, waiting behind Lily to get a look at Ben.

The kids were still really curious about this man who kept showing up to take their mother out on dates, especially Jackson.

Lily slowly opened the door as Ben stood there with a bouquet of while lilies.

"Pretty…" Lily said, referring to the flowers.

"Oh… I just found these lying out here. Someone must have dropped them." smiled Ben.

"Sure you did. My mom is going to love 'em," Lily said.

"I hope so. How are you all doin' tonight?" Ben asked, as he walked into the foyer area.

"We're fine," said Jackson. "Where are you taking my mom tonight?" Jackson blurted out.

"Wherever she wants to go," Ben replied.

"You sure are coming here a lot." Hope giggled, standing on the sofa. Lily gave Hope a stern look.

"Tired of me already, are you?" Ben replied.

"Nah, you can come over," Jackson said.

"Well, I appreciate that. So, how's school going?" Ben asked, looking at Jackson.

"I don't like handwriting," Jackson said, bouncing down on the couch next to Hope.

"What's wrong with it?"

"It's hard. I don't like it," replied Jackson.

"I like school," said Hope proudly, taking a moment to remove her wrinkled thumb from her mouth.

"Well, that's good," Ben said while looking around and wondering what to say next. Just then Sarah came down the stairs. Ben watched her wondering if this nervous feeling in his stomach would ever go away. Her hair was straight and tied back into a ponytail that bounced behind her every time she moved. Ben stood staring, as Sarah walked straight up to him, looking at the white lilies in his hand.

"Are these for me?" Sarah asked.

"Yeah, well, they were giving them away at the grocery store."

"Oh, good thing you were there to grab 'em."

"That's what I thought," said Ben.

"Thank you, Ben. They're beautiful. Let me put them in some water." Sarah then headed into the kitchen and bent down, almost as if in slow motion, as Ben watched her flip back her hair and bring a clear vase out from underneath the sink. She slowly filled it with water as she turned and smiled at Ben.

"What?" Sarah said.

"Nothin'... Nothin'," Ben said, embarrassed she had caught him staring.

Lily smiled as she watched Ben watching her mother. Jackson and Hope settled in front of the television with a bowl of popcorn. Lily walked over and sat on the loveseat.

"Are you ready?" Sarah asked.

"Whenever you are, pretty lady," Ben said, as Sarah smiled back at him.

"I'll be back early. I have my cellphone if you need anything."

"Okay," Lily said, as she headed toward the television to put their movie in.

Hope then came running over to give Sarah a hug.

Then without warning, Hope suddenly turned toward Ben and reached around his long legs, giving him a hug. Ben, surprised, found himself in an awkward embrace, unsure of where to put his arms. Hope stood looking up at Ben almost as if she were about to salute him and said, "Bye, Ben."

"Bye, Hope," Ben said, as Hope giggled and ran back to the living room floor.

"See you, guys," Ben said, waving and looking over at Lily and Jackson, then turning to head for the door.

Sarah joined him, looking back at the kids and making sure the door was locked as they walked out.

Once they were out, Ben grabbed Sarah's hand and strolled with her toward his truck.

"Did I react okay?" Ben asked. "I wasn't expecting a hug from her."

"You did fine. Hope is very loving. I'm afraid she attaches herself to others rather quickly. It is her way of telling you she likes you."

"Oh, I'm glad. So, where do you want to eat?" Ben asked, changing the subject.

"Oh, it doesn't matter to me," Sarah responded.

"I heard about this great Japanese place. You want to try it?"

"Sounds good to me."

"Great, let's go," Ben said. Then he turned toward Sarah, leaned down and softly kissed her, holding her chin with one hand. "I wanted to do that as soon as I saw you come down the stairs."

"You did?" Sarah said, grabbing the back of Ben's head, and bringing his broad shoulders down toward her as she kissed him deeply.

"Wow," said Ben when he leaned back. "Gets better every time."

Sarah just smiled. "Yes, it does."

"Shall we go, my lady?"

The restaurant had dim lighting and was filled with Japanese architecture and artifacts. The women all wore elegant kimonos and wood sandals with socks. Their faces were all painted white, with dark red lipstick, and their black ebony hair was tied up in a bun on top of their heads.

Ben and Sarah were seated around a table that faced a large, sizzling grill. The cook had on a large oversized white chef's hat and matching apron. He amazed the crowd by flipping two large knives around his body while cutting up vegetables and meat right in front of them.

After a three-course meal, they headed for a quiet place at a nearby bookstore, where they sipped on hot chocolate. They tried to converse quietly, but broke out in laughter every few minutes, to the annoyance of those around them who were engulfed in their books and laptops.

The two ended up in Sarah's driveway again, this time ending up in a heavy make-out scene that left them looking more like a couple of lovesick teenagers.

"I better go in," Sarah finally said.

"What are you doing tomorrow?"

"The kids and I usually head to my parents after church."

"How would you like to come out to the farm tomorrow?"

"I'd like that. My parents will have the kids."

"They can come out too," Ben said.

"Thank you, but I think I'd like to wait on that."

"That's fine. They can come out another time."

"I just think we should get to know each other first before the kids start getting attached to you."

"Whatever works for you."

"Well, we have church, but I could probably be there by 1:00."

"Great, we'll have a late dinner out there, and you can meet my parents."

Sarah suddenly felt a chill at the mention of meeting Ben's parents. "Your parents, huh?"

"Too scary?"

"No, no, it's fine," Sarah said convincingly.

"I'll call you tomorrow with the directions."

"Sounds great. I can't wait," Sarah said.

Ben got out of the truck and walked Sarah to the door. Sarah turned to look back at Ben. The full moon and the lights from the YMCA that was across the street lit up the area where they stood.

Sarah leaned into Ben as he grabbed her, pulling her close to him, kissing her passionately. Sarah felt herself getting lost in his arms, struggling to keep her composure.

"I could get used to this," Ben said, grabbing a strand of Sarah's hair and gently placing it back behind her ear.

"So could I," Sarah whispered, slowly making her way to the door.

"Goodnight, Ben," Sarah said, still holding the door open.

"Goodnight, beautiful," Ben responded. And he stood watching Sarah slowly close the door.

Sarah moved to the side window and watched Ben make his way back down the sidewalk and disappear into the night.

Chapter Twenty-Eight
The True Beauty of the Farm

"Mom, we're going to be late!" Saline shouted.

"No, we're not. I have to greet today. We have to be there on time."

Saline bounced down the stairs, her brown hair in waves that came midway down her back. The small 5'1" senior had on one-inch heels to add some height to her petite frame. Lily followed in flats and leggings, complemented by a multicolored sweater Saline had outgrown and handed down to her. Lily, so thin she looked almost an inch taller than she actually was, stood at only 5'2". Hope sat on the couch with her Tinker Bell backpack, trying to stuff five Barbies into her bag. She had on her shiny purple dress and white tights with matching purple shoes that had a velcro strap. Lily stood next to her, trying to get Hope's hair into a ponytail and then wrap it in a purple ribbon. Jackson leaned down trying to gather his Rescue Hero action figures and a movie into his Spider-Man backpack. His baggy blue jeans lay over his shoes, dragging in the back. He finally stood up pulling his jeans up by the waist and pulling down his blue polo shirt.

"I'm taking my car, Mom, because I have to work after church," Saline said, as she headed toward the garage door.

"Okay, I'm dropping the kids off at Grandma and Grandpa's after church. Let's go guys. We're going to be late," Sarah said, as she and the kids all headed for the door one by one.

"Where are you going after church, Mom?" Hope asked.

"I'm just going to visit Ben for a little while."

"Can we come?" Jackson asked.

"Not this time, sweetie. But Grandma said they're having pizza today."

"Yay," yelled Hope and Jackson, already envisioning the hot cheesy pizza between their lips.

"Do I have to go?" Lily asked.

"You don't want to?" Sarah said, feeling bad she was leaving them with her parents.

"I just don't want to be there all day."

"I'll be back early. Do you want me to see if Saline can pick you guys up earlier?"

"No, I guess it's fine," Lily said.

The church service seemed to run a little longer than usual. Sarah found it hard to concentrate on the sermon, anticipating her visit to the farm and meeting Ben's parents.

The church was a remodeled private school that they had bought and fixed up. The sanctuary was surrounded – floor, ceilings, and walls – by dark oak wood, the kind you would find in an old playhouse auditorium. The large wooden benches were separated into three sections with the middle section being the widest. The stage took over the whole west side of the auditorium. There was a balcony where people sat on the far-east end of the sanctuary that formed a 'C' shape. The large stained-glass windows covered the north side, exposing a palette of vibrant colors and religious scenes that drew one's eye to the north.

When they arrived, people were just starting to enter as Sarah rushed to the southeast door to help with greeting. Lily and Jackson took a seat in the family's regular spot, and Hope helped Sarah pass out the church bulletins for that day. Parishioners entered, smiling at Hope as she leaped in front of them to be the first one to greet them, handing them their bulletin.

After the service, Sarah took the kids to her parents. Sarah went in to say hello. Her stepdad took this chance to rib her about her plans with Ben.

"So, you headin' to the farm, are ya?"

"Yep, I am."

Dan – knowing the kids would be hungry – slapped the foot rest to his recliner down in order to grab the phone to call for pizza. "Well, don't forget to slap them pigs and hogs."

"They don't have pigs and hogs."

"Oh well, I'm sure those cows need some cleaning up after," Dan continued, undeterred by Sarah's quick responses.

"I'll probably let Ben take care of that."

"So, you're going to meet the in-laws, are ya?"

Sarah shuffled the kids in, taking off their jackets and shoes. "They're not my in-laws, yet."

"Oh, not yet huh, got that noose over his neck and trying to tighten it, are you?" Dan continued to tease her.

"Oh, you…" Sarah said, acting disgusted.

"Oh, don't mind him… he's just a mess, that man is," Claire said as she came in, going through some pizza coupons. "You go and have a good time, sweetheart. The kids will be fine here. We're going to watch a movie and have some pizza."

After saying bye to the kids, Sarah headed for the front door. "Okay. Well, I better get going. I have a long drive."

"How far is it?" her mother asked.

"Oh, about 30 miles, I think."

"Yep, that's about right," her stepdad interjected. "Long way to go for a date, isn't it?"

"Well, I'll find out," Sarah said, making her way to the door.

"Bye, Mom," Lily said.

Jackson and Hope – preoccupied with the thought of Grandma's homemade cookies – made their way to the kitchen.

"I'll see you guys later."

"You have fun. Don't worry about a thing," Claire said, trying to comfort her daughter.

Sarah headed for her vehicle and was soon headed west on Interstate 70. She hadn't been west of Topeka since she was a small girl. She took out the directions that Ben had given her, trying to make sure not to miss the exit.

The sun was shining that day although Sarah, who was always cold, could feel the cold air surrounding her vehicle. Sarah never cared much for winter. Summer was her favorite season. She loved the sun. She loved the warmth it shed on her skin and could sit out in it for hours. Fall and spring, of course, were beautiful, but neither compared to the warmth of the summer sun. Sarah thought about Ben, excited about the prospect of finally seeing the farm he talked so much about. Ben was a cold-weather guy, and summer was his least favorite season. Sarah smiled to herself as she drove, thinking that they seemed to have almost nothing in common.

The four-lane highway seemed to go on forever when Sarah finally spotted the Alma exit. After exiting, Sarah headed south and toured the winding roads of the country side. Ben had said the town was considered the city of native stone due to its large original stone walls and buildings. Sarah caught sight of some stone walls standing three to four feet high in front of various homes, each home separated by miles in between. The stone walls, marked with historical signs in front of them, advertised their authentic roots.

Sarah finally made it into town and pulled up to a flashing yellow stoplight in the middle of Main Street. Ben had said to go straight past the stop light and follow through to the next street, which she did. Ben's street was wide enough to drive three semi-trucks through. He had told her it would be wide because initially – when the town was built – his street was supposed to be the main street, but somehow it ended up being moved a street over and the town, for some reason, just kept his street at the same width. Sarah turned right and made a U-turn, turning in front of a quaint little two-story, gray house with white trim, which by the street number on the outside, she knew to be Ben's. As soon as she parked, she caught sight of Ben coming out of the front door, looking at his watch, smiling and pointing to it.

"You're late," Ben said, unable to contain his excitement.

"Sorry, I had to drop off the kids. It took a little longer than I thought."

"No, you're fine. I'm just giving you a hard time. Would you like to come in?"

"Sure."

Ben, excited to be showing Sarah around his home, led Sarah into the small foyer that may have originally been meant to be the dining area. The old beige carpet, spotted with stains, led to a large stone fireplace with a huge set of deer antlers above it. The small, dark paneled living room seemed drab and unkept, not cluttered just dusty. The kitchen, which was immediately seen upon walking in the front door, had been updated with a dishwasher and more modern conveniences and fairly new cabinetry. A three-shelf plant window sat right in front of the sink, which contained what seemed to be dying plants. Sarah smiled at Ben as she looked around, noting that this was definitely a bachelor's house.

"Well, this is it," Ben said proudly.

"It's nice," Sarah said, trying to sound convincing.

"It's not much, but it's just been me all these years."

"Well, it certainly has a manly air to it," Sarah said, trying to think of something positive to say about the home.

"Yeah... well, I gave it my best."

"The deer antlers help a lot," Sarah said.

"Oh, I used to hunt all the time. I find it hard to make time for it anymore. Those were from when I was younger, not that I'm old or anythin'."

"Of course not." Sarah smiled.

"Well, shall we go?" Ben said, holding out his left arm toward the back door.

"Sure," responded Sarah.

"My parents are probably waitin' dinner on us."

They both headed toward the back-sliding glass door, stopping just before opening them.

"Now... you know the farm isn't any type of 'South Fork.'"

"South Fork? Oh..." Sarah said laughing, remembering the old television show called *Dallas*.

"It's just a small farm comparably."

"Oh darn, I was expecting South Fork." Sarah giggled, finding it funny that Ben thought she had such high expectations as they both made their way to Ben's truck.

"Sorry to burst your bubble," Ben said, climbing into the driver's seat, hoping Sarah was not totally turned off by the current state of his home. Ben knew he had let things go. He just kind of gave up after Christine left. He didn't feel a need to keep up the place for himself. The only time the place got cleaned was when he could manage to pay Rachael to come over and take care of it.

"No, you had told me it was a small farm, but you all grew up there, right?"

"Yep, all four of us, with three bedrooms and one bathroom," Ben said proudly, as he backed the truck out of the car shed and drove onto the main road.

"I can relate. We never had more than one bathroom growing up. You learn to wash fast."

"That you do," said Ben.

On the way out to the farm, they drove through the small town. It was just as Ben had described it: the two small banks and pizza place next to the hardware store and small ice cream shop. There was even a small county museum. The Alma Co-Op sat next to the museum; Ben pointed it out when they passed by.

After they left the main street, they headed out to a two-lane winding road passing by farm after farm, acreage spread out in all directions with a small home usually placed right in the middle.

The leaves were beautiful this time of year as they passed pasture after pasture. Hills that lined the landscape with the vibrant colors of fall sat in the distance, displaying a background of blue sky and cumulus clouds that lazily passed by. Ben held Sarah's hand as he drove, pulling her closer to him. He suddenly turned off the paved road and headed back east on an old dirt road, canopied by sycamores that reached out above them, concealing the road from the sky.

The bumpy road led to a clearing which displayed a bridge Ben referred to as *The Low Water Bridge*. He said this was based on the fact that the bridge sat so low. You actually had to drive down to the bridge to get across, but it was still high enough to go over the small creek that ran below it. Large branches and logs laid in the creek's rushing water, bobbing up and down trying to maintain their position against the strong current. The bridge, really just a slab of concrete, had cracks and chunks of concrete missing, showing its age and usage.

"Now, you don't come through here when we have a heavy rain," Ben suddenly said, as if to warn Sarah.

"Oh, why not?"

"Because the bridge won't be here."

"Oh… good tip."

"Yep, many have gotten washed away foolishly trying to make it across this bridge."

"Really?"

"Well, not a lot, but there have been a few."

"Gotcha," Sarah said, trying to sound as if this new information was extremely beneficial to her. She sat still in wonderment of this new world surrounding her. Growing up in the city, Sarah didn't see a whole lot of country, and farms were something she saw only on television.

Ben – leaning back with his arm around Sarah – suddenly blurted out a familiar term that Sarah had heard him say before, but had not been able to decipher until this exact moment.

"Ho-hum…" Ben sighed.

"What did you say?" Sarah said, now curious as to what this term meant.

"What?" Ben looked over at Sarah inquisitively.

"You said ho-hum."

"No, I didn't." Ben now turned his attention from the road to Sarah, wrinkling his forehead.

"Yep, you did, and I've noticed you say that a lot."

"I do? Never noticed it."

"I just wondered what it meant."

"I have no clue. Must just be a habit," Ben said, not giving it a second thought.

"Well, it's cute."

"Well, thank ya… I'll try to say it more."

"Okay…" Sarah laughed and sighed, "Ho-hum."

"Stop that." Ben laughed. "You know you're kind of ornery."

They made their way up the hill after going over the bridge and were surrounded by fields on both sides.

"These are ours. We've got corn on the north side and beans on the south over here," he said, pointing toward the south. "My dad bought this place right after my mom and him were married. He slowly added on land as they started having kids."

"Well, I was expecting a much smaller place," Sarah said.

"There are bigger farms. Ours is really not that big," Ben said humbly.

"It sure looks big to me."

The truck headed around a curve and passed by three farmhouses. They approached a red gate and turned on to the rock road heading further east up to a small white farmhouse surrounded by a beautiful garden that displayed an array of wildflowers. There was a vegetable garden to the west, and cattle lined the fence on the other side of the garden, where pasture met the homestead.

"They look like they're glad to see you," Sarah said, talking about the mooing cows that now had made their way slowly across the field and gathered along the fence that faced the farmhouse.

"Yep, they always are. They know who feeds 'em." Ben looked over toward the field, watching the familiar sight.

"There are quite a few."

"Yeah, and this is only a portion. We keep some north and south of here. Shall we go in?"

Sarah hesitated for a moment. "Okay. I have to say, I'm a little nervous about meeting your parents."

"Well, don't be. What's not to like?" Ben said, getting out of the truck.

"True. I hope they see it that way," Sarah said nervously, as she opened her door and climbed down from the truck.

As they came up to the screen door, Ben stuck his head into the kitchen to say hello and Sarah came in behind him. She noticed a plump elderly woman with darker hair by the stove and an elderly man with white, feather-like hair sitting at the table. Ben's mom, not used to having company, had put on her best blouse and slacks, and even had on some makeup. His dad sat in his same old gray slacks with black suspenders that held his pants onto his thin, withering frame.

"Nice to meet you, young lady," Larry said as he looked up from the remote control to the television that sat in his trembling hand. Sarah looked over as Larry seemed to be trying to replace the batteries in the remote.

"Hello," Sarah said back.

"Oh, I'm sorry. Dad, this is Sarah. Sarah, this is my dad, Larry, and my mother over there by the stove is Cathy."

"Nice to meet both of you," Sarah said enthusiastically, trying to make a good impression.

"We are so glad you could join us," Cathy commented, putting her hands in her apron as she waddled over, shifting her weight from one side to the other.

"Whatcha doing, Dad?" Ben asked, now heading over to the table.

"Oh, the remote went bad so I'm trying to replace the batteries," Larry announced, smiling, as if putting the batteries in the remote was quite the accomplishment.

"Need any help?" Ben asked.

"No, no, I got it," Larry said proudly, not wanting to look incompetent in front of Sarah.

"Okay, you let me know if I can help."

"Is there anything I can help with?" Sarah said, turning toward Cathy.

"Well, I don't know… if you wanted to get some water and silverware on the table, that would help," Cathy said, as if she were unsure if that was too much to ask.

"All right," Sarah said, looking for the glasses as Ben pointed to the cabinet next to the sink. Sarah shook her head in acknowledgement of Ben's guidance and quickly discovered their location. "Here they are."

"So, what you two been up to?" Ben asked.

"Oh, just getting ready for dinner," Cathy answered.

"So, what we havin', Mom?"

"Meatloaf, nothin' special," Cathy answered.

"Oh, I love meatloaf," Sarah said. "It smells wonderful."

"So, are you from Topeka, Sarah?" Larry suddenly blurted out.

"No, not originally. I grew up in Kansas City."

"You're a Kansas City gal, huh," Larry said.

"That she is, Dad," Ben said, laughing while picking up a cracker and some cheese that was set out as an appetizer. "You need any help, Mom?"

"No, no I got it," Cathy said, turning now to bring the meatloaf over to the table.

Sarah noticed some other empty bowls next to the stove and went over to the stove to see if she could help with the sides.

"I can scoop these into dishes if you'd like," Sarah said.

"Sure," Cathy said.

"Looks wonderful," Sarah said, trying to compliment, Cathy.

"Thank you." Cathy gleamed over any praise of her cooking. She had always taken pride in setting an appetizing table and though she wouldn't admit it, she loved the compliments that came with it.

Sarah sat as the family before her grabbed each other's hands and bowed their heads naturally as if they had done this a thousand times before. "Bless, O' Lord, this food for thy use, and make us ever mindful of the wants and needs of others." They all said in unison, "Amen."

"Well, I'm not shy," Ben said, as he reached for the meatloaf. "Here you go, Dad." He then turned to his mom. "Mom, here's your piece."

"Thank you," his mom said.

"Sarah, here you go."

Sarah thanked Ben as they each filled their plates. They sat at the small round table just inches from one another, holding a conversation, mostly about Sarah and her inexperience with farm life.

Cathy looked over at Sarah as she saw her son light up at each new glance. She smiled as she hoped this was the woman she had been praying for. Cathy knew that she and Larry wouldn't be around forever, and she was worried about what would happen to her youngest son when they were no longer here. She had feared he was intent on living a life alone.

She observed the gentle way her son rubbed Sarah's arm and back as if they had been together for years and how Sarah smiled back at him, clenching his hand underneath the table. Cathy had a feeling this city girl was capturing her youngest son's heart.

After they finished their supper, Cathy and Larry found it hard to hide their excitement about having a new person in their kitchen. Sarah came in like a breath of fresh air, if only for a moment, lighting up the humdrum that they had become so accustomed to. Each new story left them sitting on the edge of their chair as Sarah explained what had brought her to Topeka and where she had come from.

Sarah enjoyed the company of Ben's parents. His dad – being the character he was – kept the conversation interesting with jokes of Ben's antics as a boy. Cathy laughed shyly, explaining each occurrence with the pride a mother has when explaining the upbringing of her child. Ben sat back enjoying the conversation as he felt his parents being drawn to the same traits that attracted him to Sarah: her honesty, her gentleness, and her compassion. Larry also commented to Ben what a looker she was, which didn't hurt anything. Ben's dad then expressed a familiar term that made Sarah laugh, as he leaned back in his chair after dinner and sighed, "Ho-hum," while he rested his pipe onto his lips.

They finished their supper, and Sarah looked at the clock remembering her promise to pick the kids up early.

"The dinner was wonderful, Cathy."

"Well, I'm glad you enjoyed it."

"Oh, I did. You'll have to give me your recipe for that meatloaf."

"Oh, it's easy," Cathy said humbly, overjoyed at the comment. "I'll get it ready for you and Ben can bring it out to you."

"Thank you."

"Well, Larry, you take care now and stay out of mischief," Sarah said while trying to stand from her chair to make her way over to the door.

"Oh, that's no fun." Larry smiled.

"True," Sarah answered back. "Well, it was very nice meeting both of you."

"Come out anytime," Larry told her.

"Thank you, I will." Sarah smiled.

"We are glad to have the company," Cathy said, almost feeling an urge to hug Sarah. Ben grabbed Sarah's coat from the coat rack and helped her put it on.

"I'll bring her out again," Ben said sincerely. "I promise."

"You do that," Larry said, putting his pipe back into his mouth.

"Anytime," Cathy joined in, wanting Sarah to feel welcomed.

Ben and Sarah slowly headed out of the door into a cool afternoon breeze. The truck, parked a little way up the drive way, was sitting underneath a large elm tree whose branches overhung the area.

Ben, having forgot his jacket, went back in as Sarah made her way to the truck, admiring the view of the hills surrounding the farm. The hills were blanketed with the vibrant colors of fall. The smell of the cattle rose from below the farmhouse as the cows made their way over to the fence, staring at Sarah. The mud beneath their feet broke away with each heavy-laden step, as steam rose from their noses, all of them now mooing in Sarah's direction.

Ben suddenly came out of the farmhouse as Sarah turned her head slowly back now facing him, but leaving her body at an angle. The wind picked up at just that moment as Sarah stood surrounded by the oranges, reds, and yellows of the trees, her long brown hair flowing in the wind. Sarah's figure-forming jacket seemed to accentuate her thin silhouette. She stood looking at Ben as he suddenly stopped for a moment, lost in the scene, almost breathless, thinking he had never seen the farm look so beautiful as he did at that moment. Sarah smiled back at him and for the first time in a long time, Ben knew he was falling in love.

Chapter Twenty-Nine
Ghosts of the Past and the Future

Sarah squinted her eyes, looking underneath her visor, as she drove down the street toward her duplex. Her eyes gravitated toward the large white pickup truck sitting in her driveway. As she got closer, the familiar business advertisement that she had helped design jumped out at her from the side of the extended cab pickup. It was Jack.

She hadn't heard from Jack in weeks. Sarah felt her heart start to beat rapidly as she clicked open the garage door, maneuvering her large SUV around his truck and into her two-car garage that was still loaded with boxes on either side of her vehicle.

Sarah heard the sound of laughter coming from inside even before she opened the door. She entered into the kitchen to find Jack sitting there in her living room with the kids.

"What are you doing here, Jack?" Sarah said, as she slammed her purse and keys on the kitchen counter.

"I came to see the kids."

"You should have called first," Sarah said, trying to remain calm.

Jack then got up and started to walk toward her. Sarah wondered why in the world Jack thought it was okay to just barge into her home. She crossed her arms in front of her, waiting for an explanation.

"I'm sorry," Jack said. "I wasn't thinking, but Sarah, I need to talk to you."

"What is it?"

"Can we talk in the kitchen, alone, please?" Sarah turned around reluctantly after seeing the kids' hopeful faces.

"All right, but then you'll have to leave. You can take the kids for a little while if you want, but I don't want you here."

"Sarah... I wanted to tell you how sorry I am," Jack said, looking into Sarah's eyes and taking her hand as she snatched it back from him. Images of the past few months started flying through Sarah's thoughts.

Sarah backed up from Jack, feeling that he was getting too close to her.

"You can't just show up here. This isn't your home."

"I've been thinking about us," Jack said, moving closer to Sarah.

"It's too late for us, Jack. You made your decision a long time ago," Sarah said angrily, peeping around the corner to see if the kids were watching. And they were.

"I didn't know what I was doing. I didn't realize what I was giving up."

"And how is that my fault? And Kelly, where does she fit into all this?"

"It's over between us. I made a mistake. Sarah, I'm so sorry. I'm just asking for another chance."

At that moment, the doorbell rang. Sarah hesitated for a second, trying to make sense out of what Jack just said to her. She began to walk away from him, as images began to blur. Jack's words rang out again and again through her thoughts, *Sarah, I'm so sorry*. His words seemed to be coming from a distance, and then suddenly he was laughing and talking with the kids again. Rage filled her thoughts as she headed toward the front door. The doorbell rang again and again, a nagging, recurring ring, over and over again. Sarah finally reached the door, but the door wouldn't unlock. It was jammed. Sarah struggled with the door as the bell kept on ringing.

She looked back at the kids who were still seated in the living room, but none of them made a move to help her. They just sat there with Jack.

Sarah finally managed to unlock the door, but it seemed heavy for some reason. Sarah didn't seem to have any strength. She struggled to open the door, pushing and pulling to get it to open. Jack came up behind her trying to help her, but she shook his hand loose from the knob.

A glaring light blared into Sarah's duplex as she finally got the door open. An image slowly took shape of a young blonde woman. It was Kelly. She was standing there in a red dress that accentuated her large chest. She stood there glaring at Sarah. Jack moved past Sarah and took Kelly's hand as they slowly began to walk down the narrow sidewalk toward Jack's truck.

"Jack! Jack!" Sarah screamed out. "You said you were sorry! You said you were sorry!"

With that, Sarah suddenly sat up in her bed, perspiration surrounded her forehead as she grabbed at her chest, feeling her heart running rampant.

She took a couple of deep breaths, feeling her body shaking. She felt a deepening anger build inside her, one she had come to recognize, overtaking her like a disease penetrating her organs, slowly trying to kill her.

She wanted to strangle Jack. She could feel his neck pressed between her fingers. She sensed the hatred building inside her as she tried to slowly catch her breath. The silence of her bedroom drummed inside her head.

The dreams of Jack came often. Sarah found it strange. Even when she was not thinking about Jack, he always seemed to make his way into her dreams. The dreams she loathed the most were the ones when they were back in Nebraska, and it was as if nothing had ever happened, and they were a family again. When she had these dreams, it was as if Jack had never left, and then she would wake up alone.

She was afraid to tell Ben about her dreams for fear he would not understand. She didn't understand them herself. She sat and wondered why she didn't dream about Ben. It was almost always about Jack.

Sarah laid her head back on her pillow and tried to get back to sleep.

She tried to fill her thoughts with Ben, but somehow knew Jack would eventually make his way back into her dreams.

Her feelings for Ben grew stronger with each new encounter. Sarah could only hope that someday, Ben would somehow make his way into her dreams and stop the tremendous ache that came along with remembering her previous life.

Sarah and Ben's relationship started to blossom, and they felt it was time to do more together with the kids. Ben wanted them to come out to the farm. He secretly hoped they would love the countryside as much as he did.

Ben knew how close Sarah was to the kids. She was a great mom. He knew he didn't have a chance with Sarah if the kids rejected him. He was aware of everything they had been through as a family, and he tried to think of ways he could lighten their load.

The kids were already becoming closer to Ben, especially Hope and Jackson. They seemed to be craving a male figure in their life, but Ben, not being around younger children all that much, had almost no idea what to do with them.

Sarah and Ben decided to take them out to the farm one Saturday morning. They wouldn't be able to stay long because Ben had to work that afternoon. The day was supposed to be warm and sunny, but a cold front moved in at the last minute. Ben arrived early, just as he said he would, asking if Sarah and the kids still wanted to venture out into the weather. Saline was at work, but the younger three sat saddened that their adventure may have been halted by the rain.

"Well, guys, do you still want to go out to the farm with Ben?" Sarah asked them, already guessing what the answer would be.

"Yes!" they all shouted in unison.

"Well, let's get a move on," Ben said, as he waited patiently while Sarah searched for the kids' rain boots and jackets.

Jackson and Hope decided it would be fun to try and climb up Ben while they were waiting. Hope started up one side. Ben helped her, releasing her at almost waist height, setting her down carefully on to the couch as she giggled. Jackson started up the other side. Ben caught him hanging him upside down by his feet as Jackson laughed uncontrollably and Ben placed him a little less gently on to the floor.

Sarah turned around and looked at the trio. They all pointed at each other, blaming one another for the ruckus, the tall one smiling and pointing down. Sarah had to smile at the way Ben seemed to fit in a little too well with that age group.

Lily laughed as she watched them roughhousing and felt a sense of joy at the fact that Ben was doing things with her younger siblings that her father would have normally done.

"I found my boots," Lily said.

"Great, let's get going," commanded Ben.

Jackson and Hope then headed toward Ben for more roughhousing.

"Jackson and Hope, put your coats on and let's go," Sarah said firmly.

Ben looked at them and shook his shoulders up and down. Hope and Jackson reluctantly headed over to their mom. After everyone was dressed, they loaded themselves into Ben's truck and headed west toward the farm.

The weather was a little bit cooler than they all had hoped, and a heavier rain had started to set in, making the farm a muddy mess. Sarah's clan all climbed out of Ben's truck as they stopped at the farmhouse for a moment to talk to Ben's parents. After tracking in a little too much mud into Cathy's kitchen, they all figured it was time to head out. Ben's feed truck, which had only a bench seat across the front, made it a little cramped. Sarah looked at Ben, wondering how he was planning to get them all into this small confined area.

"It'll be fine," Ben said assuredly.

"Okay, everyone in," Sarah said.

Jackson made his way in first to be sure to sit next to Ben, followed by Lily and Sarah. Hope would sit on Sarah's lap. Ben climbed in last, trying to grab the stick shift sitting between Jackson's legs.

"See, nothing to worry about." Ben laughed.

Sarah tried to smile as she looked over the crowd of bodies.

They headed straight for the field next to the homestead. The yearlings spotted the familiar sight of the feed truck and headed over to the edge of the fence that lined the vegetable garden.

Ben jumped out of the truck, feeling the cool air hitting him in the face. He quickly lifted the hood of his jacket up over his head to block some of the cold wind coming his way. He disconnected the electrical wire, tossing it to the side, and rushed back to the warmth of the truck.

"Here we go," Ben announced as he climbed back in. The children looked on in anticipation.

The truck dug into the mud, sending it flying in every direction as Ben hit the windshield wipers trying to clean off the glass. The cattle formed a mob around the truck, moving only after getting bumped by the truck. Their black dripping noses bumped up against the windows as the children stared at them in amazement.

The yearlings varied in color and size. There were some with snow white faces and some with brown and white spots, but most were black in color. Their long tongues reached out over their noses, wiping away the liquid making its way out into the cold. A stream of steam came out of their nostrils as their heavy-laden hooves broke away at the mud underneath them. "Doesn't that hurt them?" Hope asked, wondering why Ben kept hitting them with the truck.

"Nah, they have pretty tough skin," Ben replied. "They are still pretty young. We just separated them from their mothers, so they are still a little unsure of what to do. These here are called yearlings."

"Why yearlings?" asked Jackson.

"They're only a year old," replied Ben.

"Only a year old, and you took them from their mother?" Lily asked.

"Afraid so," Ben said, realizing this may seem strange to the kids. "They'll be all right. It just takes some getting used to. At night you can hear their cries, the mothers crying out to their young and the yearlings answering them."

"Really?" Jackson asked.

"Yep. I know it used to keep me up at night. My parents are used to it by now."

The cattle swarmed around the truck as Ben maneuvered the wide vehicle toward the large steel feeders lined up in a row. The feeders were about eight feet long and lined up next to each other like a long steel canal. The feeders, bent and broken from years of dedicated service, sat ready to take on the yearlings.

Ben got out and dropped a funnel down on the side of the truck as the pellets started to fly out of the large steel bin that encased them. The pellets hitting the large steel feeders sounded like a hailstorm beating on the top of a roof. Ben pulled the truck slowly forward, honking at the yearlings to move them out of the way. The cattle slowly filed in behind the truck, inching their way to the feeders, to receive the sweet wheat pellets.

Ben suddenly stopped the truck and got out and lifted up the funnel, which blocked the pellets from escaping and turned the truck around and headed across the field to a large hay feeder. The rusted feeder, which was shaped like a funnel, held what looked like straw leaking out on all sides. At that moment, the children became aware of the large round bale of alfalfa that was loaded on to the back of the truck.

Ben slowly backed up to the feeder and pulled a lever that started large steel arms moving on each side of the truck that grabbed the large bale and rose it up and over the steel feeder, releasing the bale into the center.

The children turned around to watch Ben as he hopped out of the truck and climbed up on the side of the feeder with a switchblade in his hand, cutting off the twine that held the round bundle of alfalfa. Ben pulled the twine from the hay, hand over hand, as the twine slid out from the bale with ease.

Ben, upon completing his task, wound the twine up into a ball and tossed it into the back of the truck.

"What's he doing, Mom?" Jackson asked.

"He's putting a bale out for the cattle," Sarah answered.

"But, didn't we already feed them?"

"Yes, we did, but they need more than just the pellets." Sarah smiled.

"Oh…"

After feeding the cattle, Ben headed north to pick up another bale. Coming up on several bales stacked one on top of the other, Ben slowly backed up the truck as the large steel arms slowly grabbed a fresh bale and loaded it on to the back of the feed truck.

The kids sat watching in wonder. They all were silent except for Jackson, who was full of questions about the farm. Ben answered Jackson's questions with patience and laughter, enjoying Jackson's obvious curiosity.

"Stop asking so many questions," Lily said, taking advantage of a time Ben had stepped out of the truck.

"Don't tell me what to do. I am not asking that many questions, am I, Mom?" Jackson turned to Sarah for confirmation.

"Lily, leave your brother alone. He's just curious," Sarah said.

"He's going to make Ben tired of us, and then he'll never bring us out again," Lily said.

"Jackson is fine. Ben doesn't seem to mind," Sarah said, trying to reassure her.

"Mom, are we almost done?" Hope asked.

"Yes, why?" Sarah asked.

"I'm tired, and I'm cramped in here."

"It's just a little longer."

"Quiet!" Jackson said to Hope. "You want him to take us home?"

"No, but I don't have any room," Hope said discontentedly.

"It'll just a little longer," Sarah said.

Ben returned to the truck after removing the twine from a bale of alfalfa. The children turned and watched as the bulls made their way slowly to the feeder. Their shiny black coats sparkled in the cool, frosty air. The bulls stepped steadily into the mud as steam rose from their noses. They turned and looked grazily at the truck load of people and then contently returned back to their meal.

"Well, we're all done," announced Ben. "How'd you like it?"

"It was great," Jackson said. "Can we come back?"

"Sure," Ben said proudly.

"It was awesome," Lily said.

"I have to go to the bathroom," was Hope's only comment.

"Alrighty then, we better get back to the farm in a hurry," Ben said, smiling at Sarah.

Sarah wondered if the kids had bothered Ben during his work. He seemed so patient with them. She smiled as she saw Ben and Jackson carrying on a conversation. Jackson thrilled to be able to be a part of a man's world again. Jackson seemed so distant sometimes. He was missing something. Sarah thought it was Jack. But maybe it was just a dad.

"All right, to the farm we go. Thanks for coming out with me today, guys," Ben said, as the farm truck made its way toward the white farmhouse.

And amidst the cold wind and rain, the darkness and the fog, and unbeknownst to them, a new kind of family was cramped into that old farm truck. One who would meet the challenge of the rocky road before them, slowly making their way home.

Chapter Thirty
I Prayed for You

Red, green, gold and silver, the twinkling of white lights, the holiday season had somehow made its way into one of the most tragic years this family had every known and Sarah and the kids were left having to face unknown waters… their first Christmas without Jack.

Jack had always been the one to take the kids out to cut a fresh tree for Christmas. He spoiled the kids, year after year, with things they didn't really need. Jack would be the one taking pictures and filming the children while they opened gifts Christmas morning, but none of that would happen this year. This Christmas would be different as they all struggled to form new traditions, in an unfamiliar place, a million miles from where they had once called home.

"So what'cha thinking about?" Ben asked Sarah, who was staring off into space.

"Oh, nothing," Sarah answered, wanting to spare Ben the sad details of her ongoing family drama.

"So… what do you have planned for the kids this year… I mean for Christmas?" Ben asked while taking another sip of his Pepsi. They were in the small Italian family restaurant that had become a sort of refuge for the two of them. A place they went when they wanted some alone time. There were candles lit on each table. Soft music played in the background. In the spring and summer months, there was an open patio that was situated on the north side that overlooked some downtown shops and small businesses. There was always fresh bread on the table, and a smell of oregano that floated around you as soon as you entered the door.

"Not much," Sarah said, twirling her Alfredo noodles.

"Well, how can I help?" Ben asked.

"I don't know."

Ben took Sarah's hand into his. "Well, what do the kids need?"

"Coats and clothes, mostly."

"Oh, I'm sure the little ones are expecting some toys."

"Yeah, I'm sure they are," Sarah said, feeling a little sorry for herself and letting her eyes wander around the room.

"How about a tree? Do they want a tree?"

Sarah's eyes then brightened as if Ben had read her mind. "Actually, I've been worried about that. I mean in the past we had always bought a real tree, I mean before we moved here. I just wasn't sure how to manage it this year."

"I can get one."

"Well, I hate to ask…"

Ben stopped Sarah from speaking by taking his hand and softly placing it over her lips. "Sarah, let me help you."

"Okay," Sarah said, feeling somewhat indigent, as if she were relying too heavily on this man who had every right to just walk away.

She looked at Ben in a way she hadn't before.

Her eyes began to water. She grabbed her napkin, trying to wipe them before Ben noticed. She was dumbfounded at this farmer who seemed to know what she was thinking even before she did. A man who was becoming more and more of a miracle in their lives.

"You make a list of what else they need, and we will get it together. I won't take no for an answer," Ben said.

"All right," Sarah said, now staring at Ben from across the table.

"What?" Ben asked.

"I'm just not sure how I got so lucky. How I met someone so wonderful."

"Oh, I'm sure you'll start to see my shortcomings soon enough. I'm just trying to rack up some points before you do."

"No, really, you seem perfect. Why are you still single, Mr. Thompson?"

"I've been saving myself all this time for you." Ben smiled.

Sarah laughed. "Oh, and your first marriage?"

"Well, you were taking a little long to get here."

Sarah hesitated for a moment. "I love you," she suddenly blurted out, without thinking about it. It just came out naturally, like breathing. As if all this time those words had been building up in her heart, but her brain kept pushing them away, afraid to take a chance, afraid of what they would mean if she said them out loud, terrified that Ben would run out of the room as fast as his feet would carry him once they were released. But there they were, for everyone to see and there was no turning back.

Ben, not sure he had heard her right with all the commotion in the restaurant, said, "What did you say?"

"I love you," Sarah said with tears in her eyes.

"Are you sure?" Ben said with his eyebrows lowered, as if the words were somehow a dream, something unexpected in a world where he thought love would never exist for him again.

"What does that mean?" Sarah asked, not understanding his response.

"I just mean, there are so many other men that you could have."

"Is that all you have to say to me?" Sarah asked, now grabbing Ben's hand.

"No… I mean… Sarah, I've loved you from the first day I saw you," Ben gasped. "I just never imagined you would feel the same way about me."

"And I never allowed myself to believe that I would actually find you. I prayed for you, you know," Sarah said, looking at her napkin and then lifting her eyes to meet Ben's.

"What?"

"I prayed for you. You're the answer, the answer to my prayers. I love the way you look at me. I love the way you care about the kids. You are one awesome catch, Mr. Thompson."

"No… I'm the lucky one. You're so kind, Sarah. You could have your pick of anyone. What are you doing here with a guy like me?"

"I think I'm telling you I love you."

"I love you, too," Ben said, as he leaned over the table to kiss Sarah, sending his glass tumbling forward, bouncing on his plate with a loud clank, allowing the caramel colored liquid to escape and make its way down the side of the table. Ben quickly stood up, wiping his lap off, which was now drenched with Pepsi.

"Dang it." Ben laughed. "I'm pretty smooth, ain't I?"

Sarah sat there laughing, trying to help Ben clean up the mess.

Ben, embarrassed and frantic, kneeled down to soak up the liquid that had made its way to the floor. He then hesitated and popped his head up over the table cloth, looking at Sarah. "I prayed for you, too."

Chapter Thirty-One
Reality Check

They say that divorce feels a lot like the death of a loved one. You have this hole in your heart and the emptiness is there, but that person is not six feet under; they're still walking around. This aspect probably makes divorce more difficult, because you know the person you loved is still alive, but for reasons out of your control, they are choosing to not be a part of your life anymore. They are choosing not to love you.

Sarah's children were grieving the loss of their father, and Sarah, being the parent the children felt safe with, received the brunt of their pain. The tears and later the anger that comes along with the feeling of loss, is always directed at the parent that stayed.

This became all too real the weekend Sarah's parents invited Ben to join the family for Sunday dinner. Lily had become more and more distraught as the Christmas season approached. Jack, who had continually promised to come and see the children, broke promise after promise and Sarah was left picking up the pieces.

Ben had agreed to meet Sarah and the kids at their duplex that afternoon with the intention of giving them a ride over to Sarah's parents.

Lily, who tended to hold her feelings in, lashed out that day at the only parent she felt safe enough to break down with. The parent that stayed.

"Did Dad call, Mom?" Lily shouted down the stairs, struggling to get on her sweater.

"No, why, did he tell you he would?" Sarah answered, while trying to get Hope and Jackson out of their church clothes before Ben got there. Sarah then reached into the dryer, pulling out some of Jackson's jeans. Jackson, annoyed that Sarah tried to help him put them on, took them into the bathroom and shut the door.

"He told me he'd send some money two weeks ago," Lily said, growing more agitated by the minute.

"Well, you can try and call him, sweetie," Sarah answered while combing Hope's hair.

"No, I'm not calling him," Lily shouted.

Sarah knew why she was angry. Lily was a lot like her. She held everything in and then like a time bomb would eventually just explode. Lily had faith in everyone. She had faith in her father, and again and again he continued to let her down.

"Lily, there's nothing I can do if your father chooses not to answer his phone."

"I need a new dress for my music concert."

"What's wrong with your old one?" Sarah asked, trying to hold Hope still.

"It's too short. I'm growing, you know, Mom."

"I know. Does Saline have something you can wear?"

"No!" shouted Lily.

"I have a black skirt you could wear," Sarah said after finishing with Hope.

"It's too big on me. Have you seen how much weight I've lost? Do you even notice?"

"Yes, Lily, and you don't need to shout!" Sarah said, rolling her eyes and putting her lipstick back into her purse. Sarah knew Lily wasn't really mad at her. She knew it was the situation Jack had placed them in.

Hope and Jackson sat down on the couch quietly watching television as the mounting tempers started to flare. Just then the doorbell rang and Sarah headed over to open the door hoping that Ben could not hear the shouting from the front yard.

"Hey," Ben said, as he leaned down to kiss Sarah. "How are you today, beautiful?"

"Okay, come on in, honey. I have to warn you, we're having some issues today."

"Issues? What's wrong?"

"Just stuff…" Sarah said.

Lily made her way down the stairs. Ben looked over at Jackson and Hope. He waved, but the look on their faces told Ben something was about to happen, but Ben didn't know exactly what.

Lily, who was usually very friendly toward Ben, only gave him a slight glance.

"I'm sick of having to call him. I am not calling him ever again." Lily, now giving in to her emotions, had started to tear up. She snatched a tissue from the counter and tried to wipe away a loose tear.

"Who is she talking about?" Ben leaned down to whisper in Sarah's ear.

"Her dad."

"Oh." Ben then made his way over to the couch where Hope and Jackson were sitting. He sat down quietly next to them, now understanding their queer looks.

"Okay, we can go, I guess," Lily said in disgust, stomping around trying to find her jacket.

"Sweetie, we will find you something to wear."

"It's not just that," Lily said, aggressively searching through the closet for her jacket, "He doesn't care. He doesn't care about any of us." Lily, now overwhelmed with emotion, snatched her coat out of the closet and threw it over her shoulders, trying not to make eye contact with anyone.

"Sweetie, there is nothing we can do about it right now. You have to get used to the idea that he is not going to be around like he used to."

"I am used to it. I'm used to it up to here!" Lily said, snapping her hand above her head.

"You two are awful quiet," Ben whispered to Hope and Jackson.

"We didn't want to get into the fight," Jackson responded.

"Oh… good thinking," Ben said.

"Are you guys ready to go?" Sarah asked, now realizing how agitated her voice sounded to the three on the couch.

Ben stood up quickly in a military stance, as though he was about to salute.

"Ready when you are, dear," Ben announced, trying to lighten the mood.

Lily stomped toward the front door. Sarah grabbed her coat, embarrassed that Ben had to be witness to Lily's outburst. Ben walked over to Sarah, helping her on with her coat and giving her shoulder a tight squeeze, kissing her gently on the back of her head. Sarah looked back at Ben and smiled.

"Where's Saline?" Ben asked.

"She had to work."

"Are you okay?" Ben asked.

"Yeah… just… I'm sorry you had to see this. We'll be fine."

"Fine?" Lily said, overhearing her mother. "Can you try to get a hold of Dad?"

"Lily, he doesn't answer my calls," Sarah said, now making her way to the front door. "But yes, I'll try."

"He doesn't answer mine either, or Jackson's, or Hope's. Why is he doing this?" Lily asked, as new tears formed in her eyes.

"I don't know, sweetie. We'll try to reach him later."

After they were all buckled into the truck, Ben started to pull out of the driveway. Lily sat in the middle, staring out into space. Ben could see the tears forming in her eyes through the rearview mirror. He had to fight the urge to tear up and tried to turn his eyes toward the road. Sarah, staring out the front windshield, worried that this might be a little too much reality for Ben.

"Dad doesn't care about us," Lily blurted out.

"Sweetie, you cannot let him do this to you."

"Do what?"

"You cannot let him destroy you. Your happiness," Sarah said, trying to turn toward the back seat to look Lily in the eye.

"I'm not! It's just hard," Lily said, her lips quivering.

"There is nothing we can do about it right now," Sarah said calmly.

"I can do something about it. I will let him know exactly how I feel," Lily said, as she crossed her arms in front of her, every now and then, taking her hand up to her eye to wipe away a tear.

"What are you going to do?" Jackson asked, now concerned and trying to wiggle out of his seat belt so he could face Lily.

"I'm going to tell Dad exactly what I think of him, if I ever talk to him again."

"You can't do that!" Jackson suddenly shouted.

"Why?" Lily shouted back. Sarah then turned back around to try and defuse the situation.

"Mom, tell her she can't do that!" Jackson shouted at the top of his lungs, this time toward Sarah.

"Jackson, stop shouting," Sarah said, trying to calm him down. Ben then wondered if he should pull the truck over.

"She can't do that!" he shouted again.

"I can too!" Lily shouted.

"No, you can't, because Dad will never call again if you do!" Jackson cried out.

"Do you want me to pull over?" Ben asked quietly, wondering if Sarah needed to talk to the kids before they drove any further.

Sarah shook her head no. Ben continued down the road, watching the kids from the rearview mirror. Ben tried to comfort Sarah by holding and squeezing her hand.

"Okay, I won't," Lily finally said. "Jackson, did you hear me? I won't."

"Okay," Jackson said, wiping the tears streaming down his plump cheeks as he tried to pretend he was not crying.

Ben clutched Sarah's hand as she looked back at him.

"I'm sorry," Sarah said.

"What are you sorry for? It's okay," Ben said, as he quickly looked over at her. He then gripped her hand tighter. "I understand."

After a few minutes of silence, Ben suddenly blurted out, "Anyone up for ice cream after dinner?"

"I am!" Hope took her thumb out of her mouth and smiled.

Ben then turned and smiled at Sarah.

"We'll call that by ear," Sarah said.

"Ah… but Mom, I want ice cream," Hope pleaded.

"Okay, ice cream it is." Sarah tried to smile looking over at Ben as he pulled her closer to him, hugging her with one arm, the truck now silent as they pulled onto I-70, heading east toward their grandparents' home.

When they finally arrived, Jackson and Hope had forgotten all about the episode in the truck, but Lily, still solemn, dragged herself into the house. Sarah apologized again to Ben as he reaffirmed that he understood.

They entered into her parents' home and the aroma of what smelled like roast filled the living room. Sarah's mother came down the hallway from the kitchen and her stepdad kicked the footrest down on his recliner, making a loud clanging noise as he stood up. Ben and Sarah came in behind the kids. The children, after saying hello, disappeared into their grandparents' bedroom to watch television.

The décor of ceramic figures and fake flowers filled the walls and tables of the rather large living room. Dan was slightly shorter than Ben, standing at about 5'10. He had a small bulge in his midsection that made its way over his belt. His thin hair was cut to within millimeters of his scalp in a type of crew cut.

Ben immediately noticed a spring in Dan's step as Dan walked toward him. Dan, an avid walker, walked every day, rain or shine, at the local mall, meeting up with other walkers to discuss the current events in Topeka. Ben stuck out his right hand to meet Dan's as they both neared the end of the couch.

"So, she finally got you out here, did she?" Dan said while shaking Ben's hand.

"Yes, sir, she did."

"I hear you been putting her to work at the farm."

"Yes, sir, she's a might good help if you are needin' someone to keep you company."

"Keep you company? She told us you had her out there slappin' them hogs."

"No, afraid not." Ben laughed. "She might'a been pullin' your leg on that one. We don't have any hogs."

"No, I'm just kiddin' ya, Ben. Nice to meet you," Dan said while shaking Ben's hand and slapping his shoulder. Ben noticed Dan's strong grip.

"Well, you know Sarah just has to say the word, and we can put her to work out there," Ben said, talking about Sarah as if she wasn't even there.

"What?" Sarah butted in.

"You need an extra job anyway," her stepdad commented. "You only have two at the moment."

"That's okay. I'll manage without any help from you two."

"Yes," Claire said, as she entered the conversation, "She has enough jobs as it is." Claire smiled and held out her hand to Ben. Ben noticed Claire's slight wobble as she walked toward him. It reminded him a lot of his mother's walk. Claire wore large glasses that didn't seem to quite fit her face. Sarah had said that she resembled her mother a lot, but Ben was having a hard time seeing the resemblance.

"Just ignore him," Claire said, pointing to Dan. "He's a mess, that one is."

"Okay," Ben replied, not knowing what else to say.

"He likes to give everyone a hard time," Claire tried to reassure Ben.

"Come on in and sit a while," Dan said, as Claire took Ben's coat.

"Well, I want to thank you for havin' us over," Ben said, as he made his way to the large floral couch surrounded by stuffed animals. Ben and Sarah had just sat down on the couch when the pressure from their weight brought an avalanche of stuffed animals down around them.

"Oh, don't mind them. This man wins these things out of those machines," Claire said, as she took a seat in her recliner. "I am running out of places to put 'em."

"Those machines?" Ben asked.

"Yeah, the ones with the stuffed animals inside," Claire answered, now smiling at Ben.

"Oh, yeah. Well, you must be pretty good. I never get anything out of those machines," Ben said, trying to acknowledge Dan's accomplishment, while throwing his arm around Sarah, bringing her closer to him.

"Yeah, I have hit a few. It's something to do when we're out," Dan said proudly.

"Yeah, but now I have to find room for all of 'em. They're coming down around our ears, as you can see." Claire laughed.

Family pictures lined the four walls of the room. There were various people unknown to Ben that stared at him from all angles. Ben found one of Sarah and pointed to it as Sarah smiled and explained it was her high school senior photo.

"Got more of those things in the bedroom, if you're needin' any," Dan said.

Ben finally realized that Dan was pointing at the stuffed animals.

"No, no, but thank ya. Ah… the kids don't want 'em?" Ben asked, looking at Dan and then back at Sarah.

"No, their mother said they have more than they can fit in their rooms now," replied Dan.

Ben then looked back at Sarah.

"Well, they do," Sarah said.

"So, Sarah, tells us you farm in Alma," Dan said, trying to make conversation.

"Yes, sir," Ben replied.

"Do your mother and father still live out there?" Dan asked.

"Yes, they do. They're not in the best of health so my brother and I take care of the farm and check on 'em."

"Oh, well, then it's nice that they have you two around," said Claire.

"Well, we figure they took care of us all those years, and now it's our turn to take care of them."

"That's how it should be," Dan said, trying to maneuver this footrest down. Dan finally gripped it sending it down with a bang.

"Well, supper is pretty much ready if you all want to come in the kitchen," Claire suddenly announced.

"Let me help you set the table, Mom," Sarah said, leaning over to kiss Ben before getting up.

Dan looked on as the two women made their way down the hall.

"She's a good girl that one," Dan said, looking toward the hallway where Sarah and Claire had just entered. He then leaned over to try and shut off the television.

"Oh, I know that," Ben said, leaning forward with his elbows on his knees, sensing a conversation starting.

"They've been through an awful lot these past months. Those kids are really great kids. I would have anyone of them any day of the year."

"They sure seem to be, sir," Ben answered.

"Oh, they are. Ain't any better around," Dan bragged.

"I haven't been around kids all that much. I've been on my own for a pretty long time," Ben said, now rubbing the lower part of his chin, which was slightly unshaven, giving off a rasping sound.

"I was the same way as you. It's funny. I didn't have any children of my own, but I sure seemed to have adopted an awful lot of 'em."

"Really? I thought you had children."

"Nope. I would never have guessed someone would be calling me Grandpa one day, but I kind of like the idea now. Especially with those kids," Dan said, looking directly at Ben. "I'd do anything for 'em."

"Well, I think very highly of 'em too. Sarah and the kids have really had quite an impact on my life."

"Oh, you don't have to tell me, brother. I was a bachelor till I was almost 34. My first wife had four kids, all boys."

"Really? If you don't mind me asking, what happened to her?"

"She died. Liver cancer."

"Oh, I'm sorry."

"No, don't be. I have four great stepsons and their families, and now I have Claire and her two daughters and there's a brother, but he doesn't come around much. Daughters I thought I would never have. Sarah is special, though," Dan said, as he looked around at all the photos, as if trying to find proof in all the different faces that lined the walls.

Ben looked around at the photos. "You don't have to tell me that, sir. I've never met anyone like her."

"And you won't again. You seem like a good man, Ben. I just wanted you to know that I know a little bit about what you're going through."

"It's all been good for me. Without Sarah and the kids, I would be spending another night alone. I went from having no one to worry about but myself, to her and the kids. I never really thought I would have children."

"Me neither, brother, me neither. Now how about we get some chow," Dan said, while slapping Ben on the back.

"Sounds good, Dan. I'm right behind ya."

Chapter Thirty-Two
The Most Wonderful Time of the Year

Ben's company Christmas party was approaching, and this year Ben couldn't help feeling like a five-year-old waiting for Christmas morning. He had never brought a date to the Christmas party before. For years he went alone, his time spent sitting and watching other couples out on the dance floor. He would usually bow out early and end up at a casino – lost in the miles and miles of faces – his isolated state, hidden within the crowd.

Sarah, still working at the department store, hadn't bought herself anything new for quite some time and wanted to splurge for a new dress for the Christmas party. Her older dresses were all too big, and Sarah found herself swimming in them as she wondered how she ever fit in them in the first place.

On her break, Sarah headed to the clothing department to scope out the sale racks. Searching through the miles and miles of dresses, she finally spotted what she thought was the perfect one. The dress had an outer layer of black lace that overlaid a shiny beige material. When she tried the dress on, it was a little more form fitting then Sarah thought it would be. Her friends' reactions to the dress were not what she expected. They immediately noticed how well the black lace dress melted around Sarah's curves and petite waist.

"It's perfect," Gina said. "Simply scandalous."

"Scandalous?" Sarah questioned. "I was going for conservative."

"Well, you missed that by a long shot," Kate said, while placing some new perfume sets into one of the glass cases and then closing the door. "No really, it's perfect, Sarah. Every man in the room is going to have his eyes on you."

"You think it's too much?" questioned Sarah, now turning from side to side in front of a nearby mirror.

"No… No…" they both said at once.

"It's on sale. I can get it for about $22.00 with my discount."

"It's perfect, sweetie. Ben is going to love it," Gina said.

"Okay… I'll get it." Sarah then headed back into the dressing room to put her work clothes back on before the manager caught them goofing off.

The night of the Christmas party, Sarah was extremely nervous. Jackson and Hope were downstairs playing while Saline and Lily helped Sarah get ready.

"Which shoes are you wearing, Mom?"

"I'm going to wear these," Sarah said, as she slipped on a pair of black satin pumps with pointed tips.

The girls watched their mother dress for her date. The scene was familiar and unfamiliar all at the same time. The girls reflected on when they were little and they would help Sarah get dressed for a date with their father. Now it was with Ben. They couldn't help but remember their father at a time like this, and wondered why he would ever leave someone like their mother.

"That dress looks like something they wear on *Desperate Housewives*." Lily laughed.

"What?" Sarah said, now getting even more nervous.

"It kinda does, Mom," Saline added. "But it looks great."

The doorbell suddenly rang. Jackson and Hope raced to answer it. They asked who it was before they attempted to open the door. They stood and giggled as they waited for a response.

"It's Ben."

"Ben whoooo…?" Jackson said, trying to cover his mouth with both hands while giggling.

"Ben, your mom's date," Ben answered, aware he was the object of Jackson's mischief.

"What's the password?" Hope said, joining in, as she continued to giggle, barely able to restrain her laughter.

"Jackson! Hope!" Lily screamed while descending the stairs. The two quickly receded to the living room, hiding behind the sofa, as Lily headed over to the front door to open it.

"Jelly bean!" Ben yelled at Lily, unaware that the two little ones had removed themselves from the foyer.

"Jelly bean?" a startled Lily questioned.

"The password." Ben smiled.

"Oh… sorry about them. Mom's almost ready." Lily moved to the side to allow Ben in.

Saline was upstairs helping Sarah pick out some earrings. "Mom, you look awesome. You are going to be the prettiest one there."

"Okay… I'll take your word for it."

"Augh… Mom, just go and have a good time."

Ben had made his way over to the couch and was holding Jackson upside down when Sarah descended the stairs.

"Ben who, huh…?" Ben said while juggling Jackson.

Jackson giggled while screaming, "Put me down! Put me down!"

Ben then looked up and gently lowered Jackson to the carpet. The kids slowly sat back up on the couch. They were all now looking at Sarah.

"Wow…" was all that Ben could manage.

"Do you like it?" Sarah said, combing her hair down with her fingers.

"Yeah… I like it," Ben responded. Jackson took advantage of the situation and tried to blindside Ben after jumping off the loveseat. Ben grabbed Jackson and flopped him back onto the loveseat playfully.

"That's enough, Jackson," Sarah said, afraid that Ben would grow tired of Jackson's antics.

"Oh, he's fine, dear," Ben said, as if reading Sarah's mind. "He doesn't bother me."

"Okay…" Sarah said, immediately realizing that Ben had called her 'dear' again, the words making her heart melt.

"Well, are you ready to go?" asked Ben, now even in more of a hurry to get to the Christmas party.

"I am."

"Wait," Saline said. "We want to get a picture of you two by the tree."

The two of them moved closer to the Christmas tree.

Sarah glanced at the tree, remembering the night that they had put it up…

Ben and the kids had hauled the large tree into Sarah's living room almost a week ago. It was completely decorated now. The kids, not able to restrain themselves, had decorated it that day.

After they brought the tree in, they had debated on where to put it, finally deciding to place it by the fireplace.

Jackson and Hope, too excited to sit still, began going through the Christmas decorations, pulling them out one by one. Sarah had several ornaments the kids had made over the years: stars with glitter missing, Rudolph with one antler, and a Santa that was missing his red hat. Each of these had a special memory for her, especially the ones with the pictures of her children pasted on the front. These she would never part with.

Sarah remembered how Saline and Lily sat and diligently unknotted all the lights. She thought about how she and Ben took turns going around the tree with the white strings of lights, making sure there was no empty space on the tree. When they were finished, Sarah had stepped back and watched as Ben helped the kids place the ornaments on the tree and slowly and patiently lifted Jackson and Hope up high so they could place some of the ornaments on the top half.

After all the decorations were on, Ben lifted up Hope so she could place the angel at the very top. On the way down, Hope spontaneously kissed Ben on the cheek, thanking him. Ben immediately turned red. He then made his way over and sat next to Sarah as the lights were turned on.

As the lights twinkled in the darkness, they all gathered around the tree and realized that this was a moment they didn't think would exist anymore. A moment that they thought they had lost. That night a calmness started to transcend this new little family – a familiarity that shouldn't have been familiar at all, had begun.

Sarah was brought back from her thoughts of that day by the flash of Saline's camera. "Got it," Saline said.

After the pictures were taken and goodbyes were said, Ben rushed Sarah out of the duplex. The hotel, where the party was being held, was located in the heart of downtown Topeka. Sarah slid into Ben's truck and sat in the middle of the bench seat, right next to Ben. Ben placed one hand on Sarah's thigh, caressing the rounded edges and the other hand on the steering wheel.

"You look very beautiful tonight," Ben said, turning and smiling at Sarah. Ben then lifted his arm and placed it around Sarah, drawing her closer to him.

Driving through the abandoned streets of the downtown area, Sarah caught notice of the small coffee shops and restaurants she didn't know existed in Topeka. The old brick buildings, lined with large glass windows, stood toe to toe with the modern cold architecture, the two battling it out for the rights to their own turf.

Right in the heart of the downtown area stood the capitol. Large stone staircases that faced north, south, east, and west stretched out in each direction. A large, topaz-colored dome set on the top, holding a golden Indian figure with a bow in his hand, bending back the bow ready to release his arrow into the air, sending it right toward the North Star.

The hotel was set on the east part of the downtown area. Sarah and Ben pulled up to the front parking lot. They both just sat in the truck for a moment, not saying a word.

"Well, shall we go in?" Ben finally said, taking Sarah's hand in his and bringing it up to his lips, kissing her hand softly.

"I'm ready when you are."

Ben opened his truck door and Sarah came sliding out behind him. Ben automatically held out his arm and Sarah latched on to it. They entered the large glass doors and headed toward a large multi-colored stone fountain that stood just outside the banquet rooms. Ben, unable to sustain his excitement, proudly walked into the banquet room with Sarah on his arm.

He was immediately greeted by friends and co-workers. People who had seen him show up to the Christmas party year after year alone. The women seemed to look at Ben differently with Sarah on his arm. The men, who once felt sorry for Ben, now stood in envy, as Ben and Sarah strolled across the floor to a large round table in the front of the dance floor.

Sarah gazed at her surroundings; the banquet hall was everything she had imagined. Chandeliers hung from the ceiling, giving off a soft glow. There were miles of round tables in every direction covered with white tablecloths. A gold tree-shaped centerpiece stood in the center of each table. The desserts were already placed on the table consisting of chocolate cake or cheese cake, the white china blending in with the tablecloth. People were dressed in festive Christmas colors, the women in party dresses, and the men in slacks and suits. As they neared their table, they were immediately welcomed by Ben's friends.

"Well, look who it is," Ronnie said, giving Ben an ornery grin. Ben headed for one of the eight chairs to pull one out for Sarah. Sarah stopped to shake Ronnie's hand as he headed over to where Ben and Sarah were standing.

"What?" Ben said.

"Nothing, nothing, you overachiever, you," Ronnie said, nudging Ben in his side. "He doesn't have any manners this one, so I'll introduce myself. I'm Ronnie, the good-looking friend."

"The heck you are," Chuck interrupted, catching the last of Ronnie's speech as he came up behind Ben and Sarah.

"That would be me, I'm Chuck, nice to meet you, Sarah." Chuck, a lot younger than Ronnie and Ben, leaned in to kiss Sarah's hand.

"Ah none of that," Ben teased Chuck, pulling Chuck back by his shirt.

"What, I was just introducing myself." Chuck laughed. Chuck then turned toward Sarah, winking at her. "What are you doing with this guy anyway?"

"Oh, you know, he's kind of cute in a scruffy, tall drink of water kind of way," Sarah said without hesitation.

Chuck smiled. "I like her. Does she have a sister, Ben?"

"Yes, she does, Chuck, but you aren't going to be meeting her." Ben laughed, now pulling out Sarah's chair. Sarah sat down, enjoying being the center of attention.

Just then, Ronnie's date pulled him back to his chair and leaned over the table to introduce herself, "Hi, Sarah, I'm Camille."

"Nice to meet you Camille," Sarah said, noticing how young Camille was. Ronnie, seeing another co-worker, immediately took off to talk to them, leaving Camille to manage on her own.

Just then a middle-aged man in a baseball cap, shirt and tie, made his way to the table. Ben stood up as the man came closer.

"Sam, how ya doin'?" Ben asked, "You're all dressed up tonight."

"You're looking pretty spiffy too, Ben. Did she pick out your clothes for you?" Sam said, giving Sarah a thumbs-up. Sarah smiled overhearing him.

"No, I picked them out myself, thank you very much."

"Sure you did." Sam put out his hand. "Nice to meet you, Sarah, I'm Sam, and this is my wife, Patty."

Patty, a short woman with flaming red hair, leaned over to shake Sarah's hand. Patty spoke very softly, so low that Sarah had to strain to hear her over the background noise.

The two men conversing back and forth, continued to give each other a hard time.

"They're always like this," Patty said.

"I figured." Sarah laughed.

Sarah then noticed a slightly bald man with a prominent nose and glasses headed toward their table. He moved swiftly, pulling at his tie and announcing that he was late, rushing as if the place were on fire.

"I couldn't find a dang parking place," Alex said, not noticing the new face in the crowd. "Those idiots wanted to park my car. I said no way. You never know what they're going to do with your car."

"Yeah, Alex, it's not like they do that for a livin' or anything," Ben said sarcastically, looking over toward Alex.

"Well, I don't know. I don't trust 'em. So, I had to park across the street and walk over," Alex blurted out, while taking his seat, flicking his napkin out to wipe the sweat from his brow. Alex, then noticing Sarah, turned to greet her. "Well, you must be the Sarah we've heard so much about."

"Yep, that's me."

"Nice to finally meet you." Alex put out his hand out to shake Sarah's. "We've been telling this numbskull to bring you around."

"I wanted her to get to know me before she met the kind of guys I hang around with," Ben said. "You know, I didn't want to give her the wrong impression."

"Well, it's too late now," Ronnie shouted out, laughing. "Hey, when does this dinner start anyway?"

"I don't know," proclaimed Alex. "Hey, Ben, you won't mind if I borrow Sarah for a dance or two, would you?"

"You stay away." Ben shook his finger at Alex.

"What, you don't trust me? That hurts, Ben."

"No, I don't." Ben laughed.

Ben's friends seemed to get a kick out of embarrassing him and then bragging him up to Sarah, all at the same time. Sarah could feel how much they cared for him.

Even Ronnie made a comment after accidentally calling Ben cheap in front of Sarah. "You won't find anyone one better than that one," Ronnie amended himself. "Ben is the best, ain't no better."

Ben was even shocked with the comment. He sat and grinned as his friends fawned over Sarah.

Things started to simmer down as dinner started. The plant had hired a DJ, and he began to play music as soon as the dinner was over. A variety of prizes were handed out throughout the evening. Staff cheered as one employee after the other went up to claim their prize. In between all of this, Sarah, who loved to dance, dragged Ben out to the dance floor every chance she got.

As the evening came to a close, Ben took Sarah's hand and led her to the dance floor on the last slow song of the night. Ben held her close as he smiled and waved to friends around him. Ben looked down at Sarah, proudly feeling that he had the most beautiful woman in the room in his arms. Ben stared at Sarah for a moment. "Thank you," he said.

"For what?"

"I am just so proud to be with you tonight."

"Well, I'm glad, honey. I am proud to be with you, too."

"I love you, Sarah,"

"I love you, too."

Ben held her close as they moved to the rhythm of the song. Ben tried to remember the last time he had felt this happy.

Chapter Thirty-Three
The Definition of Family

The next morning, Ben's mind filled with thoughts of Sarah and how beautiful she looked at the Christmas party. But as doubt began to raise its evil head, there were times he began to question himself. He wondered if he should have let his guard down so easily. He wondered whether or not he was opening himself up for heartache again. He began to believe the lie…

Ben thought about how he would recover from Sarah and the kids if for some reason his and Sarah's relationship didn't work out. Ben just wasn't sure he had any new beginnings left in him.

Just a few short months ago, he had resolved himself to the idea that he would be alone for the rest of his life, then she happened… they happened. He began to doubt whether he could be the father the children needed or the man Sarah deserved.

These thoughts flew through Ben's head as he entered the rock driveway of the family farm, hoping to get some feeding taken care of.

When Ben had completed his chores, he stopped by his parents to see if they needed anything before he left.

"Oh, the market has grapefruit on sale." Cathy picked up the sale ad. "Do you mind pickin' us up a couple, son?"

"Nah, Mom, you know I don't mind."

"I just thought you might have plans today," Cathy said.

"No, I have to be back out here later to work cattle with Mike." Ben walked over and grabbed a freshly baked cookie from the plastic tub his mom set on the kitchen table.

"Oh, that's right," Cathy said, realizing what day it was.

"I told you Mike and Ben were comin' out," Larry mumbled, juggling his pipe between his lips.

"I don't know where my mind is these days," Cathy answered, shaking her head.

"Ah, don't worry about it, Mom. I can't seem to remember what day it is anymore either, and I'm a little younger than you two." His mom and dad snickered at Ben's comment.

"Oh, I meant to tell you that Lindsay and Mitch are coming in for Christmas," Larry said. Ben, who hadn't seen his sister in a while, lit up with the news.

"Oh, they are? Well, that's a nice surprise."

"Yep, they called yesterday, said they would be here Christmas Eve," Larry said.

Ben then asked about his brother who lived in Colorado, "What about Brian and Sheryl?"

"Yeah, they're coming too, bringing the whole family." Larry took a moment to refill his pipe.

"Great, well, I got that week off anyway, so I'll be able to spend some time with 'em."

"Yeah, your mom here is already planning the meal."

"Well, nothin' wrong with being ready," Cathy said.

"Oh, I know, Mom. Well, it'll be good to see everyone. I'll plan to be here."

"Well, what about your lady friend?" his dad said, as he took a drink from his coffee. "You two don't have plans? You could always bring her."

"Nah, I think she has plans with her family. I'm pretty sure anyway," Ben said, not sure he wanted to introduce Sarah quite this soon to his siblings. "Well, you two take care of yourselves till I get back."

"We will," his mother answered, taking some dishes to the sink.

Ben headed back into town hoping to get a nap in before meeting Mike later.

After the divorce, Ben had made a promise to himself. He promised himself that no other woman would sleep in his bed unless he could honestly trust her, unless he felt that she was the one. He eventually came to the realization that this woman didn't exist, but that was before Sarah.

He entered his home through the sliding back doors and headed for his bedroom. The floral wallpaper still sagged in the corners and the empty bed that had carried him through all those years, no longer looked so appealing. It would never compare to Sarah's soft skin.

Ben laid down on his bed and found himself longing for Sarah to be next to him. It took him longer than usual to fall asleep. The bed felt cold and empty; so much so that if Sarah had called and asked him to drive back to Topeka just for a few hours, he would have. These thoughts ran through his mind as he finally settled into an exhausted sleep.

The alarm sounded and Ben hit it groggily, straining to open his tired eyes. Ben got up, taking off the layers of blankets that kept him warm. He sat up on his bed looking out the south window. It would be a good day for working cattle.

The sun was bright and warmed his face as he made his way to his truck heading back out to the farm to meet Mike.

As the days turned into weeks, Ben began to leave Sarah's complex later and later. It seemed to be getting harder and harder for either of them to say goodbye.

The holidays were quickly approaching. Sarah's favorite season, Christmas, was just around the corner. She was actually looking forward to having Christmas this year, which was an unexpected surprise. She had thought it might be a difficult Christmas for her and the kids, but then she met Ben. He somehow made the first Christmas without Jack just a little bit easier, or so she thought...

One evening, Ben stopped by after work. Sarah, without hesitation, and with a glimpse of excitement in her voice, blurted out what she had assumed Ben had been wanting to hear. "So, what time will you be here Christmas Eve?"

"Christmas Eve? Honey, I thought I told you. My family is getting together. My sister Lindsay and her family are coming, and Brian and Sheryl are driving in from Denver."

"No... you didn't tell me," Sarah hesitated. "That's okay. I understand. So, can you be here on Christmas Day. The kids like to open their gifts early and I wanted you to see their faces when they open your gifts. I can have them wait until you get here."

"Well, I was kinda hopin' we could get together after Christmas to open gifts with the kids."

"After Christmas?" Sarah said.

"It's jus' my family isn't always able to get together on Christmas, but this year we will all be at my parents and I was hoping to spend it with them. I thought we could do our Christmas the day after," Ben hesitated, as he tried to read Sarah's reaction.

Not being able to hide her emotions, Sarah's disappointment was obvious. "Well, I guess I assumed you wanted to spend Christmas with us... with me."

"I do. It's just my family is all in town. Honey, you're making too much out of this," Ben pleaded.

"Too much out of this?" Sarah then stopped to look at Ben as he walked toward the front door, getting ready to head back to his place.

Maybe she was, but at this point Sarah didn't care. Thoughts flew through her head as she realized she and the kids would be spending Christmas without him and somehow this fact didn't seem to bother him in the least.

"What? What did I say?" Ben asked.

"I already told my parents you would be there," Sarah hesitated for a moment, reflecting on her parents' reaction after hearing the news that Ben wouldn't be coming.

"Honey, can't we get together the day after Christmas? I never told you I would be here for Christmas."

"Yeah, I guess I just assumed you wanted to be with me. With us." Sarah then looked up at Ben, giving him a stern look. "So, that's the day you set aside for me? The day after Christmas."

"Honey, I am not going to miss this time with my family. You have to understand." Sarah, now more hurt than angry, turned away from Ben, trying to hide her disappointment. "Okay, how about I meet you at your parents' later Christmas Day."

Sarah, more relieved, turned back toward Ben. "Can you be there by three? That's when my parents want to eat, and I can keep the kids from opening your gifts until then."

"Three, that's awful early, honey. How about six?"

"We're eating at three," Sarah said, still disgusted that Ben didn't feel the need to be with her at all.

"Okay, okay, I'll be there at three," Ben said, feeling like he had no choice in the matter.

"All right," Sarah sighed. Had she been wrong about him? Had she so misjudged his feelings? She felt ill as she felt Ben kiss her cheek, and without a word, he walked to the door and slowly opened it and closed it behind him.

Ben called Sarah on the way to work the next day, hoping to come over that night. Sarah refused his request, making up an excuse that she was tired and had to get to work early the next day. Ben didn't question her response. He knew he had upset her, but he felt like she was being a little unreasonable about the whole thing. After all, what did she expect him to do, give up his time with his family?

It was hard to tell Ben not to come over, but Sarah was too hurt to see him at that point. She felt she needed time away from him. She needed to think. She wanted to give him time to think. Maybe they were moving too fast. Maybe it was too fast for Ben. Sarah was ready for a relationship, but possibly Ben wasn't. Maybe he would never be. She prayed about it, asking God to forgive her for being so irresponsible with her feelings once again.

Ben called later that day to see if Sarah was still angry with him.

"Hi, dear, how was your day?" Ben asked Sarah.

"It was fine," Sarah said coldly.

"Do you want me to come over later?" Ben said, hopeful that Sarah would change her mind. He still felt he had done more than his share of trying to make everyone happy. She would just have to understand about this one thing. After all, he had a family too.

"No, I have stuff to get ready for the kids, and I'm having my parents over Christmas Eve." Sarah felt bad about telling Ben no. She just couldn't face him right now. She started to feel the rejection all over again. He still felt his family, his brothers and sisters, were more important than she and the kids. Maybe they were. Maybe Ben just wasn't ready for them.

"Oh, okay. So, I'll see you on Christmas Day then?"

"I guess," Sarah said, too upset to get anything else out.

"Sarah, I am trying here," Ben said.

"I know you are," Sarah answered him. Silence then followed.

"There's something wrong. Why are you acting this way?" Ben asked, trying to get at why Sarah wouldn't talk to him. Ben felt that she just expected him to give in.

"What does it matter? We are just friends anyway," Sarah blurted out.

"Dear, that's not what I meant," Ben said, trying to make Sarah see his side.

"Oh, then what exactly did you mean? You didn't even invite me or the kids over to your family's Christmas celebration."

"I don't think that would be the best time to introduce you all to my family."

"Why not?"

"Well, we just started seeing each other. Can't you understand I just want to be with them this one time? You'll meet them eventually."

Those words stung Sarah like a wasp to her heart, the lump in her throat grew larger with each new comment. His family. Her family. She struggled with why she had let herself get so attached to this man. Why she had let herself fall so hard, so soon.

"Oh, I can understand. Don't worry about coming Christmas Day. My family will be fine without you," she said.

"Sarah, I said I would come Christmas Day."

"Do whatever you want, Ben."

"What does that mean? Sarah, you are being ridiculous."

"I'm being ridiculous? Here's ridiculous for you." Sarah then hung up on Ben. Ben tried to call back several times, but Sarah refused to take his calls.

She felt rejected all over again. It was as if Jack had happened all over again. Ben obviously didn't feel the way about her and the kids that she thought. She couldn't imagine not spending Christmas with Ben, after all they had been though, after all they had meant to each other. It was as if her heart was breaking all over again. And this time, it wasn't from Jack…

Chapter Thirty-Four
The Promise

Christmas Eve came and went. Having not seen Sarah, Ben called her that morning to reassure her he would be at her parents' house later that day. Ben, feeling he had no choice but to leave his family's celebration early, told Sarah he might run a little late, but he would be there.

Sarah and her mother spent the day cooking and baking. The kids looked forward to a big Christmas dinner as three o'clock rolled around. Saline had asked Sarah if after dinner she and Lily could drive to Kansas City to visit their father's side of the family. Jack was going to be picking up Jackson and Hope after dinner to take them. Sarah agreed, feeling the heartache of divorce all over again.

"So, your fella's coming about three, huh?" Dan teased Sarah.

"Yeah," Sarah said, looking at the clock which read 2:30.

Dan returned to the oven. "Okay, well, this bird should be ready by then."

Dan had got up early to cook Christmas dinner for Sarah, Ben, and the kids. His other kids rarely showed up anymore having families of their own, so he looked forward to cooking for a big family again.

"Well, I hope Ben's hungry." Dan sat down to watch the football game on the television they kept on the kitchen counter.

"Well, he's coming from his family's dinner so I don't know how hungry he will actually be."

"Where are the kids anyway?"

"I think they're watching a movie in your room."

"Claire! Claire!" Dan yelled out.

As Sarah's mother answered back, "Yeah, I'm right here, you don't have to shout!"

"Get busy on the gravy, woman," Dan said, without looking away from the television.

"It's right here." Claire moved over toward the stove. "If it had been a snake, it would have bit you."

"I'll get the table set, Mom." Sarah moved through the small kitchen, reaching into the cabinet for plates and silverware. Sarah went around arranging all the plates on the table, setting a place for Ben next to her. She thought it was funny that Ben hadn't called her yet. He usually called her when he was on his way. Sarah quickly checked her cellphone to make sure it was working.

She set down the china her parents used on special occasions. It probably wasn't real china, but that's what they called it. Actually, Sarah and Jack had given them these dishes one Christmas, ages ago. It was a beautiful pattern with silver trim and a floral pattern displayed around the edges. Sarah took out the water goblets and set them on the table. She and the kids had waited to open gifts until Ben got there. Sarah knew the kids also wanted to see his face when he opened their gifts to him. The gifts for Ben were nothing special, just socks and gloves, but they had saved the money themselves from chores and school grades, and the kids wanted to make sure Ben was included on this special day.

It was close to three when they started to get all the condiments out of the refrigerator. The rolls would be put out last to assure they were warm. Hope came in and helped Sarah with the silverware. Sarah then set out some tea in a pitcher. Sarah's family never set all the food on the table like Ben's family did. They formed an assembly line and went through the stove and island picking up deviled eggs, turkey, potatoes, and other traditional sides.

Three o'clock finally rolled around and Dan began to look at his watch, trying to soothe his stepdaughter's disheartened looks as she sat watching the clock.

"He probably ran into trouble at the farm. He'll be here any minute."

"I know. He told me he would be here, so..." Sarah said.

"Are we going to eat now, Mommy?" a hungry Hope asked.

Jackson then came in behind her. "Yeah, I want to eat, I'm hungry."

"Just give your mother a second. We're going to wait a little while on Ben," Dan said, now growing concerned himself.

"Mom, we have to be out of here by five," Saline said.

"I know. We'll just give him a couple of minutes."

Sarah sat in one of the empty chairs, trying to look like she wasn't worried. She made conversation and joked with Dan and her mother as the large hand on the clock slowly made its way down.

"Smells good, Grandpa," Lily said, as she came bouncing in.

"It should. You know your grandma cooked most of it," he said jokingly.

"She did not," laughed Jackson.

"Oh, yes she did," Dan said, teasing Jackson. "She was up at five o'clock this morning putting the turkey in."

"Don't you believe him," Claire said, now rubbing Jackson's shoulders.

As that old clock stuck 3:15, they all decided to go ahead and get their drinks. After another fifteen minutes of pouring tea, pop and water into glasses filled with ice and making side salads, the group decided to go ahead and start. Sarah, embarrassed that she had told her parents Ben would be there, tried to put on a happy face as she slowly gathered food that she had no intention of eating.

They all sat down and grabbed one another's hands as they took turns giving thanks. Sarah had originally thought about giving thanks for Ben, but changed her mind as her disappointment got the better of her.

Dan questioned the kids about their visit to Kansas City. The kids had missed spending time with Jack's family and were anxious to see them again. Jack came from a large family. He was the oldest of eight. His close-knit family was something Sarah missed the most. She was very close to his siblings. They had become her family also. But that all ended with Jack's one act. The children leaving was only a reminder of the fact that she would no longer be able to spend Christmas with them.

After everyone had finished, Sarah and the children made their way to the living room to open gifts. When she entered the living room, Sarah glanced at the grandfather clock. The long hand of the clock now rounding the six read four-thirty and the children would be leaving soon. Sarah's sadness over the situation became more and more apparent as she started to shut down during the opening of the gifts. Sarah tried to look happy as she opened the small box the girls had given her. She was surprised by the one-hundred-dollar gift card that lay inside the small box, as Saline and Lily lit up with pride. Wanting their mother to receive something special for Christmas, they had got their father to send them money to purchase the gift card.

Ben had bought the kids very considerate gifts. He purchased Saline a cellphone. Saline lit up as she opened the box. "Oh, Mom, I love it. Tell Ben I said thank you."

Lily opened her gift, discovering a pair of boots she had seen at the mall that were much too expensive for Sarah to purchase. "How did he know?" Lily said, and instantly put the boots on. "Tell Ben thank you when he gets here, Mom."

"I will," Sarah said, now smiling, remembering how thrilled Ben was to get the kids things they wanted.

Jackson and Hope had already opened their gifts of toys and were playing with them as the clock rang out a loud five chimes.

"We hate to leave, Mom, but we need to get going before it gets too dark," Saline said, trying to conceal her excitement, as she and Lily gathered their things, thanking their grandparents for dinner.

"I know. You need to get on the road. I'll be fine. You all go and have a good time."

Sarah then got Jackson and Hope's things together. Jack called saying he would pick them up in a few minutes. Sarah hated speaking to Jack especially now when she felt so alone. She was very short with him on the phone, trying not to let on that something was bothering her.

Jack arrived and came in to say hello to Dan and Claire. Claire always greeted him with the same enthusiasm she always had. Dan was more reserved as he spoke to Jack only when Jack spoke to him. Jack, sensing something was wrong with Sarah, asked again if it was okay to take the kids. Sarah responded it was fine and helped the two younger ones to gather their things and then waved goodbye to them from the door.

After the kids were gone, Sarah headed into the living room where her mom and stepdad had settled in front of the television. They didn't know what to say. They knew it was probably something unpreventable that kept Ben away, but their words fell flat as Sarah's spirit grayed and she didn't think she had the strength to drive home. She tried not to show her sadness as she pretended to be watching the movie. And a deafening silence filled the room.

Six o'clock rolled around and Sarah fell into an exhausted slumber. When she awoke at 7:00 pm, Sarah laid on the sofa contemplating returning to her empty home. Feeling she needed to be alone, she began to gather her things. The disappointment of not hearing from Ben was just too much.

"You don't have to leave," Claire announced, as she came over to sit by her daughter, placing her hand on Sarah's knee.

"I know, Mom, thanks, but I just want to go home," Sarah said.

"I bet something happened. I bet he's on his way right now," Dan said, trying to lighten the mood. Sarah smiled back at him. "You watch, he'll call you, and everything will be fine," Dan said while changing the channel.

"Oh, Dan, I'm watching that movie," Claire blurted out.

"Okay, okay," Dan said as he changed the channel back.

"No, you two watch your movie. Everything was wonderful. I'll call you in the morning. I'm a little tired. I'm just going to head home."

Dan and Claire sat helpless as Sarah rose and hugged them goodbye and headed out the front door to spend her first Christmas evening alone. Somehow not having the kids around made the rejection even worse. Sarah faced an evening of watching television alone and then curling up into an empty bed.

Sarah entered her vehicle looking around to see if she saw Ben's truck. He had never been this inconsiderate before, and something told Sarah it wasn't some emergency that kept him away.

Sarah pulled away from the curb, wiping away tears she had spent all evening trying to hold back, when suddenly, Sarah's phone started going off. She dried her eyes and checked the name on the screen which read *Ben.*

Chapter Thirty-Five
My Old Friend, "Doubt"

"So, hear you are seeing someone." Ben's sister, Lindsay, announced to the group after dinner.

"Yeah, that's the rumor," Ben answered reluctantly.

"Well, tell us more, brother," his older brother, Brian, edged him on.

"It's going well, but I don't want to jinx it. You know me. She may get tired of me anytime now."

"True," Brian said, as he continued to rib his younger brother. "We do, but we have to put up with having you around."

"You're hilarious, Brian," Ben joined in at his own expense.

"So, she hasn't gotten tired of you yet?" Lindsay continued.

"Nope. Not yet, but it's only been a couple of months. Still time... still time."

Rachael, his niece, overhearing the conversation, joined in, "Well, I think she likes you, Uncle Ben. You should have brought her; I wanted to meet her."

"Well, Ben here wasn't sure if they would all fit," Mike continued jokingly, aware that the others did not know about Sarah's extended family.

"All fit?" his sister inquired. "Is she a large woman?"

"No... no..." Ben continued, "Well, the thing is, she has four kids."

Silence filled the room as pictures of their bachelor brother around four kids flashed through everyone's minds.

"But they are very nice kids," Cathy immediately interjected.

"Oh, you've met them, Mom?" Lindsay continued.

Larry then answered for Cathy, "Yeah, Ben here brought them out, and Mom and I had dinner with Sarah. She's very nice," Larry added. "And she is pretty easy on the eyes, too," he said, smiling.

"Ohhh..." his siblings answered in unison.

"There's nothing wrong with children. I have four of them myself," Cathy butted in, beginning to get annoyed with her children.

"No… no… we know that, Mom," Lindsay added. "Ben, we are now positive this woman is a saint to be putting up with you… and with four kids on top of that. I am already impressed." She laughed.

"Yeah… yeah…" Ben said. "Well, don't get your hopes up. It's all new. We haven't been dating all that long."

"You should have brought her," Debbie added. "I wanted to meet her."

"Maybe next time," Ben answered, trying to change the subject and move things along. "Well, anyone up for dessert? Mom, Dad, you all have gifts to open here."

"We got time… no hurry," Larry answered as they all settled into the living room and the clock read 3:00 pm.

Ben thought about his promise to Sarah and wondered what he should do. He played with his phone in his pocket, debating on whether he should call her or not. He knew she would be angry that he wasn't already on the way. Ben let go of his phone and sat down with his family, joining in on the conversation. Ben played games with his nieces and nephews and lost track of time as the evening got away from him.

He had convinced himself that Sarah would just have to understand his need to be with his family as he sat back and enjoyed their time together and figured Sarah was doing the same. After all, Sarah had the kids to enjoy… Ben only had the family before him and if for whatever reason Sarah decided to walk away, Ben would still have them.

Before he knew it, he looked up at the clock that read 7:00 pm, and it occurred to him that it was a good forty-five-minute drive to Sarah's parents' house from the farm. Ben, to the amazement of his family, said some quick goodbyes and without an explanation, headed out to his truck. He debated on whether to call Sarah now or to just show up and pray she has been too busy with her family to realize how late it had gotten.

Ben decided to try and call, for the mere fact that he didn't want to show up at her parents if Sarah wasn't there, the situation being awkward enough. And if she was still there, she might go easier on him if her parents were around. He decided it was worth the risk. He dialed the number and held his breath as he debated about what he was going to say, continuing to hear the phone ring and ring…

Chapter Thirty-Six
And Then There Was Pride

Sarah looked down at her cellphone and continued driving. She knew Ben would head to her parents' home thinking that she was still there, especially if she didn't answer her home phone. Sarah pulled in her driveway and looked down at the clock which was lit up bright white. It read 8:00.

She entered the silent duplex. She didn't even bother to turn on any lights.

She walked hearing her footsteps hit the tile floor as she collapsed on the bottom stair. Tears filled her eyes as she thought of her kids now with her ex-in-laws, eating desserts and celebrating the day, opening gifts. Her ex-sister-in-laws would be sharing their recipes as they passed around the desserts. The guys would probably get into a fight with all the women, as they pretended to argue about whether they should watch some sappy romantic comedy or a football game. The women always won. They would finish off the evening with board games and margaritas after all the kids were in bed.

Sarah looked around her empty room as she heard her cellphone ringing again. She picked it up seeing that the call was coming from her parents.

"He just left here," Dan said, as fast as the words would come out. "He said he was heading to your place. I told you he would come."

"Okay, Dad. Thanks for calling."

"You cheer up now. Everything will be all right."

"I know. I'll call you later."

Sarah decided she needed to leave. She ran frantically up the stairs, grabbing shirts off hangers, leaving the hangers swaying on the bar. She moved to the bathroom dropping miscellaneous items into a small black bag. She dialed Tiffany's number as she packed, praying that Tiffany would pick up.

"Hi," was all Sarah heard on the other end of the line. "How are you?"

"Fine, hey, what are you doing tonight and tomorrow?" Sarah asked in a hurry.

"Nothing really," Tiffany said, hearing the urgency in Sarah's voice. "We got all our holiday stuff done. We're all just relaxing."

"You feel like some company?" Sarah said, hoping Tiffany could sense her desperation.

"Yeah, that would be great. When are you coming?"

"Is right now okay?"

"Right now is perfect. We haven't had a girls' night in a while. Feel like getting some chips and salsa?"

"That would be great."

"So, when will you be here?" Tiffany asked.

"I just have to finish packing and I'll be on my way, so about an hour and a half."

"Great. I'll get ready to go out."

"Okay, see you soon…" Just then the doorbell to Sarah's duplex rang out again and again, as Sarah quickly ended her conversation. "I'll call you when I'm almost there."

Sarah had forgotten she had given Ben a key in case of an emergency, when she heard the downstairs lock *click* and the door open.

"Sarah… are you here?"

Sarah thought about not responding for a moment when she suddenly felt herself being drawn down the stairs.

"Yeah, I'm here."

"Hi, honey, how was your Christmas?" Ben said, moving closer to her as if it were three o'clock… and everything was fine. "I went to your folks' home…"

"I know you did," Sarah interrupted him.

"Oh, did your dad call?"

"Yeah…"

"Well, I got here as soon as I could," Ben said, trying to move closer to Sarah for a hug. Sarah moved back, almost pushing him away.

"Oh, you did? Do you know what time it is?"

"Honey, I told you I might be running late," Ben said, trying to down play the last few hours.

"No, late is 3:15 or 3:30, late is not eight o'clock," Sarah said, now crossing her arms in front of her. Sarah, too angry to speak, was trying not to burst into tears. She knew they were coming, tears of anger, not of sadness. These tears she was all too familiar with, tears of disappointment.

"Oh, I didn't realize it was that late," Ben said, regretting the words as soon as they were released, as Sarah stood there thinking, *Does he really think I'm that stupid?*

"What, did the clock in your truck suddenly stop working?"

"Honey, I was with my family. Time just got away from me."

"Oh, it did, huh…" Sarah said, now moving closer to Ben. Ben feeling her anger backed up a little, meeting the back of the sofa.

"I told you I was going to be with my family. I don't see anything wrong with that."

"Oh, you don't? Even though you told me you would be at my parents' at 3:00 and I sat there like a fool waiting for you!"

"Sarah, calm down," Ben said, holding his arms out in front of him.

"I don't want to calm down."

Ben stood for a minute, contemplating what he should say next.

"Well, what do you want me to do, Sarah? I didn't mean to upset you." After a few minutes of silence, Ben blurted out the words he would soon come to regret, but it was too late, they were already out floating in the air, "Do you just want me to leave?"

His words resonated around the room. And at that moment, he said exactly what she was feeling. Sarah hadn't known what she wanted until that exact moment. That was exactly what she wanted. Without knowing it, Ben had given her the words she was searching for. "Yes, I want you to leave, and I want you to leave right now. And give me my key back."

"Well…" Ben said, searching for words that didn't come. "Sarah, I just wanted to be with my family. You're being unreasonable."

"Unreasonable? I'm not being unreasonable. I'm doing you a favor. I'm just sending you back to your family. Now you can have all evening with them. Oh, and take tomorrow too."

Ben stood there speechless. His stubborn pride was winning the battle. He slowly took the key off his key ring and handed it to Sarah.

Ben waited for a moment looking at Sarah, hoping she would change her mind. He then slowly made his way to the door. He stopped and looked back, but said nothing. Sarah followed behind him silent, too angry to speak.

Without a word, Ben opened the door and left, looking back only once he was outside. He took a few steps forward, and was suddenly startled by the loud sound of Sarah clicking the lock on her door behind him. He looked back again, staring at the cold door.

Part of him wanted to go back and beg Sarah for forgiveness, but the other part of him couldn't bring himself to admit that he may have been wrong. Ben got into his truck, loudly slamming the truck door.

"If that's how she wants it, fine." Ben pulled away, hitting the gas. "I'm not heading home," he said to himself. He headed north up Highway 75, breaking all of the speed limits, trying to leave the memory of what had happened far behind. He headed to the one place that always welcomed him with open arms, the casino.

Chapter Thirty-Seven
The Road to Forgiveness

"I just wanted to let you know I'm heading to Kansas City to visit Tiffany for a day or so," Sarah told her mother while struggling to reach for the toll both ticket.

"To Kansas City? What happened to Ben? Didn't he come over?" Claire stammered.

"I told him to leave. He wanted to spend time with his family, and now he has all the time in the world with them."

"Sweetheart," Sarah's mother said softly. "He made a mistake. You shouldn't be that hard on him. After all, he did end up coming over."

"No, Mom. I'm done with making excuses for men. I'm done with putting up with what I don't have to. That just showed me how much I meant to him."

"Sarah, he's a good man." Claire moved away, so Dan couldn't hear her conversation with Sarah. "You shouldn't be so hard on him."

"I'm going to let you go now, Mom. I've got to drive." Sarah needed to get off the phone, afraid of what she might say in her state.

"Okay... okay. Just think about what I said, sweetheart."

"I've got to go, Mom. I'll call you later." Sarah hung up the phone, sorry she had called her mother. She couldn't get the conversation out of her mind as she thought to herself, *even her mother didn't think she deserved any better.* The highway was long and pitch black. It gave Sarah time to think as lighted images before her suddenly became blurs in her rearview mirror. She thought about Jack and the kids together with Jack's family. She thought about Ben heading back to his family, as she tried to figure out what exactly was God's plan for her.

Pulling up to Tiffany's house, Sarah exited her vehicle, lugging in a suitcase and makeup bag. Tiffany, seeing the lights enter her driveway, stood at the door happy to see her old friend. The two women hugged as Tiffany put her arm around Sarah, walking her into the kitchen.

Tiffany's two youngest children were playing video games as they both came over to say hello to their Aunt Sarah. Tiffany and Sarah had decided long ago that each other's kids would call them aunt and their husbands uncle. Richard, Tiffany's husband, was Uncle Richard to Sarah's kids. The two couples, who met before they had kids, grew to share a unique bond. Coming to Tiffany's was like coming home, and Sarah and Tiffany quickly retreated to the family area just off the kitchen where they could be alone.

Tiffany, ecstatic to see Sarah again, started their long conversation off, "So what's new?"

"I think I broke up with Ben."

"Oh, I'm so sorry, Sarah, what happened?"

"He didn't show, Tiffany. He didn't show for Christmas dinner. Well, I mean he did, but it wasn't until eight o'clock. I had already left my parents and was on my way home when I finally heard from him."

"Did he say why?" Tiffany inquired, now bringing a large brown pillow in front of her and hugging it.

"No. He just said he wanted to be with his family," Sarah said, brushing her long bangs out of her face.

"Had he asked you to join him there?"

"No. He insisted it was too soon for us to meet his whole family."

"Oh. I'm so sorry, honey. Do you still want to see him?"

"I don't know. When he came over, I was so angry I couldn't even see straight."

"What happened?"

"He came over, and we got into a huge argument. Well, it was really me more than him. He just stood there holding his ground, like he was right."

"That's because he really thought he was right."

"I know. He showed no remorse, not a speck of consideration for my feelings. It was so unlike him." As the words left Sarah's lips, it was the first time she had thought about how unlike Ben his actions really were. Ben really was a caring person. Sarah knew this better than anyone. He cared about her and the kids, and that's why none of his actions that night made any sense.

Tiffany hesitated for a moment then brought her hand against the side of her face as if she were having an epiphany. "Maybe it was something else."

"Like what?"

"Maybe he's still afraid of getting too close to you. Maybe he's afraid of his family's reaction. I don't know, maybe he's afraid you're going to leave him, too."

"I suppose."

"Well, we have all night to think about this. How about we get out of here and go and have a snack somewhere?" Tiffany said, hopping up from the sofa.

"I'm ready whenever you are."

Sarah slowly started to put her Christmas Day behind her. But trying to find an open restaurant that served margaritas on Christmas Day was harder than the two women anticipated. They finally found a small family-owned Mexican restaurant that was open. The two women headed in and ordered chips and salsa, and two frozen margaritas.

"What did he end up getting the kids for Christmas?"

Sarah went on to explain the cellphone Ben had gotten Saline and the expensive boots he bought for Lily and the numerous toys the two had picked out for Jackson and Hope.

"Oh, he must be in love," Tiffany said.

"I thought so. It's just so unlike him to do something this inconsiderate."

"Maybe he just made a mistake. It happens. So, what did you do when he finally showed up?"

"I was furious. And then he tried to play it off like it was nothing." Sarah hesitated as the waitress came by to see how the two friends were doing.

"Thanks, we're fine," Tiffany responded, hoping that the waitress would get the message. The waitress smiled and walked away.

"He asked me if I wanted him to leave and I said yes."

"Boy, I bet he was sorry he said that," Tiffany proclaimed, snickering at her friend.

Starting to regret her actions, Sarah asked, "Do you think I went too far?"

"No, not at all. I mean, you can't let him treat you like that," Tiffany said.

"My mother doesn't seem to think so," Sarah sighed.

"Why, what did she say?"

"She thought I should have forgiven him on the spot, like I have to put up with someone treating me like that. Like no one else will want me."

"Don't you believe that. I mean, I'm sure that's not what she meant, but you did the right thing. He'll call you, you watch. You haven't heard the last of Mr. Ben."

Just then Sarah's phone lit up, and both women looked over at the screen as a name glared back at them. Sarah squinted her eyes at the screen as the name slowly came in to focus. The name on the screen read 'Dave.'

"Dave?" Tiffany said, "Who's that? Is he the one...?"

Sarah looked back up at Tiffany as she wondered what to do. "Should I answer?"

"Yes, just see what he wants."

Sarah juggled the phone in her hands as she struggled to open it before it stopped ringing. "Hello."

"Sarah, hello, Merry Christmas!"

"Hello, Dave, Merry Christmas." Sarah, looking at Tiffany, shrugged her shoulders in disbelief.

"I am sorry to call so late, I was just thinking about you and the kids and wanted to wish you all a Merry Christmas. How are you?"

"I'm good. How are you?"

"Well, you know, the kids just left to go back to their mom's house and I was just going through my phone and your name came up and I thought what the heck. So... anyway... did you have a nice Christmas?"

"Yes, it was fine." Sarah then looked at Tiffany raising her hands in question as Tiffany giggled at the irony. "My kids left with their dad, too."

"Well, I know it is late, but I wondered if you would be interested in getting some dessert and maybe coffee or hot chocolate. I know a great place open on Christmas evening. I mean, only if you want to. Do you have plans?"

"You know it is great to hear from you, Dave, but I'm currently in Kansas City visiting a girlfriend. We are actually having dinner right now."

"Oh, I'm so sorry. I didn't mean to interrupt. I just thought I would take a chance. I won't keep you. Do you mind if I call you some time? I mean, just as friends."

"I guess that would be all right."

"Okay, well, I'll try you sometime next week. It was great to talk to you. You have a great evening, Sarah."

"You too, Dave, bye."

Sarah hung up the phone and looked over at Tiffany in disbelief. "Wow, that was strange how he just called out of the blue like that."

"I know. Maybe it is a sign. Isn't he the one you broke up with to go out with Ben?"

"Yeah, that's him."

"You kind of liked him, didn't you?"

"Yeah, I did, but there was something about the way he ended up divorced that bothered me. He didn't seem to be totally honest with me."

"Oh, well, that's not good. He certainly seems to want to reconnect with you. Are you going to go out with him?"

"I don't know," Sarah said, glancing around the restaurant as if something was missing. She pictured Ben beside her and her hand in his. She remembered the way he always sat on the same side of the booth as her, like a couple of teenagers, because he said he liked being near to her. She thought of his face expression as he left her duplex and wondered if it was really over, and if she would ever see him again.

"Well, are you?"

"I'm not sure..."

The next day, Sarah awoke from a surprisingly restful sleep. It was just beginning to be light outside as she rolled over on to her side looking out the back window of Tiffany's house, which displayed massively large oak trees whose shadows reached into the interior. A slight breeze swayed them in the wind as Sarah sat and watched the shadows creak in and out of the room. She thought about Ben and wondered what he was doing at that very moment.

Sarah dragged herself out of bed and got her things ready to shower. Tiffany said she would be up early so they could head out for breakfast. Sarah checked her phone and found no missed calls as she made her way to the guest bathroom and turned the water on to an almost scorching temperature and watched the steam rise from the tile.

Sarah felt its warmth and stood there letting the water cover her, running her fingers through her hair, pressing it back against her head as she slowly turned, letting the water run down her back.

At that moment, Sarah's cellphone suddenly went off. The ringer was set on low so she wasn't able to hear it through the pelting water. Sarah stood absorbing the peaceful pellets onto her skin as she slowly began to wash her hair.

After showering, Sarah quickly got ready to go out. Tiffany came knocking at the door at 8:30 am sharp.

"Hey, are you ready?" Tiffany whispered.

"Yeah," responded Sarah as the two made their way to the garage, the rest of the house still in a deep slumber from a late night.

Sarah then glanced down at her cellphone, thinking that she should call and check on the kids. She saw that she had a missed call. Looking at the phone, Sarah smiled when she saw it was from Ben.

"He called, didn't he?" Tiffany asked, seeing Sarah's face light up, acknowledging that she had been right.

"Yeah," Sarah exclaimed softly.

"Well, tell me what he said," Tiffany barked, almost as excited as Sarah.

Sarah then began to play the message as Tiffany leaned in to hear:

"Ah... Honey, I've been tryin' to get a hold of you. I'm out at the farm. Sorry if the message is a little jumbled, I'm not sure what type of reception I'm gettin' out here." (A sound of wind suddenly washed across the mouth piece).

"Um… I not sure if you are gettin' my calls, but I just wanted to talk to you if I could. Ah… I'll try you back later. I love you…"

"Ah… he sounds like he really misses you," Tiffany said.

"Yeah, but I'm not sure I am ready to talk to him yet," Sarah said.

"Yeah, but it's nice to know he wants to talk to you," Tiffany interjected, as they both entered her vehicle.

"Yeah, it is."

Chapter Thirty-Eight
A Familiar Road

After Ben had left Sarah's duplex, he drove straight to the casino and found himself in the midst of other single men and women trying to find an escape from the holiday season. Ben, still agitated at Sarah's stubbornness, quietly debated if he had made the right decision. Ben wondered if he could return to the life he had known before Sarah. The life that seemed all too familiar, as the past now surrounded him like a bad dream.

He collected his losings and headed to cash out, looking around the smoke-filled room, feeling the loneliness of the crowd. There was the man pushing a portable oxygen machine, and a woman with gray hair and a long floral dress who played two machines at once, and who smiled at Ben as he passed by. The ringing of slot machine bells sounded around him as lights flickered on and off, simultaneously without end. Ben stopped to refill his drink and headed for the exit.

After arriving home, he found it hard to go to sleep. He flicked on the television, surfing through the channels trying to find an old western or poker tournament. Finally realizing there was nothing worth watching, Ben clicked off the television. He stared out his large bedroom window at the full moon that hung right above his bed. Ben thought about Sarah and suddenly reached beside him to find an empty space. He turned, grabbing a pillow, bringing it close to him, and he closed his eyes, hoping to fall asleep as memories of the past few months rushed through his thoughts, making their way into his dreams.

Awaking from a sleepless night, Ben arose from his bed wanting to believe that last night was just some sort of nightmare. Ben headed for the shower trying to wash off the smell of smoke that had embedded itself into his hair and skin from the casino.

As the water began to fall, Ben's breathing became short and labored. He felt dizzy as he grabbed on to the walls, afraid he was going to pass out. He tried to stay standing, bending over and coughing. He took several deep breaths before he regained his composure, looking through the thousands of clear drops beating against his face. He glared out the steam-filled shower doors onto the paneled walls of his bathroom. The brown seemingly moving closer to him as he gripped onto the towel bar, trying to clear his vision as the room closed in.

Ben slammed the shower doors open, quickly drying himself off. He had to refrain himself from running outside, while wearing only a towel and breathing in the fresh, clean air. He sat on his bed, hunched over trying to catch his breath, looking at the digital clock on his table. It read 7:00 am. Was it too early to call Sarah? Would she even talk to him? Ben sat reliving his actions as he fell back into his bed, sinking the palms of his hands into the sockets of his eyes.

"You idiot. What did you do?"

He decided he would try and call Sarah on his way out to the farm. The sky was as cloudy as Ben's brain, as he entered his truck dialing Sarah's number, misdialing and then dialing again, hearing the phone ring and ring.

After several failed attempts, Ben decided to leave a message.

Ben had taken four days off work to spend with Sarah after Christmas, and he now sat and wondered if he would ever see her again.

As in the past, Ben could always find ways to keep busy, to keep his mind from wandering. Chores were always needing to be done. Cows needed fed. He had to check on his parents. The tractor and the flatbed needed the oil changed. Yeah, Ben knew how to keep himself busy. He just didn't know if he knew how to live without Sarah.

Ben entered the two-lane highway leading to the farm with memories of Sarah filling his thoughts. He suddenly hit his steering wheel with his fist in disgust, taking his eyes off the road for a moment, causing his truck to slowly drift into the north bound lane at the exact moment a semi-truck was heading his way. The large truck blared its horn.

Ben, hearing the warning, yanked the steering wheel to the right, causing his truck to swerve onto the shoulder toward the decline. Ben, realizing he was heading downhill, pulled the wheel back toward the left, skidding to the shoulder of the road. Luckily for him, there had been no other traffic coming in either direction.

Ben leaned into the steering wheel, burying his face into his arms for a moment. Lifting his head, he slowly put the truck into drive and pulled back onto the road.

Shaken, Ben arrived at the farm just as his brother Mike was leaving their parents' house. Mike waved him down, as Ben slowed down beside him.

"Hey, brother, how was your Christmas with Sarah?" Mike asked, afraid that he and the family may have overstepped their limits when discussing Ben's relationship with Sarah that night.

Ben, unable to hide his ill humor, was not up for small talk that morning. "It went fine, Mike. I'm just going to head out south to finish up some fencing."

"No hurry, brother. We aren't planning on having cattle out there 'til spring. There's really no rush…"

Cutting his brother short, Ben said, "I know. I just thought I would get started, that's all."

"Well, it's up to you, but I can really handle it out here today if you got things you need to do," Mike said, thinking Ben might have had plans with Sarah, being that he spent the Christmas holiday with them. Ben, not wanting to go into details, became a little short with Mike as his agitation from his current situation got the best of him.

"I said I got it, Mike," Ben snapped.

"Okay, if you need any help, let me know." Mike then stepped back from the truck, as Ben sped off to the barn to collect some tools.

Mike, feeling his brother's sadness, stood and watched as Ben loaded the truck and headed off down the road, scattering leaves and dirty snow behind him.

Ben headed across the concrete bridge that the city put in shortly after Ben was born. The bridge was located just west of the farmhouse. As the story was told to Ben, the city had to get his dad's permission to build onto a section of their land in order to get the new bridge in. His dad, knowing that the city had to build the bridge, agreed to let them do so if they would build him ten-foot concrete walls around his well. Larry had already built six-foot walls, but feared that if they had a flood, the walls would not be tall enough to keep out the contaminated creek water. The city agreed. And Ben's family had fine running water ever since. And the city, well… they got their bridge built.

Ben drove over it, looking over the concrete sides that had shiny steel posts across the top. The cold winter water ran slowly through the creek, melting the snow-covered ridges as it passed by. In the spring, this area was one of the most beautiful on the farm. Water that rushed down this rock-filled creek, gave nourishment to plants and animals alike all year long.

He sighed as he drove over the creek, remembering how he got lost in its vastness as a kid, heading out to the creek with his fishing pole or catching crawdads, a different world, all in itself, untouched by the worries of contemporary life. Ben had always thought that this was what heaven must be like, at least his heaven.

After arriving at his destination, Ben lowered the steel post into the ground and got out the worn, rusted post driver that had been handed down to him and Mike from their father. The driver had a hollow, cylinderical body with a large handle on each side and was sealed on one end. Ben stood the post vertically onto the ground and covered the top of the post with the post driver. He then used both arms to raise the post driver up and pounded it down onto the steel post, over and over again, letting out an exceptionally loud grunt with each new strike.

The wind that rushed and howled around Ben's head, threatened to make him retreat to the warmth of his truck. Defying the loud screams of the blustery wind, Ben tied the hood of his jacket tighter under his chin.

He grabbed his cellphone, checking it to make sure it was still working. It was. He stuffed the cellphone back into his jacket pocket in the hopes that Sarah might call.

Ben succeeded in aligning a row of posts on the east side, but because of the frigid cold, he found himself giving into the ambush of Mother Nature and headed back to the truck sooner than he would have liked to. Ben thought about heading back home, but didn't want to be left with time on his hands, time to think.

He picked up his cellphone, checking for calls and tried to call Sarah again. She did not answer. He left another message. Ben took off his gloves, throwing them to the floorboard. He then hit the steering wheel so hard, he rocked the truck forward. Ben sat staring out at the empty field. The grass had patches of snow left on it. The trees now bare, shook, fighting back at the howling wind. Ben reached down to grab the gloves off the floorboard, swiping them up in one fierce motion. He then headed back out into the sting of the wind, feeling the cold air beat against his face.

Not being a coffee drinker, Ben hadn't brought anything hot to drink. He figured he might stop in to visit his folks on his way in and maybe grab a cup of his mother's hot chocolate. The thought of the hot chocolate set Ben to working faster as he anticipated the warm, smooth liquid warming his cold and achy body. Ben worked until he could no longer see his hands before him. He then started to gather the leftover posts, throwing them back into the bed of the feed truck. He started the engine, threw the truck into reverse and quickly backed out of the field.

Pulling up to the farmhouse, he sat for a moment watching his mother through the small north window of the kitchen. He watched her as she brought over a fresh cup of coffee for his father. He caught a glimpse of smoke rising just in front of the window and assumed it was from his father's pipe. After a moment, he exited the truck and slowly started walking toward the house, entering into the kitchen.

"Hey, Dad, how's it goin'?" His parents were just finishing up supper, his mother already at the sink washing dishes.

"How's it goin' out there?" Larry exclaimed.

"Oh, just fine, been workin' out on the south fork tryin' to get the posts into the ground," Ben replied.

"What, on a day like this? You're probably frozen to the bone. You want me to make you up some hot chocolate, son?" Cathy asked, already headed to the cupboard to retrieve it.

"That would be great, Mom," Ben said, as he sniffled and grabbed a tissue off the table to wipe his dripping nose.

"I thought you'd be in Topeka," Larry said, relighting his pipe.

"Nah, Dad, I needed to get some work done."

"Oh, didn't you have plans with Sarah?" Cathy asked nonchalantly, somewhat concerned.

"Yeah, but she had some things she had to get done. I'll probably see her while I'm off," Ben said, now getting up to wash his hands.

Cathy's demeanor sorrowed as she reached for the milk to put in the hot chocolate. "Supper's still on the stove. It's sloppy joes," Cathy added.

"You know, I might take you up on that, Mom. That sounds really warm."

"Go right ahead, take as much as you want," Larry said, trying to maneuver the remote control around for the television, his trembling hands fighting him all the way.

Ben got up, moved across the kitchen and gathered a bun and some steamy sloppy joe sauce.

"If I had known you were havin' this, I would have come in a lot earlier." Ben laughed, feeling the familiarity of his parents' home come rushing back. Ben finally began to relax, tired from his long day.

"So, you comin' out tomorrow?" Cathy inquired, trying to inconspicuously find out if he was still seeing Sarah.

"Yep, I think so anyway. Why, you need somethin' from town?" Ben questioned, as he took a bite of his sandwich and then reached to gather some leftover potato salad.

"No, no, just thought if you were goin' into Topeka, you could grab us some sale items." Cathy turned back toward the sink of dirty dishes, now anticipating the worst.

"Well, give me your list, Mom, and I'll try and grab what you need. I'm really not sure I'm goin' tomorrow, but I'm sure I'll be out there sometime."

"No hurry, just thought if you were goin' to be there anyway," Cathy said, now downhearted, believing the worst and afraid to ask.

"Well, son, did you get much done?" Larry inquired.

"Yep, got the whole side of the road done," Ben said proudly.

"Well, that's quite a feat on a nice day, let alone a day like this," Larry praised his son.

"Yeah… well… it's done," Ben said, hoping they wouldn't bring up Sarah again.

"Thought you had taken a couple of days off to visit that pretty lady friend of yours," Larry smirked, his pipe bouncing between his lips.

"I probably will, just not today."

Larry sensed he had hit a sore spot with Ben and quickly changed the subject.

"I hear they keep puttin' more and more lights out in town. Is that true?"

"Yep, I guess they're tryin' to get business for the antique shops. Tryin' to compete with the plaza lights in Kansas City, I reckon," Ben kidded.

Larry smirked while holding his pipe. "Guess so, son, guess so."

The three visited and reminisced about the Christmas holiday and the weather. Being that he was in no real hurry to get home, Ben relaxed in his parents' living room. Cathy and Larry enjoyed the company and figured whatever happened between he and Sarah was Ben's business.

After a couple of hours, Ben said his goodbyes. He headed out the kitchen door and into the raging wind. He sighed as he made his way to his truck not wanting to go home, but too tired to go anywhere else.

Ben finally made his way to his bed after showering and shaving. He clicked on the television, trying to keep his mind busy as he noticed the same moon glowing outside his window again. He wondered what Sarah was doing at that moment. He questioned if she would ever answer his calls again. He dreaded falling asleep because of the dreams that were most assuredly waiting for him as thoughts of Sarah filled the crevasses of his slumber.

Chapter Thirty-Nine
Faith, Hope, and Love

Sarah and Tiffany re-entered the silent, darkened kitchen from the garage door of Tiffany's home. The women, still full from a large dinner, decided to watch a movie. The two friends only made it halfway through the movie, as they found themselves falling asleep on the couch.

Sarah gently shook Tiffany as Tiffany snapped her head up, startled.

"I'm going to bed," a sleepy Sarah whispered to her friend.

"Me too." Tiffany rose and headed toward the DVD player.

Sarah began to collect her purse and shoes as she turned toward Tiffany. "Thanks for today," she said.

"Not a problem. It was fun. Are you leaving in the morning?"

"Yeah, the kids will be home in the afternoon, and I need to get home before they get there."

"Okay," Tiffany stated, feeling her friend's uneasiness about Ben. "You know, everything will be all right. He'll call again."

"I know. Good night, Tiff." Sarah headed upstairs thinking about her children. She felt like she had made another mistake. She had brought yet another man into her children's lives that they would have to say goodbye to. Her old friend 'failure' was laughing at her once again as regret started to bring her down, filling the depths of her soul.

Sarah entered the guest room and realized that Ben had not called since six. She walked over to the large window looking out into the darkness. She picked up her cellphone looking at his number. She then laid it back down on top of her purse. Consumed with indecisiveness, she started to get ready for bed.

She climbed into bed and put her head down over her knees and began to pray. She felt the tears start to race down her cheeks as she wiped each one away, preventing them from reaching their destination.

She gathered one of her pillows, hugging it, pulling it into her as she pressed her head down onto her pillow and slowly fell into a tear-filled slumber.

Sarah awoke a little more refreshed than the day before as she realized she needed to get back to Topeka, and to her life. She said goodbye to Tiffany and climbed into her vehicle, not looking forward to the long drive that would give her time to think, time to regret, before she had to face the questions from the kids.

Thoughts of the last couple of months filled her mind as she drove along I-70, hoping that her phone would ring one more time. Looking down at her phone, she cursed it. She wanted to throw it across the car, but she was afraid she would end up breaking it and the kids would not be able to get in touch with her.

Sarah was reaching the halfway mark when her phone suddenly lit up. Not looking at the caller, Sarah juggled the phone, dropping it twice as she swerved into the other lane.

"Hello, hello," Sarah said, hearing a dead silence on the other end and then suddenly…

"Sarah? Is that you?" It was Jack.

"Yes, it's me," Sarah said, now disheartened. She didn't want it to be Jack. She sat silent as Jack started rambling details off that she was halfway listening to.

"I'll drop them off in about two hours if that's okay?" Jack finally said.

"Yeah, that's fine," Sarah said, trying to sound normal.

"Are you okay?" Jack asked, as if he expected Sarah to just spill her guts to him.

"I'm fine," Sarah said annoyed. "I'll see you in two hours."

The day turned even more gloomy as clouds filled overhead. Sheets of rain slowly started to pour down onto Sarah's vehicle as if heaven's buckets were being released, which was unusual for this time of year. Low flying gray clouds covered the toll booths heading into Topeka. Barely able to see through the heavy downfall, Sarah tried to concentrate on the road before her as she made her way through Topeka. The rain was so heavy, Sarah had to pay special attention to the lines along the road in order to stay in her lane. She finally made it to her street as the rain showed no signs of letting up.

"Just great," was all she said as she pulled up into the driveway, attempting to hit the garage door opener when suddenly someone came out from around the corner of her garage. Startled, Sarah stretched to form the image that was before her. The tall image slowly moved toward her car. As she looked closer through the blanket of rain, she realized, through the haze, it was Ben.

Sarah smiled as tears began to fill her eyes. She reached over to the window control and slowly rolled down the passenger side window as the rain started to fill the now open space, soaking the passenger seat.

"What are you doing?" Sarah shouted at the sight of a soggy Ben standing in the driveway under the torrential rain.

"I thought I could stay away from you. I thought I could go back to the way my life was before you, but…" Ben struggled to talk through the pelting buckets of rain.

"But what?" Sarah said, as Ben headed to open the passenger side door, opening it and letting in even more rain.

"I can't. Sarah, you have to forgive me. I didn't understand what I was giving up. I'm so sorry."

"What are you talking about? You need to get in here. You are soaking me and the car."

"Oh, yeah… but there's one more thing."

"What? What are you doing?"

Ben then stepped away from the door, closing it as Sarah's breathing stopped. She looked down to see if she had the car in park as Ben slowly made his way in front of her car heading to the driver's side of the vehicle. Once he got there, he opened the door and knelt down on one knee, in the pouring rain, displaying a black box. He opened the box which contained a silver ring.

"Sarah Harris, will you marry me?"

"Marry you?"

"Yes, I'm so sorry. I won't ever take this love for granted again. Will you forgive me?"

Sarah, without thinking, suddenly jumped out of the car and into the soaking rain as they clung to each other – the farmer and the single mom.

"Yes, yes, I'll marry you… you crazy man. I love you."

"I love you, too. Don't ever lock me out again. I can't lose you." Ben took Sarah's face into his hands, kissing her among the millions of raindrops. "Sarah… you are my life."

Epilogue

Four months later, Ben and Sarah were married. Friends and family gathered to witness Sarah and Ben's road finally become one. They were married at Faith Bible Church. Sarah insisted on a ceremony that included the kids.

This was not just a ceremony between Ben and Sarah; it was the coming together of a family. It was as if God had sent Sarah to this lonely farmer with no children, and sent Ben to Sarah and the kids to become the father and husband he didn't know he was capable of being. And at the end of this road, there was a fantastic celebration, a sharing of themselves as they had become witness to what God can truly do with broken people… and broken roads.

Saline and Lily, the only bridesmaids, held a bouquet of blue carnations and white baby breath. Jackson, the ring bearer, walked down the aisle in a black suit and silver tie, and a black eye from a mishap the day before with a neighbor kid that left Jackson the target of a tree branch. The swelling, although somewhat dark in places, was practically unrecognizable in the pictures. Hope, the flower girl, walked down the aisle wearing a white dress and a cubic zirconia studded crown she said made her look like a princess.

In the back of the church, Sarah and her stepdad stood as they prepared to walk down the aisle.

"I told you it would all work out," Dan said, trying to think of something profound to say. Dan stood, continually trying to stretch out the collar of his starched white shirt.

"Yes, Dad, you did," Sarah said, not feeling nervous at all.

"You know, I'm very proud of you."

"Oh, Dad," Sarah said, giving him a hug.

"Now don't you go to cryin'. I won't have you blamin' me for your makeup being ruined."

"I won't," a now tearful Sarah said.

"Well, shall we go?" Dan said, now stretching out his arm.

"I'm ready," she said, trying to wipe the corners of her eyes with a tissue her stepdad handed to her.

Sarah stepped out in her simple, strapless, white gown and made her way up the aisle. She could sense Ben watching her. He looked at her as though this was the very first time he had ever seen her. He was breathless, and Sarah loved this about him.

The ceremony was short and included one of Sarah's favorite bible verses.

Pastor James stood before their friends and family and reflected on Sarah and Ben's journey. And he began... "How miraculous is our God who brought these two people together, against all odds, these two people whose roads came together in the parking lot of a restaurant, neither one knowing what God had in store for them. Ben here had given up on love. He had resided to the fact that he would be alone for the rest of his life, childless. And look at him now, four kids and counting."

The crowd then let out a brief roar of laughter. Pastor James hesitated before beginning again, "And Sarah, who endured grief that no one should ever have to face, the grief of a broken family, yet Sarah, through all of this, never underestimated the love of her Lord and Savior. She saw Ben when there was no Ben. She could have become bitter and given up on life, but Sarah chose life. She chose love. She had faith that God had better plans for her. She had faith God would send her down a road that would bring her eventually to Ben, so let us all see these two once broken roads as an example of what miraculous acts our God is truly capable of."

Pastor James then hesitated and he looked at the couple standing before him and smiled. "I have been asked to read one of my favorite verses that particularly pertain to these two people standing before me. It was written I believe to symbolize how love should be between a husband and a wife, between a parent and a child, between a brother and a sister, or between friends or for a stranger. This verse is from 1 Corinthians 13:4-7 and it reads: *Love is patient, love is kind... it does not envy... it does not boast... it is not proud... it is not rude... it is not self-seeking... it is not easily angered... it keeps no record of wrongs... love does not delight in evil but rejoices with the truth... it always protects... always trusts... always hopes... always perseveres... always perseveres...*"

The ceremony continued as both Sarah and Ben's families looked on and delighted in the fact that they had found one another. Pastor James, now coming to the end of the ceremony, signaled for Ben to turn to Sarah. Ben took Sarah by her hands, squeezing them and then gently lifted his hands to her face, taking it into his hands. He kissed her longingly as the crowd cheered and clapped. Ben and Sarah then turned toward the crowd, making their way out of the large wood sanctuary. They headed out the door where a group of people stood, blowing bubbles that floated up and around them.

The reception was held in the lower level of the Pink Elephant Restaurant where they had first met. The large open reception area housed the dinner and dance. The room soon filled with family and friends, enjoying a miraculous celebration of life and love.

The time came for the first dance. Ben walked out to the center of the floor while the DJ made the announcement. Sarah, who had been talking to the Granges, turned around to see Ben holding out his hand for her to join him.

The DJ then announced, "I am now proud to introduce for the first time as husband and wife, Mr. and Mrs. Ben Thompson."

The crowd clapped as Ben took Sarah into his arms, swinging her around, as if they had been dancing together all of their lives.

Ben brought Sarah close to him and whispered to her softly, "God bless my broken road." He then lifted Sarah in his arms, twirling her in circles as the lights became blurred. Ben then softly placed Sarah back on the ground and kissed her softly.

Their new beginning.